# THE
# WHISPER
## OF
# STARS

# THE
# WHISPER
## OF
# STARS

CRISTIN
WILLIAMS

First published in Great Britain in 2025 by Gollancz
an imprint of The Orion Publishing Group Ltd
Carmelite House, 50 Victoria Embankment
London EC4Y 0DZ

An Hachette UK Company

The authorised representative in the EEA is Hachette Ireland,
8 Castlecourt Centre, Castleknock Road, Castleknock, Dublin 15, D15 XTP3,
Republic of Ireland (email: info@hbgi.ie)

1 3 5 7 9 10 8 6 4 2

A CIP catalogue record for this book is
available from the British Library.

ISBN (Hardback)  978 1 399 62131 1
ISBN (Export Trade Paperback)  978 1 399 62132 8
ISBN (eBook)  978 1 399 62134 2
ISBN (Audio)  978 1 399 62135 9

Typeset by Input Data Services Ltd, Bridgwater, Somerset

Printed in Great Britain by Clays Ltd, Elcograf S.p.A

MIX
Paper | Supporting
responsible forestry
FSC
www.fsc.org    FSC® C104740

www.gollancz.co.uk

*For the disillusioned.*
*May you find within yourself the courage to shine.*

# PART I

—

*Daughter Of The Revolution*

# Resistance

```
                 REFUSE
             FEAR AND    RESIST
           WEAKNESS.  EVERYONE
           SILENT IS  GUILTY OF
           CONDONING  VIOLENCE
     AND       HATE.  WE MUST     REBEL.
       ANARCHISTS        FIGHT   BECAUSE
       BLOOD SPILLED       ON     FACTORY
       FLOORS CRIES OUT FOR       JUSTICE
     AND SLAVERY OF A PEOPLE  DEMANDS    REVOLT.
    WE EXPECT    DIGNITY AND  EQUALITY   FOR ALL
   WORKERS.          FAITH   AND LOVE   SUSTAIN        ,
   US, AND PASSION           CONQUERS   SORROW.
   A HEART STRIPPED OF ALL    SELFISH   DESIRES
   WILL STAND. COURAGEOUS     ACTS    LIVE ON
     AFTER MARTYRS PERISH,
      AND THE LIGHT OF OUR    REVOLUTION
       MAY FLICKER OR WANE    BUT SO LONG
       AS THERE IS BREATH   IN OUR LUNGS
        IT WILL NOT GO OUT.  OUR BATTLE
          CRY IS FREEDOM, EVEN FROM OUR
          PRISON CELLS. WE WILL NEVER
            BEND, THOUGH OUR BODIES
              MIGHT BE BROKEN. WE
              SACRIFICE OUR LIVES
              ON AN ALTAR OF HOPE.
```

# Chapter 1

## *Katya*

If Red Square was the beating heart of Moscow, the square at Lubyanka was the carotid artery – the best place to take the city's pulse. Perhaps that's why Vladimir Lenin chose it as headquarters for the Cheka, his secret police force. The new communist government commandeered the Rossiya Insurance Building, an elegant neo-baroque structure built in a cheerful shade of yellow brick.

By day it cast a sunny face on the bustling crowds of Moscow.

By night its doors opened like jaws, devouring those doomed ones accused of counterrevolution.

Deep within Cheka headquarters, one Doctor Aleksandr Vasilevich Barchenko conducted paranormal experiments in the top-secret offices of the Extraordinary Commission. It was September of 1923, and Yekaterina Efremova had been awake for seventy-six hours, a new record.

Curled up in the corner of a tiny concrete cell, Katya listened to the eerie notes of a distant violin. It might've been the sleep deprivation making her imagine things, but, in the music, she felt the weight of the ghosts haunting these halls – voices silenced, heartbeats stilled, thousands upon thousands of lives cut short by the firing squad in the basement. Or by something worse.

Seventy-six hours was her longest resistance yet, more than three days without sleep, without food, and with only enough water to keep her alive. Now fatigue turned her blood to syrup, slow and heavy as it flowed through her limbs. Her thoughts became sticky, and hunger tightened her stomach into something hard and knotted, like an old winter root.

When footsteps sounded outside her cell, Katya already knew she'd give them what they wanted. Once again she would trade part of her soul for a pill to make her sleep and the meal she would wake to.

The lock gave with an ominous clank, and the hinges of the iron door shrieked like banshees as lamplight spilled into the tiny concrete cell. Petrova's burly form filled the doorway, her frizzy grey hair sticking out the edges of her white nurse's cap.

'On your feet,' Petrova ordered.

Thus began their hourly ritual. Petrova clamped an iron collar around Katya's neck to prevent her from casting a spell. They'd learned that precaution the hard way, after Katya nearly killed a nurse and two guards in her first escape attempt.

Katya winced when Petrova raised her arms to secure the collar – the woman's body odour could wilt roses.

'Have you ever considered scented soap?' Katya asked. 'Or perfume, perhaps?'

'Walk.' Nurse Petrova prodded Katya's spine.

Katya felt the intensity of Petrova's hatred focused on her back as she raised her chin and strode out through the iron door of her cell. She navigated the familiar labyrinth of hallways. Two guards stood sentinel outside the lab. Their fingers moved to the triggers of their rifles as Katya passed by. She put a swagger in her step when she entered the lab, knowing it would irritate Doctor Barchenko.

Said doctor had his back to her. He bent over the chemistry

table to examine a flask, his jowls hanging.

'Ready to co-operate?' he asked without bothering to look up.

Katya had been ready, but his indifference stirred her outrage. If guilt tormented Katya, Barchenko ought to be plagued with regrets. He should have blisters of remorse and boils of self-reproach. But, of course, he didn't. The worst ones never do.

When he finally looked at Katya, he had the nerve to appear bored. Had destroying lives grown mundane, or was he just tired? Every hour they'd dragged Katya into this lab was an hour of sleeplessness for him as well.

'What, no threats?' Katya clicked her tongue in mock disapproval. 'If you have a limited supply of colourful ultimatums, you really ought to space them out more, like pills. Or didn't they teach you that in medical school?'

Barchenko tensed at the mention of medical school. Katya regularly wove that phrase into their clashes, though she never knew why it bothered him so much.

'Co-operate and we'll feed you,' he said flatly. 'Your stubbornness hurts no one but yourself.'

Katya's stomach twisted at the suggestion of food, but he was wrong about this resistance only hurting her. To get funding for this lab, Barchenko must have promised Lenin the secrets of the occult served on a silver platter. Unfortunately for Barchenko, his primary test subject was a defiant anarchist who resisted him at every turn.

'I'll tell you what,' Katya said, as if she were in a position to bargain. 'Make Nurse Petrova promise to bathe before work from now on and never eat stinky cheese again. Then we'll negotiate my co-operation.'

The nurse dug her fingernails into Katya's arm, but the pain was worth it. Barchenko's lips shrank like prunes – she'd cured him of indifference.

'Take her back to her cell,' he ordered the nurse.

'That won't be necessary,' Katya said sweetly. 'We're both tired. And if there's anyone in the world who needs beauty sleep, it's you. Might as well get this over with.'

Barchenko's jaw clenched. After a long beat, he ordered the nurse to prepare the experiment.

Katya struggled half-heartedly while the nurse dragged her towards the curtain splitting the lab in half. Beyond it, a wooden desk formed a barrier between two reclining chairs. Phonographs, cameras and other various pieces of equipment cluttered the space.

Petrova shoved Katya into one of the lab chairs, fastening her so tightly that loose skin bulged around the leather straps on Katya's wrists and ankles. Pain pulsed up Katya's limbs, but she flashed a smile because nothing would annoy the nurse more.

Petrova left to retrieve their next victim, and Katya closed her eyes against the dizziness. She hadn't hallucinated yet, but that wouldn't be far off. Blinking several times, Katya focused through the haze. She must have blacked out. When her vision cleared, the new test subject had already been strapped into the other chair.

Katya didn't mean to look at him. She should have averted her eyes, knowing how much harder this would all be if she let herself see the other test subjects as people. But something about this one captured her attention.

It wasn't just that he was young – late teens like Katya or maybe early twenties – but that his face was all soul, a little more alive than other people's. Katya might've expected to see a face like that in a museum, perhaps painted in a garden scene of a handsome knight seducing a tender maiden. Not here. He didn't belong in this lab, with his tousled brown hair swirling like paint strokes, and his lush eyebrows softening the chiselled lines of his cheeks and jaw. His rich brown eyes radiated warmth and good cheer.

If Katya had seen him somewhere else, anywhere else, she'd be pulling out her poetry diary to try and capture something of his essence on the page.

What a shame he'd ended up here.

Last time it was an old Siberian shaman, Number Twenty-Nine. By the time Katya had finished casting Doctor Barchenko's latest attempt at an incantation, the shaman was slumped in his chair. Red veins webbed the surface of his unseeing eyes, and his mouth had frozen in a pain-filled grimace, like an Italian Renaissance portrait of the damned.

His face and her spirit could have been twins.

In her ten months here, Katya had seen twenty-three corpses strapped to the chair on the other side of the séance room.

Spellcraft was a complicated magic. It took years of study to master the charovnik arts, and even then an incantation could be temperamental. Words are symbols, after all. They mean something slightly different to each person based on individual perceptions and experiences.

No matter how much Katya argued with Barchenko, pointing out the years of guided study most charovniki undertook before ever attempting their own spell craft – study she herself had not yet mastered – the doctor persisted in this ignorant experimentation.

Sending Petrova out of the room, Doctor Barchenko perched on the wooden stool by his desk. He yawned and tiredly rubbed his forehead as he reviewed his notes. Then he switched on the phonograph. 'Eighteenth of September, 1923. Test subjects Two and Thirty, experiment number one.'

Doctor Barchenko turned to the dark-haired young man. 'Relax and follow my instructions. This is a harmless first exercise, nothing more.'

'Harmless? I'm sure you dragged me through a maze of hallways and multiple locked doors for the sake of my health.' Number Thirty tilted his head and offered Doctor Barchenko a smile with the feel of an invitation. *Tell me all your secrets*, it seemed to say, *you know you want to*. He raised an eyebrow and asked, 'Why am I really here?'

'Co-operate and you'll be allowed food, sleep and a comfortable room. Don't co-operate . . .?' Barchenko thumbed toward Katya. 'You'll end up like her.'

When Number Thirty looked at Katya, his lips parted in a small gasp. Of recognition? Surely it couldn't be that, yet his eyes traced the lines of her face with keen interest. Katya felt a moment of shame. There were dark circles under her eyes, and she couldn't remember the last time she'd bathed. She squirmed in her restraints, expecting that at any moment his expression would turn to one of disgust. Instead his thick eyebrows drew together in concern. He stared at her trembling fingers.

'I'll co-operate.' He lifted his gaze to meet Katya's, and the compassion radiating from his eyes made her want to cry. In that moment, she felt not only looked at, but seen. The warmth of his expression hardened as he turned to Doctor Barchenko. 'So long as you give her what you promised me – food, sleep, and a comfortable room. Can't you see she's starving?'

Doctor Barchenko waved a dismissive hand at the young man's concerns. 'You'll both be fed after the experiment, I assure you.'

Number Thirty weighed those words, his eyebrows pressing together to form a crease above his nose.

'It's true.' Katya looked away as she said this, her guilt like a lump of hot iron in her gut, searing her from the inside out.

She'd been brought to this lab for one purpose. Lenin's government wanted to reengineer the human soul, to take away greed, rebelliousness and doubt. The future utopia they envisioned was populated by numb and mindless followers, men and women who worked tirelessly while asking no questions.

These experiments were intended to control minds, but so far Barchenko had only managed to crack them. Twenty-three experiments had led to twenty-three corpses sitting opposite Katya in the séance room.

In casting Barchenko's spells, Katya became the 'something worse' than the firing squad in the basement. She ought to die rather than co-operate, but that would mean failing her mother completely, rendering both of their lives' work null and void.

Katya couldn't bear to wrap her mother's legacy in a burial shroud, so she survived, a traitor to every ideal she once held dear.

By refusing to be a martyr, Katya had become their monster instead.

She would indeed be given food and rest after the experiment, but, despite Barchenko's assurances, Number Thirty wouldn't survive it. Her guilt sharpened into an acute ache. For months, no one had looked at Katya like a human being, and certainly no one had spoken out against the way she'd been treated. How could Katya live with herself if she went through with the experiment, knowing he would die? He was too young, too *alive*, to end up like the others, used and then discarded like a broken doll.

Katya might not have much power in this place, but perhaps she could force Barchenko to choose a different test subject.

Katya rallied for one more fight, another hour of resistance. She'd made it seventy-six hours, why not seventy-seven?

Doctor Barchenko began as he always did, by hypnotizing the test subject. This prevented them from resisting Katya when she cast Barchenko's spell.

Barchenko counted backwards from a hundred. Katya blacked out during the eighties, and again at sixty-three – her body might not last another hour. She dug her fingernails into her palms until pain cut through her like a shock.

*You are Yekaterina Efremova,* she reminded herself. *You are a daughter of revolutionaries, and you will stay awake.*

When Doctor Barchenko's voice trailed off, Katya assumed she'd blacked out again. Fatigue covered her like a rain-soaked blanket. She opened her heavy eyes. Barchenko lay slumped over the desk, the phonograph still recording. This had to be a hallucination. Katya shook her head and blinked several times, but it was true.

Doctor Barchenko had fallen asleep.

Katya's mouth went dry. She swallowed, but the lump in her throat refused to budge. Number Thirty stared at the ceiling, transfixed.

Katya struggled against her restraints, pain pulsing upward from her wrists when the leather straps broke her skin. She couldn't escape, but she could make sure Barchenko never hurt anyone else.

First Katya had to get the iron collar off her neck. That wouldn't be too hard since they'd fitted it when she first arrived at the lab and then proceeded to starve her for ten months. Katya tipped her chin down into the ring, feeling at the clasp with her lips and tongue until she pried it open. A wave of relief washed over her as the iron dropped onto her lap and then rolled to the ground with a clank.

Barchenko twitched at the sound.

Katya held completely still, her muscles tensed in anticipation of punishment. She let out a long sigh when Barchenko's breathing evened out again.

She turned her thoughts to the task before her. Katya's

mother had taught her that human beings were made of three parts: body, soul and spirit. The body existed in the physical realm, limited in its perceptions by what could be seen, heard, tasted, smelt and touched. Sixth sense gave a vague awareness of the spirit, our eternal and divine self, which dwelled in the Otherworld, the unseen realm where magic came from. The human soul was the gateway between the two.

Katya's magic became possible when she opened her soul to the Otherworld. As her spirit reached through that gateway, divine power flooded Katya's body, bringing with it the potential to affect change on the natural world. As a charovnika, Katya channelled that power into words.

Most of the spells Katya had used in the past came from her mother's expansive grimoire. Since crafting original spells was such a complicated art, most charovniki relied on ancient incantations written in Old Russian or Byzantine Greek. Katya had memorised a dozen or so of these incantations, meditating on the meaning of each word until the spells painted pictures in her mind that she could bring to life with her words.

One of her memorised spells was an archaic Greek incantation that altered the flow of blood in a person's body. Though intended to heal circulation disorders, Katya's mother had tweaked the spell for use in political assassinations. Forcing a rapid flow of blood to a man's head caused a haemorrhagic stroke, a death that appeared natural.

To cast this spell, Katya would need more strength than she had in her exhausted and starving state.

She turned to Number Thirty.

All the test subjects were volshebniki, magical folk. But this young man wouldn't be so expendable if he were a charovnik spell-caster like her. He might be a vedun sorcerer or perhaps a koldun healer. Whatever magical ability Number Thirty possessed, Katya would have to make use of it, and quickly.

Closing her eyes, Katya recited a zagovor, an Old Russian incantation passed down from her mother. She always chanted these lines before attempting spellwork, letting her mind blur into a trance-like state until the world around her fell away and her soul became a doorway inching open. The words were like her own personal key, unlocking the Otherworld so her voice could draw from her spirit's power.

*'My soul, like the branches of the World Tree,*
*Weave the seen and unseen into one whole.*
*Be to me a gateway to the Otherworld,*
*That I may harness the powers of creation.'*

As she recited the spell a few times, she felt it – the blurring of her eyes and sharpening of her spirit. When the room came back into focus, an ethereal light glowed at the edges of her vision and tingling warmth spread through her blood.

'Relax now,' she ordered Number Thirty, and he slumped more deeply into the chair. 'And open your soul to the Otherworld.'

The air in the séance room became charged, and a slight buzzing filled Katya's ears. She opened herself to draw from his power, but it crashed into her like a cresting wave, leaving her breathless. It came as turmoil with all the chaos of jazz, and she knew she had made the right choice in trying to save him. Never before had she encountered a soul so immense. It felt as though a dam had broken, and, through this young man, magic flooded the room. Katya fought to keep her focus, channelling that power into the words of her spell.

*'Lalo pros ten kardian sou,'* Katya began. She repeated the opening words a few times until her tongue tingled and magic pooled in her diaphragm. When she was certain of the spell's potency, she continued. *'Hoi epesin outoi, hos litho trokhoidei, to rheuma tou haimatos tes zoes sou hodegeitosan—'*

Doctor Barchenko shifted. Katya froze. The lenses of Barchenko's spectacles magnified his eyes as they opened. He rubbed the rolls of skin at the back of his neck, pausing mid-motion when he noticed the iron collar on the floor.

'*Ty suchka*,' he growled. *You little bitch.*

Slamming his hands on the desk, Barchenko pushed himself up to standing.

'Wait.' Katya's voice sounded small, like a child's drowned out by roaring thunder. Barchenko was the storm, ten months' worth of swallowed hatred swirling to the surface as he crossed the room in two violent steps.

Katya gasped in a breath as his hands clamped around her throat. Wrath twisted Barchenko's face into a snarl. He leaned on Katya's chest. Choked her. Pressure clogged Katya's ears. Her eyes bulged as she struggled. The leather straps cut into her wrists and ankles.

She'd ceased funnelling Number Thirty's magic but had left him open to the Otherworld. Power pooled until the air glistened. The static buzzing became a high-pitched ring.

Barchenko squeezed harder. Beads of sweat formed on his upper lip. His hot, minty breath puffed against Katya's cheek. *This is the end.* She'd pushed too hard, and he'd snapped.

Darkness crept in around her vision. Then the shadows shifted. The vice around Katya's throat released. Breath came to her in gasps, burning inside her throat and lungs. Tears blurred her vision.

'Lyudmila,' Barchenko turned toward something behind him. 'The tranquilisers!'

Everything hurt when Katya raised her head. A broken leather strap shot across the floor, landing near her iron collar. Katya lifted her eyes. The breath in her chest went still.

Number Thirty wasn't a charovnik, a vedun, or a koldun – he

was some sort of shape-shifting wizard. The magic transformed the pale, dark-haired boy into an adolescent brown bear. He'd burst his leather straps and now stood on hind legs, grunting in annoyance at Doctor Barchenko.

'Lyudmila!' Barchenko shouted.

The bear's grunts became a distressed moan. Barchenko raised his hands defensively. He screamed when the bear swiped its mighty paw, flinging Barchenko across the room. He landed facedown, unmoving as blood pooled around him on the white tile floor.

Dropping to all fours, the bear pawed the ground as his eyes – one blue and one brown – fixed on Katya.

She tried to speak. Lacing magic through gentle words would calm the bear, but her throat was swelling closed from Barchenko's attack. She couldn't find her voice. The bear raised his head, his black nose snuffling her direction. Trapped by restraints, Katya froze as the creature lumbered forward.

Nurse Petrova flung the curtain open, a tranquiliser gun in hand. She shot a dart in the bear's flank. With a bellow, the creature charged at the nurse, swaying dizzily for a few steps before toppling to the ground.

Petrova looked from the unconscious bear to Doctor Barchenko's unmoving form to the iron collar lying on the floor.

Then she turned on Katya.

# Chapter 2

## *Dima*

For as long as he could remember, Dima Danilov had been searching for a story. His grandfather said it was a holy calling, the purpose that gave shape and weight to every skomorokh's life. Danilovs were one of five remaining families who could trace their lineage to the People of the Bear, whose storytelling magic was passed down from one generation to the next.

In ancient times, Skomorokhi minstrels travelled alongside their bear companions, performing stories, songs and illusions. Skomorokhi saw history as a great tapestry, continuously being woven. Every life a thread. Every choice a stitch. They dedicated themselves to the art of storytelling, carrying the tales of one generation to the next and reminding the people of Rus that they belonged to something far bigger than themselves.

Dima found threads of that tapestry in everyone he met, often capturing some aspect of their story on the pages of his sketchbook. But he yearned for something more. It was a feeling akin to homesickness, the sense that his soul longed for something more tangible than the small threads of story he wove into his art.

He wanted an epic, a tale that would ripple across minds and hearts – a story to change the world.

He'd never expected to find the first threads of it in a covert government lab.

When he'd been arrested in Kazan a few months back, Dima had thought he was a goner. But when he saw the girl sitting opposite him in the séance room, Dima knew he wasn't going to die. Not yet.

Though they'd never met, Dima recognised her. He'd sketched her likeness three times in the year before his arrest. He often had a minstrel's dreams, true ones, of the past or of the future. When he sketched his visions the next morning, his drawings weren't just portraits – they were premonitions.

Sure enough, he'd survived the first experiment unscathed. Or, mostly unscathed. Dima felt like he'd been hit by a train, but he was still breathing. A salty crust sealed his eyes closed, as though he'd cried himself to sleep.

The last thing Dima remembered was the doctor counting backwards from a hundred. A dreamlike haze shrouded everything afterwards. Every muscle in Dima's body ached, and his senses had sharpened so he could smell not only the ammonia used to clean the lab but also the body odour of a woman moving about on the far side of the room. He also smelled a mix of metals – tin, lead and . . . heated iron?

Dima cracked his eyes open, then blinked. His bleary vision came into focus. A thick chain coiled around his chest four times, securing him to the table he lay upon. Was that why he hurt so much? Iron had a binding effect on magic. It caused a reaction in the blood and considerable pain to any volshebnik it touched.

Though pain radiated below his skin, the ache went deeper than iron could reach – bone deep. It was the agony of being remade, of a skeleton reshaping and flesh reforming. He'd felt this pain twice before. Once on the day his family died, when

Dima discovered the skomorokh ability to change into a bear was more than an ancient legend. The second time was months later, after he'd roamed the forest all summer, hibernated all winter, and awoken in the spring, a boy once more.

Now it had happened again.

Turning his head, Dima's vision blurred and then refocused. He was still in the lab, but in a different room, a smaller one. In one corner, the nurse with frizzy grey hair – Petrova, the doctor had called her – held a glowing red soldering iron.

Dima shifted, sending a stab of pain through his limbs. A scan of the room confirmed he was alone here with the nurse.

'The girl?' Dima's throat was so dry his voice came out as a croak. 'The one from the experiment . . . where is she?'

At the mention of the girl, the nurse's nostrils flared. That seemed to have been the wrong thing to ask. Dima would have to approach from a different angle.

'Sorry, I'm confused.' Dima shrugged as much as the chains would allow. In his experience, friendliness was often reciprocated. He tilted his head and offered the nurse his most disarming smile. 'What happened during the experiment? I don't remember anything.'

Petrova's glare eased into something softer.

'The experiment went wrong.' Nurse Petrova averted her eyes, but Dima noted the shiver that moved up her spine along with her words.

Wrong how? Did something happen to the girl? Dima shifted on the table, trying to look in the nurse's face. Pain knifed through his muscles at the movement. *Right*. Dima did know what happened in the experiment. The bone-deep pain spoke volumes. That must be why he'd been chained to a table. They were afraid of him, afraid because he'd shifted into a bear. But then what happened?

Dima closed his eyes as a wave of vertigo swept over him. His stomach began to roil as the darkest parts of his imagination offered images of what bear claws might have done to the beautiful girl he'd dreamed of three times.

Nurse Petrova unplugged the electrical soldering iron. Dima's mouth went dry when she wielded the glowing hot iron and stepped towards him.

'What's that for?'

'Just doing my job.' She avoided his eyes as she perched on a stool beside him.

An iron collar and a coil of soldering wire rested on a work table. Nurse Petrova set down the hot iron and fitted the collar around Dima's neck. He flinched at the new source of pain. Though he tried to move away, the chain held him firm. Once the nurse had the collar in place, she began melting the wire with the hot iron and filling the creases.

She planned to clap him in iron, permanently.

With a sense of horror Dima wondered what it would be like to have iron stinging his skin at all times.

'Wait.' Dima's brow furrowed and he cast a pleading look at the nurse. 'Please don't.'

Nurse Petrova gritted her teeth and brought the soldering iron back to the wire, trapping Dima's magic within iron.

# Chapter 3
## *Natasha*

Natasha didn't need to hear footsteps to know he was coming. She felt it in her violin, in the way the vibrations shivered through her bones. As her fingers slid from major notes to minor ones, the music filling her cell took on an eerie quality. A light gust of air swept up her back as the door opened then shut. Natasha slid the bow languidly over a string in a mournful closing note, almost like a howl – the perfect way to greet the wolf behind her.

Commissar Boky might look like a man, but Natasha understood his true nature. His scent flooded her senses, something of wind and wild places, of soil, root and unfallen snow. Though fear raised the hair on the back of her neck, Natasha took a steadying breath, curved her lips into a serene smile, and turned.

Her gaze moved up him. The meticulously polished shoes. The simple military uniform. The gauntness that had come from a brush with tuberculosis but in his new life marked him with the lean elegance of a predator.

Natasha raised her eyes until she stood face to face with the most dangerous man in Russia.

Comrade Gleb Boky, also known as 'The Cipher,' ran the Bolsheviki spy network. His simple clothes belied his importance in Lenin's regime. While other bureaucrats requisitioned mansions and palaces, living in vulgar extravagance, Boky had moved into a single-room flat. He drove the government-issued automobile of a common policeman. That's what made him so dangerous. Not just his obsession with the occult and his penchant for dark magic, but that Gleb Boky was a true believer in communism, and a disillusioned one at that.

He would do anything to create the utopia he'd expected the Revolution would usher in. For two years in the lab, Natasha had experienced first-hand the lengths he would go to make Russia match the vision in his head.

Boky looked ageless, neither old nor young, a striking man rather than a handsome one. His pale blue eyes appeared almost grey, two cold stones boring into Natasha. She always worried he could penetrate her thoughts and secrets when he stared at her in his unblinking way. Though she carefully schooled her features into a mask of calmness, her heart thundered in her chest and her knuckles turned white as she gripped her violin in one hand and her bow in the other.

What did he want? Boky had observed her experiments a handful of times, but in the two years she'd been imprisoned in the lab, he'd never visited her cell.

'Commissar.' Natasha tilted her head coyly, letting her long, red hair spill over one shoulder.

'Natasha.' His deep, breathy voice made her name sound as though it had been carried upon the wind.

Danger prickled up her spine, but she'd flirted with that before. When Boky's eyes shifted away at last, the squeezing feeling in her chest released and Natasha took a deep breath. He stepped further into her cell. Natasha shakily set her instrument on her desk and watched him examine her space.

Commissar Boky's eyes skimmed over the bed, dressed with wool blankets and feather pillows. His gaze lingered on the easel in the corner with oil paints carefully arranged in its tray.

'You've done well here.' Boky ran one of his long, scarred fingers along the tops of the finished canvases stacked beside the easel. 'I hope you feel we've treated you fairly.'

Every comfort in this room had been given Natasha by Doctor Barchenko for her co-operation. As if she'd had any choice but to do what they wanted.

As a vedma witch, hers was a magic of ritual. Natasha spent the better part of her childhood apprenticing under her aunt, and there were few people in Russia who could claim the depth of esoteric knowledge Natasha had attained.

That made her a valuable government asset.

At first, Barchenko asked for small things. She spent months imbuing amber beads with protection spells, so those who wore them couldn't be enchanted or hexed. Then they requested her help identifying Lenin's enemies. Natasha used a divination ritual to expose spies and treasonous plots. Many counter-revolutionaries faced the firing squad in the basement of the Lubyanka building with Natasha's word as the only evidence of their guilt.

It had taken great restraint not to avenge herself on her own enemies, but her aunt had taught Natasha patience. Many a powerful person was toppled because they didn't have the discipline to bide their time.

Barchenko's demands had taken a darker turn of late. He'd been experimenting with a forbidden shamanic ritual, one that required human sacrifice. It took several attempts and many lives lost before Natasha succeeded in turning a common Red Army soldier into a volkolak, a wizard empowered by dark magic to shapeshift into a wolf.

Natasha wasn't proud of what she'd done, but no matter what they demanded of her, she complied.

By becoming helpful – and then invaluable – she'd survived.

Eventually she would escape.

Boky was staring at her again. Had he asked something? Admitting she hadn't heard him would show weakness. Instead, Natasha shrugged with an air of mystery. A twitch in her left eye spoiled the effect. Isolation had wrecked her nerves, and the spasms were becoming more frequent. Her fingers were trembling again, too. Natasha tucked them under her arms and leaned against her desk in what she hoped was a casual stance.

'As I was saying.' Boky clasped his hands behind his back. 'You've done well in this lab, but I've decided there's another way you can make restitution for your crimes against the people.'

By 'crimes' he of course meant that Natasha had been born an aristocrat. Yes, she'd technically been engaged in treasonous conspiracy when they arrested her, but anyone else would have faced the firing squad for that. Natasha's name, not her actions, condemned her to the lab.

'What do you want me to do?' Natasha kept her voice casual, though her stomach clenched. The most recent rituals she'd performed in this lab had brought nightmares to life – what worse thing would Boky ask of her now?

'I'm searching for something. I intend to transfer you, so you can help me find it.'

Natasha took care not to let her interest show. A transfer would mean fresh air and sunlight on her face for the first time in over two years. More than that, it meant possibilities: of getting news from beyond these walls, of reordering her circumstances – perhaps even of escape.

'And what is it you want me to find?' Natasha asked.

'The *what* is not your concern. All you need to worry about is who.'

Commissar Boky pulled a small, square photograph from his jacket pocket. The photo had lost its crispness from too much handling. Natasha's gift of foresight stirred inside her, and she sensed this photograph didn't only contain a person – it contained Boky's obsession. She imagined him fingering its edges as a nervous tick and staring at it in every solitary moment as though it contained a cipher, the only one he couldn't crack.

When he handed her the photograph, Natasha clamped her jaw to keep her mouth from dropping open. The face in the photograph was nearly as familiar to Natasha as her own countenance. This girl had been an obsession of Natasha's before her arrest, though not for the same reasons as Commissar Boky. Did he know? Was that why he brought her this proposition, to torment her?

'Her name is Yekaterina Efremova,' Boky said.

Natasha already knew that name – she'd cursed it a thousand times, at least. Had Boky said it to gauge Natasha's reaction? She looked up at him through her lashes, but his attention was fixed on the photograph. Perhaps he didn't know of Natasha's connection to Katya, though it seemed like quite a coincidence that Boky would bring this photograph to her of all people.

'She has information I need.' Boky plucked the photo out of Natasha's fingers and returned it to his pocket. 'I want you to get close to her, befriend her – and report her movements to me.'

'You want me to be your spy.'

'Yes. If you succeed, it will prove your loyalty to the government.'

'And what is my loyalty worth?'

'Freedom,' he said. 'Help me find what I'm looking for, and I'll release you.'

His words tasted like lies. Natasha's knowledge of vedun magic made her a valuable asset to the government, and her name made her a dangerous liability – too dangerous for them to ever let her go. Still, a transfer would create possibilities. If Natasha was strong and cunning, as she'd been taught to be, this could be her chance to take back everything she'd lost.

# Chapter 4
## *Katya*

Katya woke to impenetrable darkness. Her heartbeat hammered a cruel rhythm on the inside of her skull, and her body vibrated with the movement of a train hissing over tracks. Reaching out, her fingers collided with rough wooden boards. She was being transported inside a sealed crate, like an animal.

Katya gave up pushing against the boards when her pain sharpened. It felt like an invisible blade had lodged in her throat, stabbing when she moved and scraping with every breath she took.

Horror washed over her when she remembered Barchenko's meaty fingers closing around her neck. Katya still smelled the mint on his breath, still saw the murderous gleam in his eyes as he squeezed the life out of her. If the other test subject hadn't shapeshifted, Katya would have died in that lab.

*I'm still alive,* she reminded herself, forcefully dispelling the memory of Barchenko's attack. And, given his state when Katya had last seen him, Barchenko was probably dead. He could never hurt her again.

Katya took stock of her injuries. Besides her damaged throat, open wounds ringed Katya's wrists and ankles from her struggle against the lab chair's restraints. She touched her face, finding it swollen and tender from near asphyxiation.

The train whistled and screeched to a stop, releasing a rush of steam. She'd arrived at her destination, but where might that be? Katya's stomach twisted. With hunger, perhaps, and fear. She forcefully pushed beyond those primal instincts and took hold of something more useful – her defiance.

Whatever horrors awaited her in this new place, Katya would confront them with her head held high.

As two men hauled her crate out onto the train platform, Katya shook off the remaining fog of the tranquiliser.

Men muttered curses as they discussed what ought to be done with her. Apparently, someone had written 'Special Delivery' on Katya's crate. When it came to the Extraordinary Commission, *special* meant dangerous, and everyone knew it.

Eventually someone pried the crate open with a crowbar. Katya hissed as a flood of light and cold stung her eyes. Five armed guards surrounded her. That would be a minor obstacle if she had access to her magic, but her voice was trapped inside a swollen throat.

A guard grabbed the back of Katya's shirt and lifted her onto feet as wobbly as a new-born fawn's. Her muscles had weakened with disuse, but she locked her knees and managed to stay upright. Whatever happened, she refused to lose face in front of these bastards.

As she threw back her bony shoulders and raised her chin, Katya forced her eyes to suffer the brightness and get a good look at her surroundings. Rows of wooden sheds, a barbed wire fence with thick northern forest beyond it – they'd sent her to a camp of some kind. Katya hadn't expected to end up outdoors, breathing fresh pine and salty sea air. She definitely hadn't expected to be wearing a school uniform, as though time had snagged and looped back to ten months ago.

Before her was a sea. *Which sea?* She had no way of knowing how long she'd been unconscious or calculating how far she'd travelled.

In her physical state, she'd never outrun the guards for long. Could she hide if she somehow reached the forest? A guard prodded Katya with his rifle, urging her towards a steamer waiting at the dock. Smoke rose from its stacks in lazy wisps, and the crew bustled about the deck, preparing to set sail.

Katya's chances of escape would lessen exponentially if they got her on that ship. Feigning dizziness, she spun in a circle to gauge her chances. Too many guards. Even if she darted between them, she'd have five bullets in her back before she reached the tree line. She had no choice but to obey them. For now.

One of the guards held out Katya's leather schoolbag, which she hadn't seen since her arrest. She swiped it and lurched toward the dock. The armed guards fanned out behind her.

Stepping onto the gangway, Katya shivered as freezing wind stung her exposed skin and whipped through her tangled blonde hair. She pretended to lose her balance and caught herself on the handrail, peering over. A crust of ice already banked the harbour, thick enough to cause injury before plunging her into frigid waters, if she jumped.

'Keep moving.' A guard's rifle barrel jabbed Katya's back like a metal finger.

He flinched when she glared at him over her shoulder. The guard ran a nervous tongue over his lips as though tasting danger in the air. Katya couldn't escape. Not here. Perhaps she'd find an opportunity wherever this boat was taking her to. But that didn't mean she'd make it easy for them to get rid of her. Channelling every drop of her anarchist defiance, she flashed a wicked smile.

'Go,' he ordered.

'Make me,' she said in a hoarse whisper that sent a stab of pain down her injured throat.

Katya gripped the handrails, the cool metal instantly numbing her fingers. *I'm going to get myself shot,* she thought vaguely, but it felt good to resist, almost intoxicating. Her body might be weak, her voice silenced, but they hadn't broken her yet. Fighting back wouldn't change anything, but sometimes it was the only way to remind herself she was still alive.

A sailor lumbered down the gangway, hooked his thick arm around her middle, and hauled her onto his shoulder like a coil of rope, a thing instead of a person. Katya clutched the schoolbag as the sailor carried her aboard and dumped her onto a platform halfway down the companionway. He strode back up to the deck without a second glance.

Five men were seated on two wooden planks attached to either side of a stairway leading down to the hold. A din rose from behind the locked door, voices moaning of crushed ribs or crying out for air.

The prisoners' desperate voices clawed at her conscience as she pulled up her threadbare stockings and situated herself on the splintered wood of the platform, hugging her schoolbag to her chest. The men seated on the platforms regarded Katya's injuries with some mix of pity and morbid interest. Katya glared at them one by one until they turned away. When her gaze fell on the person beside her, she let out a small gasp.

It was the shapeshifter from the lab, Number Thirty. He'd been immersed in a sketchbook on his lap while she descended the stairs, his long fingers moving a pencil over the page in sharp, practiced strokes. Now he watched her, his dark hair spilling out from beneath a newsboy cap to partially obscure his face. His lush brows gathered above his nose in an expression of concern.

'What happened to you?' His voice sounded nearly as devastated as her body felt.

Katya swallowed, and the movement sent a stab of pain through her throat. Speaking to the guard had been a mistake, one she wouldn't repeat. She shook her head and pointed to her injury.

Number Thirty brushed the hair back from his face, his pencil still dangling between his fingers like an extension of his hand. His brown eyes were gentle, soulful, deep. An iron collar encircled his neck, and Katya winced with sympathy when she noticed it had been soldered shut, locking away his magic.

Instead of sterile lab clothes, he now wore grey trousers held up by braces, a white collared shirt and a wool greatcoat. Katya wished she'd been dressed so sensibly when they arrested her.

'Don't I know you?' A middle-aged man on the other platform squinted at Katya. She shrugged noncommittally at the same moment his face lit with recognition. 'You're Svetlana Efremova's girl.'

*Svetlana Efremova.*

That name still held such power over Katya, more potent than any incantation in a charovnik spellbook.

*Svetlana Efremova*, turning up at resistance meetings with rouge on her lips and magic on her tongue.

*Svetlana Efremova*, brave and brilliant, with a fierce compassion for the poor and a hatred of all injustice.

Katya's complicated feelings about her mother had become impossibly tangled since Svetlana's murder last year.

The men on the platforms watched Katya with interest. They must be Politicals, members of various parties that had fought together for the just world the Revolution promised and then splintered apart after the Bolsheviki took over.

Most Politicals had been a little bit in love with Katya's

mother. Hell, Katya had been in love with her too. A hungry kind of love, panging with want of affection and twisting with need. She'd grown up in the shadows cast by her mother's blazing light, catching whatever scraps of attention she could.

Svetlana had been like the winter sun – the brightest thing in Katya's world, yet too remote to provide any warmth.

'You *are* Svetlana's daughter, aren't you?'

Katya shifted on the platform, suddenly feeling the hardness of the boards and the way the splintery surface scratched at the skin between her hem and stockings. She didn't want to think about her mother.

As though sensing her discomfort, Number Thirty drew the man's attention away from Katya. Leaning forward, he offered the kind of smile that put people at ease and gave them the sensation of sitting beside a fireplace with someone they'd known all their lives. He introduced himself as Dmitri Danilov, Dima for short.

'I'm Sergei Istomin.' The Political nodded toward Dima's iron collar. 'What's that about?'

'I think it's because I made some . . . *improvements* to communist propaganda posters.' A ghost of a smile haunted Dima's lips.

'You're a Political?'

Dima's smile faltered. 'I'm a Cossack. And an aristocrat – about as counter-revolutionary as they come.'

Sergei lowered his gaze, looking uncomfortable.

Katya scooted a few inches away from Dima.

Cossacks had been the tsar's best warriors, entirely complicit in enslaving Russia's workmen and peasants. Whatever interest Katya had in him withered, shriveled, blew away.

He'd shown her kindness in the lab, and she'd saved his life because of it. But now, knowing who he was, Katya understood that Dmitri Danilov could only ever be her enemy.

'Bad luck, I know.' Dima winced dramatically and shook his head, as though he were more surprised than anyone to find himself on the wrong side of the Revolution. He seemed to have a knack for reading people, and his comment went a long way in breaking the tension between him and Sergei. 'Any idea where they're sending us?'

'Solovki,' Sergei said.

Solovki was a nickname for the Solovetsky Islands, an archipelago in the White Sea and a place of pilgrimage in Russia for centuries. Considering that the sea froze over to make the islands unreachable for most of the year, it wouldn't be an easy place to escape from.

'To the monastery?' Dima asked.

'It's a prison now.' Turning to Katya, Sergei's eyes softened, and he said more gently, 'Don't worry. They've set up a separate facility for Politicals. There'll be good food, clean sheets, even a library. The guards aren't allowed to harm us in any way.' He glanced down the companionway towards the door of the hold, behind which the other prisoners had given up pleading for help. 'Now *we're* the protected class – what a change that is.'

Katya flashed him a disbelieving look.

'It's true.' One of the other men leaned around Sergei to address her. 'We're administrative prisoners, not convicts.'

'The Whites are finished, and Lenin's no fool,' Sergei said. 'He won't risk the foreign press stirring up trouble.'

The Whites were the anti-communist army that opposed the Bolsheviki after the Revolution, made up of Cossacks, the former aristocracy, and forcibly conscripted peasants. Katya knew the Civil War was over – it had been in the papers before her arrest last autumn. It made sense that Lenin would now want his political enemies out of the way while he cemented his hold on power.

*So, they're putting us on an island.*

Katya imagined a quarantine where the sickness was having education and the wrong sorts of ideas.

Everything felt off – where she was, what she was wearing, the schoolbag full of possessions they'd withheld from her in the lab but returned now. Katya took a long inhale. Briny sea air sliced down her injured throat and burned a cold fire in her lungs.

At least there were other anarchists imprisoned on Solovki.

When she was eight-years-old, Katya spent a summer at an anarchist commune. Her mother had been sentenced to five months at the Smolensk women's prison for inciting a riot. Before beginning her sentence, Svetlana brought Katya to a large country estate an hour's drive from Petrograd where several dozen anarchists lived together. There she gave Katya into the charge of a kind-looking woman called Marina.

Though Svetlana's absence ached like a sore tooth, Katya remembered that summer as one of the happiest of her childhood. She had abundant playmates. They'd spend their days exploring the countryside or swimming in the lake. They valiantly ventured into the forest in search of mushrooms, which often evolved into epic games of tag or trench warfare with boys on one side and girls on the other, hurling pinecones at each other instead of grenades.

After supper, Katya would abandon her playmates' games and join the adults sitting on the lawn to enjoy the cool evening breezes and late light. Katya learned to play chess from Uncle Vova, an old physicist turned radical. She liked that he never let her win, and that he talked to her as though she were his intellectual equal.

She'd listen to the debates that inevitably sprung up each evening as the adults shared ideas and bottles of wine. These discussions sparked Katya's interest in history, philosophy, geopolitics and literature. More than that, she learned that even though the anarchists shared common values, individual members could – and should – think for themselves. Disagreement was never discouraged.

*It's how minds stay sharp,* Uncle Vova said one night when Katya had been distracted from their game by a particularly heated exchange.

That summer taught Katya to be curious, to thirst for knowledge and think for herself.

It also taught her what a mother was supposed to be.

Warmth radiated from Marina's eyes whenever she looked at her children. She sang them songs, told them stories, plaited their hair. Sometimes she'd pull them into her arms and kiss their cheeks for no other reason than that she loved them.

Katya began to ache, not just for the absence of her mother but with the realisation she'd hardly had a mother at all. Svetlana left Katya home alone for long periods. She half-listened whenever Katya spoke, rarely looking her in the eye. If Katya hugged her mother, Svetlana stiffened, tolerating her daughter's nearness for the space of two breaths before pulling away.

Katya wondered if Svetlana didn't know how to be a mother, but that didn't make sense. Svetlana Efremova, born Svetlana Balakina, had been one of the anarchists' best operatives. She incited riots, broke political prisoners out of the Peter and Paul Fortress, and stole intelligence from government officials. Their comrades talked about Svetlana as though she were an atheist saint – their golden lady, harbinger of the Revolution.

A woman like that must know how to be a mother. That meant the problem must be Katya.

Katya vowed to change. When her mother got out of prison, Katya would be tidy, obedient and helpful. She'd earn her mother's love.

In the meantime, she thrived at the commune, surrounded by honorary aunts, uncles and cousins. For the first time in her life, Katya had felt true belonging.

Now, as the steamer carried her toward Solovki, Katya thought imprisonment might not be all bad. She'd spent the last two years of her mother's life in hiding, completely isolated from the people they'd known and loved. Svetlana died, but Katya still had family – other anarchists bound to her not by blood but by their shared ideals.

Joining them might be like coming home.

Katya opened her school bag and took inventory of her belongings. Rifling through her possessions felt surreal, like reaching through time to touch her old life. Katya found the waist-length raincoat she'd been wearing when they arrested her. It was meant for autumn rather than winter but better than no coat at all.

Removing the coat revealed books resting in the bottom of her bag – a collection of fairy tales, the textbooks she'd had on her during her arrest and one other.

Her poetry diary.

For a long moment, Katya stared at the leather cover, cracked and flaking from so much use. The lab might have been half-way bearable if she'd had pen and paper. She'd composed a hundred poems in her head, but with nowhere to write out her heartbreak, the words settled in her soul like stagnant water. Without poetry, she'd lived a slow poisoning.

Katya carefully picked up the diary. Opening to a blank page, she ran a finger over the textured paper. She was tempted to flip backwards, to read over the last poem she'd written, as she always did before starting something new. But there was no going back to ten months ago.

She returned the diary to the bag. There might not be enough ink in the world to purge her conscience, to transform the evil she'd seen and done into lines and stanzas. But Katya was a poet, and so she would try. Later, though. In solitude.

Right now, she needed to pay attention. There was something out of place among her returned possessions.

Beneath her schoolbooks and poetry diary, Katya found her old book of fairy tales, a book that hadn't been in her bag when they arrested her. How did it end up here?

Katya flipped through the book's pages. She paused when she noticed a dark brown splotch. *Dried blood?* As she continued turning pages she found more splotches, as though someone had leafed through the book with bloody fingertips.

Pressing a hand over her mouth, Katya took a shaky breath. Everything within her stilled, the flow of time slowing to a trickle. The steamer still rocked, her heart kept on beating, but this felt like a threshold – a moment that would change everything.

Bracing herself for what she would find, Katya flipped through the remaining pages. There, beside the back cover, was a message in Svetlana's swirling handwriting. It must have been written on the day of Katya's arrest – the day Svetlana died.

Слушай шепот звезд. *Listen to the whisper of stars.*

The whisper of stars was a weather phenomenon in the Siberian winter, a tinkling sound made when breath turned to ice. The Yakut people believed if you spoke during the whisper of stars, your words would freeze as they left your lips and fall into the snow. Then later, during the spring thaw, anyone walking by might hear your secrets.

Before she died, Svetlana left this message for Katya to find, like words fallen into the snow during the whispering of stars.

Katya flipped through the blood-marked pages, wondering if the book contained a cipher. That would be just like her mother.

Whatever secrets awaited her, Katya felt as though Svetlana had reached through the grave to grab Katya's shoulders, shaking her awake. The steamer was nearing Solovetsky Island, and Katya took in every sound and smell with heightened awareness: screaming gulls overhead, ice scraping wood as the ship navigated the harbour, faint undertones of smoke carried upon the sea air.

This message meant Svetlana had made one last plan to save Russia from tyranny. It was up to Katya to decode it. Perhaps this plan was exactly what the anarchists needed to breathe new life into the resistance.

Katya looked up the companionway toward the cold, blue sky and the gulls flying free overhead. She was still a prisoner, but something stirred within her, something that had lain dormant for a long, long time – something that felt like hope.

# Chapter 5
## *Dima*

Dima would die on Solovetsky Island. His existence rather inconvenienced the Bolsheviki, after all. They couldn't have aristocrats wandering around Russia with their titles of nobility and claims to ancestral lands, so it seemed their solution was a death island in the middle of a frozen sea. Dima couldn't decide if that was better or worse than the French and their guillotines. Better, probably. At least Dima had time. Days, weeks – months, if he was lucky. Hopefully enough time to find a story worth telling.

When a sailor shouted down the companionway for them to disembark, Dima tucked his sketchbook back into his leather satchel. The pages contained portraits he'd drawn on the streets of Kazan.

At present, Dima's sketchbook also contained an enigma.

Dima waited for the Politicals to climb off the platforms and follow the sailor up the companionway to the deck. He kept his eyes lowered until the anarchist was partway upstairs. A quick glance after her showed her tangled blonde hair tied in a messy bun as she climbed the steps. The sight of her back gave Dima the all clear to hop down from the platform and follow the Politicals above deck.

When he'd started dreaming of her, Dima spent hours

wondering who she was, where she was, why sadness pooled in her eyes and defiance stiffened her chin. But in all the times he'd imagined her, he never thought she might be his enemy.

*An anarchist.*

The memory of the day the Red Army came to his family home bubbled in the back of Dima's mind like a pit of blackest tar, ready to coat his thoughts in darkness. That's why Dima refused to think about it. Also why he avoided looking at the face he'd memorised long ago.

Dima's dreams meant their stories were connected somehow, but it couldn't be a love story. Or even one of friendship. To befriend an anarchist would be a betrayal of his family, who had died at an anarchist's hand.

A gust of freezing wind struck Dima's face as he emerged onto the deck. The sprawling monastery complex spread before him, enclosed within a medieval fortification. Rising above the immense stone walls, dozens of mystical white towers stretched towards the sky, like an illustration of a fairy-tale palace. But the image was tainted – the onion domes that once ornamented the churches' tips were blackened and damaged from a fire that still smouldered in the largest buildings.

Something twisted in Dima's gut at the sight of the fire-damaged monastery. Not that it surprised him the Bolsheviki had set fire to one of the holiest places in Russia. They'd destroyed everything else, after all. But it still hurt to see it.

That grief sharpened when counter-revolutionaries were herded like cattle out of the steamer's hold. Dima and the Politicals had been ordered to wait. He stood slightly apart from them, his heart in his throat as the counter-revolutionaries streamed down the gangway: princesses and barons, scientists and merchants – people who, because of their titles or education, might pose a threat to the communists' hold on power. Dima was tempted to lower his eyes to keep from being overwhelmed by heartbreak, but he forced himself to look, to witness those pathetic figures – exhausted, bedraggled, and headed for hard labour. Just like Dima.

Guards separated the prisoners by gender and led them to a bathhouse. There they washed themselves in shifts while guards deloused their clothes. Dima's belongings were returned to him smelling of sulphur. The scent mingled with the smoke hanging in the air, creating an atmosphere of fire and brimstone as a guard led the way to the monastery gates.

Dima followed the crowd between rows of residential cells and workshops, then finally through an arched entrance to the monastery's kremlin, the innermost fortress where administration buildings and churches surrounded a large courtyard.

Crossing himself, Dima looked up at the three primary churches of Solovetsky. They gleamed white in places and were blackened where the fire had destroyed several towers and onion domes. For centuries, Solovetsky had been a place of miracles. Even now something stirred in the ground about Dima's feet, and in the wind cutting through his clothes to sing against his skin – something awake, alive.

*Magic.*

There was power here. Dima's grandfather sometimes spoke of places where the curtain separating the realms thinned like gossamer. Perhaps Solovki was one such place.

Dima stood amongst the counter-revolutionaries in the courtyard, while the anarchist and the other Politicals waited slightly apart. Guards clad all in black with sheepskin greatcoats and military caps smoked cigarettes and laughed with one another while the prisoners waited for whatever they'd have to endure next.

At last the door to the main administration building swung

open. An enormous man stepped through it. He had the look of a sailor, walking with the lurch of someone who might be thrown off balance at any moment. The thick muscles of his shoulders and arms bulged beneath his uniform. The guards put out their cigarettes and stood at attention, saluting as the enormous man passed by.

He stopped before the crowd, rocking from his toes to his heels as he regarded the new arrivals with bloodshot eyes. Slurring his words, he said, 'Welcome to Solovki, you wretches. I'm Camp Commander Nogtev, in charge of this special purpose camp.'

He started to say more but seemed to lose his train of thought.

'Here.' One of the guards offered Nogtev a small stack of folders. 'The Politicals.'

'Eh? EH? Speak up,' Nogtev barked.

'Files.' The guard raised his voice. 'For the Politicals.'

'*Dah.*' Nogtev swayed off balance when he moved to swipe the files.

'Allow me, Comrade Camp Commander.' Another guard stepped forward, barely concealing his disgust at his superior's drunken display. He took the folders and shouted loud enough for everyone in the courtyard to hear, 'Politicals and party men, step forward when I call your name.'

The guard opened the first folder and called out, 'Istomin, Social Democrat.'

Sergei stepped forward, and the guard continued calling out the names listed in the files. *Kruglikov, Menshevik. Pudovkin, Social Revolutionary. Naumovich, Socialist Zionist. Umskin, Social Revolutionary.*

And then he had no more files to read from.

The anarchist stood alone.

Dima couldn't help it then – he looked at her. She'd changed from when Dima first began to draw her, and even since he saw her in the lab. Her cheeks were sunken in with hunger, her lips chapped with thirst. Eyes that had been sad when Dima first sketched her now looked downright haunted. Her jaw worked back and forth as though it hurt to swallow, and finger-shaped bruises crossed her throat.

Who had strangled her? Dima tried to remember what happened in the lab, but a dream-like haze of forgetfulness cloaked everything after the doctor hypnotised him.

The anarchist looked pleadingly at Sergei and the other Politicals. Instead of speaking up for her, they averted their eyes and followed the guard leading the way out of the courtyard.

Terror crossed her face in the moment she realised they would abandon her, but then she put her shoulders back and raised her chin. Defiance blazed from her bloodshot eyes, and Dima's heart panged. If his magic weren't locked inside him by the iron collar, he'd have been compelled to draw a portrait of her courage.

The hope of safety was being taken from her, the promise that Politicals would be given comfortable lodgings and protection from all harm. If she was doomed to hard labour like the counter-revolutionaries, Dima doubted she'd survive it. She wasn't only injured, but starving. A long imprisonment had left her emaciated and weak.

This wasn't right. Dima watched the Politicals crossing the courtyard, willing them to speak up for her. Not a single one turned to look back.

'You, girl,' Nogtev said gruffly. 'Why are you standing over there?'

'I'm an anarchist.' Her face contorted with the pain of pushing words through her injured throat.

'Eh?' Nogtev stepped toward her. 'Speak up.'

She curled her hands into fists as she forced words out, louder this time. 'Yekaterina Efremova, an anarchist.'

*Yekaterina*. Dima finally had a name to go with the face in his sketchbook. Not that it mattered. With any luck, they'd find her file and send her to the political prison, where she'd be safe.

The guards flipped through the files that came with the new arrivals.

'Found her.' One of them pulled a file from the stack and placed it in the director's hand. Nogtev glanced over it.

'You're classified counter-revolutionary.' Nogtev slurred his words as he pointed toward the crowd of prisoners. 'Stand over there.'

How was that possible? Even if Katya wasn't an anarchist herself, being Svetlana Efremova's daughter should have been enough to shield her from hard labour.

Katya stood her ground. A yellow-haired guard pulled a curved bat from his belt, smiling like he hoped Katya would give him a reason. She opened her mouth, but then winced in pain. Giving Nogtev her name must have caused Katya's throat to swell even more. She couldn't speak, and none of the Politicals had spoken for her.

Dima hesitated. Katya was an anarchist, and anarchists had killed his family. She was also the girl whose face appeared in three of his skomorokh dreams. He couldn't pretend that didn't matter.

Dima stepped forward.

When Comrade Nogtev's cruel eyes turned his way, Dima's heart began to race.

'Her mother was the activist Svetlana Efremova.' Dima projected his voice, though it cracked at the end. 'Lenin ordered political prisoners and their children to be kept separately, unharmed.'

The silence that fell over the courtyard was a living thing, a quiet with a pulse. The guard with yellow hair tightened his grip on the curved bat. Dima's survival instincts warned him to lower his head and rejoin the safety of the crowd. But Katya hadn't stood down, so neither would he.

'Here's the first thing you need to understand.' Nogtev's lip curled into a cruel smile. 'There is no Soviet authority here, only Solovki authority. The civil war is finished, and you people lost. Now we can do whatever we want to you.'

Nogtev shoved a cigarette in his mouth. His hand wavered drunkenly when he struck a match. After a few attempts he connected the flame to his cigarette and sucked in, exhaling smoke.

Cold dread crept over Dima as Nogtev said, 'So we're going to play a little game.'

# Chapter 6

## *Katya*

Katya stood frozen as Comrade Nogtev took prowling steps toward Dima Danilov. Why had he spoken up for her? They'd misclassified Katya, yes, but the Bolsheviki would think twice about harming someone with her political connections. Dima, on the other hand, was both a Cossack and an aristocrat – two things that made him an enemy of the people.

'Look there. The monastery's old hermit cells.' Nogtev waved his cigarette toward one end of the courtyard. 'Beside each is a supply hole, just the size for a man to squeeze into. And this mean bastard is Comrade Smolensky.'

The yellow-haired guard took another step forward, swinging his bat in practice strokes.

Nogtev gripped Dima's arm.

*Look away*, Katya's reason warned. *There's nothing you can do.* Katya shouldn't care what happened to this stranger. He'd spoken up for her though, and she felt oddly responsible for him now.

She needed to get their attention away from Dima. Though she couldn't speak, she strode forward.

Another guard lifted his rifle and smashed it into Katya's back, dropping her to her knees. Pain reverberated through her body. He hit her again, and she timbered. Her cheek collided with the cobblestones. The guard wedged his knee between her shoulder blades, pinning her to the ground.

'Make her watch,' Nogtev ordered.

The guard grabbed her hair, tugging her face upward.

'Here are the rules. Once this young man squeezes himself into the hole, he'll be safe. But until then, well . . .' Nogtev nodded toward Smolensky, who swung his bat in demonstration. 'I'm not a monster, though. I'll give him a three-second head start.'

With a tiger's smile, Nogtev released Dima's arm.

'One.'

Dima hesitated.

'Two.'

Shocked into motion, he sprinted across the courtyard, swinging his satchel off his shoulder and wrapping the strap around his wrist.

'Three.'

Smolensky gave chase, boots pounding the cobblestones, bat clenched in a white-knuckled fist. Katya exhaled. By the time the steam of her breath cleared, Smolensky had caught up. He swung the bat overhanded like a mallet – a blow meant to force Dima to the ground.

Dima skidded out of the way. The bat missed him. Twisting, he swung his leather satchel at Smolensky's cheek. It knocked the guard's head sideways.

Smolensky kept up a steady stream of angry-sounding Polish while he disentangled himself from the bag's strap. Dima sprinted toward the hole. Maybe he didn't need help. He was making it, he was . . .

Smolensky lifted the bat overhead and sent it spinning through the air. A thud echoed through the courtyard followed by a collective gasp. Dima clutched his ear as blood dripped through his fingers. He staggered a few steps.

Smolensky retrieved the bat and cracked Dima's ribs with a brutal swing. Katya felt that crack deep in her spirit, and she knew. Her mistake wasn't trying to help, but wanting to. Compassion was an indulgence of the weak. To survive this place, Katya had to be harder than the iron collar around Dima's neck. She had to cloak her heart in steel.

Katya closed her eyes. Pressed down by the guard's knee like a pinned butterfly, she focused on the cold seeping from the ground into her skin, chilling her blood. She imagined the numbness of a winter night spreading frostlike through her mind. If only she could conjure a roaring January wind to drown out the sounds of Smolensky's bat pounding flesh, cracking bone. That wind would sweep away all thought and memory of Dima's pain-filled cries, covering them like a drift conceals footprints in snow.

When the beating ended, Katya kept her eyes closed a few moments more. Had Smolensky stopped because Dima had dragged himself into the hole, or because he'd never do anything ever again?

The guard unhanded Katya's hair and then released the pressure on her back. Grabbing her schoolbag, Katya pushed herself up to standing. No corpse lay on the ground. Dima must have reached the hole alive.

A vicious smile sliced across Smolensky's face as he strutted through blood and returned to Nogtev's side. Nogtev nodded his approval. Flicking away his cigarette, he faced the crowd.

'I trust no one else will be giving us trouble.' He paused for effect before saying, 'Good. We have a special guest with us, so you people better be on your best behaviour.'

Nogtev signalled to one of the guards who opened the door of the Father Superior building. The man who entered the courtyard with a smooth, predatory gait was slighter of build than Comrade Nogtev, but the way the guards all straightened left no doubt to his importance.

There was something familiar about him. Katya squinted, and recognition turned her blood cold. *The detective.* Seeing him took her back to that rainy afternoon last autumn.

Katya's memories of that day were charcoal sketches across papery thoughts, all dark streaks and blurred edges. She recalled her bicycle dropping in wet grass the moment she saw the ambulance wagon outside their building. The medics were sharing a cigarette, their backs to the wagon as though it contained something too terrible to face.

Katya had rushed into the building and taken the steps two at a time but stopped when she saw the wide-open door to her flat. The last few stairs had creaked beneath her boots and her dread. In one dizzy flash she saw paint splattered across their living room wall – only later would she understand it had been blood.

She'd been intercepted on the landing by a police detective with eyes as grey as the November sky. He had the gaunt look of a tuberculosis case that never fully healed, and he wore a wrinkled raincoat and a military cap with a red star on the front.

'You must be Yekaterina,' he'd said. 'A bad business, this. A wet affair.'

'Wet affair' was slang for a robbery gone wrong, code for a crime that shouldn't have been possible. Svetlana refused to live like the rich while working on behalf of the poor. She had patches on the elbows of her coat, and her most valuable possessions were stacked haphazardly on a bookshelf.

'Do you have any family I should call?' The detective placed his hand on Katya's shoulder – a comforting gesture, though something inside her squirmed.

'There's no one left,' Katya admitted.

'You'd better come down to the station and answer a few questions.'

That was how she'd found herself in the backseat of a government-issued automobile, staring out the window as the darkening city streaked by. Instead of police headquarters, the detective brought Katya to the Cheka building at Lubyanka Square. A lift carried them to an upper floor where dozens of guards watched as they passed through labyrinthine hallways and into the laboratory. Doctor Barchenko awaited Katya there, a tranquiliser shot in hand.

This officer had delivered her to the lab. Now, on the day she'd been transferred, here he was again. What was a Moscow police officer doing in Solovki?

'This is Commissar Boky,' Nogtev announced, 'Head of the Special Department of the Extraordinary Commission oversee-ing this camp. He wants to say a few words.'

Everything inside Katya stilled. Shock engulfed her, and realization bit deep. Commissar Boky had lied. He was a senior Bolshevik official, not a police detective. Head of the special department, and 'special', of course, meant dangerous.

*Listen to the whisper of stars,* Svetlana's final message warned.

Now she had Katya's full attention.

'I welcome you new arrivals to the beginning of your re-education,' Boky announced. 'We call this a 'Special Purpose Camp', but what, you may ask, is that purpose? We will turn you criminals and class enemies into perfect Soviet workers. Consider this a grand experiment, a micro-society mapping the path to utopia.'

Boky's wolfish gaze roved over the assembled crowd. He smirked suggestively, as though hard labour were something erotic.

'In the past you have rested your feet on the backs of the peasants. The time has come to make amends.' Commissar Boky raised a fist. 'Labour will be your purgatory, pain your redemption.'

Instead of applause, the prisoners gaped at him. Boky seemed to savour their dismay. When his eyes fell on Katya, they lingered. Katya's skin crawled, but something told her he'd enjoy seeing her afraid. She lifted her chin and stared unflinchingly back.

'Thank you, Commissar.' Nogtev stepped forward, his cruel eyes scanning the crowd. 'Tomorrow you begin working off your crimes against the Russian people. Now get out of our sight.'

# Chapter 7
## *Katya*

*When the shepherds become wolves, the sheep must lead themselves.*
That old anarchist catchphrase rose to the forefront of Katya's
mind as Commissar Boky strode back into the administration
building. Her thoughts flurried, swirling with questions she had
no answers to. Why had she been misclassified? Why had Boky
left the comforts of Moscow to come to Solovki? And what
had Svetlana meant by her final message – *listen to the whisper
of stars?*

Katya had to set those thoughts aside for the moment. Starving, badly injured, and now sentenced to hard labour – none of
her questions mattered if she didn't survive.

If Katya's allies knew she was on the archipelago, they'd
demand her transfer to the political prison. She had to get word
to the anarchists somehow, but, for the moment, she simply had
to make it through her first day.

The guards ordered the men and women into separate groups,
leading them in different directions. Katya fell in with the
female convicts. The aches in her body sharpened with every
step, and her throat had swelled so much she could barely
swallow.

Still, she tried to take note of her surroundings. The monastery compound was an enormous maze of churches, residential

buildings and workshops, surrounded by immense stone forti-
fications. Katya assumed the walls would be used to lock them
in, but the guards led them out through the main gates instead.

They trudged alongside the stone harbour, over pebbles
and patches of grass. At the end of a plank walkway stood a
rectangular wooden building with white framed windows and
a green roof. This used to be the monastery's guesthouse, but
now it would house female convicts.

Outside the entrance, the guards explained the new rhythm
their lives would fall into. A morning bell would wake them
each day. They would then have an hour to return to the monastery, queue up for morning rations, and assemble in the main
courtyard for roll-call. Their company would be assigned a work
detail each morning and expected to labour for a minimum of
ten hours per day, after which they would receive a hot meal.

Anyone who missed roll-call would have their rations cut
in half. Failure to report to duty for three days would lead to
further cuts.

Work or starve – that was the choice set before them.

The guard's voice grew distant as a ringing filled Katya's ears.
Her legs ached. A dark film crept in the edges of her vision,
but she closed her hands into fists and forced her back to go
ramrod straight.

Just as Katya thought she might faint, a strong hand steadied
her. The stranger laced Katya's arm over her shoulders and
propped her up.

Katya turned to look at the young woman, whose black
hair was covered by the ugliest headscarf Katya had ever seen.
When Katya peeled her eyes away from the hideous scarf, she
understood why she'd wear such a garment. The woman had
also smeared dirt on her cheeks, but that didn't conceal the
perfect cut of her cheekbones nor dim the luminosity of her big

brown eyes. Beauty could only be a liability in a prison where men outnumbered women twenty to one.

As if to drive that truth home, the guards announced that the women should step forward for inspection when their names were called, then enter the barrack and find an empty bed. This 'inspection' consisted of the guards leering at each woman before assigning her a monetary value: half a rouble for the elderly, a rouble for the young but plain, two roubles for the beauties.

After a handful of women had passed this degrading inspection, an old lady stepped forward of her own accord. Though short, plump, and walking with a cane, her perfect posture made her appear taller than she was, larger than life. Her elegant black coat had thick puffs of fur at the collar and sleeves, but they were matted and soiled after her difficult journey to Solovki. The contents of a single suitcase clutched in her hand were likely the only possessions she had left in the world.

'Wait your turn,' the guard ordered, a low note of warning in his voice.

The old woman merely leaned on her cane, glaring at the guards like they were very small, foolish boys.

'What's the meaning of this?' She waved at the list in the first guard's hand with an air of exasperation. 'What are the roubles for?'

'That's how much each of you would go for as a Petrograd whore.' The second guard laughed, elbowing his companion.

Under the old woman's disapproving gaze, the first guard didn't join in. He squirmed, a flush rising to his cheeks. When the old lady continued staring at him, he snapped. 'What are you looking at, old woman?'

'Your mother's shame,' she said calmly, never taking her eyes from his.

The second guard's laughter died away at that statement. 'Go and stand with the others until we call your name.'

'I'm here now,' the old woman said. 'The name's Witte. Matilda Ivanova Witte.'

The first guard found her name on the paper and made a mark beside it.

'And? How much do you think I'm worth, young man?'

'Nothing.' He didn't meet her eyes.

'I'm worth nothing?'

'No, babushka.' The flush on his cheeks deepened. Even his ears turned red. 'I meant that you may enter the barrack without inspection.'

'Why thank you.' Matilda Ivanova's voice dripped with condescension. 'But I believe I'll stay right where I am until this "inspection" is complete.'

Matilda Ivanova set down her suitcase and leaned on her cane, earning Katya's begrudging respect.

Deference to elders was deeply ingrained in Russian culture. It was generally accepted that young people ought to listen to those who had lived long enough to know better than them. Still, it took guts for Matilda Ivanova to stand up to two armed guards.

The roll-call continued, but there was no more leering or assigning monetary value to the female inmates.

Each woman who passed into the barrack met Matilda Ivanova's eyes, nodding their thanks or blinking twice in a gesture of friendliness. The lovely young woman who had propped Katya up squeezed Matilda Ivanova's hand in gratitude after her name was called.

When they called Katya, she nodded to the old woman and stepped into the guesthouse, turning down a hallway and entering an open door. The barrack was a long room with three-tiered bunks lining either wall. She manoeuvred the narrow aisle until she realised with dismay that the beautiful young woman had saved a space for Katya in the bunk beside hers.

She'd removed the headscarf, and her black hair hung long and shiny as silk. With her tan skin and dark eyes, she looked like someone from the Caucuses – Armenian or Georgian, perhaps.

'That looks painful.' She nodded toward Katya's throat. Then she extended her hand. 'My name is Tsisana, but you can call me Sana. All my friends do.'

'I'm not your friend,' Katya whispered as she lowered herself onto the bare wooden planks of her bunkbed.

Katya couldn't afford the luxury of friendship.

She might be wearing a school uniform, but she was lifetimes away from the hopeful teenager who'd basked in the glory of the Revolution. Six years ago, when revolutionary forces toppled the interim government, Petrograd had become a city of heroes. Her streets and taverns were filled with songs of triumph. The air had seemed abuzz with hope and possibility, and Katya had been in love with life, in love with love. She'd kissed boys behind bleachers in auditoriums where her mother was speaking and filled her diary with poems dedicated to whichever revolutionary's son had infatuated her that week.

Katya cringed when she thought of that girl, her heart wide open to the world, not realizing how thoroughly it was about to be broken. When the Bolsheviki took over, the sweetness of victory turned bitter, and now here Katya was – alone in the world, but wiser. She wouldn't tempt grief by lowering her guard.

Friendship and heartbreak were sisters. Better not to care.

Katya unhooked a lantern and brought it with her as she laid down on the bunk, purposefully turning her back on Tsisana. She took out her book of fairy tales, and searched for clues on the pages Svetlana's bloody fingertips had touched. At first she'd assumed her mother left them while flipping through the book, but the marks were deliberate thumbprints.

Svetlana had chosen those pages intentionally.

Katya reached for the pen in her schoolbag and opened her poetry diary to the next blank page. She jotted down the page numbers Svetlana had touched, then she worked methodically to try and crack the code. 'C' for слушай was the nineteenth letter in the alphabet, so she wrote down the nineteenth word on the first page Svetlana had marked. She did the same for the other letters in the message – but there were twice as many blood-marked pages as letters. The message came out as nonsense.

Katya ran the message through two substitution ciphers. With the Caesar, every letter moved three places down the alphabet. The monoalphabetic cipher was more complicated, in that the letters would remain the same distance apart from one another, but could be moved to any part of the alphabet. Neither cipher worked. Any more elaborate cipher would take time for Katya to crack.

Interestingly, the page numbers written out looked almost like a code: 3-7-14-15-22-29-34-36-40-44-53-61-65-75-82-91-95-100-102-108-112-116-124-131-140-144-151-153-163-171-180-186.

The book was over three-hundred pages long, but the marks stopped abruptly at page one-hundred-eighty-six. Again, that seemed deliberate. Katya examined every single page in the light, looking for clues. When she got to the final page where Svetlana had written *Listen to the Whisper of Stars*, she found slight indentations below the text. Katya smiled, despite everything.

She'd been eleven when her mother taught her how to leave secret messages with lemon ink. They were in hiding. A new arrest warrant had been issued for Svetlana's involvement in the assassination of a war official. Svetlana, restless and irritable, paced the safe house like a caged tiger. Katya, on the other hand, was delighted to have her mother all to herself. *Can you teach me to make invisible ink?* Katya had asked on their third day in hiding. Svetlana had paused her prowling steps. She sighed with resignation and said, 'Why not?'

Svetlana wrote her a secret message in lemon ink. It had felt like magic when Katya held the paper over a flame and letters appeared. *Hello little turtle.* 'Little turtle' was Svetlana's nickname for Katya.

A few days later, the tsar's secret police found them. Svetlana was convicted of the assassination and deported to a penal colony in Siberia. She only managed to escape and come back to Petrograd after the Revolution. With her mother gone, the anarchists sent Katya to a girls' school where she could spy on the daughters of the bourgeoisie.

Those were lonely years, but once in a while an envelope would arrive from Siberia with a seemingly empty paper inside. Katya always felt a thrill when she held those papers over a flame and found the messages her mother had written for only her to see.

Now Katya fought back tears as she lifted the glass from the lantern and held her book over the flame, careful not to burn it. The hidden message on the page became visible.

*1436*
келья

ГЦЪШ РФЭ ИИ Г Т С Н Й Б Н Б О М А

Katya stared at it for a long moment. The number didn't mean anything to her at first glance. The word on the second line was 'cell' – but what kind? A prison cell? A monastic cell? An anarchist cell hiding in a safe house? And what did the labyrinth mean? The letters on the last line had to be code of some kind.

As Katya stared at the revealed message, something moved in the shadows. Katya went stiff. Closing her book, she grabbed the lantern and swung it out, casting light in the night-dark room. A set of eyes gleamed, reflecting the flame for the briefest of moments.

Katya was on her feet, lantern held out in front of her. A woman stood just a few steps from Katya's bed. Katya thrust the lantern out further, and light flickered across the woman's freckled skin – it danced like fire through her loose-hanging auburn waves.

The stranger was younger than Katya thought at first, around Katya's age. Though scrappy and malnourished, the redhead had an aristocratic forehead, excellent cheekbones, and a narrow, slightly off-centre chin. Her eyes were open graves. That stare held a thousand deaths within it, cold enough to send a chill into Katya's soul.

*A witch*, Katya thought, unsure how she knew that.

The girl tilted her head to an odd angle, like a broken doll's. Then she smiled, wide and wicked, showing the sharp edges of her teeth. She stepped towards Katya, leaned over the lantern, and blew out the flame. A puff of kerosene smoke filled Katya's senses. Darkness washed over them. Katya held the book tight against her as the girl's footsteps passed by. In the faint moonlight trickling in through the window, Katya saw her climb onto the bunk above Katya's and lie down.

Katya watched the girl's silhouette for a long moment, then got back in bed. She situated the book of fairy tales beneath her so no one would be able to take it without waking her up, though after so many unsettling things had happened in one day, Katya doubted she would sleep at all.

# Chapter 8

## *Dima*

Dima shivered on a stone floor. When he opened his eyes – or rather opened his *eye,* since the left one had swollen shut – darkness engulfed him. Memories of the beating gripped him with the sharp claws of a nightmare. The first blow had hurt the most, when Smolensky threw the bat at Dima's head. A throbbing ache now radiated from that spot. When Dima probed the wound, his fingers came away sticky with blood.

The blows that followed blurred together. Dima remembered trying to focus through dizziness, crawling toward the supply hole attached to a hermit's cell. He felt the echoes of the beating all over his body. Bruises, aches, swollen flesh and a stabbing feeling in his side that likely meant cracked ribs.

He was lucky to be alive.

Lying on his back, Dima breathed through the pain of his headache. He felt around for his satchel before remembering he'd flung it at Smolensky's head. What would he do without his sketchbook? The iron collar stitched pain into Dima's neck, and his fingers felt unbearably empty without a pencil or paintbrush.

Regret twisted Dima's gut as he felt around the cell, just in case someone had thrown the satchel in after him. He didn't find it, but he did feel something odd – a small engraving on the stone floor.

His fingers traced over circular lines.

Dima pushed himself up to sitting, wincing as the ache in his ribs sharpened with the movement. The stone marked by the engraving shifted slightly when he put weight on it. Dima wobbled it a few times before fitting his fingers in the crease and lifting. The stone concealed a shallow hole with something inside it. Dima pulled the object out. Though the darkness of his cell made identification impossible, it felt like some kind of square pouch made of soft, worn leather.

He would have to wait until morning to see what it was.

Dima slept badly. The iron collar cut him off from his minstrel's dreams, leaving only a recurring nightmare. *His paintbrush tumbling from his fingers and two red spots appearing on his canvas, spreading like pools of blood.* Dima woke up before the nightmare could play out, haunted by a memory he couldn't bear.

He lay in the darkness, trying to think of better times. He recalled boyhood visits to Kyiv, where his grandfather worked as a professor of history and folklore at the Imperial University of Saint Vladimir.

Dedushka believed all a person needed to know could be learned from folk tales. *If you don't know the trees, you may be lost in the woods,* he would say, *but if you don't know the stories, you'll be lost in life.*

Even now Dima could close his eyes and picture Dedushka at his cluttered desk, hard at work on an epic poem. He used to mould texts like clay, kneading and shaping until every line reflected its truest self. Then he'd lean back, smoking his pipe and watching the ink dry, as though the words were likely to misbehave if he didn't keep an eye on them.

Dima's favourite visits were in summer. Whenever thunderstorms rolled over the city, Dedushka would take Dima and his siblings to the university's solarium so they could watch the spectacle through the glass ceiling. He'd sing folk songs between puffs of his pipe. Preparing them for the future, he called it.

Years later, Dima would wonder if he knew. When Dedushka tucked the covers tight around him and kissed his forehead, did he tell stories about children turned into beasts or frogs or crows because he suspected that, one day, Dima too would be cursed?

Dedushka had never turned into a bear. And the curse was not transformation in and of itself, but the horrors preceding it. Every member of Dima's family had died in one terror-filled afternoon, and nightmares had plagued him ever since.

Perhaps that's why Dima yearned for a story. He needed there to be a reason he survived when everyone he loved had perished. Rationally, he knew violence and death held no special purpose, but his heart ached to create something his family would be proud of – because if his life mattered, their deaths might not have been in vain.

When the coming dawn lessened the shadows in Dima's punishment cell, he could finally examine the pouch he'd found beneath the loose stone. Setting it on his lap, Dima untied the laces. The pouch opened into a large vellum rectangle.

*A map.*

The title, written in golden ink, said: The Gates of Solovetsky. Artistic renderings depicted the islands of the archipelago with angels standing guard over each one. Instead of being topographical, the map diagrammed the ancient stone labyrinths that dotted these islands. Bolshoi Zayatsky, though a much smaller island than Solovetsky itself, was drawn largest of all, owing to the fact that it had the most labyrinths.

Beside each labyrinth were lists of names and dates going back centuries. Dima scanned the names. The earliest date on the map was 1429, written beside the names Herman and Savvatiy, the first monks to live on Solovetsky Island.

Beside another labyrinth was written: *Zosima – 30 May, 1436.* Zosima officially founded the Solovetsky Monastery that same year.

As Dima scanned the names beside each labyrinth, he began to recognise some. Mystics, faith healers, revolutionaries – men who made pilgrimage to the Solovetsky Archipelago and went on to live extraordinary lives.

A prickling sensation spread over Dima's skin when he found a familiar name.

*Yelezar Kerdeyevich Danilov – 15 July, 1661*

That was Dima's ancestor, one of the most famous sko-morokhi in Russian history. Yelezar had served as minstrel to the Cossack folk hero, Stenka Razin, who led a peasant revolt against the tsar in 1670.

Legends claimed Yelezar Danilov wrote a first-person account of Stenka Razin's life. The Danilovs had been searching for that manuscript for two hundred and fifty years. They never found it, but still Dima's dedushka had been determined to continue Yelezar's work. Alongside giving lectures at the university, Dedushka obsessively researched the life of Stenka Razin.

As Dima ran his finger over the name of his many-times-great-grandfather, his skomorokh magic stirred inside him, despite the iron around his neck. There was something special about this archipelago. He'd felt it when he first set foot in the monastery.

Some of the most significant names in Russian history were written on this map. Their stories began here, and finding this map felt like a beginning for Dima as well. He wanted to live before he died on this island, wanted the thread of his life to somehow matter in the great tapestry that was Russia.

Dima traced his finger over the lines of the labyrinth beside his ancestor's name and an idea came alive within him, bringing with it a rush of energy. He tapped his fingers on the map, unable to hold still. What if he went to Bolshoi Zayatsky? Maybe seeing the labyrinths for himself would help him understand why a pilgrimage to this archipelago made the men listed on this map extraordinary. Maybe going there would make Dima extraordinary too.

As Dima continued studying the labyrinths and the names beside them, he found another familiar one.

*Stepan Timofeyovich Razin – 15 July, 1661.*

That was him, Stenka Razin, the Cossack folk hero Yelezar had served. Stenka meant 'Little Stepan', a nickname given to Razin ironically because he stood a head taller than most men. Just like the others on this map, Razin's story began in Solovki, on the same day as Yelezar Danilov's. They must have come here together.

Tracing his finger to the names below Razin's, Dima found the most recent name written on the map.

*Svetlana Nikolaevna Efremova – 20 October, 1922.*

A chill spread over Dima's skin. Katya's mother had come to the archipelago last year. Did Katya know? This might explain why Dima had dreamed of her so many times. He hated the idea of being connected to an anarchist in any way, but their pasts were rooted on this archipelago. Their futures must be intertwined as well.

Still, why did she have to be an anarchist?

The taste of bile crept up Dima's throat as the memory of what anarchists had done to his family threatened to surface. He suppressed it, refusing again to think about that day.

Instead he considered what this map could mean.

Perhaps all his wanderings had led him to this path of providence. All his life he had searched for a story, and now, at last, he found himself in its opening act.

# Chapter 9

## *Natasha*

A bell rang in the distance, and Natasha's eyes snapped open. She froze like prey at the sounds of movement, but then it all came back – Boky's proposition, her transfer and spying on Katya before falling asleep on a hard wooden bunk.

She sat up. All around the room women rose from their beds, gathering their affairs and wrapping scarves around their hair as they prepared to face the coming day.

Natasha curled her knees up to her chest and watched them. After two years in a lonely cell, it felt odd to wake up surrounded by other people. She couldn't let herself be distracted by the strangeness of it, though – she had a job to do.

Spying on Katya would be far easier if she had supplies for her witchcraft. Usually, Natasha could learn everything about a person by stealing a follicle of hair and a treasured possession. Or else she could gain preternatural insight while playing her violin. But no, Boky wanted her to befriend Katya, no matter how distasteful she found that prospect.

As a violinist, Natasha understood discipline. Sometimes you had to play the notes of the music set before you, reining your talent into the composer's vision. Here in Solovki, Natasha couldn't be the woman with a grudge against Yekaterina

Efremova. She had to play the song of duplicitous friendship that Boky had requested.

Her problem was figuring out how to become Katya's friend.

Natasha knew how to be charming. She simply mimicked the person she was talking to, adopting their energy, gestures and manners of speech. She essentially became a mirror. People liked her because she reminded them of their favourite person – themselves.

That could never work with Katya. If Natasha made herself as closed-off and jaded as the anarchist, they'd never even have a conversation. No, if she wanted to mine Katya's secrets, she needed to become someone else. Since Katya had spent her life trying to help the poor and oppressed, maybe that's what Natasha should be. Weak, pitiful, vulnerable. The type of person Katya might feel compelled to take under her wing.

Scanning the room, Natasha observed the other prisoners. Most were still getting ready for the day, exchanging the nervous glances and timid smiles of strangers thrown together. Natasha studied those smiles – closed-lipped if they merely shared a look, showing teeth if in response to something spoken. That seemed easy enough to replicate. The shy glances wouldn't be a problem either, so long as Natasha's eye didn't twitch.

Natasha found the most frightened-looking mouse in the room, a plump middle-aged woman cowering in the corner. Imitating the woman's wide-open eyes and creased brow made Natasha feel pathetic. She supposed that meant her disguise was complete.

Natasha slid down from the bunk. Katya looked up from her poetry diary, her eyes narrowing.

'Good morning.' Natasha curled her shoulders forward to make herself smaller. 'I wanted to apologise for last night.' She offered a nervous smile, barely more than a spasm of her lips. 'I didn't mean to spy on you.'

'Didn't you?' Even though Katya's damaged voice didn't carry above a whisper, she still managed to fill those words with mockery. Rising, Katya faced Natasha squarely, shoulders back, chin jutting.

'No, of course not!' Natasha let her already frightened eyes go even wider.

'Who are you?' Katya demanded.

Natasha considered lying, creating a weak name for the pathetic girl she was pretending to be, but her hatred ignited. She couldn't smother her outrage at what this girl's mother had done to her father.

'Natasha,' she said, all meekness gone from her voice. There it was, a breadcrumb for Katya to follow, if she had the wits.

'Natasha who?'

Natasha's eyes darted upward, as though the answer to that question waited above her head. She obviously couldn't give her real name, so she set out another breadcrumb. 'Natasha Georgiyevna Bobrinskaya.'

Katya crossed her arms.

'You're Yekaterina, right?' Natasha cowered slightly as she spoke. 'I heard you say that yesterday. Can I call you Katya?'

Katya shoved past her, bumping Natasha's shoulder. 'I'd rather you didn't speak to me at all.'

After Katya strode to the door and stepped out into the cold morning, Natasha straightened her slouched posture. That had gone abominably. Natasha should have been more careful last night. When Katya swung out the lantern and saw her, Natasha may have lost any chance of comradery, no matter how good an act she put on now.

She had to find a way to salvage this.

'All right, girls.' An old woman with a cane stepped towards the door, the filthy hem of her tattered fur coat dragging at her feet. 'Let's find our breakfast.'

She led the others outside, and Natasha joined the group. Their shoes crunched over frozen grass and gravel as they made their way from the guesthouse to the main monastery complex. The old woman asked around until she discovered the ration line and led the women to the queue.

Katya joined back up with them at roll-call, after which a guard led the new female arrivals to a cavernous laundry room. The monastery's waterwheel pumped a continuous stream of near-freezing water into a dozen basins with washboards. A mountain of dirty hospital linens filled the centre of the room – a mountain that would have to be moved before the women would be allowed to stop work.

They all lined up for instructions, but the guard's voice faded to the background as Natasha watched Katya. The anarchist's knees trembled, and her eyes grew unfocused, as though she might faint. Natasha was thin after two years of imprisonment, but Katya looked to be starving.

Perhaps this was her way in. Instead of being a weak girl in need of rescue, Natasha would do the saving. If Natasha helped Katya survive hard labour, the anarchist would owe her. Eventually, Natasha would manage to form a friendship and extract the information Boky wanted.

The women grabbed dirty sheets from the pile and took their places at the sinks while the guard positioned himself by the exit. Natasha waited to make her move. Katya's knee buckled as she tried to take a step. Just when Natasha was about to swoop in and keep her from falling, a hand steadied Katya.

'Vodka and cabbage,' said a beautiful young woman.

Katya looked bewildered as the woman draped Katya's arm over her shoulders, bracing her up by the waist.

'For your throat. Cabbage to reduce the swelling and vodka to relieve the pain – it's an old remedy my grandmother taught me. I can't promise I'll be able to get some, but I'll ask at evening rations.' She guided Katya toward the furthest sink and gently leaned her against the wall. 'Just rest. I'll cover your work quota.'

Natasha's jaw clamped tight as the stranger's kindness obliterated her plan. She would never get close to Katya. Even if she did, Natasha doubted Katya would willingly reveal her secrets.

That meant Natasha would have to take them.

Rather than going to a sink, Natasha strode to the door. The guard moved to stop her, but then he recognised who she was and let her pass. Natasha headed towards the monastery kitchen to gather supplies for her witchcraft.

All violinists can play the notes they're given, but the truly great ones know when the time has come to improvise.

# Chapter 10

## *Dima*

Footsteps sounded outside Dima's cell. Quickly stashing the map beneath the loose stone, Dima forced himself to stand, even though the movement made him acutely aware of every injury on his body.

Orange light filled the creases of the door, and the footsteps stilled. A key turned in the lock before the door creaked open. A lantern inched into the cell, followed by the man carrying it.

Dima exhaled a relieved breath at the sight of a scraggly-bearded monk in a black cassock. The monk had a grim face. His blue eyes radiated such sadness that Dima's fear was swept away by compassion. Dima recognised too well the signs of grief so immense that it shattered the soul.

'I'm Father Iosef,' the monk said. 'I've come to take you to the infirmary. Can you walk?'

Dima managed a lumbering step forward. When he lost his balance, the monk braced Dima up.

'The guards are busy overseeing work details, but there are still two administrators working in the kremlin. We'll have to be quiet.' Father Iosef guided Dima out into the corridor.

Having to avoid guards meant this monk was helping Dima against the administration's orders – and probably risking his life to do so. Dima tried to thank him, but the pain took his breath away.

He could only grit his teeth and focus on putting one foot in front of the other. His breaths became ragged, and his heartbeat knocked against the inside of his skull. Father Iosef helped Dima up a flight of stairs. By the time they reached the top, Dima's knees quaked.

Dima perked up when they passed a doorway leading into a printing workshop where an old lithograph machine gathered dust.

They continued further along the corridor. When Father Iosef opened one of the doors, the smell of ammonia assaulted Dima's nose, followed by the subtler odours of blood and sickness.

Dusk had dimmed the windows, so only a few hanging lanterns offered light. Three rows of wooden cots lined the long, narrow room, crammed so close together that the doctor would have to turn sideways to fit between them.

Dima couldn't see well enough to guess how many patients occupied the cots, but he heard their moaning and laboured breaths. Father Iosef guided Dima to an empty bed. His ribs gave a sharp stab as he sprawled onto his back, head spinning. Father Iosef hung the lantern from a hook above Dima's bed.

'What's this?' A man in a white medical coat came out of the shadows.

Upon seeing Dima, he arched his brow at the monk. 'You're going to get us both killed, you know that right?'

'I'll take the blame if anyone finds out.'

The doctor gave the monk a dubious look that seemed to say, *As if that would make any difference.* He sighed as he looked Dima up and down. 'What happened to you?'

'I made the acquaintance of Comrade Smolensky.' Despite

his spinning head, Dima mustered a sardonic smile. 'Or, more accurately, I became very well acquainted with his bat.'

'He needs help,' Father Iosef said.

'Clearly.' The doctor hesitated a moment before huffing with resignation. 'Bring me snow, Father. A lot of it.'

'You're a good man, Doctor Tarasov.' The monk patted the doctor's shoulder as he left.

'They lock up the morphine, so I've nothing to give you for the pain,' Doctor Tarasov told Dima as he helped him strip off his jacket and shirt. 'But I'll try to bring down the swelling and keep your wounds clean as they heal.'

'You have my thanks.' Dima made the motion of tipping an invisible hat, since he'd lost his newsboy cap during the beating.

'Thank me by telling no one I helped. Otherwise, I'll be the one bleeding in a punishment cell – or worse.'

Doctor Tarasov left to get supplies. Lying there, a sense of unease spread through Dima, his skin prickling with the feeling of being watched.

From the bed beside him, half cast in shadow, the ghostly-pale face of a middle-aged man stared at Dima. A strap from the ceiling elevated his arm, which had been amputated at the wrist, the stump wrapped in thick bandages.

Dima greeted him warmly, but the man didn't seem to hear.

'He doesn't speak,' Doctor Tarasov explained as he returned with a basin of fresh water and a linen cloth. 'Not anymore.'

'What happened to him?'

'Lost his mind in the forest.' Doctor Tarasov began wiping the dried blood and dirt from Dima's wounds. 'He chopped off his own hand with an axe.'

Dima recoiled from the horror of the image the doctor's words painted in his mind. 'Why would he do that?'

'He said he wanted a few days off.' Doctor Tarasov shook his head. 'You treat a man like an animal long enough, he'll start acting like one.'

Dima wished he didn't have iron around his throat. Then he could dream of this man's past and perhaps call him back to the person he'd been before the prison broke him. Was he a husband? A father? What was his profession? What were his passions? Though Dima stared into those too-wide eyes, he found no spark of life within them.

As Doctor Tarasov continued cleaning Dima's wounds, Dima thought back to an evening after the Revolution when his grandfather had come home with a tidy paper bag pinched in his weathered fingers. Dedushka had returned from Kyiv to their estate in the countryside nine months earlier. The university had closed its doors at the onset of the Revolution, as though wooden planks and brass locks could keep the Red Terror from seeping through the cracks to spill the blood of the intelligentsia.

Even though he had no lectures to give, Dedushka went out every afternoon. He'd return with food sometimes. More often he came home with stories of how their friends and neighbours were bearing up in this new world the Revolution had created.

Dima's stomach had grumbled hopefully at the sight of the paper bag. It didn't look very big, but maybe Dedushka had found a few potatoes at least. The paper crinkled as Dedushka opened the bag. He pulled out a small, round tin of shoe polish. Dima couldn't contain his disappointed sigh.

Dedushka patted the seat beside him on the sofa. 'Come sit by me, Dimochka. We might not have anything to eat, but we can still polish our shoes.'

Then his grandfather taught Dima how to clean the dust off his shoes, how to polish and buff them. Dedushka even finished with a spit shine. By the time they were done, their shoes looked brand new.

Dima was still hungry, of course, but he felt a bit better when he put his shoes on. His family had lost almost everything, but here was a bit of dignity they could claim for themselves.

'That's how hope grows,' Dedushka had said. 'In the soil of little things, the things that remind us we're more than what we suffer.'

As Dima lay in the infirmary, he wondered what would have happened if the amputee beside him had been given shoe polish – maybe a bit of soap or a book to read when he wasn't working. Could he have endured longer before his mind cracked?

After Dima's family died, he'd ended up in Kazan. There he found work as a printer's assistant, a job he had for three years before his arrest. Dima could work a lithograph machine in his sleep, and so he wondered . . . what if he used the monastery's printer to share a piece of art with his fellow prisoners?

It might not be much, but it was the only morsel of dignity he had to share.

Father Iosef returned with a blanket full of snow.

'I brought you this, as well.' Father Iosef held up a metal file. He must have stolen it from one of the workshops. 'That collar can't be comfortable.'

'There's an understatement if I've ever heard one.' Dima took the file with gratitude. 'When Lenin spoke to his chekists of the need for "iron discipline", I don't think he meant it literally.'

The corner of the monk's lips twitched into something that could almost pass for a smile. Dima considered that a small victory. His mother always called Dima her entertainer, often with exasperation at the lengths he would go to make people laugh. Perhaps because of his skomorokh blood, he found nothing more rewarding than connecting with another person in a way that brought them joy, especially if that person wore their sorrow as plainly as Father Iosef did.

Dima held the metal file close to his heart as Doctor Tarasov set cold compresses over his contusions. Once he freed himself from the iron collar, Dima could dream again. And with his magic untethered, he could use that lithograph machine to sprinkle joy throughout the camp, where the prisoners so desperately needed it.

'Rest for a while,' Doctor Tarasov said. 'Father Iosef will have to take you back to your cell before the evening bell, but you can sleep here for now.'

It didn't take long for Dima to sink into a shallow, dreamless slumber. When he woke up, Dima removed the lukewarm compress of melted snow from his face. He stared up at the ceiling with his one good eye, thinking about the lithograph machine, the map and what it meant that Katya's mother had visited the island last year.

When Father Iosef returned to take Dima to his cell, he asked about Svetlana Efremova's visit to the archipelago.

The monk crossed himself when he heard Svetlana's name.

'She shouldn't have been here at all,' Father Iosef said. 'It was strange. Women had never been permitted in the monastery, but the brothers let her in. None of us questioned it until afterwards, when it felt as though a fog had been lifted from our minds. I think she bewitched us somehow.'

'What did she do here?' Dima asked.

'She spent most of her time in the library.' Father Iosef shrugged and held out his free hand in a gesture of helplessness. 'My memories of those days are dreamlike, hard to grasp. She may have borrowed a fishing boat to visit outlying islands, though I'm not certain.'

That would make sense. Svetlana's name on the map suggested

she'd visited the labyrinths on Bolshoi Zayatsky. Why, though? And what had she been looking for in the library?

'Can you think of anything else?'

Father Iosef shook his head, but then paused as something occurred to him.

'She did ask about the hermitess who lives on the island, Valentina Pavlovna Kryukova. Perhaps Svetlana Nikolaevna visited her.'

That name raised the hair on the back of Dima's neck. Kryukovs were one of the five remaining families with skomorokh magic – could this Valentina Pavlovna be a skomorokh like Dima?

'Is she still here?' Dima asked as he and Father Iosef descended the stairs.

'I don't know.' Father Iosef shrugged again. 'Her *izba* is on the east side of the island, surrounded by bogs and only reachable in full winter. It's possible the Bolsheviki haven't found her yet.'

They reached the bottom of the stairs and headed for the door of Dima's cell. 'Is there anything else you can tell me about Svetlana Nikolaevna?'

Father Iosef stiffened at the name.

'I can tell you many of my brothers would be alive today if not for her. The Bolshevik navy arrived on the archipelago while Svetlana Nikolaevna was still here. When our watchmen spotted the armada on the horizon, Svetlana Nikolaevna panicked. She said they were coming for her. Not long after, a fire broke out in the library.'

'I thought the Bolsheviki burned the monastery.'

'No, it was her. She started the fire, and then she left. The brothers of the Solovetsky Monastery blinked and shook their heads, as though waking from a dream. We found ourselves with a navy outside our walls and a raging fire within it. Perhaps we could have held off the Bolsheviki if not for the fire. This monastery has withstood years-long sieges in the past. But so many of us were fighting to save the churches that we couldn't defend our walls. The Bolsheviki breached the gate, and the slaughter began. More than half of my brothers lost their lives that day.'

Dima's heart ached for the monk. He knew what it meant to lose a family, and so he hoped Father Iosef could feel the sincerity of his condolences.

Back in his cell, Dima felt for the loose stone. He took out the map, tracing his fingers over the leather as he considered the implications of Father Iosef's tale.

Svetlana must have been searching for something on this archipelago. But why burn down the library before she left? Dima thought of all the blackened walls and towers, so much history gone up in flames. There had to be a reason, and a reason too for Dima dreaming of Katya three times. As much as he didn't want anything to do with an anarchist, Katya had a part in whatever destiny was unfurling around Dima.

Both Dima's ancestor and Katya's mother had gone to the labyrinths. Dima wanted to follow Yelezar's footsteps, but he sensed he wouldn't find the answers he sought, not without Katya.

Dima turned his mind to the task at hand. Getting to the island of labyrinths was a problem for another day. Right now he needed to free himself from the collar binding his magic. Dima found the seam where the iron had been soldered shut and began the tedious process of filing through it.

# Chapter 11
## *Katya*

Katya leaned against the wall, her head still spinning. Tsisana carried an armful of linens to the sink and began scrubbing them. Within seconds, the ice-cold water turned her hands a painful shade of red.

'Why are you helping me?' Katya whispered.

'So you don't get yourself killed.' Tsisana raised a perfectly shaped eyebrow. 'You have a problem with that?'

Katya exhaled a long breath, releasing the urge to fling Tsisana's mercy back in her face. Stubbornness was another luxury Katya couldn't afford, along with friendship. She shrugged her consent, but the Georgian girl's self-satisfied look raised Katya's hackles.

'This doesn't mean we're friends,' Katya said.

'That's too bad. It might have been interesting to befriend an anarchist.' A smile turned Tsisana's heart-shaped face radiant. She winked as she said, 'Just don't blow anything up in my general vicinity, and we'll call it even.'

One of the women raised her voice in song, a folk tune about the death of the forest in autumn. Others joined in, harmonising in a minor key that made the sound haunting and sad. It set the mood as the women scrubbed, syncing their movements with the beats and lilts of the music.

Katya huddled against the wall, weak and only surviving the day by the kindness of her enemies.

Before the Revolution, life had shone golden upon Russia's favoured sons, those few born with everything, their boots made to stand on the chains of men born to nothing but sorrow.

Would these women despise Katya if she explained Revolution was supposed to level the ground so everyone might feel sun upon their faces? Anarchists wanted to push power as far downward as they could, but wolves circled below them. The Bolsheviki snatched power and then proceeded to make a mockery of the revolutionaries' ideals.

They'd dreamed a just nation and found themselves in a nightmare no one could wake from.

Now here she was, surrounded by aristocrats. Only *they* were the ones labouring in despair, their bellies groaning with want. Was this justice? Had the Revolution delivered them their due, or was the wheel of oppression still rolling, just crushing someone else now?

The women continued singing their heartbreak as the hours passed. The laundry room had darkened with twilight by the time the mountain of linens had been washed. Looking around, Katya saw that the women's hands were red, chapped and painfully stiff.

When the guards dismissed them, the women headed for the ration line. Though she was starving, Katya's throat still hurt too badly to eat.

Instead she returned to the guesthouse and sprawled out on the wood planks of her bed, dizzy and exhausted. To distract from her gnawing hunger, Katya continued puzzling over the cipher until the other women returned.

They carried kerosene lamps, fanning out into the room as each sought her own bed in silence and exhaustion. Katya closed her book and tucked it away as Natasha – if that was her real name – climbed up onto the bunk above Katya's.

Tsisana knelt by Katya's bedside, setting a bundle and a lamp atop the wooden planks. She removed her scarf, and her long, black hair fell loose. In the glow of the lamplight, her beauty looked otherworldly, like an icon of a saint rendered by a master painter. She studied Katya's injuries with concern etched into her brow and compassion shining out from her dark brown eyes.

Maybe her kindness *was* genuine, though Katya didn't dare to trust it.

Katya's bed shifted as Matilda Ivanova sat beside Tsisana.

'What have they done to you?' Matilda Ivanova's soft wrinkles deepened as she studied Katya's neck. While Tsisana arranged supplies on the bed, Matilda Ivanova reached for Katya's hand. Though she ought to refuse being touched, Katya was too tired to protest. The old woman's weathered skin felt almost like paper as she laced her fingers through Katya's. Matilda Ivanova said, 'I'll help you fill your work quota tomorrow. You don't have to get through this on your own.'

'I'll help, too,' said a middle-aged woman sitting on the next bunk over.

'So will I,' added a Polish girl from across the room.

Voices echoed these sentiments all around the barrack as the ladies promised to share the load of Katya's labour while her injuries healed. Tears stung Katya's eyes. Here were her enemies, offering her kindness. Katya wished more than believed she could receive it without her heart being touched.

Tsisana numbed the skin of Katya's throat with vodka. Then she began to chant Hail Marys while resting gentle fingertips on Katya's neck. A soft power tingled against Katya's skin everywhere Tsisana touched, penetrating deeper with every repeat of the chant – healing her tissue, releasing her pain.

Tsisana must be a kolduna. She'd mentioned the remedy she would use on Katya came from her Georgian grandmother. Most villages had a wise woman who inherited the family book of remedies and the healing touch.

When she'd finished chanting, Tsisana made a compress of cabbage leaves to reduce the swelling of Katya's throat and put a crown of birch twigs on her brow to relieve the headache. Katya relaxed into the sound of the women's voices.

Tsisana told Matilda Ivanova about growing up the middle daughter of a Georgian count who split his time between their estate in the Caucuses and a townhouse in Paris. Though she'd trained as a nurse with the intention of becoming a nun, Tsisana's plans had abruptly changed course last year when a dashing Mexican nobleman attended a dinner party at her family's Paris home. Rafael Fernández-Villaverde, son of the count of Valle de Orizaba, had been on his way to Egypt to take up the post of his country's ambassador. One simmering look across the dining room table changed everything for them both.

'We were married this spring,' Tsisana said. 'Since the Civil War had ended, we decided to visit Tbilisi on our honeymoon tour. I wanted Rafael to meet my grandmother and see my father's ancestral lands, but we arrived to find the house had been requisitioned. The Red Army arrested us on sight. I've been sentenced to three years' hard labour, and Rafael . . . I don't even know where he is.'

Her voice cracked, and Matilda Ivanova put an arm around Tsisana's shoulders.

'They wouldn't dare to kill a foreign ambassador,' Matilda Ivanova assured her. 'Once your husband sends word to his government, you'll both be released.'

'I hope you're right.' Tsisana's eyes glistened with unshed tears. 'What about you? What's your story?'

79

'My surname is Witte,' Matilda Ivanova said.

'Are you the Countess Witte?' Tsisana asked, and the old woman nodded.

Her husband, Count Witte, had been the tsar's minister of finance. He'd pushed for Russia to become a constitutional monarchy, using his influence to bring protections for workers, peasants and Jews. Even Katya's mother had spoken well of him: *If Petrograd were filled with men like that, there'd be no need for revolution.* Yet here was his widow, being punished as an enemy of the people.

'Witte means white. It turns out that when the anti-Soviet forces call themselves the White Army, even a name can be counter-revolutionary.' Matilda Ivanovna smiled sadly. 'I got five years.'

Katya closed her eyes, trying to take calming breaths so that injustice wouldn't set her blood to boiling. What kind of government sends people to prison because of their name?

Other women shared their experiences with the Soviet justice system. Most had similar tales: terrifying arrests, sham trials, guilty (*always* guilty) verdicts, and sentences of three to ten years' hard labour. The trials gave an air of legitimacy to the government's plan of putting their enemies in concentration camps.

What did it mean that all these women had such similar experiences after their arrests, while Katya's had been cloaked in secrecy? No charges, no trial, no sentencing – and then she'd been misclassified as a counter-revolutionary. If they hadn't given her a release date, would they ever let Katya go?

A high-pitched bark cut through the din of women's chatter. Everyone fell silent. They listened to the husky's insistent yaps and howls, and then other sounds, quieter sounds. Boots marching. The thud of a rifle butt pounding flesh followed by a pained moan. From behind the guesthouse came the crunching of shovels breaking frozen earth and the hiss of soil being flung away.

Katya stood and peered out the back window. Commander Nogtev shared a flask with three other guards as twenty male prisoners dug a wide hole.

While the sounds of shovels filled the night, the women stood vigil – some watching through the windows, others sitting stiffly on their beds. Eventually the dog tired of barking. The barrack felt like a tomb. A strange, sepulchral silence fell over them.

By the time the prisoners were chest-deep in the ground and still digging, it became clear what purpose the hole would serve. Tsisana prayed quietly, but Katya could do more than that.

Thanks to Tsisana's ministrations, the swelling had gone down in Katya's throat. It still hurt, but, if she could speak, she could cast a spell to stop the evil unfolding outside the window.

Starting at a whisper, Katya began chanting the words of the zagovor she used to open her soul to the Otherworld. It took several repetitions, but power gradually began to flow into Katya, pooling in her diaphragm.

'That's good enough,' Nogtev shouted. 'Everybody out.'

After scrambling from the hole, the prisoners lay their shovels in a pile. They were ordered to stretch out their hands as a guard moved down the line, touching an iron object to the men's skin. Testing them for magic. Only one prisoner reacted, revealing himself as a volshebnik when he grimaced and pulled his hand back from the iron's stinging touch. Two guards took the volshebnik's arms. They dragged him away to devil-knows-where.

'Remove your shoes,' Nogtev ordered the remaining prisoners before taking a long swig of vodka. The prisoners looked at one another. Their expressions were those of doomed animals unable to fathom the trap closing around them.

Katya had to help them.

Svetlana had never taken the time to properly train Katya. Instead she helped her memorise the spells that would aid her in her work for the anarchists, things like assassination, stealth and memory manipulation.

She'd also learned an incantation for influencing emotions, which she often cast while Svetlana gave speeches, so the audience would feel the words more deeply. Katya's throat burned as she began to cast the spell, her intention focused on filling the guards with feelings of compassion.

Nogtev finished drinking and wiped his mouth with the back of his hand. 'Now take off your clothes.'

A sob escaped an old man's lips. The guards circled the prisoners, bullying them into doing as they'd been told.

Katya's spell wasn't working. The words left her lips, but she sensed them missing their mark. With horror, she realised what was going on. Svetlana always carried a protective talisman to guard against attacks from other volshebniki. These guards must have something similar.

Even with all the power of her magic, Katya couldn't save these men.

Having dug their own grave, the men lined up at the edge of it. Naked. Trembling from cold and fright. Some weeping, others wide-eyed with shock as the guards took aim. One prisoner, bearded and thin with hunger, looked to the window of the women's barrack.

Katya swore their eyes met.

She couldn't save him, but she could lessen the horror of his last moment. Katya chanted the spell again. This time she thought of Marina, the anarchist who watched over Katya when her mother was in prison. She gathered from her memories all the warmth of love and comfort she felt when held in Marina's arms, weaving that feeling into her spell.

The bearded man's expression shifted into a countenance of peace. A moment later, gunshots broke the silence and he fell forward.

Nineteen men dead. Nineteen lives ended, just like that.

The scent of gunpowder lingered long after the guards marched away with the dead men's clothes.

A tear slipped down Katya's cheek. She swiped at it and tried to hold back the horror and grief rising in her like swelling tides. The women returned to their beds, stunned to silence.

Katya lied down. In all the months she spent in the lab, she hadn't cried. She'd been afraid if she started she might never, ever stop.

Now she couldn't help herself. Grief streamed within her like bitter waters, rising to the surface. She covered her face with her hands as sobs wracked her body and tears began to flow.

Legs swung over the side of the bunk. Natasha dropped to the floor, her long red hair pulled atop her head in a loose chignon. She knelt at Katya's bedside. At first Katya thought Natasha meant to comfort her. Then Natasha's arm snaked out. She yanked Katya by her hair.

Pain pulsed over Katya's scalp. She screamed, and pain tore through her swollen throat. With cold determination Natasha fisted Katya's hair with one hand and clutched her chin with the other. Katya tried to twist and scramble away, but Natasha held her fast.

'What are you doing?' Tsisana scrambled off her bunk. 'Let her go.'

Natasha leaned in. She licked a tear from Katya's cheek. Then she released her. Katya scuttled off the bed, falling in a heap on the floor. All her outrage rose into her glare as she wiped her face with the cuff of her jacket.

'You should be more careful.' Natasha tasted her lips and then looked at Katya, her blue eyes as dark as the twilight outside the windows. 'It's never wise to share your sorrows with a witch.'

'She's mad,' one of the women declared, her high-pitched voice carried upon the uneven rhythm of her sobs.

This wasn't madness. Natasha must be a vedma witch. While kolduni healers used natural remedies, and the powers of charovniki spellcasters were in their voices, the veduni practiced a magic of rituals. Many of the old aristocracy were vedun sorcerers, involved in secret societies.

Though most vedun magic revolved around rituals, the word itself meant 'knower.' They were masters of divination and fortune-telling.

How many of Katya's secrets would Natasha be privy to, simply by the taste of her tear?

If Natasha was indeed a vedma, she was likely part of one of the oldest aristocratic families in Russia.

'Who are you?' Katya whispered, clutching at her aching throat.

'You're asking the wrong question.' Natasha tilted her head coyly. 'You should be asking what I want and how we could help each other.'

Though Katya was physically tired and emotionally spent, she rose to her feet. She raised her chin and met Natasha's eyes.

'I don't care what you want. And I refuse your help.'

'You think we're so different?' Natasha's face tightened with scorn. 'You congratulate yourself for surviving hell when you were only in the lab for ten months. That's only a fraction of what I went through.'

A shiver moved up Katya's spine. 'Who are you?'

'When you were labelled Number Two in the lab, did you never wonder who came before you?' Natasha leaned towards Katya, her voice low and dark. 'I am Number One – Doctor Barchenko's first victim.'

# Chapter 12
## *Natasha*

A secret kept could be powerful, but sometimes the true art of espionage was knowing when to give one away. Natasha would never work her way into Katya's confidences, so she made a play for the next best thing: her curiosity.

*I am Number One – Doctor Barchenko's first victim.*

A hundred more questions glittered in Katya's eyes. That was the power of a secret revealed. When the not knowing became unbearable, Natasha would have Katya right where she wanted her.

For now, Natasha tilted her head and spread her lips into an unhinged smile. Whispered conversations filled the room. The other women thought Natasha had lost her mind. Perhaps she had, a little. Two years locked in a laboratory will do that to a person. Natasha might not be entirely sane, but she knew exactly what she wanted.

Natasha's end goal was her greatest secret of all. She'd buried it deep, like the inner part of a nesting matryoshka doll. A secret within a secret within a secret within a secret. Her enemies would have to peel back a hundred layers of pretence before they found her true motive.

Natasha strode out of the guesthouse, leaving Katya's questions unanswered. She'd got what she needed. That tear, still salty on her lips, would reveal much about Katya's past once Natasha had time to play her violin. Tackling Katya had also provided a distraction – Katya hadn't noticed Natasha swiping the folded paper stashed inside her book. Natasha concealed the paper in her sleeve, its crease scraping slightly against the soft skin of her wrist.

Stepping outside the guesthouse, winter washed over Natasha. The cold numbed her face and tightened the two puckered scars on her back, old bullet wounds. No stars glittered in the sky. There would be snow tonight.

Though prisoners were only allowed to enter the monastery through the Nikolski Gate, Boky had organised an alternative route for Natasha to bring him news. She prowled alongside the fortress walls, headed for the Svyatya Gate.

There she knocked five times – two slow, three fast.

A latch turned, and the wooden gate creaked open just enough for Natasha to slip through. She tipped her head down so her hood concealed her face as the passed the guard and strolled through the tunnel beneath the fortress walls.

Natasha entered the administration building from a back door that led into a darkened kitchen. She paused to listen for any sounds. The building should be empty. Guards would either be drinking or still occupied after the evening's death march. Boky was known to enjoy a glass of wine and a book after dinner, so Natasha should be able to move about undetected. If anyone caught her, she had her excuse tucked inside her sleeve.

Natasha made her way to Boky's office and closed the door behind her. Only then did she dare to light a kerosene lamp. Sitting at Boky's desk, Natasha pulled the pins from her chignon, letting her hair fall loose. The drawers were locked, so she used one hairpin to hold the bottom of the lock in tension and a second to fiddle with the pins until the lock gave.

Natasha opened the drawer and lifted a file onto the desktop, labelled *S.N. Efremova*. Beneath it, Natasha found Boky's stash of occultist paraphernalia: black candles, a variety of crystals, a mirror and chalk. Natasha pocketed the chalk, but the other items were of little use to her.

Vedun magic manifested differently in men and women. Male sorcerers joined secret societies where they worked their way deeper and deeper into the mysteries of the occult. A vedun would learn to bind corrupted spirits to his will, sacrificing parts of his soul in exchange for power. The mightier the spirit, the more it cost the vedun who wished to master it. These spirits would aid their master in rituals, alchemy and divination.

A vedma need not trade her soul – she gleaned power from her connection to Damp Mother Earth.

Natasha had spent much of her childhood in her Aunt Sonya's workshop, where hundreds of herbs and flowers hung drying from the ceiling. Brown glass bottles and jars cluttered the wall-to-wall shelves.

Though Aunt Sonya spent hours teaching Natasha to prepare ingredients for rituals or to mix potions in that workshop, they usually performed magic in the bathhouse or outdoors, connected to the nature that empowered them. Natasha learned to be guided by moon cycles and seasons. She would dance beside a bonfire on the summer solstice, naked as the day she was born and crowned with a garland, her menstrual blood flowing to the earth and her hair loose to the wind. In those midnights of untamed freedom, Natasha discovered the depths of her own power. Then she began to believe what Aunt Sonya said about her destiny.

Those summer nights felt a world away from where Natasha now found herself, imprisoned in the Russian north. At least she'd escaped the lab. The freshness of falling snow and crisp wind had revived Natasha to an extent, but they only made her hunger even more for freedom.

She could take her freedom, of course. Natasha had allies on this island that Boky wasn't aware of. If she wanted to, she could leave on the next ship out.

But if Natasha ever hoped to rise to the destiny Aunt Sonya had groomed her for, she needed to gather as much power to herself as possible. Whatever Commissar Boky sought on this archipelago could be the key to the future she envisioned.

Natasha started sliding the drawer closed but paused when she noticed books tucked beneath the crystals. There were three science fiction novels: *Doctor Black*, *Out of the Darkness* and *Waves of Life*. From the description, Doctor Black seemed to be the story of a scientist's quest to discover a mythical underground kingdom where the ancients hid their knowledge.

A closer look at the front cover made ice creep through Natasha's veins. All three novels were written by A.V. Barchenko – the doctor from the lab.

According to the author biography, Barchenko wasn't a doctor at all.

Natasha gripped the edge of the desk to steady herself. She'd dug graves inside herself for the horrors of the lab, buried them as deep in her subconscious as she possibly could. But seeing Barchenko's name on those books unearthed those caskets and made bile crawl up her throat. The man who'd experimented on her was a fraud, a novelist posing as a medical professional as he tried to bring his science fiction stories to life.

Commissar Boky had given Natasha to Barchenko, even though he knew the 'doctor' was no doctor at all.

Natasha would make him pay for it.

She turned her attention to Svetlana's file. It contained photographs of Svetlana's murder scene as well as a list of dates and locations going back four years. Had Boky been monitoring Svetlana all that time? The last entries on the list were telling.

*16-21 October, 1922 – subject tracked to Solovetsky Island.*
*3 November, 1922 – subject terminated at Moscow residence.*

Why had Svetlana Efremova been here in Solovki? Did her trip to the archipelago have something to do with her death and whatever Boky was searching for on these islands?

Boky's spidery handwriting filled the next page. It held tables, charts, and calculations. These must be attempts at cracking Svetlana's cipher – failed attempts.

This had to be why Boky wanted Natasha to spy on Katya. He'd brought Svetlana's daughter here and given her the book of fairy tales with the cipher inside, hoping Katya would crack it.

*He's coming.*

The thought forced itself to the front of Natasha's mind, her magical foresight warning her of danger. She returned the papers and photographs to Svetlana's file and shoved it back into the desk drawer. As Boky's footsteps sounded in the hallway outside, Natasha used her hairpins to lock the desk. She hurried to stand on the other side of it.

Natasha took steadying breaths as she watched the elegant double doors of Boky's office. She had to be calm and measured. Boky required a different approach than Katya. Not a wide, wicked smile, but a mysterious curve of the lips. Not an unblinking stare, but half-lidded eyes concealing a thousand secrets. The best way to deal with Gleb Boky was to become an object of fascination, an enchanting enigma. She would be safe from him as long as she held his interest – and not a moment longer.

The door creaked open. Natasha tilted her hip and leaned against the desk in a way she hoped looked relaxed and somewhat sensual. Lantern light spilled through the doorway and then there he was, a gaunt man with a predator's grace, smelling like the forest. Wildness hid behind his pressed uniform and polished boots, something of tangled roots and crisp winds, of the prickle of pine needles and the lazy amber flow of oozing sap.

Commissar Boky personified Natasha's nightmares, every horror of the last two years. Even more so now that Natasha knew he'd let her be experimented on by a fraud. Still, she locked every morsel of fear and revulsion inside herself, another secret to keep.

Boky prowled towards her, a muscle ticking in his jaw.

'What are you doing here?'

'This and that,' Natasha said with a flirtatious shrug.

Boky's hand caught her throat. He swung her sideways and slammed her against the wall, so hard the wooden beams trembled at her back. Then she was pinned, both by his cold fingers around her neck and his colder eyes fixed on hers.

Despite her racing heart, Natasha didn't let her coy smile slip. Not when she felt his fingertips sharpen into claws. Not when a low growl sounded in his throat. She'd been in this situation dozens of times with the other volkolaki, the wolves they'd created in the lab. Fear would only fuel his transformation, so Natasha forced herself to remain calm.

'Why. Are. You. Here?' Boky spoke through his teeth, revealing elongated canines.

'To bring you this.' Natasha pulled out the paper concealed in her sleeve.

Boky turned his head to sniff the paper. He released Natasha, though not before his claws sliced her throat. She pressed her hand over the shallow cuts to stop their bleeding as Boky moved the paper into the lantern light. His human curiosity overtook the wolf's instincts, and the danger of transformation receded as he carried both paper and lantern to his desk.

Allowing herself one ragged breath of relief before regaining her composure, Natasha followed after him.

'What is this?' Boky pointed at the paper. His claws had vanished. Natasha's gaze snagged on the knobby scars that marred his fingers, then she followed his fingertip to the spot on the page he indicated.

*1436*
келья

ГЦЪШРФЭИИГТСНЙБНБОМА

'She found that in her book, written in invisible ink,' Natasha said.

'Hmm,' was his only reply. If the message meant anything to him, he didn't let it show. 'What do you make of her?'

His slate-grey eyes pinned Natasha again. As always, his stare issued a challenge. Natasha met it for a long moment, as though she had nothing to hide. Then she lowered her gaze, making him feel like the alpha. If she wanted to outplay Boky, she had to let him believe he was the one in charge.

She considered his question. What *did* she make of Katya? In some ways, Natasha saw a reflection of herself. They were connected, after all, though it was dangerous to even think of that connection in Boky's presence.

Besides that, they'd both been through trauma and loss.

Natasha would have a clear understanding of Katya's losses later on. She'd need privacy to make use of that stolen tear.

Whatever tragedies lay in Katya's past, they shaped Katya differently than Natasha's had her. Grief made Natasha like that tear drop, always moving, always changing shape, slipping past every obstacle and trap set before her. Katya's grief had made her a fortress, with walls erected around her heart and mind. But no gate could withstand the battering ram indefinitely.

'She's smart,' Natasha said. 'Strong – but not unbreakable.'

'Indeed.' Boky's lips quirked up as he jotted the invisible ink message onto a separate paper. Then he refolded Katya's paper and held it out to Natasha. 'Stay close to her. If anything changes, report to me immediately.'

Natasha dipped her head in agreement and turned towards the door.

'Oh, and Natasha.' The smile he offered her was terrifying, that of the wolf beneath his skin. 'I give second chances, but never a third. If I catch you spying on me again, it will be the last thing you ever do.'

# Chapter 13
## *Dima*

Dima was a canvas, one that had been painted with bruises. Shivering on a bench in the corner of the infirmary, he scrubbed at the dirt and sweat coating his skin. Then he rinsed himself with lukewarm water. Beneath the grime he found spots of yellow, green, purple, black, blue – he had every shade of injury, all in various stages of healing.

Father Iosef had brought Dima here twice more in the past week so Doctor Tarasov could clean and bandage Dima's wounds. They'd managed to stave off infection.

'You *should* make a full recovery,' Doctor Tarasov had said earlier that night. A troubled look crossed his face, though, and Dima knew why.

*Hard labour.* Two words, ten measly letters, but they might spell Dima's doom. Tomorrow Dima would be released back into the general population. That meant long days in the frozen forest. It meant swinging axes and hauling logs, despite his cracked ribs. It meant his unhealed injuries might become permanent.

Tonight was his last chance to rest in the infirmary, but Dima had already decided to pursue something more important. Now that he was clean and freshly bandaged, Dima pulled his clothes back on.

He nodded his thanks to Doctor Tarasov, unhooked one of the lanterns lighting the room and slipped out the door of the infirmary. Making his way down the hall, he entered the printing workshop and closed the door behind him.

Dima hung the lantern on a hook and took in his surroundings. Aside from a coating of dust and ash, the lithograph machine seemed to be in working order.

Dima found a large cupboard filled with printing materials: gum arabic, talc, asphaltum, carborundum, linseed oil and pigments. Hundreds of papers lay ready in a stack, perfectly sized for the printer. Best of all, Dima found a collection of black-tinted beeswax crayons of various thicknesses.

Pulling one of the large stone slabs out onto a trolley, Dima sprinkled carborundum grit onto the surface and ground the stone's surface with a large metal disc. Once the stone was smooth and level, Dima rinsed it off and stared at the blank slate for several minutes.

A warm, peaceful presence spread through him. As Dima's vision simultaneously sharpened and expanded, he began to see what the stone wanted to become.

He recalled an ancient poem Dedushka used to sing when the family gathered at the fireside on cold winter nights. It was the story of how the skomorokhi came to be. Dima pictured those words scrolling down the middle of the stone with artistic renderings on either side.

With the final image in mind, Dima picked up a fine-tipped beeswax crayon and began to write.

> 'Tis said when Rus was yet unnamed
> and wizards sang to sky and sea
> that man and bear a union claimed
> through bond of soul and memory

In farthest north this magic dwelled
Beneath the soil of root and cave
In winter's sleep the bear beheld
what man finds only in his grave

The Otherworld, where magic sings,
that reservoir of heaven's wealth
Thus as he wakes the bear doth bring
Mankind a share of life and health

The poem continued. As Dima wrote each stanza on the stone, his magic painted images in his mind. At first he saw the taiga in winter, the pines and spruce branches heavy with snow. Then a village came into view, where bears and people lived together. A strapping boy wrestled playfully with an adolescent brown bear while a pair of younger girls threw snowballs at them both. Cub and child were equals here, and humanity's connection to the land felt complete.

Dima wrote of a changing world, of conquering armies and the greedy stretching out of cities. The bears became too wild and the humans too tame. Men lost their connection to nature, and, with it, the blessing of magic bears brought from the Otherworld when returning from their winter slumber.

The People of the Bear would have been lost to time if not for a forgotten island where man and bear still lived as equals. When once an islander ventured out into the wide world, he returned to his home as an old man and conveyed all he had seen. Humanity had lost its stories and its sense of magic had grown dull.

It was too late to restore what had been lost, but the islanders resolved to help mankind remember. Before they left their home, daggers sliced across hand and paw, and the people mingled their blood with bears in an oath of eternal kinship.

These skomorokhi devoted their lives to stories, traveling the world as holy minstrels. At their life's end, it was said they did not go to the grave but transformed to live a second lifespan as a bear.

Dima wrote the final verse:

> Skomorokhi share blood with bears
> All history is theirs to know
> The threads of myth they freely share
> For stories link us soul to soul

With the poem complete, Dima started on the accompanying artwork. On one side of the poem, he planned to draw half a man's face, on the other side half a bear's. He outlined their shapes, then allowed his skomorokh magic to pull him into a trance-like state.

Focusing on the bear, Dima conjured an image in his mind of what the sacred animal symbolised. As the poem suggested, ancient Russians believed that, as bears hibernated, their souls lived in the Otherworld, where magic comes from. Dima imagined the bear's eye as a window into that unseen realm, a connection to the divine.

After using various sizes of crayons to achieve lifelike shading and a razorblade to add detail to the fur, Dima turned his attention to the outlined man.

Here Dima wanted to draw a person the prisoners could relate to. Not a hero in a fairy tale, but someone real. Dima drew a man who had known hunger and pain. There were lines of grief edging his eyes, hinting at the absence of those he had loved and lost. Because of his obvious hardship, his raised head emanated dignity and the lively spark in his eye made glorious the courage of his survival.

*Yes,* Dima thought, *this is what I want the prisoners to feel.*

Dima stayed up all night. After finishing the artwork, he prepared the stone for printing. He brushed talc over the crayon then painted on a gum layer, massaging the products to drive the beeswax's grease into the surface of the stone. Once the gum dried, Dima used a solvent to remove all the excess wax.

When he'd worked as a printer's assistant, this had been the most nerve-wracking part of the process. His stomach always squeezed when the solvent erased every trace of the artwork. This was the step of faith. If Dima had done his job well, the poem would still be there. Though invisible now, ink should cling to the grease Dima had worked into the stone.

Dima mixed linseed oil with pigment. After applying a thin layer of greasy asphaltum, he rolled out the ink. Sponging away the excess revealed the poem and artwork, exactly as Dima pictured them.

Dima smiled despite his exhaustion as he moved the stone onto the lithograph machine and began printing copies.

# Chapter 14

## *Katya*

A week after arriving on the island, when her throat was nearly healed, Katya ripped a page from her poetry diary and wrote 'Dear Julia'. Then she carefully crafted a paragraph of text that would appear as nonsense to anyone unaware that Julia was the alias of the anarchist contact person in Berlin. Only someone who knew of Julia's real name would be able to crack the code and read Katya's letter.

She'd been paying close attention at roll-call, noting that a group of adolescent boys rowed supplies to the political prison every other day. If one of them carried her letter to the anarchists, her allies would demand her immediate reclassification.

As the morning bell rang out from the monastery, Katya folded the note and slipped it in her pocket. It felt heavier than it should.

After that first day in the laundry room, the women had spent the rest of the week harvesting peat. They waded through the frigid, wild bogs of the island until they came to a mining site that had been drained. There the same shovels that less fortunate prisoners used to dig their own graves were placed into their chapped hands. They spent hours driving the shovels into the turf with all their might, cutting away bricks that could be dried and burned for warmth.

The women tried to help Katya, taking turns labouring at her side so the guards wouldn't notice how few bricks she managed to cut compared to everyone else. Still, the labour wore Katya ragged. Hunger squeezed her belly in a clawed fist, and the cold worked its way into her bones until she felt like a ghost, a shadow of herself.

Though the guards didn't notice Katya falling behind on her work quota, they did notice Tsisana.

Their second night on the island, Smolensky, the Polish guard who beat Dima on arrival day, strolled into the women's barrack. He'd washed his face and combed his blond hair back. He took off his hat as he approached Tsisana and invited her to join him for dinner.

Tsisana politely refused.

The next day at roll-call, Tsisana learned she'd been reassigned from hard labour to a coveted position as an infirmary nurse. Smolensky returned in the evening, asking her to dinner, which she again declined.

After that, Smolensky did not ask.

Katya and Tsisana sat together one evening, Tsisana applying a compress to Katya's throat. Four guards swarmed into the women's barrack, guns drawn.

The cabbage leaves she'd been pressing to Katya's neck tumbled from Tsisana's trembling fingers. The guards called out three names of women whose presence was required in the kremlin. When Tsisana's name was called, she met Katya's eye.

Katya grabbed Tsisana's hand. She began to chant, first the zagovor that opened her soul to the spirit world. Then she cast an incantation for memory manipulation, planning to confuse the guards so they might forget their purpose in coming here.

Katya conjured the spell with all her might, letting magic stream from her lips. She sharpened every word with her full focus and intention, casting them over the guards like a net. Somehow, her words missed their mark.

Once again, the guards were immune to her spellcraft.

'Thank you for trying.' Tsisana's bottom lip trembled as she squeezed Katya's hand, then she rose and smoothed her skirt. Her expression held equal parts fear and resignation as she joined the two other women being led out into the night.

They returned a few hours later with hollow eyes. No one said anything. No one had to. Instead, the women quietly did what they could for them – tending wounds, making tea, offering small gestures of care and solidarity. Katya climbed into Tsisana's bed, holding her as she sobbed herself to sleep.

Now, Katya couldn't help feeling this coded letter represented a betrayal, that joining the anarchists meant leaving these women behind, leaving Tsisana behind.

She had to do it, though. Even with the women helping her, Katya wouldn't survive much longer. She needed rest and good food to recover her strength – both of which she would receive if classified as a Political.

Tsisana laced her arm through Katya's to walk as a pair toward the monastery, their boots crunching over frozen grass.

'The steamer returned last night,' Tsisana said, her tone a strange mix of yearning and dread.

A new batch of prisoners meant a possibility that her husband had arrived on the island. Seeing him had been all Tsisana wanted, but now that prospect held trepidation as well.

On their way to line up for morning rations, Katya noticed prisoners gathering around something hung on the wall. Tsisana followed as Katya shouldered her way into the crowd, looking up at the large paper. She only meant to scan the page, but it drew her in. There were two images – half a man's face on one side, half a bear's face on the other – with a poem between them.

The bear caught Katya's attention and wouldn't let go. It opened a window in her mind, bringing to life her connection to the Otherworld.

These weren't just drawings, they were icons steeped in magic.

Several printed copies had been hung around the courtyard, and everywhere Katya looked she saw prisoners affected by the art. Some were crying, others looked inspired.

A skilled volshebnik had printed these, and they'd taken a great risk doing so under the administration's noses. Katya couldn't help but be impressed.

She herself had never shared her poetry after the fear her mother instilled in her when she was nine years old.

Before then, Katya had no idea her mother was a charovnika.

Most women started their day by fixing their hair and makeup. Svetlana Efremova did that too, but she also spent an hour each morning chanting quietly under her breath. Katya knew not to disturb this meditation, despite being unaware its purpose was to open Svetlana's soul to the Otherworld.

The magic she received turned Svetlana radiant, golden-haired and glowing.

They were living in a Petrograd safe house, a home base from which Svetlana went out into the city each day in her secret work for the anarchists. She'd been released from prison a few months earlier, and Marina had offered Katya the chance to stay at the anarchist commune, the chance to be part of her family. Katya had been happy there, and Marina had all the warmth Katya wished for in a mother.

But she wasn't Svetlana.

Perhaps even then Katya thrived on a challenge, determined to create love where it didn't exist. Or maybe her mother's allure had so captivated Katya that she accepted loneliness and rejection just for the chance to be near her.

She thought if she worked hard enough, Svetlana would learn to love her. Katya cleaned their flat, cooked their meals, walked to school and back without accompaniment, and never interfered with her mother's work.

To fill the lonely hours while Svetlana was gone, Katya began journaling. She'd write out all her ugly thoughts – her stubbornness, her loneliness, her insecurities and fears – so that they didn't spill out in her mother's presence. After reading a volume of Pushkin, Katya tried writing a poem. Something clicked into place, and new life stirred within her.

In poetry, Katya discovered the language of her soul.

She wrote every day, pouring her heart out in her composition book. Afterward, it would feel as though part of her spirit was drying on the page along with the ink.

While Katya revelled in this effervescent creativity, Svetlana wilted.

Svetlana's skin and hair lost their lustre. Dark circles formed under her eyes. After multiple failed missions, she stayed at home. She'd pace back and forth in the living room, chanting under her breath. Then she'd knock over lamps or slam cabinets when her meditation failed to produce the golden glow it used to. Katya began to prefer loneliness to this frazzled and volatile version of her mother.

One day Katya came home from school to find their apartment ransacked. She stood in the doorway, gaping at the overturned furniture and scattered papers. Hearing no sounds, Katya cautiously stepped deeper into the safe house.

She followed the trail of destruction to her bedroom.

Svetlana sat on the bed surrounded by crooked drawers and strewn clothing.

'Mamochka?' Katya stepped deeper into the room but stopped short when she saw the outrage radiating from her mother's bloodshot eyes.

'I knew something in this flat was draining my magic. I thought someone put a hex on me, hid some kind of amulet or rune stone in here to make me weak.' Svetlana tapped her brittle fingernails on the book in her hands – Katya's journal. 'Turns out it was you.'

Katya stood like a criminal awaiting judgment. Surely her mother would be repulsed by the truth of Katya's soul, written in the pages of her diary.

'You're quite the little turtle, aren't you?' Svetlana said. 'There's far more to you than the shell you show the world.'

'I'm sorry.'

Svetlana's chapped lips tightened in annoyance.

'Don't apologise. I assume you were unaware of the spellwork in your poems?'

The confusion on Katya's face answered her mother's question.

'Sit down.' Svetlana patted the bed beside her.

Then she began to explain the world of volshebniki, the magical folk of Russia.

According to Svetlana, there were two categories of volsheb-niki – those born from a bloodline with inherent magical abilities, and the other, more common type of magician, who learned their abilities through apprenticeship.

'Everyone has some capacity to learn magic,' Svetlana said. 'Though for centuries, its secrets have been hoarded by the aristocracy.'

For the second group of volshebniki, magic was like any other skill. Mastering it required both natural aptitude and knowledge. Artistic ability was a good indicator for aptitude, since artists instinctively opened their souls to the

Otherworld during the act of creation. For that potential to develop into magical ability, the artist needed years of study and practice.

There were four types of learned volshebniki. The bogatyri were heroes of old who wielded a type of elemental magic, but they no longer existed in modern Russia. Kolduni, village wise men and women, passed their knowledge of rituals, healing, and herbs from one generation to the next. Vedun sorcerers and vedma witches practiced a magic of ritual and divination, their knowledge fiercely guarded among the upper echelons of the aristocracy.

'Then there are the charovniki. Like me.' Svetlana handed Katya her composition book. 'And like you.'

'Me?' Katya took the book with trembling fingers.

'Most spellcasters are gifted with words – poets, writers, actors and orators. But I've never heard of an untrained charovnika putting as much magic into her words as you've done there.' Svetlana dipped her head, indicating towards the composition book. 'I suspect that's to do with your father.'

Katya had asked about her father dozens of times, and Svetlana always refused to answer. Now Katya held very still, afraid to even breathe too loud lest she break whatever spell was making her secretive mother be open with her.

'All you need to know about him is that he's in the first category of volshebniki, those with magical bloodlines.'

Two groups were part of this category. Skomorokhi, whose blood still carried the remnants of an oath made with bear-kind. And the Rurikidi, like Katya's father.

Rurik, a Viking prince who ruled over Novgorod a millennium ago, founded a dynasty that lasted twenty-one generations. Legends claimed that Rurik's mother seduced the god of fortune. That's why the princes of Rus were called Dazhbog's grandchildren, and also why the dynasty lasted so long – they were descended from a demigod.

Whether truth or fable, the legend explained the particular magic found in Rurikid blood, a magic that allowed those who possessed it to draw power from volshebniki around them, adding it to their own abilities. That was why Rurikid monarchs were avid patrons of the arts. They filled their courts with master sculptors, painters, dancers and composers – and from them drew the supernatural authority that added legitimacy to their reigns.

'You've been draining me of power,' Svetlana said, 'drawing it into yourself and then pouring it out on the pages of your journal.'

Katya's eyes widened. The taste of bile crept up the back of her throat. 'I didn't mean to. Mamochka, I'm sorry.'

'I told you not to apologise.' Svetlana reached for Katya's chin, turning her face to look into Svetlana's fierce eyes. 'Never apologise for being strong. Never.'

Katya nodded. Maybe she'd been wrong about the pathway to her mother's heart. Trying to be a perfect daughter had only made Katya easier to ignore. This was the most Svetlana had looked at Katya in months.

'This changes everything.' Svetlana spread her fingers over the cover of Katya's composition book. 'No one can know about this, Katyushka.'

Katya was taken aback by her mother using such an affectionate nickname. There was no warmth in her countenance, but maybe it was a sign that she *did* care. Maybe the magic they shared would form the bond Katya yearned for.

'You mustn't show your poetry to anyone,' Svetlana said. 'Not ever. And you'll have to stop going to school. I'll keep you with me at all times. To protect you.'

From that day forward, Katya became her mother's shadow. She accompanied Svetlana to political meetings, surveillance missions and even assassinations. Since she withdrew from school, her education came mostly from books, supplemented by sporadic lessons given by other anarchists or by Svetlana herself. Though Katya continued to write poetry, Svetlana crafted an incantation Katya could use to regulate her Rurikid magic, drawing power from the Otherworld rather than from her mother.

Svetlana still didn't love Katya, not with the warmth and affection Marina had for her children, but she seemed to respect her daughter's strength. Katya told herself that was enough, and, for the next few years, it was.

Taking one last look at the artwork hanging on the wall, Katya turned away from it. She sometimes wished she could share her art with the world like that volshebnik had. What was the point of writing, after all, if no one ever read your words? But Katya's apprenticeship had been far from complete when her mother died, and she wasn't trained enough in the arts of symbolism to predict what affect her words might have on those who read them.

Tsisana fell in beside Katya as they joined their company assembling for roll-call. Prisoners streamed into the courtyard, and Tsisana stood on her tiptoes. She scanned the faces of the new arrivals, her shoulders slumping when she realised her husband wasn't there.

The women of the thirteenth company sighed with relief when told they were assigned to the laundry room again – scrubbing linens in frigid water was a lesser torture than harvesting peat. They left the courtyard and followed a path around the cathedral.

'I dropped something back in the courtyard.' Katya separated her arm from Tsisana's and made a show of checking her coat pockets. 'Go on without me.'

Tsisana tilted her head, dark eyes searching Katya's face. 'You're leaving, aren't you?'

Katya regarded her for a long moment, then nodded.

'I'll cover for you if the guards ask where you are.' Tsisana reached for Katya's shoulders and pulled her in, kissing her left cheek and then her right. 'I wish you all the luck in the world.'

'Thank you . . . Sana.'

At Katya's use of her nickname, a smile spread over Sana's face, summer-warm and beaming. It was the first time Katya had seen her smile since the guards took her away five nights ago. Katya's heart was in her throat as she turned back the way they'd come.

Instead of returning to the courtyard, she hung a right. Katya chanted her zagovor as she went, filling herself with magic. Then she cast a spell in archaic Greek.

'*Krypton pros panta omma to blapton moo.*' *Hidden to every eye that means me harm.* '*Siopilon pros pav ous akouon meta kakis gnomis.*' *Silent to every ear listening with ill intent.* '*Akhyron pros ten rhina zetousa mee.*' *Scentless to the nose that seeks me.*

A buzzing sensation spread over Katya's skin as the spell cloaked her from any enemies she might encounter. It might not help if all the guards carried talismans, but it was a precaution Svetlana had hammered into Katya from a young age.

Katya made her way through the part of the monastery housing male prisoners. The three-storey brick cell buildings loomed over her path as she jogged towards a back gate leading out to the lake harbour.

Outside the gate a long patch of grass bordered the monastery walls. Beyond it a body of crystal blue water glistened. There were more than six hundred lakes on Solovetsky Island, many of them connected by canals leading to and from this harbour. They allowed travel to anywhere on the main island, by boat in the summer months and by dog sled in winter.

Several rowboats were tied to a rickety wooden dock, and the juvenile prisoners stood on a grassy patch beside it, while two guards read out their orders.

Katya stepped out onto the grass, cautiously at first. Her spells had rebounded twice recently – first when she failed to stop the executions and again when she couldn't protect Tsisana.

Her muscles coiled like springs, ready to make a run for it if the guards noticed her. She took one step, and then another. One of the guards' eyes roved over the prisoners, the trajectory of his gaze passing over Katya.

He didn't see her. That meant not all of the guards carried talismans. They must be reserved for the more senior men in the administration, like Smolensky and Nogtev.

Katya strode towards the group of prisoners, approaching them from behind. One of the boys turned at the sound. He stood at the back of the group, smoking the world's thinnest cigarette.

His eyes widened at the sight of her, and Katya raised a finger to her lips, warning him to silence. Since her spell protected her from the senses of those with ill intentions, this boy must be someone she could trust with her letter.

Stepping up behind him, she slipped the letter into his fingers and whispered in his ear.

'Please, will you give this to the anarchists?'

He glanced between the guards and Katya, confusion on his face. When he nodded, Katya pulled a bundle from her pocket and handed it to him.

'My tobacco ration, for your trouble.'

Katya hurried away, hoping her absence in the laundry room

hadn't been noted. She entered the gate and turned. When she veered into an alley, she nearly collided with someone.

Stumbling back, Katya took in muddy black boots, a long sheepskin coat, and a medal of valour pinned to its chest. The reek of vodka assaulted her nose as she looked up into the hard, cruel face of Commander Nogtev – whose eyes were fixed on Katya.

# Chapter 15
## *Katya*

The camp director saw Katya, despite the cloaking spell still vibrating over her skin. A string of amber worry beads protruded from his coat pocket, glowing with an otherworldly light.

That must be the talisman rendering Katya's magic ineffective.

Katya apologised and tried to go around Commander Nogtev, but he stepped sideways to block her path.

'What are you doing here?' Despite the early hour Nogtev's booming voice was already a little slurred.

Since she couldn't use spellwork, Katya's best chance of getting out of this was trying not to piss Nogtev off. Lowering her gaze, she noticed a reddish tinge to the mud caking Nogtev's boots. Blood, probably. She had to consciously think about making breath go in and out of her lungs, of keeping her shoulders from curling in with tension. At least she no longer had the letter on her person – as far as the camp director knew, Katya had done nothing wrong.

'I'm on my way to the laundry room, sir.'

'Eh?' Nogtev asked. 'Speak up so I can hear you.'

'I'm going to the laundry room.' Having to raise her voice stripped it of meekness, and Katya's tone ignited a spark of hate in Nogtev's small, blue eyes.

'Then you have no reason to be here.' Nogtev stepped closer.

'I got lost,' Katya said. 'It's because I was hurrying to find my way that I ran into you. I apologise again.'

Dipping her head into a nod she hoped passed for respectful, she stepped around him. Thick fingers coiled around Katya's upper arm. Nogtev yanked her off the walking path. The back of her head slammed against the brick wall as he forced her against the cell block. Pain exploded across her skull and stars danced in her vision. Nogtev pinned Katya to the wall with his thick forearm across her chest.

'I know who you are, witch,' he said, 'I knew your whore mother.'

Katya cringed from the smell of his breath, putrid with vodka and the slight tinge of last night's vomit. But his nearness created an opportunity. If she could steal the beads from his pocket, he'd be at the mercy of her spellcraft.

'You knew my mother?' Katya discreetly moved her hand toward the talisman.

'Excuse me, Comrade Nogtev,' said a cautious male voice.

'Go away,' Nogtev barked over his shoulder.

The man didn't move on. Nogtev turned to glare at the prisoner interrupting him. It was Dmitri Danilov, out of the punishment cells for the first time since his beating last week. His cheeks appeared swollen. Deep bruises beneath his eyes had begun yellowing at the edges. His proud, aristocratic nose had been broken. Its crookedness was a reminder of what he'd suffered, all because he spoke up for Katya.

'Commissar Boky sent me to find you,' Dima said.

'I'm busy.'

Katya's fingers found the beads. In a quick movement, she lifted them from Nogtev's pocket, concealing them in the sleeve of her jacket.

'He said it's urgent,' Dima was saying. 'He asked you to come right away.'

Katya had begun chanting the first lines of a spell when a frustrated groan rose from deep in Comrade Nogtev's thick throat.

'This isn't over,' he said in Katya's ear before he released her and stalked off.

When he was gone, Katya rested her head against the wall, closed her eyes and breathed in and out a few times, willing her heartbeat to slow. The beads were unnaturally warm against her wrist. She pulled them out and examined them – fourteen amber beads strung together, all of them glowing. Katya supposed the light came from the power of her own spellcraft that had been absorbed by the protective charm worked into the talisman.

She would have to make note of which guards carried beads and which didn't. Though, perhaps it didn't matter. Once the anarchists got her letter, she'd be transferred to the political prison where none of them could touch her.

Katya shoved the beads in her pocket, then she gingerly felt the lump on the back of her head, smearing blood on her fingertips.

Dima stepped closer, his brown eyes watching her with concern. Once again he'd intervened on her behalf, but this time she hadn't needed his help. She could have handled Nogtev on her own.

'I'm fine,' she said shortly, looking away from the intensity of his gaze.

His face was a mess of swelling and bruises, an ugly brown scab crusted his split lip, and his dark hair was matted on one side. Yet there was still something about him, a vibrancy of spirit that both drew Katya in and discomfited her.

'I'm glad I ran into you,' Dima said.

'I never asked you to speak up for me.' Katya crossed her arms. 'So if you're expecting me to thank you, you'll be waiting quite a while.'

'Now why would I go looking for a thank you when I've already received my reward?' His lips curved into a crooked smile as he motioned to the bruises on his face. 'Don't worry. I'm sensible enough not to expect gratitude from an anarchist. I did, however, find something that you ought to see.'

The excitement sparkling in his eyes looked like trouble, and that was the last thing Katya needed. She pushed away from the wall and moved to brush past him. Dima caught her wrist. If he'd grabbed her, she would have yanked her arm free and kept going, but his fingertips were gentle whispers against Katya's skin.

'Please,' he said. 'I just need a minute of your time.'

'You're an aristocrat. Why should I listen to anything you have to say?'

Dima sighed. 'Is every conversation with you an argument?'

'I tend to get argumentative with people who represent everything wrong with the old Russia.'

'I represent *everything* wrong with Russia?' Dima pressed a hand to his chest as though flattered. 'I had no idea I was so influential. So symbolic.'

'Cossacks were influential. Then they used their military might to enslave people. That's why you ended up here.'

'And you're what – just visiting?'

'I'm biding my time.'

She thought of the letter already on its way to the political prison in the pocket of the juvenile delinquent. Another day, maybe two, and she'd be safe.

Dima leaned in conspiratorially, raising an eyebrow as he

asked, 'What if you could do more than bide your time?'

He pulled an ancient-looking square pouch from his coat pocket. After looking both ways to make sure no one was coming, he untied the laces.

The pouch opened into a map depicting the archipelago's labyrinths. Beside each labyrinth were lists of names and dates going back four hundred years. Despite her efforts to remain indifferent, the map awakened her intrigue.

'Who are they?' She ran a finger along a line of names.

'Mystics and faith healers. Heroes and revolutionaries. Ordinary men who made the pilgrimage to Solovki and went on to lead extraordinary lives.'

'I don't see what that has to do with me.'

'Look there.' Dima pointed to one of the labyrinths of Bolshoi Zayatsky. Katya read the names: a few she didn't recognise from the fifteenth century, a sixteenth century travelling mystic she'd read about once, the legendary folk hero Stepan Timofeyovich Razin and . . . Katya gasped.

There, in handwriting so familiar it drove a quill into Katya's heart, it said: *Svetlana Nikolaevna Efremova – 20 October, 1922.*

Katya held her breath until her lungs burned. Buzzing filled her ears, and the moment took on a dreamlike quality as she stared at Svetlana's name. Her mother had been here in Solovki. She'd visited the island of labyrinths and held this very map in her hands.

Two weeks later, she was murdered.

'Where did you find this?' Katya asked breathlessly.

'In the hermit cell where they kept me after my beating.'

'A cell?' Katya's voice drifted as her thoughts went to the clue she'd found in lemon ink.

'Yes. Hidden beneath a loose stone with an engraving on it.'

'What kind of engraving?'

'Something round. Maybe a target or—'

'Or a labyrinth.'

A chill moved over Katya, lifting the hairs on her arms as she thought of the hidden message Svetlana had written in her book.

*1436*

келья

ГЦЪШРФЭИИГТСНЙБЛЯОМА

Katya scanned the ancient map until she found the name Zosima – beside it was written 1436, the year he founded the Solovetsky Monastery. The clues in lemon ink were meant to lead Katya to Solovki – and to this map. But what did the code beneath the labyrinth mean?

'I managed to pilfer a couple of these from the infirmary.' Dima pulled two official-looking documents folded up into squares. 'They'll allow us to leave the monastery. The fishing boats aren't strong enough to carry us to the mainland, but Bolshoi Zayatsky isn't far – we should make it without a problem.'

'Hold on.' Katya shot to her feet, ignoring that one of her stockings slid down into a pile around her ankle. 'Not only are you talking about the kind of thing that could get you a bullet in the head, you mistakenly used the words "us" and "we". There is no "us", and the only thing "we" are doing is going our separate ways.'

'Aren't you curious about what they found on that island?' Dima reverently folded the map and tied the leather strings. 'It's risky. And of course you don't have to come. I just assumed you would want to when you saw your mother's name.'

Katya closed her eyes, tried to think. One of the clues in the book of fairy tales was meant to lead Katya to this map. Svetlana went to Bolshoi Zayatsky two weeks before she died – she must have left something there for Katya.

'All right.' Katya huffed out a breath and pointed an accusatory finger at Dima. 'But if this is some kind of trick or trap, you'll beg to be put back in that punishment cell if only to get away from me.'

'Noted,' he said with that crooked smile.

'And this doesn't mean we're friends, *Dmitri*.' Katya made a point of avoiding his nickname. 'I'm going for my own reasons, not because you asked me to.'

'Fine by me, *Katinka*,' he said, using an overly-familiar form of Yekaterina.

Dima handed over her pass to leave the monastery with a gentlemanly flourish. This might be a mistake, but Katya couldn't resist following her mother's footsteps.

Katya and Dima made their way back to the lake harbour. They showed their passes and were allowed to take a fishing boat and two oars. Rowing out into the island's system of channels, they turned south, heading for the island of labyrinths.

# PART II

---

*Wolves Of Solovki*

# *Prey*

```
            I
          HAVE
          HEARD
      OF MONSTROUS
      PREDATORS, MEN
       WARPED BY EVIL,
          TRANSFORMED  INTO
          BEINGS OF   VIOLENCE.
          HERE IN SOLOVKI
          GUARDS ARE DANGER
           CLAD IN LAMBSKIN
           COATS, DARK WOLVES
           IN SHEEP'S CLOTHING.
           THEY PROWL THROUGH THE
           PRISONYARD, HATRED BARING
       FANGS OF STEEL, CLAWS OF MALICE.
       THEY ARE BANISHED HERE LIKE WE ARE.
        WE FOR EXISTING, THE WOLVES FOR DEVOURING.
          WHEN A PARTY MEMBER BEGINS TO CRAVE INFLICTING PAIN,
             WHEN HIS THIRST FOR BLOODSHED BECOMES UNQUENCHABLE, HE
               IS BOUND FOR THE ARCHIPELAGO, DESTINED TO JOIN THE PACK.
               I  SENSE WICKED, DARK MAGIC AT WORK IN THEIR WRATH, AND I
               AM  ALWAYS WARY, KNOWING I WILL BE THEIR VICTIM. IT MAY BE
                 NOW  OR TOMORROW BUT THEIR THREATS ARE NEVER GIVEN IN VAIN.
                  BIT  BY BIT MY COURAGE WITHERS HERE.   BRAVE MEN MADE WEAK
                  BY   BEATINGS     HAVE SPILLED THEIR   BLOOD IN THE SNOW.  I
                  THE    ENDLESS                         MOURNER, WAIT. I  AM
                  WHO    SHADOWS                          FOLLOW, ALWAYS   FEAR
                  AND    FEAST                            OF GRIEF. MY     PAIN
                  WHY    I CAN                            NEVER OPEN  .I HATE
                  AND    HOWL,                            HEART BEATS    EVEN
                  WHEN   CLAW                             FAST SHREDS    ME
                  OF     TIME.                            IN SORROW,
                  RAGE   NEED                                ONLY FESTER.
                  TOO    FAST                                AGING OF
                  OLD    OPEN                                    ACHES.
                  AND    NOW                                   CREEP
                HUNGRY  WOLVES'                             INSTINCTS
               TO SATE   TEETH                            OF KNOWING
                                                         I AM PREY
```

# Chapter 16

## *Katya*

It was early October, but the wind carried all the fury of mid-winter. Every gust sliced through Katya's raincoat like a whip. Her teeth clattered even as her muscles burned from rowing. Tangled forest spread from either side of the canal, and the smell of pine hung in the air. Breathing it cleansed Katya's lungs from the remnants of the crowded barracks.

Sunlight trickled through the forest canopy, casting dancing beams of light and shadow. Katya watched them play across Dima's back as he rowed. Without meaning to, Katya let her gaze drift up to the dark locks of hair curling slightly at the nape of his neck.

He glanced over his shoulder, catching her staring. His expression shifted faster than the wind blowing through Katya's coat. One second his thick brows were pressed low in concentration, the next they lifted with amusement. A smile spread crookedly over his lips.

'Like what you see?'

Dima did look good. Even with the broken nose and the bruises still visible from his beating, his face had the semblance of a sculpture that could be admired at any angle. That didn't mean Katya was interested, though. She couldn't be interested in an aristocrat. A Cossack, no less.

'You're not horrible to look at,' Katya finally said.

Their canoe drifted along with the currents as Dima watched her over his shoulder, squinting like an artist trying to focus on some detail in his muse. 'Can I ask you a question?'

'Why?' Katya's eyes narrowed. She closed herself to exposure the way a camera lens shuts out all but a pinprick of light. It was reflexive, a habit reinforced by years of secrecy.

'Because that's what normal people do when they're getting to know each other,' he said with a chuckle.

'You know who else asks unnecessary questions? Spies and informants.'

'What if I assure you I am neither informant nor spy?' Dima grinned over his shoulder as he pulled the oars.

Katya arched a brow.

'Come on, indulge me. I want to know what's next for you, after Solovki. Will you study, work, or maybe do . . . I don't know, radical things that anarchists keep busy with?'

Katya's mind went straight back to Kronstadt. Artillery blasts and machine gun fire still reverberated in her memory. She'd failed the resistance then, and her remaining hope died the next year, alongside her mother. With most of her allies killed or imprisoned, there was nothing left for Katya in Russia. If she left Solovki, she would flee to Germany or France, where small pockets of expatriated radicals still worked to undermine the Bolsheviki.

Thinking of what Lenin and his regime had done to Russia made Katya's heartbeat kick up. A gust of wind made her shiver, but the cold couldn't tamper the heat of her growing rage.

Dima watched her over his shoulder. He stared as though he could read every emotion on her face. Feeling exposed made her fury simmer. She had a sudden urge to scorch him with it.

'If I get off this island I will fight for a free Russia,' she said fiercely.

Dima was an aristocrat. He probably thought things were better before the Revolution simply because they were better for him. Privileged people were like that – selfish, clinging to power, not caring that their wealth rested on the backs of broken men. She hoped he would mock her, argue with her, make himself a target for her to unleash her righteous indignation.

'A free Russia.' Dima tested the words on his tongue, looking up at the sky as though those words painted a vision he could faintly see. 'Now there's something worth fighting for.'

Katya thrust the oars into the water and rowed fiercely, annoyed that he'd agreed with her. The ache in her shoulders sharpened into an acute, throbbing pain, but she pulled the oars even harder with the next stroke. Her muscles would have to suffer her wrath since Dima refused to rise to an argument.

'What about you?' she snarled. 'What will you do when you get out?'

'Now this is progress,' Dima said cheerfully. 'I asked you a question. Then you asked me one. You're getting the hang of this "how normal people get to know each other" thing.'

Katya gritted her teeth. A hundred insults rushed through her head, but Dima spoke before she could choose an appropriate one.

'It's like you said earlier. I'm a Cossack aristocrat, symbolic of all that was wrong and unjust about old Russia – never mind that I was fifteen when the Revolution changed everything. I hadn't quite got around to oppressing the proletariat, but here I am, an enemy of the people nonetheless.'

Though his tone was light-hearted, it had an edge. Pain rested just beneath his playful delivery – Katya could sense it mirroring her own. But if he wanted to make her feel sorry for him, it wouldn't work. 'You didn't answer my question.'

'I'm getting to it.' Turning on the rowing bench, he bowed

stiffly. 'Technically I am Count Danilov, so feel free to address me by my formal title of nobility.'

'I might prefer not talking to you at all.'

Dima shook his head in disappointment. 'And here I thought you were starting to like me.'

Katya glared at him.

'Anyway,' he said with that crooked smile. 'I'm under no illusions that they'll let me survive this place. There is no "after Solovki" for people like me.'

His words found the cracks in the shield she'd placed around her heart. How could he be so jovial and easy with a smile while convinced he was going to die?

They rowed on in silence. Soon the forest canopy opened up and the canal turned into a harbour. Their small vessel still took on water as they headed westward out to sea.

Dima was right. This canoe could get them to the nearby islands, but it would never make it to the mainland. There was no escaping Solovki – not for either of them.

Several bare islands dotted the horizon, rising from the sea like grey tortoise shells. Rounding Bolshoi Zayatsky, they stayed a distance from shore to avoid sand banks and the jagged sheets of ice already crusting the island. At the southwestern point, a small, onion-domed chapel marked the location of the harbour.

Wind raged around them, howling in their ears and slicing through their half-soaked clothes as they reached the dock. Dima tied the boat, scrambled onto it and offered Katya a hand, which she ignored. Shivers wracked her body as she climbed out of the boat without his help.

'There's a storm coming.' Dima shouted over the wind. He pointed westward, where dark clouds gathered on the horizon. 'We won't have much time if we're going to make it back.'

They sheltered beside the church to block out the wind

enough for Dima to open the map. Though Katya huddled in her coat, it only reached to her waist. Her stockings were soaked, and her skirt left her legs exposed. She was shivering violently by the time Dima found their location and worked out which direction to go.

Looking Katya over with concern, he asked, 'Do you want my coat?'

'I'll be fine,' she said, though her teeth clattered.

A path led inland, lined with moss and cushion plants stretching between scattered groups of shrubs and boulders. Katya followed Dima, her head lowered against the wind as they trekked north.

'I see them,' Dima shouted to be heard over the gusts.

The first labyrinth was visible ahead, a circle of moss-covered boulders with dual curving lines creating a maze-like pattern within it. Dozens of circular labyrinths dotted the landscape, some several metres wide.

'I wonder what they are,' Katya said.

'I believe they're gateways.' Dima held the map up reverently. 'Doors of power, where a person can touch the Otherworld and hear the echo of God's own heartbeat. Don't you feel it?'

Dima held out a hand, palm down. At first Katya only felt the shivers rattling her bones. When she closed her eyes, a tingling sensation spread over her fingers.

'I'd like to walk the same labyrinth as my ancestor,' Dima said. 'I believe it's off to the left. Svetlana's is the fourth labyrinth beside the path, straight ahead.'

Katya met Dima's gaze for a long moment, and then she nodded. Her heart beat a slow, steady rhythm to the songs of wind and waves. The power buzzing against her skin intensified as she walked beside each labyrinth, and lessened when she passed them by.

She paused at the entrance of the fourth labyrinth and took a deep breath. The shroud separating her from the Otherworld felt threadbare, ready to split open.

Gravity shifted as Katya stepped into the labyrinth. The force tethering her to Damp Mother Earth pulled sideways, drawing her deeper. The wind died away. Warmth enveloped her, as nurturing as a mother's embrace.

She closed her eyes. The labyrinth guided her along the lines of the path. Her mind entered a trance-like state. As her feet treaded in one world, her spirit drifted into another. Katya felt a poem gathering at the edges of her consciousness.

Katya's boots still crunched over sand and ice, but in her mind's eye she stood on a precipice. Darkness gathered in the abyss before her. The words of her poem stretched out into a bridge no thicker than a tight-rope, written in pure starlight. Katya understood she needed to cross this void, but the strand of hope seemed too slender to put her feet on.

Katya took a step back.

A wave of vertigo washed over her, and she opened her eyes. Her boot caught the edge of a moss-covered rock. As she fell to her knees, her connection to the Otherworld severed. Wind snatched the warmth from her skin, and she shivered as she left the labyrinth.

She'd hoped there would be a clue of some sort, but she saw no sign of Svetlana having been here.

Dima waited a short distance up the path, his hands shoved into his pockets and a haunted look in his eyes.

'Did you see anything in the labyrinth?' Katya asked.

'Yes.' He glanced over his shoulder. His eyebrows furrowed, as though he feared whatever he'd encountered in the labyrinth might come after him.

'Are you all right?'

Dima swallowed and nodded stiffly.

Katya considered probing further, but then she reminded herself she shouldn't care. Instead she reached for the map. 'Can I see that again?'

Dima handed it over and then angled his body to block the wind. Katya found the diagram with Svetlana's name beside it and compared the shape of its curves to the one she'd walked. They matched.

'I was so sure there would be a clue,' Katya said. 'Something to explain why my mother hid that map.'

'Hiding the map isn't the only thing she did.' Dima hesitated, looking at Katya as though weighing how she might react to something unpleasant.

'What do you mean?' Katya gripped the map with shivering fingers.

'The date on the map.' Dima stepped closer and pointed to Svetlana's name. 'The twentieth of October last year – that was two days before the Bolshevik fleet arrived in Solovki. The monks told me Svetlana hurried to leave the island when she saw the armada – but not before setting fire to the monastery's library.'

'No.' Katya shook her head. Svetlana would never burn a book, let alone a library filled with priceless medieval manuscripts. *Unless there was something in that library she didn't want the government to find.*

Katya chewed on that for a minute and looked at the map again. It was then she noticed a name beside a different labyrinth.

*Viktor Mikhailovich Ivanoff* – one of the aliases Svetlana used in written communications. The handwriting resembled Svetlana's, and the date said 8 July, 1704, exactly two hundred years before Katya's birthday.

Here was the clue she'd been looking for.

Thrusting the map into Dima's hands, Katya raced towards the shore. Angry waves crashed against the crust of ice lining the island, and the wind gained force as Katya reached the other labyrinth. There was no moss or lichen here, only sand, ice and grass sprouting up between the rocks. Katya ignored the labyrinth's power and crouched as she made her way through it, testing every rock and lifting the loose ones.

Dima joined in, working the other direction. They met in the middle where bigger rocks lay in a heap. Taking turns lifting stones off the pile and setting them to the side, they eventually found something wrapped in oilcloth.

Katya's hands scraped against rocks as she pulled the object free. She sat down with it on her lap and looked at Dima.

Despite what had clearly been a troubling experience in the labyrinth, excitement sparkled in Dima's dark eyes, matching the fizzy feeling in Katya's belly. She reverently unwrapped the oilcloth. Inside she found a journal resting on top of a book so old that the leather binding had warped and faded. Oddly, part of the book was missing. Someone had sliced the end of the manuscript clean off. The whiteness of the thread used to resew the bindings suggested it had been done recently.

Taking a deep breath, Katya opened the book. It was written in Greek, a language she'd never learned beyond a few memorised spells. When she opened the journal, Katya saw her mother's handwriting swirling across the page. It seemed Svetlana had begun translating the book. The title read:

### THE CHIEF OF BEGGARS
*by Yelezar Kerdeyevich Danilov*

'I can't believe it.' Dima knelt beside Katya 'My ancestor accompanied Stenka Razin all through his pirating years and during the peasant revolt. Then he disappeared without a trace. There were rumours he'd written a book about Stenka Razin. We've never been able to find it. Not until now.'

Katya lifted her gaze to Dima's, swept up in the wonder of his expression and the awe in his voice. How odd that Yelezar's descendent should be the one to find the map leading to this book. Was that a coincidence, or had Dima brought her here by design? Katya assumed Commissar Boky had spies watching her. Could Dima be one? The guilelessness in his expression made that hard to believe. Still, Katya had to be careful.

Svetlana had wanted Katya to find this book. Why, though? What did a Cossack rebel who'd lived centuries ago have to do with the resistance against the Bolsheviki? What secret did this book contain that cost Svetlana's life?

A raindrop landed on Katya's cheek. She wrapped the manuscript and journal in the oilcloth and tucked them inside her coat.

'Let's get back. Then we can decide what to do with these.'

'We won't make it.' Dima nodded toward the sea. The darkening clouds dumped rain not far offshore. It looked like the clouds themselves were streaking down towards the choppy waters.

Staring out at the coming storm, Katya's heart sank.

They trekked back to the onion-domed chapel, seeking shelter. A porch led into a small wood-panelled room with two glass windows on either side. There was no furniture, and the altar took up half the space. Crossing himself as he entered, Dima found ceremonial candles and lit one.

They would be safe here at least, but Katya couldn't stop shivering. Her stockings were stiff with ice. Sitting down on the edge of the altar, Katya pulled her knees up to her chest and wrapped the flaps of her coat around herself as best she could. It didn't help much. She wouldn't survive winter unless she found better clothes. Even now, with below-freezing temperatures and a storm raging against the rickety chapel, Katya might not last the night.

'I'll share my coat with you.' Dima began unclasping buttons.

'I'm fine,' Katya said.

'You're shivering.'

'I'm *fine*.' Her glare was colder than the ice-crusted sea and twice as violent as the storm raging outside.

'Katya.' The amusement in his voice made her name sound like laughter. His lips curved into an infuriating smile. 'I know we're not friends, but choosing to freeze to death rather than lie next to me seems a little extreme, even for you.'

A sound left Katya's throat, something halfway between a sigh and a growl. Dima's wry smile grew into an all-out grin. He made a show of unbuttoning his long, wool coat. He let it slide off his shoulders, and then shook it out with a dramatic flourish, like a magician's cape. He sprawled on the floor.

'Come on, little anarchist, live to fight another day.' He patted the ground in front of him. 'I promise not to bite.'

'Well, I don't.' Katya shot him a wicked look and then dropped to her knees. She removed her coat before lying on her side, careful to stay a few inches in front of him.

Dima draped his coat over their hips and legs, Katya's over their upper bodies. Then he scooted closer. When his legs pressed against the backs of Katya's thighs, she kicked his shin.

'What do you think you're doing?' she demanded.

'Keeping you warm,' he said, 'And, though I don't know why I bother, alive.'

He scooted forward again, and every one of Katya's muscles tensed. Gently smoothing her hair to one side, Dima moved his arm to cushion her head. Then he folded his forearm up across her chest, pulling her shivering form tight against him. Heat radiated into her back, and his breath was a whisper beside her ear.

Katya's skin awakened as though from a long slumber, feeling everything far more than it should. This wasn't a romantic moment; it was survival. Yet as her shivering subsided, Katya found herself melting into the embrace.

His free hand reached over her to pick up the journal with Svetlana's translation.

'You're going to read it?'

'We may be stuck here for a while.' Releasing Katya's chest but not moving any further away, Dima propped himself up on his elbow and leaned forward until their cheeks were nearly touching. His throat was by her shoulder, so his voice vibrated against her skin when he spoke. 'And I'm curious about what's in here, aren't you?'

'Could you read aloud?'

He nodded and opened the cover. Once he'd angled the journal so the pages caught the candlelight, Dima took a deep breath and began to read:

'A whirlwind hurled itself across the steppe the night Stepan Timofeyovich came into the world. It tore the roof off the cottage of Timofey Razin and his labouring wife, Matryona, at the moment of their child's birth. People say the boy's first breath came to him upon a gust, filling him with all the wild destructiveness of a prairie wind . . .'

# Chapter 17
## *Natasha*

Natasha knelt on the floor of an abandoned cabin in the woods, her stolen chalk pinched between her fingers. A peat fire filled the space with a pleasant, earthy smell. That scent mingled with the herbs she'd strung from the ceiling and the sweet musk of decay permeating this damp and forgotten *izba*.

As soon as she'd realised Katya left the monastery, Natasha sprang into action.

She found this cabin and decided it would serve as a makeshift workshop. Herbs now dangled from the rafters, and small jars of honey, vodka, oil and vinegar rested on top of the dilapidated table beside her violin.

Having cleared the centre of the floor, Natasha drew a large chalk circle, perfectly round. Any imprecision in a protective circle could leave a vedma vulnerable to demonic attack.

Natasha drew rune marks around the circle while reciting an ancient Slavic poem that accompanied them. It had been passed down through Natasha's maternal line for generations as one of the family's most carefully guarded secrets.

Natasha threw sage into the fire. As its smoke billowed out into the cabin, she stood barefoot in the centre of the circle. She lifted the rusted bronze key off her neck, letting the chain dangle from her fingers as she held her hands straight out and began to chant in Old Russian. Natasha's soul opened to the Otherworld. Warmth crept into her feet, spreading through her blood as magic seeped into her. Natasha turned in a circle, her movements falling into the rhythm of the chant.

When she finished the verse, Natasha dropped the key necklace. It landed on the rune for ice. That meant to pause or wait. Natasha stared into the sage smoke, letting her vision blur into a partial trance until she understood the rune's message. She needn't go after Katya. Her enemy would come to her.

To complete the ritual, Natasha chanted two more times. The key landed on the gambler's rune, which meant the outcome was up to chance. She might convince Katya to forge an alliance, she might not. Finally, the key landed on the torch rune, indicating secrets would be revealed.

That made Natasha uneasy. Her plans would unravel if anyone learned her true intentions. Still, Natasha had to risk it.

*It's always been a woman who saved Russia.*

That message had been deeply ingrained in Natasha, written across her soul.

Natasha's mother had died in childbirth. The family insisted Natasha's aunt, Sofia Alekseyevna, being unmarried and determined to remain as such, should oversee Natasha's education.

Before Sofia Alekseyevna came, Natasha had enjoyed a leisurely, though often lonely, childhood with her indulgent father and a palace full of servants. Then one day a messenger arrived. Natasha had been reciting a new violin piece for her father, Georgy, as he sat in his big armchair with a pipe. Georgy let out a long sigh when he read the telegram.

'What is it, Papa?' Natasha paused her playing to ask.

Though his voice sounded pained, there was an amused twinkle in his eye as he said, 'Your aunt is coming to Strelna.'

Natasha could hardly contain her excitement. She'd never met a female relative. At dinner, Natasha studied the portrait of her mother that hung over the mantle. Would Sofia Alekseyevna be as elegant and hauntingly beautiful as Natasha's mother had been? Between bites, Natasha pestered her father for any gleanings of information about her aunt.

'She studied surgery,' he said. 'I think she's been volunteering as a Sister of Mercy.'

Before Natasha could fix the image of a saint-like woman in her mind, her father continued.

'Honestly, I don't know how they put up with her. That woman has a foul mouth and an even fouler temper.' When Natasha's eyes widened, her father added, 'But she is a good sort, beneath all her bluster.'

Just then, a loud thump sounded in the palace, that of the front door being thrown open so hard it banged against the wall. Servants' footsteps resounded through the corridors as they rushed towards the entryway.

Georgy chuckled to himself. Then he took a long drink of wine, draining his glass. He patted the corners of his mouth with his serviette before laying it across his plate and rising from the table.

'Come.' He held out his hand. 'Let's go meet your mother's sister.'

Georgy and Natasha entered the foyer to find a footman trying to remove a valise handle from the firm grip of a short, plump woman.

Sofia Alekseyevna wore a tailored jacket with a necktie and a matching flared skirt. Beneath her wide-brimmed hat, strands of greying dark hair had come loose from her messy chignon. She had a square face and none of the willowy elegance of Natasha's mother.

'Release my property at once.' Sofia Alekseyevna stomped on

the footman's toes. 'I'm perfectly capable of carrying my own luggage.'

'Peace, Sonya.' Georgy said, using a diminutive form of her name. He strode forward to kiss her cheek, a greeting she disconsolately accepted. 'We all know you're more than capable of anything you set your mind to.'

Sofia Alekseyevna reluctantly released the valise into the care of the aggrieved footman. Her hawkish eyes turned Natasha's way.

'*Itak*,' she said, '*vot doch Yulia.*'

'Good evening, Aunt.' Natasha gave a proper, ladylike curtsy. 'Forgive my rudeness, but I don't understand Russian. We always speak French at home.'

Sofia Alekseyevna cast Georgy a disparaging look. 'You've taught her to curtsy like a little doll, but she doesn't know the language of the people she lives among.'

'She's still a child.' Georgy put an arm around Natasha's shoulder.

'Not anymore.' Sofia Alekseyevna bent down to look at Natasha eye to eye. 'My other nieces and nephews call me Aunt Sonya, so you may also. Starting tomorrow, I will be your teacher. You will learn Russian, for starters, but also German, English, Greek and Old Russian. I expect you to master history, diplomacy, science, philosophy . . . and many other topics.'

It turned out the many other topics Aunt Sonya would teach Natasha were the ways of witchcraft. True to Sofia Alekseyevna's word, Natasha's soft and easy childhood ended that day.

Natasha was raised to be a weapon for the motherland, her mind and magic forged by Sofia Alekseyevna's iron will. Though her aunt was dead and gone, Natasha held fast to the responsibility instilled in her. She would do whatever she must to win her freedom and the means to achieve her goals.

For now that meant teaming up with her oldest enemy, no matter how distasteful Natasha found that prospect.

As morning sun filtered through the filthy windows of the cabin, Natasha prepared a ritual to guide Katya here. She went outside and used a pine bough to sweep snow clear of a large circle. In it she built a bonfire.

She threw herbs onto the flames. Moonwort to ward off evil spirits. Ivy and fern leaves to make the smoke smell like an invitation. Sitting cross-legged beside the fire, Natasha sang an ancient chant as she plaited a garland of birch and hazel rods. The birch represented the forging of a union, while the hazel symbolised communication and reconciliation. They would make Natasha's words more compelling when she offered Katya an alliance.

Crowning herself with the garland, Natasha stood barefoot upon the frozen earth. She took up her violin, the strings fitting perfectly into the calluses of her fingertips and the bow like an extension of her hand.

Natasha played a few opening notes, awakening her soul to the power of the earth beneath her. Like roots, her bare feet drank in the nourishment of the soil. Magic flowed into her like golden sap, filling her with power.

When she turned her thoughts to that stolen tear, Natasha tasted salt on her lips. She closed her eyes and began playing the melody of Katya's sorrows. It would beckon Katya like a siren's song, drawing her to this fireside where an alliance could be forged.

# Chapter 18

## *Dima*

A paintbrush fell from Dima's fingers. It spun twice before hitting the ground, splattering droplets of green paint across the hardwood floor. He'd been painting the view from his bedroom window on a late summer day. Wildflowers dotted the grass like sprinkled confetti. Sasha, Dima's youngest brother, pushed their sister Taya on the rope swing beneath the old sycamore tree.

Dima had been in deep concentration as he tried to capture the way light gleamed in Taya's dark brown hair as it streamed behind her.

The spell was broken by the sound of a gunshot.

Looking at the canvas now, his siblings had vanished. The swing hung unmoving from the sycamore's branches. In the painting, two crimson splotches marked where his brother and sister had once been.

Here he was again, in a nightmare as familiar to Dima as his own name. Dima rushed out of his room and down the hall. Smoke poured through the open door of his grandfather's office. Deciding to investigate, Dima coughed and raised his arm to shield his eyes from the smoke's sting.

Despite the warm summer day, Dedushka had lit a fire in the hearth and was frantically tossing in papers. Just last week he'd finished a years' long endeavour – an epic poem on the life of Stenka Razin. It was supposed to be his masterpiece, the culmination of his life's work and research. He'd already inquired with a handful of contacts about having it published, yet here Dedushka was, feeding his creation to the flames.

'Dedushka?' Dima asked.

The old man turned. The furrows of his forehead were deeper than usual, and a thick smear of ash streaked his face.

'They found me.' Dedushka's eyes looked wild as a startled animal's. 'They've come for my poem, but I won't let them have it. Go and hide yourself, Dimochka. I'm the one they want.'

'But . . .' Dima stood paralyzed in the doorway, shaking his head in disbelief. Who had found Dedushka? And why did they want his poem?

'Go, boy,' Dedushka shouted.

Dima hesitated one last moment, eyes locked on his beloved grandfather's. Then he continued along the hallway and rushed downstairs, taking the steps two at a time.

He collided with someone in the foyer – his older brother, Petya.

'Soldiers. On the driveway,' Petya said between panting breaths. His face was ghostly white, his eyes wide with fear as he grabbed Dima's hand.

They ran together.

Dima wanted to shout a warning. *Not that way! We'll get caught.* But the nightmare was a memory. It played out night after night. No matter how much Dima struggled, he couldn't change a single choice he made that day. He was doomed to relive the worst moments of his life, a silent witness to his family's demise.

*This is an unpleasant dream,* said an unfamiliar voice, resounding through Dima's memory.

Dima and Petya ran towards the side door. Dima knew what

awaited them there – a rifle held ready. The Red Army had their house surrounded.

*You needn't relive this,* the stranger's voice said. *Come with me, fellow dreamer.*

A door appeared beside Dima, opening to reveal a forest on the other side.

Dima stopped running. He tried to hold onto Petya's hand as he crossed the threshold, but his vision blurred as he stepped into the forest. When it cleared, he found himself perched in the high branches of an oak tree.

Petya was nowhere in sight.

Dima felt a familiar pang in his chest, a hollow ache. He was desperately homesick for a place and time he could never return to. But at least tonight he wouldn't have to watch his loss play out before his eyes.

Instead, he'd entered another dream.

Dima sat on the branch of an oak tree. Beside him, a teenage boy clung to the trunk. The boy wore green tights with a red tunic belted around his thin waist. Over this he wore a magnificent cloak made of blue and red patchwork squares. Each square contained the embroidered figure of a person, animal or creature of legend. Dima thought he saw an embroidered griffon flap its wings, but before he could get a better look, the boy swept the cloak to the side, revealing an injury.

He had four parallel slashes across his ribs.

A beast prowled below him, circling the tree with hunger in its yellow eyes. It was larger than an ordinary wolf, and the malice radiating from the creature felt distinctly human.

*It's a volkolak,* the stranger spoke into Dima's mind. *It devoured my master and has been tracking me for two days.*

Volkolaki were shapeshifters, dark wizards who could take the form of wolves.

*You pulled me from my nightmare into another?* Dima asked the dreamer.

*No.* The boy raised his arm and pointed into the forest. *This is the moment I first met him. Look.*

A Cossack warrior stepped through the trees. His head was shaved except for a thick black forelock, which hung over his left shoulder to brush away any devils that might try to whisper in his ear.

The whip he carried marked him as a bogatyr – a hero from the stories of old, aided by elemental magic. Runes were carved into every inch of the whip's leather, and spells bound within every knot. The weapon seemed to have a life of its own as it pulsed with power in the warrior's hand.

He stepped out into the clearing, letting his whip uncoil and slither through mid-air.

The volkolak raised its hackles.

Holding the whip in one hand, the bogatyr drew his sword with the other.

The wolf crept closer. A low growl sounded deep in its throat. Then it leapt.

With lightning in his eyes and thunder in the crack of his whip, the warrior muttered a spell as he struck the beast. The spell cleaved magic from the creature. There were now two wolves in the forest. The beast of fur and claw lay panting on the forest floor, stunned by the whip's blow. Beside it stood a second wolf, one formed of shadow, smoke and dark-as-midnight magic.

Venom dripped from the shadow creature's teeth as it growled.

Letting his sword fall, the bogatyr held his whip in both hands. For a long moment, man and magic crouched in ready stances, staring each other down. When the shadow wolf pounced, the warrior swept the whip in a sideways curve. No sooner had the wolf's paws left the ground then the whip wrapped three times around its throat.

The warrior began to chant a spell of binding while the creature struggled. With every repetition of the spell, the shadow wolf shrank and the physical wolf transformed. Paws stretched into human hands and fur gave way to skin.

The shadow wolf shrank smaller and smaller and smaller until the coil of the whip collapsed around thin air and all remnant of dark magic vanished.

Back in his human form, the wizard was an old man with a wild, frizzy beard. He stumbled to his feet and ran away.

The boy dropped to the ground with a pained grunt. Though still bleeding, his blue eyes were alive with excitement.

'That was . . .' He shook his head with awe. 'Spectacular. I mean . . . I'm lost for words, and anyone who knows me will tell you I'm never speechless. My master tried forcing me to practice silence an hour a day, for the sake of his nerves. I'd fidget so much in my efforts to keep quiet that he became even *more* nervous. Then he let me talk however much I wanted. But the way you fought that wolf left me tongueless.'

'You seem to have recovered quickly enough,' the warrior said with amusement.

'Well, yes, of course. A skomorokh who can't quickly recover his wits isn't worth his cloak, now is he?'

*A skomorokh?* Dima asked, dropping down from the tree limb. Looking more closely, he realised the embroidered figures on the boy's cloak did occasionally twitch and move as though they were half alive.

Dima had heard about story cloaks, though the skill to craft them had been lost after the great persecution when Tsar Alexei Romanov declared skomorokh magic a heresy. Before that, skomorokhi were magic wielders with powers related to stories, songs and illusions. They travelled from town to town, either as individuals or troupes, and performed at fairs and markets. Legends say that each thread of their cloak contained a living story that they had mastered the telling of.

'Aren't you a little young to be travelling on your own?' the warrior asked.

'I'm fifteen,' the boy said in a wounded tone, pulling himself up to his full height, which was significantly shorter than the bogatyr. 'And I suppose I'm not actually a skomorokh. I'm an apprentice, or I was. One day this spring my master had too much vodka and started spinning riddles during lambing. I'm sure you can imagine how that turned out.'

The warrior looked at him blankly.

'It turned out disastrously, of course! Lambing is a very dangerous time of year for storytellers, and spinning a riddle is about the worst thing you can do. Wolves have been after us ever since – both normal ones and those.'

The boy gestured vaguely toward the forest in the direction the volkolak had gone.

'We've been heading for Solovetsky Island so the monks can cleanse us from the curse of the wolf, but then my master got himself devoured, and Mishka abandoned me to go fishing in the river, so *that's* how I ended up in a tree with a volkolak slash across my ribs. Thanks for rescuing me, by the way.'

'You're welcome?' The warrior appeared bewildered by the rapid stream of the boy's words.

'I'm Yelezar Kerdeyevich Danilov.' He gave a little bow, and then gritted his teeth at the pain of the movement. 'I suppose I should have said that to begin with.'

A chill spread up Dima's spine. This was his ancestor, author of the book Katya had found in the labyrinth. Dedushka spoke of sharing dreams with Yelezar, which had led to his lifelong obsession.

This dream must be one of Yelezar's memories, and that meant the warrior could be none other than the famous Cossack folk hero, Stenka Razin.

'I'm headed for Solovetsky Island myself.' Stenka whistled, and a black stallion trotted into the clearing. 'Perhaps we might travel together.'

Just then, a bear lumbered out of the trees. The stallion whinnied and skittered sideways. Stenka drew his whip, but Yelezar laughed heartily.

'Finally tired of fishing, I see, and come in search of honey.' Yelezar's cloak billowed as he rose to his feet, wincing at the pain in his ribs. The bear sat back on its haunches, waiting as Yelezar drew a clay honeypot out of his pack and approached the creature without a trace of fear.

*Is this Mishka?* Dima asked, remembering Yelezar had mentioned being abandoned by someone with that name. Skomorokhi and bears had special kinship, often travelling and performing together. But it still surprised Dima to see the bear wrap its enormous arms around Yelezar and draw him in for a hug.

*Indeed it is.* Yelezar stuck his fingers in the honey pot and held them out for the bear to lick. *My most faithful friend, who abandons me at the first sniff of river trout but is sure to find me when he wants dessert.*

With the bear added to their company, Yelezar and Stenka began the journey northward, headed for Solovetsky Island.

\*\*\*

Dima woke slowly, his shoulder and hips aching from lying on the chapel floor. Opening his eyes, Dima's mind snapped to full awareness. He lay face to face with Yekaterina Efremova, breaths mingling in the air between them.

Katya still slept. Her head rested on Dima's outstretched arm, but she'd turned in the night. Her wrist now draped languidly across his healing ribs. Her fingertips rested against his back.

The way his skin awoke beneath her touch meant danger. Dima may have been infatuated with Katya before, when she was only a figment of his skomorokh dreams. He may have memorised every line of her face – the sharpness of her jaw, the softness of her lips, the slight dimple in her chin that only appeared when she stood in defiance. But that had been before he knew she was an anarchist.

Just like the woman who ordered his family's execution.

Stepping into Yelezar's dream had been a welcome respite from his usual nightmare. The memory of the day the Red Army came to his *dacha* haunted him. Even yesterday, in the labyrinth, his vision returned him to that darkest hour. A gentle voice spoke to him then. *Just as a putrid wound must be scraped clean before being bandaged, so too must you face this remembered horror before you can truly heal.*

Dima had broken the trance and stumbled out of the labyrinth, dismayed. He had no intention of reliving that memory by choice.

What did it mean that he dreamed of Yelezar on the same night he'd followed his ancestor's footsteps to this island? Was this the story he'd been searching for all his life, the same one that had captivated his grandfather before him?

He wished Dedushka were here right now, but that day in his smoky office was the last time Dima had seen his grandfather alive.

Now morning sunrays filtered in through the small chapel windows, lighting Katya's hair like a golden halo. Katya stirred against his arm. Dima didn't mean to watch as her dark lashes parted and her pale blue eyes blinked open. *She's an anarchist,* he reminded himself. Why did she have to be so beautiful?

'We should go.' Katya turned away from him and stood. 'We've likely missed breakfast, but we could get back in time for roll-call, if we hurry.'

'What are we going to do with the manuscript?'

Dima picked up the ancient book. Here was the story calling to his dreams, written in his ancestor's own hand. If only Dima had learned Greek, he could read it. Perhaps they could have it translated. Dima felt the loss of his grandfather's life's work almost as deeply as losing the man himself.

Was this the reason Dima had survived, to tell the story of Stenka Razin and the peasants who rose up against the tyrannical regime in Moscow to demand their freedom?

'There is no *we*.' Katya held out her hand. 'I'll take the book.'

Dima couldn't help smiling at her stubborn expression, even more so when his smile made her lips tighten with annoyance.

Katya lunged for the manuscript, so he raised it above his head.

'It was written by *my* ancestor, and my family has been searching for it for centuries.'

'Your family didn't find it,' Katya said with fiery intensity. 'I did.'

'Because I showed you the map.'

'My mother left the map there for *me*.'

Interesting. Had Svetlana Efremova been the one to hide the map? Was that before or after she set the library ablaze? Dima felt a strange sense of déjà vu. Dedushka burning papers, Katya's mother burning books – were they connected somehow?

Dima raised a brow, inviting Katya to expand on her statement. She let out an exasperated sigh.

'My mother left clues for me to follow, and that book is

one of them. It might hold the secrets to why my mother was murdered and what she wants me to do next.'

*What she wants me to do next?* Katya spoke of her mother like a general and herself as a pawn. She had far more to give the world than blind obedience. Still, he understood being beholden to a lost relative. Generations are connected, after all, in the great tapestry of souls. Threads weave together and patterns repeat. Naturally, Katya would want her mother's death to mean something.

Wasn't that the same reason Dima wanted the book, to honour his grandfather's legacy?

If the answers Katya sought were in this book about Stenka Razin, Dima might be able to help her find them. And he could certainly benefit from Katya's input if he turned Yelezar's story into an epic poem, as his grandfather had done.

'Maybe we should work together.' Dima lowered the book and held it out between them like a peace offering.

'Why?' Katya asked.

'Clearly we were supposed to meet. What are the chances that I found the map your mother hid, and that it led to my ancestor's manuscript? I can't help thinking it's—'

'Extremely suspicious?' Katya interjected.

Dima's smile widened. 'I was going to say fate.'

Katya crossed her arms, and that little dimple appeared in her chin. 'This has nothing to do with you.'

'I disagree,' he said cheerfully. 'Whatever this is about, I'm already involved. You might as well let me help you.'

'Why? What's in it for you?'

'Do I have to have an ulterior motive?'

'*Everybody* has an ulterior motive.'

Tilting his head, Dima raised one eyebrow and bit his lip, considering how to answer.

'I've been sent here to die. But I'd like to do something, for my life to *mean* something before it's over.'

One of the Bolshevik's first official policies was 'decossackization', a systematic genocide in the region of the Don. His people had been crushed, his family slaughtered – and all Dima had to offer them was a story.

Maybe Stenka Razin's courage could be a lamp to every Cossack, shining long after Dima's death.

'I want to recreate my grandfather's research.' Dima stepped towards Katya. The air between them became static, prickling across Dima's skin. 'I want to write an epic poem of the Cossacks, to remind a scattered people we were once a nation in love with freedom. And that we could be again.'

Biting her lip, Katya considered his words for a long moment, then asked, 'You're a poet?'

'Not a good one. That's why I'm hoping you'll help me. I need someone to smooth out my rhymes and fix my, uh . . .' He snapped his fingers while searching for the word. '. . . pentameter?'

'Iambic tetrameter would be a more traditional choice for a Russian epic.'

'See? I clearly need your help. And in return I'll be your resident expert on Stenka Razin. I grew up on my grandfather's stories, which means I probably know more about Razin than anyone alive.'

Katya watched him, biting her lip as she considered his proposition.

'I'll think about it, Dmitri,' Katya said finally. 'But this doesn't mean—'

'I know, my dear Katinka.' Dima's smile blossomed into an all-out grin. 'It doesn't mean we're friends.'

# Chapter 19
## *Katya*

When Katya stepped out of the chapel door, it felt like the storm that swept over the archipelago last night now raged within her. She wished Dima hadn't spoken with such passion about the poem he hoped to write for his people. She said she'd think about helping him, but her letter to the anarchists must have been received by now. They would demand her transfer, and Katya would go to the political prison, taking the manuscript and clues along with her.

At the harbour, Dima climbed into the canoe and used an oar to break the ice that had formed around it. He offered Katya a hand. Their eyes met, and something twisted in Katya's gut. A light of goodness shone in Dima, so bright it hurt to look at. His pleasant banter and warm smile had begun melting through Katya's protective layer of hostility.

Despite herself, she was starting to like this Cossack.

She didn't want to betray him by taking the book, but what else could she do?

*Maybe it's for the best,* she thought as she took his hand to step into the boat. The touch sent prickles up her arm. Heat gathered in her belly, morphing into a sharp ache at the thought of never seeing Dima again. *Definitely for the best.*

Katya couldn't befriend Dima. Nor anyone else, for that

matter. Caring about people meant having something to lose, and she'd lost too much already.

Sitting on the rowing bench, Katya took up the second oar and they cast off. She rowed hard, partly to warm herself but mostly to try and distract from her sense of guilt. Dima didn't make it easy. He kept glancing back at her as though working up the courage to say something.

Finally, he asked, 'What was it like growing up as an anarchist?'

'Why?' She clipped her word short to warn him against trespassing.

'Just curious,' he said lightly. 'Your childhood seems much more interesting than mine.'

'I doubt it.'

Dima shrugged and continued rowing.

Katya stared at his back, at the muscles shifting beneath his coat with every powerful movement. He glanced over his shoulder. Though he started to smile, it fell flat beneath the hard suspicion in Katya's glare.

'I wasn't trying to pry,' he said. 'I thought it might be nice to get to know each other.'

'Talk about yourself, if you want, but don't expect an open book when it comes to me and my past.'

'Fair enough.' Gripping the oar, Dima stood up in the canoe, setting it rocking.

Katya shrieked as freezing water leaked over the edges, pooling in the bottom of the boat. 'What are you doing?'

Dima turned on the rowing bench, amusement dancing in his eyes. 'If I'm going to talk about myself, I'd like to do so face to face.'

A blush crept into Katya's cheeks. The last thing she needed was him gazing into her eyes. A vein pulsed in her clenched jaw as she pulled her oar more forcefully than she needed to. It took a few strokes for Dima to get the hang of the rhythm now that they faced each other, but soon they were rowing in sync across the frosty sea.

Dima cleared his throat.

'In a certain village, not far, not near, not high and not low, there once lived a boy with a very boring family,' he said, using a typical fairy tale opening and projecting his voice as though in a theatre.

Katya cracked a smile despite herself. She quickly turned it into a scowl, but Dima grinned triumphantly at getting a reaction out of her.

'How many brothers and sisters do you have?' she asked.

Dima's smile faded.

Why had she asked him that? His past was a minefield she'd be wiser not to cross, and from the haunted look in his eyes, it seemed she'd already stepped on a trigger.

'Never mind,' she said.

'It's fine.' Dima rowed a few strokes. 'It's just, there used to be four of us. I'm the only one left.'

'I'm sorry,' she said. Those words didn't feel like nearly enough. As a poet, she should be able to express her compassion more elegantly, and, as a charovnika, she understood better than most people how powerful words could be. But some losses dig holes so deep that words can never fill them.

'So am I.' Dima forced a smile. 'But I'd rather speak of the happy memories.'

As they continued rowing toward Solovetsky Island, Dima told Katya stories about his family. He talked of his grandfather the professor, who had taught Dima to love history and folklore. And of his older brother Petya, who'd wanted to be an engineer.

Dima was the second born. After him came Taya, who'd

been a Francophile through and through. She loved everything French – language, music, pastries. She collected every catalogue put out by Parisian couturiers, even though Dima's family wasn't wealthy enough to order clothes from France. When she was about ten, Taya organised a fashion parade and only informed Petya and Dima after they'd agreed to participate that they'd be displaying their mother's dresses.

'And you went along with it?' Katya asked, unable to suppress her amusement.

'Oh, yes.' Dima chuckled, his eyes brightening. 'There was no point arguing with Taya, so I decided to have fun. I swished my skirts, swayed my hips . . . even attempted a pirouette.'

That won another smile from Katya, and this time she didn't turn it into a scowl. Hearing his stories made her childhood seem rather lonely in comparison.

'I always wanted siblings,' she admitted. Their rowing had taken a more leisurely pace, as though neither of them was in a hurry for this trip to be over.

'Your mother couldn't have more children?'

'She didn't want children, period. Not me and certainly not others.'

Katya spoke in a light-hearted tone, as though her mother's scorn was a source of amusement akin to the antics of Dima's siblings. Dima stopped rowing.

'I'm sorry she made you feel that way,' he said.

Katya lowered her gaze, cleared her throat. Why was she opening up to him? It wasn't like her to trust so easily, and Dima might not even be who he seemed. *Anyone can be an informant,* her mother had warned her a thousand times.

'We were talking about your family, not mine,' Katya said.

Dima hesitated for a moment, as though he didn't want to let the topic drop. Thankfully he didn't push her. He continued rowing and spoke of his brother Sasha, the baby of the family. He'd been a sweet boy who cried over dead spiders, liked to sleep curled up with the dogs in front of the kitchen stove, and followed Taya around like a second shadow.

Dima had only vague recollections of his cold and formal father, who went away to war nine years ago and never came back, but his face became luminous when speaking of his mother.

'She was happy, always singing or humming as she went about her day. If I said something, she'd stop what she was doing and give me her full attention. Whatever I had to say mattered to her. *I* mattered to her. Finances were tight with my father gone, and my mother . . .' Dima's voice cracked. 'She gave up eating meat so there would be enough money for my paints and art supplies. That's how generous she was.' Dima wiped moisture from the corners of his eyes. 'I miss her.'

'I don't know how you can bear to talk about them,' Katya said. 'I can barely stand to think about my mother. It hurts too much.'

'It hurts, but I want to remember. They may be dead, but as long as I keep their memory alive, they're not really gone.'

Katya pondered his words as they reached Solovetsky Island and rowed into a narrow canal. She did feel Svetlana with her still, a vague presence watching over her. That's why she had to solve the mystery of her mother's death and the cryptic message she'd left behind – it was her last chance to earn Svetlana's approval, something she'd rarely managed to accomplish while her mother was alive.

As they went further inland Katya began to wonder if bringing Yelezar Danilov's book to the monastery was a mistake. What if she was inadvertently bringing it straight to Commissar Boky? Wouldn't it be better to hide the book where he wouldn't find it? Somewhere that Katya could retrieve it when the anarchists secured her transfer?

'Listen,' she said. 'There's something you need to know about my mother's death.'

Katya held back as much information as she could, but she told Dima enough about Boky's involvement in Svetlana's murder to explain why they shouldn't bring the manuscript to the monastery.

As he listened, Dima's forehead creased. 'What do you want to do?'

Katya looked up to the sky and felt a tug in her spirit. Yesterday, as they'd rowed through the canals on their way to Bolshoi Zayatsky, Katya had spotted an abandoned cabin in the forest. That cabin was near enough to the monastery that she could retrieve the book when her comrades came for her.

'I might know a hiding place,' Katya said.

The tree canopy bent over them as they rowed, and Katya sensed the cabin growing nearer. Her heart contained a compass, pointing her exactly where to go.

'It's here.' Katya indicated toward the shore.

Dima leapt onto the bank and used a rock to pound a branch into the ground before tying the boat to it.

He offered Katya a hand. When she stepped up onto the frozen shore, he didn't release her. His lively brown eyes studied her face. Katya held her breath. She wondered if he would try to kiss her, then wondered if she would let him. But he only squeezed her fingers and said, 'If you ever do need to talk about your family – you know, with someone who understands what you've lost – I'm a good listener.'

Katya bit her lip. Her throat felt raw. It was an offer she couldn't take him up on – today she should be transferred to join the anarchists and then she'd never see him again – but still she whispered, 'thanks.'

They headed for the clearing where the cabin rested. Something guided Katya, as though by a tether. She didn't pause to consider how odd that was, not until the eerie notes of a violin filtered through the trees.

'I know that song.' Katya couldn't remember where she'd heard it before, but it felt intimately familiar. The music reminded her of the violin she used to hear playing in the lab, her only company besides ghosts during those lonely hours of resistance. If she'd heard this same violin in the lab, that meant . . . .

Natasha stood barefoot in the clearing, playing her violin to a dying fire.

When Katya and Dima stepped beyond the tree line, Natasha's eyes snapped open. They seemed to hold an otherworldly darkness. Her auburn hair shimmered as though it had soaked in moonlight.

'Who is that?' Dima asked warily.

'Trouble,' Katya said, though she couldn't stop her feet from carrying her to Natasha's fireside. She'd been bewitched.

Katya pulled the amber beads from her pocket, wondering why they hadn't guarded her from Natasha's witchcraft. They pulsed in her fingers, thrumming to the rhythm of the violin. Then Katya understood. The beads couldn't protect her from Natasha's power because Natasha was the witch who had crafted them.

'Well, well, well.' Natasha raised her eyebrows suggestively as she set her violin in its case. 'Here I was worried about you, and all the while you were off with a boy. Not that I blame you.' Natasha looked Dima up and down, nodding appreciatively. She shouldered past Katya and slunk toward him, extending her hand. 'I'm Natasha.'

'Dima.' He cast Katya an uncomfortable look before shaking Natasha's hand.

'So, what are you?' Natasha purred.

'*What* am I?' Dima sounded amused. 'Do you mean literally or metaphysically?'

Natasha narrowed her eyes.

'Well, do you want to know that I'm a twenty-year-old Cossack? That's literal. Metaphysically, I'm a little harder to nail down.' Dima started counting off on his fingers. 'I'm an artist. I'm a romantic. I have faith – both in God and in the good in people. I'm—'

'What are you?' Disdain dripped from Natasha's voice. 'As in, what kind of volshebnik?'

'Ah. In that case, what I am is one of the few remaining skomorokhi in Russia.'

'Hmmm.' Natasha tilted her head, considering him thoughtfully. 'A skomorokh, a charovnika and a vedma could form a powerful alliance.' Natasha met Katya's eyes. 'Whatever the two of you are planning, I want in.'

'That's not going to happen,' Katya said.

'You'll need a translator.' Natasha jutted her chin, indicating Yelezar Danilov's book. Katya hadn't meant to hold it with the title showing. 'I've studied Greek extensively.'

'That . . . would be really helpful, actually.' Dima looked at Katya, raising an eyebrow as though to ask, *Well? What do you think?*

What Katya thought was that Dima trusted people far too easily. Natasha had been spying on her since their arrival on the island. She wanted to know why.

Katya closed her eyes and began quietly chanting the zagovor she used to bring her mind to awareness of the Otherworld.

'What are you doing?' Natasha asked warily.

Katya felt her soul opening and the trickle of power warming her blood. Fixing Natasha in her mind, Katya cast an Old Russian spell that could compel a hostile witness to speak truth.

'*Lukavye glaza, lzhi ne izdavay. Dushish'sya v vozdukhe, yesli osmelish'sya. Pust' pravda zastavit tvoy yazyk.*' *Wicked eyes, speak no lies. Choke on air if you should try. May truth compel your tongue.*

The spell had to be chanted six times for full potency. Before Katya finished the second repetition, Natasha shoved Katya's chest with both hands. Katya lost her balance. As she tumbled to the frozen ground, Natasha wrenched the oilcloth bundle from her.

Dima crouched beside Katya, his brows pressed together in concern. 'Are you all right?'

Katya sat up and scanned the trees. Natasha was gone, together with Yelezar Danilov's book and the journal containing the opening chapters translated by Svetlana.

Dima offered a hand to help her up. As Katya stood, a twig snapped in the forest. They both turned, and Katya's stomach dropped.

Smolensky and four other guards came through the trees, their rifles aimed at Katya and Dima.

'Get down on your knees,' Smolensky ordered.

'I can explain.' Dima held his hands open in a friendly gesture of surrender. 'You see, we were just—'

'Get *down* on your knees!'

Smolensky moved his finger to the trigger, and the sight awoke nightmares in Katya, memories of the night spent holding vigil as men dug their own graves behind the women's barrack. Smolensky had been there. He'd murdered those men, probably with the same gun now aimed at her.

'All right,' Dima said in the tone of voice used to calm growling animals.

Dima dropped to his knees, but Katya couldn't. Wouldn't. If Smolensky meant to shoot them, he'd do it regardless of their compliance.

Katya thought to cast a spell, but a set of amber worry beads protruded from Smolensky's coat pocket, same as the ones she'd lifted from Nogtev.

Katya's words couldn't save her. Still, she refused to die on her knees. In the chance her mother *was* watching over her, Katya would make her final moments ones Svetlana would be proud of.

Though she was trembling, Katya put her shoulders back and raised her chin.

Smolensky's nostrils flared. He lunged forward and swung the rifle at Katya. Pain burst across her temple as the gun struck her face. Everything went momentarily silent. Katya dropped to her knees then toppled over, the world spinning a few times before everything went black.

# Chapter 20
## *Natasha*

Natasha watched from the shadow of the trees, her heart pounding as she clutched the books to her chest. Dima struggled, calling Katya's name as guards wrenched his arms behind his back and led him away. Katya, still unconscious, had to be dragged across the forest floor.

Comrade Smolensky lingered in the clearing. When the others were out of sight, Natasha stepped out into the open.

'Marius,' Natasha greeted him.

He took off his fur hat, running his fingers through his blond hair. His cheeks were reddened with cold, and resentment shone in his eyes as he reluctantly bowed to Natasha.

Smolensky hated all Russians. Even her. Perhaps *especially* her because of the hold she had over him.

His parents had been killed as part of the Polish resistance against the Russian Empire. After the Revolution, he'd joined the Bolshevik party and become one of the most enthusiastic participants in the Red Terror, enacting vengeance for his parents' deaths on ordinary Russians. He'd killed, tortured and raped without mercy. And when his crimes became too much of a liability to the government, they sent him to the lab at Lubyanka Square.

Now he was part of Natasha's pack.

Besides Commisar Boky, there were seven volkolaki on the island, men who had opened their souls to dark spirits in exchange for the power to transform into wolves.

Boky thought he was their alpha. Natasha let him believe that was so.

Even as a prisoner, Natasha had been planning for the future. When each of those seven men came to the lab, Natasha summoned unclean spirits, as Barchenko instructed her to. In performing the ritual, however, Natasha offered the men's souls in exchange for the spirits' service to *her*. They obliged, accepting Natasha as their master. She could command the seven shape-shifters, and they were bound to her will.

'Report,' Natasha ordered.

Though his lips pursed at the command, Smolensky obeyed Natasha, as he must.

His report offered little encouragement. Commissar Boky had been informed both of Katya's escapade to Bolshoi Zayatsky and of Natasha's plans to intercept her here. He'd sent guards to drag Katya and her accomplice back to the monastery, together with any objects they'd found on the outlying island.

This confirmed Natasha's suspicion that Boky was searching for something on this archipelago. But how had Boky known where to find Natasha?

'Did you tell Boky my plans?'

'Of course not,' Smolensky said through his teeth. 'I'm not able to betray you.'

That was true. It was physically impossible for any of her wolves to disobey her orders. Boky must have had her followed by someone else.

'Commissar Boky said we should bring you back to the monastery as well.'

Natasha considered her options. Right now Boky believed

himself the alpha of the volkolaki on the island. Natasha would be wise to maintain that illusion for as long as possible. Having Smolensky drag her back to the monastery would allay any suspicion Boky might have of the wolves not being under his control.

Except that leaving the cabin now meant giving up the chance to study what Katya found on Bolshoi Zayatsky. Natasha's aunt made sure she could read archaic Greek as fluently as French or Russian. It wouldn't take her long to study the book.

If she found what she was looking for, Natasha would have no need for an alliance with Katya or to stay on Boky's good side. She could take the artefact – whatever it turned out to be – and get off this godforsaken island before the sea froze over.

'Tell Boky you couldn't find me,' Natasha said. 'And spread this command throughout the pack: I want my enemies watched – Katya, her associate Dima and Boky as well. I expect daily reports, and, if any of them leave the monastery again, I wish to hear about it immediately.'

'*Horosho.*' Smolensky dipped his head in obedience to her command and stalked off.

Once he was gone, Natasha retrieved her violin and went inside the cabin. She built up the fire and set the books out on the table. The older manuscript was a first-hand account of the life of Stenka Razin. The journal contained Svetlana's translation of the opening chapters.

Why was Boky so interested in the life of a Cossack folk hero?

In 1630, Razin had been born in the Don Republic, Muscovy's southern neighbour. The Romanovs had risen to power after the Time of Troubles. In an effort to restore stability, Alexei Romanov created *Sobornoye Ulozheniye*, the law code of 1642. This law fettered every serf to the town or village of his birth and to the profession of his father, under pain of death.

In contrast, the Don Republic was a nation of outlaws and brigands who valued freedom above all else. They considered all men equal and governed themselves by councils of elders that were elected every year.

Any Muscovite serf who reached the Don became a free man. By the time Stenka Razin was a young bogatyr rising to prominence in the Don Republic, the Cossacks faced a refugee crisis. Every day, escaped Muscovites arrived on their lands by the hundreds and thousands, far more than their communities could reasonably support.

After his pilgrimage to Solovki, Stenka Razin decided to help those poor wretches the only way he knew how – by bringing them on an adventure.

He recruited a pirate crew who called themselves the River Wolves. In 1667, they sailed from the Don on the spring tides and began raiding the coasts of the Caspian Sea, gathering plunder that would help the refugees establish themselves as free men.

Curled like a cat in front of the hot stove, Natasha scanned over the chapters detailing the raids and adventures of the River Wolves.

She cursed when she reached a part where three pages had been ripped out of the manuscript.

Running her finger along the ripped edges, Natasha wondered what they had contained. The text cut off right after the River Wolves commandeered a flotilla of trade vessels flying the Patriarch's banners. It picked up again several months later.

Could Stenka Razin have found something on the church patriarch's flagship during that pirate raid?

If Natasha remembered correctly, the Patriarch of Moscow at that time was a charovnik spell-caster called Nikon. He'd been a monk here in the Solovetsky Archipelago. Just five years after leaving Solovki, the tsar dropped down to his knees before Nikon and begged him to become the church patriarch, the highest ecclesiastical office in Russia. It was said that Tsar Alexei didn't make a single decision without Nikon's approval – not until the patriarch fell out of favour two years before Razin's revolt.

What if Nikon possessed a relic, one powerful enough to fuel his rise to power? A relic that was stolen by Stenka Razin.

What could it be, though?

The answer must be in those missing pages.

If Katya cracked the cipher, would it lead her to the artefact Stenka Razin stole from the church patriarch?

Having this book wasn't enough. If Svetlana Efremova's ciphers held the keys to her secrets, she would ensure no one besides her daughter would be able to crack them.

Natasha had cursed Katya's name a thousand times.

She cursed her still.

But she needed this alliance.

Natasha wrapped Yelezar Danilov's book in the oilcloth, stashing it beneath a loose floorboard. She doused the fire and stepped outside, heading back to the monastery in search of Katya.

# Chapter 21

## *Katya*

When Katya came to, she was being dragged by two guards. Cobblestones scraped the fronts of her legs and shredded her stockings. The guards yanked her arms so violently that the seams of her shirt came apart, the threads unravelling just like her plans.

Pain bloomed inside her skull, and her vision kept blurring. Katya tried to think. She had to stay alive until the anarchists demanded her transfer. Just a few more hours and she would have been safe. She had to buy some time, but how? Could she pretend to have information the government wanted?

Katya tried to get her feet under her, to walk instead of being dragged. Before she managed it, the guards stopped moving. Smolensky elbowed Katya. She blinked to clear her double vision. A naked figure stood on a wooden platform, arms outstretched and tied to poles. When Katya looked at his face, an anvil dropped inside her chest – it was the boy she'd asked to carry her letter to the anarchists.

Smolensky smirked.

He'd brought Katya this way so she'd know they'd intercepted her message.

So she'd know no help was coming.

So she'd be afraid of what came next.

Now what? Katya tried to think but her head hurt too much. It felt like bees were trapped in her skull, buzzing in her ears, swarming through her thoughts, and stinging her everywhere as the blow to her cheek reverberated with a growing ache.

Smolensky dragged Katya into the kremlin, up a stairway and into a high-ceilinged room where Dima already stood waiting with guards on either side of him. She saw a desk, bookshelves and a sitting area. Before Katya had time to wonder whose office this was, the door to an adjoining room opened.

Commissar Boky, the man who'd pretended to be a detective after Svetlana's murder, prowled into the office. He wore a military uniform with pockets on either side of his chest and a medal pinned over his heart. As he came near, Katya caught his scent. He smelled like the forest – the dampness of moss, the crispness of pine, and the heady fragrance of snow carried upon a biting winter wind.

His piercing grey eyes made Katya want to lower her head in submission, but she refused that instinct. She glared at him as he looked her over, from her old boots that could use a good polish to her stockings to her schoolgirl uniform.

Boky's gaze lingered on her injured cheek.

'Leave us,' he ordered the guards. 'Two of you wait outside the door.'

When the guards let her go, Katya faltered as nausea surged through her. Her vision wavered, and the ache in her cheek pulsed along with her heartbeat. Dima cast concerned glances at her.

Boky stepped closer, reaching into his pocket. Katya flinched when he pulled something out, but it was only a handkerchief, white as the snowflakes that had begun falling outside the window.

'Go on,' he said.

Katya swiped the handkerchief and pressed it to her wound. Her cheek was swollen and sticky with blood.

'My orders were that you be brought to me unharmed, I'd like you to know that. And know also that the guard responsible will be punished.'

Boky clasped his hands behind his back, as though to appear unthreatening. But Katya sensed fangs behind his words. Danger turned the air sweet and pungent, heavy as ozone before a coming storm. She didn't trust his stillness, like that of a tiger tracking prey.

'There is, of course, the matter of you both being found outside of the prison compound.'

'That was my fault.' Dima stepped forward, smiling ruefully. 'I invited Katya to go for a walk with me this morning to talk over a proposal I've been planning to give the administration. In fact, since I have the chance to speak with you, I can tell you about it right now.'

Katya made her expression carefully blank. If Dima thought he could talk them out of this, she'd let him try. Boky stared at Dima. Most people would wilt beneath that knowing gaze, but not Dima. His expression remained pleasant, lips curved upward, eyes honey-warm and welcoming. He looked like a man about to confide in his dearest friend, not a convict about to be disciplined by one of the most dangerous men in Russia.

At last Boky blinked and said, 'I'm sure your *proposal* will be very interesting to hear.'

'I want to start a community theatre,' Dima said. 'An artists' unit that meets for rehearsals after the work day, so it won't interfere with the prison's running. We could put on shows, dance and acrobatic performances, concerts. I think it would boost the prisoners' morale, especially as the darkness of winter sets it.'

'And what makes you think the administration wants the prisoners' morale to be boosted?'

'Because you say the purpose of this camp is re-education,' Dima said. 'What's education without art?'

With his hands still clasped behind his back, Boky strolled to the window. He stood there for a long moment, watching the snowflakes fall. 'And what role will Miss Efremova have in this artists' unit?' Boky glanced at her over his shoulder. 'Do you sing? Dance?'

'I'm a poet,' she said.

'Every Russian is a poet.' Boky chuckled darkly and turned away from the window. 'It's a national affliction.'

Katya glared at him.

Boky put a hand over his heart and said, 'No offence intended. I take poetry very seriously, as every Russian must. It gets people killed, after all. Is there any other country where poetry is so common a motive for murder?'

His question settled between them, sharp with meaning. What meaning, Katya couldn't decide.

Dima had gasped at Boky's words. All the blood drained from his face, and Katya wondered if those comments were aimed at Dima rather than her. Did it have to do with the epic poem he'd asked Katya to help him write?

'I am amenable to the idea of a prison theatre,' Boky said. 'So long as the choice of play is approved by the administration and the artists maintain their work quotas. And, just this once, I will overlook the fact that the two of you were caught outside the monastery grounds, but do not expect such leniency again.'

'Thank you, sir.' Dima dipped his head in appreciation, but Katya tensed. If Boky was letting them escape punishment, it wasn't out of the goodness of his heart. What was his angle? What did he want from them?

'You are excused, Convict Danilov.' Boky spread his arm and gestured toward the door. 'The guards will see you returned to your company.'

'What about Katya?' Dima planted his feet.

'She and I have some private matters to discuss.'

Katya dragged in a long, slow breath. Being alone with Boky was the last thing she wanted, but perhaps, if she was clever, she could glean some information about Svetlana's death. Pain throbbed in her cheek and her head ached terribly, but Katya crumpled the bloody handkerchief in her sweaty hand and focused beyond the pain.

'Go,' she told Dima. 'I'll be fine.'

Worry carved deep creases in Dima's brow, but he respected her wishes and left.

'Please, sit down.' Comrade Boky gestured toward the sitting area. Then he shouted, 'Armanov, bring the tea.'

Sounds of movement came from an adjoining room. *Tea?* Katya had been bracing herself for torture, yet somehow Boky's politeness felt just as dangerous. Katya chose a chair with its back to the wall.

She set the handkerchief on the coffee table beside an open letter – *her* letter that she'd written to the anarchists. It had been decoded, every last word.

'A fair attempt.' Boky sat down. He crossed one leg over the other and folded his hands together on his lap. 'But I, of course, know Julia. I make a point of knowing everything about Russia's enemies.'

His subtle smirk said he considered Katya part of that category, and that he knew all about her too. Katya smoothed her skirt over her thighs, wiping the sweat from her palms.

An old man in a tattered three-piece suit entered with an elegant tea service on a silver tray. Setting it on the table, he offered her tea with lemon and sugar. Katya took the cup gingerly, breathing in steam before savouring the taste of sweetness and tang.

After serving Boky the old man limped back to the adjoining room and closed the door.

'I studied engineering, did you know that?' Boky took a long, slow sip of tea.

'Unlike you, I don't have a secret police force to go about torturing people for information on my enemies.'

'I thought your mother would have mentioned me. We were great friends, you know.'

He studied Katya's reaction. She tried not to have one, but her fingers clamped so hard on the handle of her teacup, it nearly snapped.

'You didn't know.' Boky's lips curled with cruel amusement. 'How interesting.'

'Is that why you were there when she was murdered? Because you were *great friends?*'

'You have questions and so do I.' Boky leaned back in his chair. 'I suggest an exchange. You may ask me one question, which I will answer honestly. Then I will ask you something, and you will tell me the absolute truth.'

This conversation had the feel of thin ice, like one wrong word would plunge her into a breathless darkness. Katya had secrets – truths which, if exposed, would give the Bolsheviki every excuse to execute her.

She weighed her danger against her need for information.

Boky sipped his tea as he waited for Katya to think. His stillness disquieted her. And beyond the lemony fragrance of the tea came his strange scent – wind, soil, pine, snow – as though he carried the Russian taiga upon his skin.

She thought of her mother's admonition, *Always learn as much about your enemy as you can.*

'You used to be an engineer.' Katya leaned back, trying to appear casual despite the tension she held in every muscle. 'What are you now?'

Boky tilted his head, considered Katya for a moment, and then nodded in acceptance of her question.

'As I said, I trained to be an engineer. I used to think magic was peasant superstition, that everything in the world could be explained, measured, controlled.' Boky spoke like a metronome, his voice set to a beat. He leaned forward, and his voice broke from its rhythm when he said, 'Then I went to Tashkent.'

Rather than being stiff and measured Boky now spoke as a gifted storyteller, shifting his tone to match his content. 'That was four years ago. On my journey there, I began to cough. Strength drained from my body, and before I could take up my official position I was diagnosed with tuberculosis. Bedridden, feverish and with lungs so swollen I could hardly breathe, I felt myself growing weaker and weaker.'

Remnants of the illness were still visible. With sharp cheekbones and a thin neck, Boky had a gaunt, hungry look about his face.

'The doctors gave me no hope, so I turned to an Uzbek shaman.' Commissar Boky shrugged and gave a mirthless bark of laughter. 'I had nothing to lose, after all. The shaman brought me to a white boulder set above a ley line. He gave me wolf meat for strength, and I ate it. Then, as though in a dream, he led me through a ceremony that drew power from the rock and made me well again. So there you have it. I am an engineer, a revolutionary, a communist – and, now, a believer in miracles.'

Katya waited for him to continue, but he didn't. Surely he was some manner of volshebnik. There was something not quite natural about his scent and predatory gaze.

Katya pushed a question past the lump forming in her throat. 'What are you, really?'

'Guess.' Boky tilted his head, eyes unblinking, lips splitting into a smile that revealed his teeth. Her heart skipped a beat when his canines elongated into fangs. Katya scrambled to her feet. Boky stood and prowled towards her. Fur began to sprout on his cheeks, and the bottom of his face elongated into a muzzle. The hunger in his eyes made her blood run cold.

She had to stop this transformation. The talisman Boky carried prevented Katya from hexing him, but spell-casting wasn't her only ability.

Katya muttered an incantation, the one Svetlana wrote to help Katya regulate the Rurikid magic in her blood. The spell opened Katya to the power in the room, allowing her to draw magic from other volshebniki.

Hijacking Boky's power should prevent him from shape-shifting.

His magic rushed into Katya alongside an intake of rotten breath. The taste of decay coated the back of her throat, and she gagged. It felt like inhaling a shadow, or a ghost. Usually Katya's blood sped up when she drew from other people's magic, but the heartbeat thrumming in her ears slowed like a musical rallentando.

*Thu-thump.* Pause. *Thump thump.* Pause. *Thump. Thump.*

Boky's face had been twisted in the agony of transformation, but he paused to watch her with curiosity.

Something was wrong.

Katya's limbs grew colder, stiffer. She licked her lips and tried to stay the course, even when Boky turned his face to the ceiling and howled. The sound was all animal, and it tensed Katya's shoulders, made fear drip like venom to paralyze her vertebrae one by one.

Her plan was working, though. As she stole his magic, his transformation reversed. Boky's back straightened and his fur slowly receded.

She exhaled a shallow gasp, her limbs corpse cold. This magic wasn't just corrupted – it felt like death itself. Katya's lips were numb and turning purple. She could hardly move her fingers. But it had worked. Boky was human again, offering Katya the cruellest of smiles.

'You're a volkolak.' Katya couldn't steady the tremor in her voice.

The signs of his transformation faded, but his eyes held wild danger.

'When the shaman performed the ritual that saved my life, he instructed me not to touch the stone of power. In my weakness, I stumbled into it. The shaman fell dead instantly, and I became what you say I am. A volkolak.'

The preternatural cold of his corrupted magic crept through Katya's veins, chilling her to the marrow. She shivered.

'Now you know the answer to your question.' Boky lifted an amused eyebrow. 'I hope you're satisfied.'

Katya tried to move, but her limbs felt wooden, corpse-like. She collapsed onto her chair and eyed Boky. 'What is your question for me?'

Tilting his head, he tapped one finger. 'I think I'll save my question for another time.'

Katya inhaled, but the tension constricting her chest made her breathing shallow. She felt confined in a too-small space, both sweating and shivering as her nerves reached their limit.

'Then why ask to speak to me privately?' she asked.

'You're interesting,' he said. 'Too interesting to be wasted on hard labour. I'd like to help you, Yekaterina.'

'You could help me by sending that letter.' She nodded

towards her decoded note left open on the table. 'I belong with the anarchists.'

'I'm afraid they don't see it that way. The anarchists revoked your mother's party membership, back when you were still a juvenile and too young to join in your own right.'

*Impossible.*

The party never would have expelled their golden lady.

'You cannot be reclassified. However . . .' Boky drew out the silence for a long, tense moment. 'You could work here in the kremlin, cleaning, administration – lighter work. How does that sound?'

The implication was clear: Boky wanted Katya where he could watch her. She'd expected to join the anarchists today, but she was stuck here with the most dangerous enemy she'd ever faced. Until she found another way to reach her comrades, she'd make the most of it. Working here in the kremlin, Katya might have a better chance of figuring out why Commissar Boky was at Svetlana's murder scene and uncovering the truth of why she died.

'Fine by me,' Katya said.

Boky smiled as though she were a pawn placed on the board exactly where he wanted it. Good. Let him underestimate her. Let him think her weak and foolish. Let him forget that Katya was her mother's daughter.

Gleb Boky could spy on Katya all he wanted.

She'd be watching him, too.

# Chapter 22

## *Katya*

Commissar Boky showed Katya into an adjoining office. Though the room held several desks and bookshelves, the only person working there was Armanov, the old man who'd served the tea. He sat at a desk, his pen moving rapidly across the pages of a ledger. He had white tufts of eyebrows, a perfectly-waxed moustache that curled on either side of his mouth, and a face lined with the laughter and sadness of at least seventy years. So engrossed was Armanov in his work that he didn't notice their presence until Boky cleared his throat.

'Oh, pardon me.' Armanov set down his pen. 'I did not hear you, Commissar. Is there something you need?'

A subtle undercurrent of contempt flowed beneath his polite words, making Boky purse his lips.

'Yekaterina will be cleaning the administration building from now on. You will orientate her.'

'It would be my pleasure.' Armanov extended a hand across the desk. 'I'm Andrei Sergeevich.'

'Katya.' She shook his hand.

When Boky left, Andrei Sergeevich waited, tilting his head to listen as Boky's footsteps retreated down the hallway. He opened his desk drawer to reveal a novel hidden inside it. He poised his pen above the ledger, ready to pretend to be writing in case Boky returned.

'What should I be doing?' Katya asked.

'As little as possible.' Andrei Sergeevich pressed a wrinkled finger to the page to mark his spot. 'That's what I do, anyway.'

'Boky doesn't notice?'

'Oh, he notices. But I saved his life once and he doesn't want to send an old comrade to hard labour. Besides, I have a bad leg – got shot storming the Winter Palace. Office work is all I'm good for, and I make a point of not being terribly good at that either.'

'You're a Bolshevik?' Katya crossed her arms.

'Used to be.' Noting her body language, Andrei Sergeevich tapped his fingertips on the desk and frowned. 'That was before the Revolution. Let's just say I didn't approve of my comrades imprisoning our allies and treating the lower class as badly as the aristocrats used to. When the Kronstadt sailors rebelled, I'd had enough.'

Katya sucked in a breath at the mention of Kronstadt, which had been a major turning point in her life as well.

'I decided if those courageous men were against us, I must be on the wrong side of things. I was there when Lenin announced our victory. My comrades cheered at the news that thousands of our former allies had been slaughtered. They even gave Lenin a standing ovation.' Outrage shone in Andrei Sergeevich's eyes. 'I stayed seated.'

'That was brave,' Katya said.

'Brave, foolish – it's hard to tell the difference sometimes.' Andrei Sergeevich smiled sadly. 'The Cheka arrested me the very next day. Now I'm here. But at least I can live with myself.'

Andrei Sergeevich went back to reading his book.

Katya stood there for a long moment, deciding what to do next.

She'd left her school bag at the guesthouse. That prevented her from working on the cipher, but being here in the kremlin gave Katya the opportunity to put her espionage training to good use.

'I should get to work.' Katya tried to sound casual. 'Commissar Boky mentioned cleaning the file room. Could you tell me where I might find it?'

Putting a finger on the page to mark his place, Andrei Sergeevich looked up. He studied Katya for a moment, and then a mischievous glint sparkled in his dark eyes.

'One floor up, second door on the left.'

Nodding her thanks, she stepped out into the hallway. Katya quietly chanted her zagovor. After several repetitions, she felt a trickle of power in her blood. Soon it was pooling in her diaphragm, ready to be laced through her words.

She then cast her spell for stealth. It was a precaution she always took, even now that she knew it wouldn't protect her from the higher-level guards who carried talismans.

Katya crept upstairs and made her way down a quiet corridor until she reached the entrance to the file room. She cast a second spell, and the door unlocked. She inched the door open and peeked inside, letting out a relieved breath when she found the room blessedly empty.

Faint light filtered in through small, arched windows. The room looked almost like a library with a narrow aisle leading the way through rows of shelves. Instead of books, the shelves held alphabetised folders. Only the first four shelves were filled. Solovki had just begun operating as a prison a few months earlier, so the fact that they'd made space for tens of thousands of files sent a shiver through Katya. Would the Bolsheviki imprison every Russian who raised their voice against the government?

Katya walked the length of the first shelf.

Natasha claimed her last name was Bobrinskaya. Kneeling down beside the shelf containing 'B' names, Katya ran her thumb along the file tabs. She checked three times, but there was no prisoner in Solovki with that surname.

So who was Natasha really?

Katya had to retrieve the book somehow.

Maybe Dima could get hold of more passes, but could Katya trust him?

Continuing along the shelf, Katya found Dima's folder. Tucked into the shelf next to it was the leather satchel he'd been carrying when he arrived on the island. It must have been confiscated after his beating.

Katya pulled it off the shelf. Inside were pencils, chalks, and three sketchbooks. Closing the satchel, Katya slung the strap over her shoulder. She may as well return his things when she next saw him.

She opened his file. Dmitri Petrovich Danilov was born on 10 March 1903 in a village near Rostov-on-Don. The file listed his people group as Cossack, his title as Count, and his political affiliation as Counter-revolutionary.

At least one of her would-be allies was who he claimed to be.

Katya's gut twisted when she read about his family members. Dima's father fell in battle during the Great War. The Red Army executed Dima's grandfather, mother, brothers, and sister on 2 June 1919 as part of the government policy of decossackization. Dima's youngest brother, Alexandr, had been only nine years old when Red Army soldiers shot him in the back of the head, as though his life meant nothing.

Katya squeezed her eyes closed, feeling like she might be sick. Anarchists had still been allied with the Bolsheviki in 1919, still believing their Revolution would birth a just society, still fighting in the Red Army against counter-revolutionary forces. It could have been an anarchist who'd executed Dima's family.

How could Dima stand to look at Katya, let alone want to work together?

Normally she'd call that suspicious, but nothing in his file pointed to him being an informant. Three months ago, authorities in Kazan arrested Dima during a raid of an illegal printing operation. When his identity became known, he'd been transferred to Moscow and handed over to the Extraordinary Commission.

Everything in Dima's file aligned with what he'd told her.

Replacing the folder, Katya found her own file.

The first page contained basic information, which thankfully didn't include her biological father's name. Katya had often asked about him. Svetlana sat her down when she was fourteen, saying they would speak of it once and then never again. She told Katya how she'd been conceived – not in an act of lovemaking, but during a feat of espionage.

Around the turn of the century, Svetlana had become obsessed with a legendary spell book called the *Volkhovnik, The Book of the Wizard*. It was an Old Russian manuscript on the arts of divination and spellcasting – one of many books considered heresies by the church.

Almost every copy of the *Volkhovnik* had been burned, but a few still remained, hidden in the libraries of monasteries or aristocratic palaces. Svetlana searched for every copy she could get her hands on, convinced that one of them was the original. That oldest version of the book was said to give whoever possessed it godlike powers.

With the book, Svetlana had believed she could single-handedly ignite the Revolution.

She spent years searching for the original *Volkhovnik* in the occultist libraries of the old nobility. She never found it, but after seducing her way into the Lvov's palace in Strelna, she fell pregnant. From Prince Lvov came Katya's ability to increase her power by drawing magic from other volshebniki. If anyone discovered Katya came from a royal bloodline, she'd have a target on her back from her enemies and allies alike.

The blank spot on her file meant Katya's most dangerous secret was still safe.

According to her file, Katya's membership to the anarchist party had been revoked on 2 April, 1921. That was right after the failed Krondstadt Rebellion, the very day Katya and Svetlana went into hiding in Moscow.

That had to be a mistake. Katya flipped through the papers in her file, but almost everything had been blacked out. Apparently her entire life was top secret.

Her file had something in common with Dima's – neither of them had a release date.

They had no intention of ever letting Katya off this island alive.

She felt numb. What had happened to make the anarchists turn their backs on Katya's family? Or maybe they hadn't – maybe the government changed Katya's status so she'd be forced to stay here under Boky's thumb.

That was the only thing that made sense.

Svetlana died still believing in a free Russia.

For however long she had left Katya would devote her life to that same cause. She'd follow every thread of information and unravel the mystery surrounding her mother's death, hoping that at the end of it, she'd find a match that could reignite the resistance.

# Chapter 23

## *Dima*

Snow fell with the dusk. Large, wet flakes soaked into Dima's hat and coat as he stood beside the ration line with a bundle under his arm. After a day spent swinging an axe in the forest, Dima's injured ribs ached. Grime coated his skin, and the cold seeped into his tired bones. Dima longed for the warmth of soup in his belly, for the weight of bread to tamp down his hunger. But though his stomach twisted, Dima waited for Katya at the front of the line, watching each prisoner as they passed.

He spotted her legs first, which was unfortunate. Katya's ridiculous schoolgirl stockings left little to the imagination, and Dima needed to forget how good it had felt to hold a beautiful woman – literally the girl of his dreams – in his arms last night. *She's an anarchist,* he'd been reminding himself all day. Those words became a desperate anthem as the line inched forward, bringing Katya inexorably closer to him.

They were allies, nothing more. Dima would *not* think about how perfectly their bodies fit together when he'd held her close, or the way the morning sunlight had turned her hair into spun gold. He ignored the butterflies taking flight in his stomach when she noticed him waiting. For once, her eyes warmed at the sight of him instead of narrowing with suspicion.

'Dmitri.' Though she used his formal name, her lips quirked into an almost smile. Progress, he supposed.

'Katinka.' Dima's mouth went dry. He cleared his throat as he fell into step beside her. 'This is for you.'

He offered the bundle, a stash of clothing with a wool coat wrapped around it. Dima had swung by the infirmary on the way back from his work detail, and Doctor Tarasov helped him scrounge up the warm clothes Katya would need for winter.

'It's not much, but—'

'Not much?' Katya looked up at him, her eyes glistening. 'You just gave me a chance at survival. That's . . .' Katya pressed her lips together. Her chest rose and fell with a heavy breath, and he could see the moment she got hold of her emotions, pushing them deep down, just like always. 'Thank you.'

'What are not-friends for?' he said as they shuffled forward with the line.

'I have something for you, too.' After glancing around to check no one was watching, Katya reached behind her. She had a leather strap across her chest. When she lifted it over her head, Dima saw the strap belonged to his satchel.

Dima's mother gave him the satchel for his tenth birthday, so he would always have his sketchbook when inspiration struck. The day the Red Army killed his family, Dima lost everything except this satchel and the sketchbook inside it, which contained Dima's last drawings of his life before.

Dima hadn't let himself grieve the loss of his satchel. There had been too much else to think about and survive. But as his fingers touched the worn leather, the texture as familiar to him as his own skin, tears sprang to Dima's eyes.

Dima stared at Katya for a long moment, stunned by gratitude. She held his gaze until his smile went crooked. Then Katya was staring at his lips. She let out a shaky exhale. The air between them buzzed with static. What would happen if Dima stepped into it, closing the gap between them? He imagined pressing his lips to hers, but then stopped himself. He shook his head to dispel the madness that had momentarily taken hold of him.

*She's an anarchist.*

'Thank you.' Dima hugged the satchel to his chest for a long moment before draping it over his shoulders.

At the front of the line, they gave their names to the guard. Since they'd missed roll-call, the monks handing out rations only gave them a half ladle of soup and a small hunk of hard bread.

Back outside, they found a quiet corner out of sight of the guards. Katya devoured her bread, and then held her nose as she drank the fish soup.

Dima ate more leisurely, chatting between bites. He realised he was purposefully prolonging his meal. Because once he finished eating, they'd go their separate ways.

*She's an anarchist.*

Though to be fair, Dima didn't know what that meant. The only other anarchist Dima had encountered was the one who killed his family. He'd read about anarchists in the newspaper, usually after they'd blown something up. Katya wasn't exactly walking around with bombs hidden in her sleeves, and she didn't seem like the kind of person who would condone the executions of children. So what *did* she stand for?

Katya was looking off to the side. Dima angled himself into her line of sight. 'Can I ask a question?'

She sighed. 'Can I stop you from asking a question?'

'Why are you an anarchist?'

He tried to make his tone one of humble curiosity, but Katya treated any question like a besiegement. Usually Dima found it easy to connect with people, disarming them with a friendly smile. Not Katya. She held the bundle of clothing like a shield, her jaw clamped tight.

'I mean . . .' Dima nervously rubbed the back of his neck, unsure how to approach someone so clearly immune to his charm. 'What do you believe in? What do anarchists stand for?'

'That's three questions, not one.'

Dima sighed, gesturing between them as he said, 'Questions are how normal people get to know each other, remember?'

Katya turned her face upward, letting snowflakes fall on her skin. He thought she might not answer, but then she closed her eyes and began to speak about a time when she was ten years old and her mother took her to visit a textile factory in Petrograd. *It's not enough to be told our people need justice,* Svetlana had said. *You need to see it with your own eyes.*

They'd walked the factory floor together. Female workers, some even younger than Katya, laboured there eighteen hours a day and slept on the floor by their workstations. With bare feet and rags for clothing, they slaved away for wages that could barely fill their bellies with bread. They would be worked until exhaustion or mishap saw them added to the mass grave behind the factory, or until they were injured and put out on the streets to beg.

'These were my countrywomen,' Katya said. 'My sisters. If I'd been born to another family, they could have been me.'

Afterwards, Svetlana had taken Katya to the factory owner's mansion – a palatial white house with a separate stable building and garage. They stood at the gold-plated gates, looking in at sweeping gardens and a perfectly manicured hedge maze. Katya hadn't understood how those people could sleep at night in their featherbed palaces while their workers lay on concrete floors.

'That was the moment I learned to hate the aristocracy.' Katya looked at Dima, her expression both fierce and tinged with regret – probably because that meant hating Dima, too. 'I read the scattered works of Bakunin. He wasn't a philosopher like Marx, but an activist, a volcano of a man erupting with holy rage. His words fell into my soul like embers, and I decided to be an anarchist – not just because of my mother, but for my own conscience.

'When my mother was exiled to Siberia, I became a messenger for the party, riding my bike around Petrograd after school. I'd deliver coded letters and drop stacks of propaganda pamphlets near factories. I truly believed that once the workers and peasants recognised they had nothing to lose except their chains, they too would join the revolution – and that's exactly what happened. Of course, it didn't turn out the way we hoped.'

'What did you hope?'

'Not for this.' Katya looked around at the darkened courtyard, her face contorting as though the state of Russia caused her physical pain. 'We wanted freedom. Of speech and the press. Political freedom, too. Anarchists planned to break up the country, liberating all the nations and people groups the Russian Empire had swallowed up. We envisioned a society not unlike the Cossacks during the time of Stenka Razin – with power pushed as far downward as possible, to the people. Also, economic freedom. Factories and farms would have become co-ops where every worker owned a share, where managers were elected and where all involved were compensated proportionally to the profits earned.'

Dima bit his lip. To him, anarchists were the kind of people who would swarm into a peaceful home, force the family outside at gunpoint and shoot them in the back of the head one by one.

How could he reconcile the evil he'd witnessed with the goodness Katya professed?

Katya spoke as someone who despised injustice and wanted

to make the world a better place, just like Dima. He couldn't overlook what an anarchist had done to his family, but was blaming Katya for what happened any different from the Bolsheviki condemning Dima just for being an aristocrat?

'What?' Katya asked defensively, and Dima realised he'd been staring.

'Nothing.' He drummed his fingers on his leg – he never could hold still when he was nervous, and everything about Katya unsettled him. 'I wish you were open like that more often.'

'Well, I'm not.' Katya huffed out a breath. She pressed her lips closed, as though she regretted having said so much. Before Dima could think of something to reassure her, she said, 'I need to go.'

Dima watched her leave with some mix of longing and relief. Opening his satchel's clasp, he ran a finger along the edges of one of the sketchbooks. He'd filled two more books since escaping arrest four years ago.

Taking out his most recent sketchbook, Dima thumbed through the pages until he found his first sketch of Katya.

In it, she stood on a rocky shore staring out to sea, wind dancing through her loose hair. Dima recognised the setting as the shore of Bolshoi Zayatsky. In the drawing, Katya clutched a bundle to her chest, which Dima now knew contained Yelezar Danilov's manuscript and the journal with Svetlana's translation.

He'd dreamed of her that way a year and a half ago. Yesterday, that dream had come true.

He flipped forward to the next of Katya's portraits. Here she was bent over her poetry diary, so focused she looked almost furious in her concentration.

Then he came to his favourite portrait, or at least the one that had been his favourite before he met Katya.

She lay with her head resting on her arm, her long hair draped across the foreground. Her lips curved in a sensual smile, and her eyes exuded tenderness. Dima had fancied himself in love with the girl in that portrait.

His first sketchbook held his past, and he'd believed this one held his future.

Now he didn't know what to think.

# Chapter 24

## *Natasha*

Natasha stood in the shadows once again. She'd entered the monastery kremlin with confidence, ready to present the translation she'd been working on all day and finalise her alliance with Katya and Dima.

She found them already together.

Warmth shone from Dima's eyes when Katya approached him in the ration line. What surprised Natasha was the answering sparkle in Katya's. Was Katya falling for this skomorokh? Natasha studied the emotion in their faces as they exchanged gifts. After they moved through the line, they were too engrossed in one another to realise they were being watched – both by Natasha and by Commissar Boky, who stood at his office window looking down at them.

A skomorokh could have been an asset to their partnership, but romance cast things in a different light. If Katya and Dima had feelings, their loyalty would be to one another rather than to Natasha.

This budding relationship was a threat – one that had to be eliminated.

Natasha glanced up at Boky's window again as a plan took form in her mind.

She melted into the crowd before Dima and Katya noticed

her. Entering the administration building, Natasha went upstairs and entered Boky's office without knocking.

As always, a shiver of fear moved over Natasha's skin as she
stepped forwards to greet the wolf.

Natasha swallowed the lump in her throat. She would sacrifice anything to achieve her goals – even her own body. She set
her face: crooked smile, half-lidded eyes, head slightly tilted.
Swaying her hips, she sauntered across the room to greet him.

Boky stood before the darkened window, preternaturally still
except for his eyes tracking Natasha's movement. A subtle shifting in his throat was the only sign that her flirtatious manner
had an effect on him. Still Natasha felt it, the spicy sweetness of
desire changing his scent as she came far closer than she needed
to for a conversation, close enough that he could reach her with
hand or claw. Natasha exposed her throat, knowing the predator
within him would find that vulnerability irresistible.

'What are you doing?' Boky said.

'I needed to see you.' Natasha raised her eyes to his and let
those words hang between them for a long moment. For this
plan to work, she'd have to clear the air about what happened
at the cabin that morning. 'I have information to report.'

'Is that so?'

'Yekaterina Efremova left the island last night, together
with another convict, Dmitri Danilov. They went to Bolshoi
Zayatsky.'

'I'm aware.' His voice deepened into a husky purr. 'My guards
intercepted them in the forest. You, however, they could not
find.'

'I'm here now.' Natasha's eye twitched. She took a steadying
breath. 'I imagine you'd like a report on what Katya found on
Bolshoi Zayatsky.'

Boky raised an eyebrow. If nothing else, she had his interest.

To keep it, she began mirroring Boky's expression and gestures, reflecting back to him the lust she'd carefully awakened. She made her eyes sleepy, her vision thickening with a sensuous haze. Her chin went slack, her lips crooked. While Boky loomed over her, leaning slightly forward, Natasha matched the angle of his upper body as she leaned away. Their chests were inches apart.

'Katya found a book her mother hid in one of the labyrinths.' Natasha made her voice as husky as Boky's had been. 'It's an eye-witness account of the life of Stenka Razin, written in archaic Greek. I've started translating it in an abandoned cabin near the south coast of the island.'

Boky's lips curved into a devilish smile.

'You're not surprised,' she observed.

'I've been tracking Svetlana Efremova's movements for years, just like I keep tabs on all significant people.'

Boky paused for a long beat, his meaningful look suggesting he'd been watching Natasha, too.

'Four years ago, Svetlana travelled to the Don region. She went to the country estate of an aristocratic family whose patriarch had been a history professor obsessed with Stenka Razin. Svetlana spent three days shut inside the professor's office. She took several of his journals with her when she returned to Petrograd.'

Natasha pressed her lips together as she considered the implications. Svetlana Efremova had been tracing Stenka Razin's footsteps for at least four years. That must be what had brought her to the archipelago last October, when she hid Yelezar Danilov's book in the labyrinths and left a map for Katya to find. The lemon ink clue was meant to lead Katya to the book about Stenka Razin, but why?

'What was Svetlana looking for on these islands?'

'Let's not forget how this alliance works.' Boky's smile shifted into a sneer. 'You're supposed to be giving me information, not the other way around.'

'Alliance is such a cold word.' Natasha rested her hand on Boky's chest, feeling the quickness of his heartbeat.

'Is it?' he asked on a shaky exhale.

Natasha turned her face upward, stopping just before their lips met. 'Perhaps we should renegotiate the terms of our agreement, make them a little friendlier.'

When Boky smiled again, Natasha saw fangs. The wolf within him was creeping to the surface. She started to recoil, but then his lips were on hers, hungry and hot. It had been more than two years since Natasha had been touched with anything like tenderness. She kissed him with all the desperation of her loneliness, so tired of being empty that she willingly filled herself with poison.

With a growl, Boky abandoned her lips and began trailing kisses up the column of her neck. His fangs scraped the tender skin but didn't draw blood. The sensation flooded Natasha, intoxicating her with a potent mix of danger and desire.

Boky kissed his way up the razor edge of her jaw, then whispered in her ear. 'What sort of agreement did you have in mind?'

'A partnership. The kind where we share information . . . and meet each other's needs.'

'And what do you need, Natasha?' He grabbed the back of her thigh. She gasped when one of his fingers extended into a claw.

'This,' she admitted, untucking his shirt. She ran her fingers up his back, feeling the crisscrossing scars of an old flogging. She wrapped her arms around him and pressed herself against his body. A deep moan escaped his lips. Natasha smiled. 'And there are two other things I need.'

'Tell me.' His hand trailed down the front of her coat, his

claw slicing the threads of her buttons. The buttons clinked to the ground one by one. Boky slid the coat off her shoulders. The cool air sweeping over her back contrasted with the heat of his body pressed against her bosom.

'I've convinced Katya to be my ally.'

Boky paused. His lips had been kissing her collarbone, his fingertips tracing the lines of her ribs. He straightened and peered into her eyes, as though searching for a sign of deception. It wasn't a complete lie. She hadn't won Katya over *yet*, but she would do so. She just needed the skomorokh out of the way.

'I want her driven out of the monastery and to the cabin where I'm working on the translation. Then I'll be in a position to spy on her if she makes any progress with her mother's cipher.'

'That might be arranged,' Boky said. 'What is the second thing you need?'

Boky's fingers slid down her ribs one by one, coming to rest at her hip. A wave of heat spread to her core. Throwing herself at Boky had seemed the easiest way to manipulate him, but she hadn't counted on her body responding like this.

She made him wait for the answer to his question. Where he had hastily sliced open her coat, Natasha took her time unbuttoning his. All the while she held his gaze in a predatory challenge, each of them determined to prove their dominance. He didn't flinch when his coat dropped to the ground. Natasha began unbuttoning her blouse, a teasing smile on her lips. She exposed herself, revealing her bare stomach and the lacy bra she'd been wearing the day of her arrest, stained rusty brown from all the blood. Boky's gaze lowered, a shudder moving through him as he reached to cup her breast. Natasha's smile widened. She'd won. Now she had him right where she wanted him.

'Here's the second thing.' Natasha rose to her tiptoes and whispered in his ear. 'I need you to kill Dmitri Danilov.'

# Chapter 25
## *Katya*

Katya walked briskly in the direction of the guesthouse, as though speed could keep her one step ahead of feelings she didn't want to examine. Why had she opened up to Dima like that? She could have left his question unanswered, or maybe told him something trite and meaningless. Instead, she'd bared part of her soul.

She blamed it on the way he looked at her. Because of Svetlana, Katya had a sixth sense for knowing when people saw her as a tool. Dima wasn't like that. Every time she was with him, Katya felt seen – as a person rather than for the ways she might be used.

As Katya continued her march to the guesthouse, she wondered about her membership in the anarchist party being revoked. Had Boky manipulated the paperwork, or had Svetlana done something to turn their allies against them?

She thought back to the year she'd first noticed her mother's imperfections – the year of the Revolution.

Some people think of Revolution as a single event, a moment in time, but Katya had experienced it as the pounding of a battering ram. Protests, *boom*. Riots, *boom*. Revolts, *boom*. Until at last the corrupt establishment splintered open and change rushed in.

In Russia, the mothers of Petrograd were the ones to finally breach the ancient gates of tsarism. They flooded the streets on International Women's Day in February of 1917, protesting the war that had stolen away their sons.

Twelve-year-old Katya joined the protests. She stood shoulder to shoulder with those courageous women who refused to back down, even when faced with aggressive police and armed troops.

Over a million Russian soldiers had been needlessly killed in the Great War, and their mothers had had enough.

Protests swelled like a tide for eight days, until the tsar announced his abdication.

Radicals commandeered Katya's school, making it the headquarters for several revolutionary groups, including the anarchists. It resembled nothing more than a beehive, with hundreds of revolutionaries swarming the classrooms and meeting halls to share information.

The constant buzz of voices fell silent one March afternoon. Katya was having lunch in the large school dining hall when everyone turned toward the entrance.

Svetlana Efremova stood in the doorway – their golden lady returned to them at last. Eighteen months of Siberian exile had sharpened her cheekbones, but she hadn't lost her lustre. Her eyes held a gleam Katya recognised as ambition.

'We've done it,' Svetlana announced.

The magic in her words prickled across Katya's skin, but why was she using spell-work on her own comrades?

'The great change has commenced.' Svetlana's hips swayed as she sauntered into the room, looking approvingly at her mesmerised audience. 'Tsarism has been vanquished, but our work has only begun. As a woman must labour to bring her child safely into the world, we must now work single-heartedly to birth a new Russia.'

All around the dining hall, radicals nodded and voiced their agreement. They would not accept the provisional government. With Svetlana as the de facto head of the anarchists, their struggle would continue until every institution had been broken down and the power returned to the people.

After her speech, Svetlana noticed Katya in the crowd.

Svetlana surprised her by pulling Katya into a tight embrace. Her kiss of greeting left red lipstick on both of Katya's cheeks.

Her heart swelling with love, Katya disregarded the calculation she noted in her mother's face. She also ignored the sense of wrongness she felt about her mother casting a spell on their comrades during her speech. Svetlana must have her reasons – no one was more committed to the cause than her.

But even as she tried to put her misgivings out of her mind, Katya thought of something she'd read in one of Bakunin's manifestos. '*If you took the most ardent revolutionary and vested him in absolute power, within a year he would be worse than the tsar himself.*'

While Svetlana conversed with several anarchists who had come forward to greet her, another of their comrades approached Katya with a message for her to carry. Svetlana grabbed Katya's wrist to prevent her from taking the note.

'I don't want you delivering messages anymore.' Authority boomed through Svetlana's voice, and Katya recoiled from the strength of her mother's magic. Svetlana smiled again, though this time it didn't reach her eyes. 'I want you with me at all times, just like before. I've missed you, my little turtle.'

Katya nodded, though the possessiveness in her mother's voice made something twist inside her. Svetlana didn't want Katya around for the pleasure of her company. Katya could be a useful tool, with the rare combination of her spell-casting skill and inherent Rurikid magic. Katya had never minded being used, so long as she could be near Svetlana, but now . . . it bothered her.

She wanted more from her mother, wanted to be seen and valued for the depths of her soul rather than for the ways she might prove useful.

Katya had to content herself with the knowledge that she and her mother both wanted the same thing. Helping Svetlana helped the cause, and so Katya accepted her role. Once again, she became Svetlana's shadow.

Svetlana had been right about the Revolution needing more time. All across Russia, 1917 was a year of birth pangs and blood. The provisional government failed to withdraw Russia from the Great War, and in July, the week after Katya's thirteenth birthday, violent demonstrations broke out in Petrograd. Prince Lvov resigned as prime minister. His successor, Alexandr Kerensky, cracked down on leftist parties like Bolsheviki, Socialist Revolutionaries, and Anarchists.

By excluding the revolutionary parties from the government, Kerensky inadvertently prepared the ground for a second wave of Revolution. In October, the coalition of Bolsheviki and Anarchists seized Petrograd. Svetlana convinced the sailors of the Baltic Fleet to mutiny and join the Red Army in storming the Winter Palace to unseat the government.

Those were days of victory.

But if 1917 was the year of anarchist glory, 1918 was the year it all fell apart.

Katya sighed as she stepped through the door of the guesthouse and stomped snow off her boots. She'd lingered so long in the courtyard with Dima that the other women had already returned to the barrack.

Natasha was nowhere in sight.

Tsisana lay on her bed, looking at her wedding photograph.

She turned at the sound of Katya's footsteps, her eyes shining with unshed tears.

'Katya?' The bed boards creaked as Tsisana sat up. 'I thought you'd been reclassified.'

'It didn't work out.' Katya sat on her bed. Only yesterday she'd written that coded letter to the anarchists – it felt like so much had happened since then, but somehow she'd ended up right back where she started.

'There you are.' Matilda Ivanova came over, her white night-dress swaying with each step. Concern deepened her wrinkles when she saw Katya's cheek, swollen and bruised from being pistol whipped.

'*Bozhe moy*,' she said. *My God*. 'What happened to you?'

'I'm fine.' Katya patted Matilda Ivanova's hand.

'You don't look fine.' Tsisana rose to her feet and caught Katya's chin in her fingers. She turned Katya's face this way and that, examining the wound. 'You could have a concussion. Did you lose consciousness at all?'

'For a bit,' Katya admitted.

She wished she could downplay the injury to avoid unwanted attention. Already the women on neighbouring bunks were craning their necks to catch a glimpse of Katya's face.

Tsisana, being both a trained nurse and a kolduna, was having none of it.

'This could be a very serious injury,' she said sternly. 'Let me see if I have anything to help.'

While Tsisana rummaged through her suitcase, Katya's gaze drifted to the upper bunk where Natasha usually slept.

'Has anyone seen Natasha?' she asked.

'Who?' Matilda Ivanova's wrinkles deepened into an expression of perplexity.

'The redhead who sleeps in the bunk above mine.'

'That's Marfa,' Matilda Ivanova said. 'Marfa Aikhenvald, part of a merchant family who works in Constantinople.'

'She told me her name is Saskia Wagner,' Tsisana said, looking up from her luggage. 'Her father is an Austrian manufacturer with business dealings in Petrograd.'

'I heard her call herself Lucia Somogyi,' another woman chimed in. 'She spoke to me with a strong Hungarian accent.'

Even though she shouldn't be surprised, Katya's heart sank.

*Who are you, Natasha?* Katya wondered. *And why did you steal my book?*

'I don't have the right supplies to treat your injury.' Tsisana sighed as she closed her suitcase. 'I'll go beg Doctor Tarasov for salve and brew you a birch tea for the pain. I want you to lie down, but *don't* go to sleep.'

'A woman in the tenth company has a kettle, if I remember correctly,' Matilda Ivanova said. 'I'll ask if we can use it.'

Matilda Ivanova pulled on a dressing gown and hurried to the neighbouring room while Tsisana left to her own errands.

Katya sprawled onto her bed of wooden planks and took out her book of fairy tales. Ignoring her pounding head, she looked over her notes from the other night. Something stood out about the page numbers Svetlana marked with bloody thumb prints: 3-7-14-15-22-29-34-36-40-44-53-61-65-75-82-91-95-100-102-108-112-116-124-131-140-144-151-153-163-171-180-186.

There were thirty-two of them, and sixteen letters in the message she'd left. Слушай шепот звезд – *Listen to the whisper of stars.*

It could be a nihilist cipher, with two page numbers corresponding to each letter in the phrase. While Katya had served as a messenger for the anarchists, she often carried numerical ciphers. If the police had ever stopped her, they'd find a series of maths equations in her notebook, nothing more. With the keyword, those numbers held information about secret meetings, names of contacts, and warnings about possible informants.

Katya took the last digit of each page number, creating sixteen numbers to use in a nihilist cipher: 37-45-29-46-04-31-55-21-50-28-26-41-04-13-31-06. She assigned a numerical value to the letters in *Listen to the whisper of stars*, based on their placement in the alphabet. С=19, Л=13, У=21, Ш=26, А=01, Й=11, Ш=26, Е=06, П=17, О=16, Т=20, З=09, В=03, Е=06, З=09, Д=05.

She drew a table with three rows and sixteen columns. In the top row, she filled in the page numbers. The keyword went in the middle row. Subtracting the middle from the top should give the cipher's solution.

| 37 | 45 | 29 | 46 | 04 | 31 | 55 | 21 | 50 | 28 | 26 | 41 | 04 | 13 | 31 | 06 |
|----|----|----|----|----|----|----|----|----|----|----|----|----|----|----|----|
| 19 | 13 | 21 | 26 | 01 | 11 | 26 | 06 | 17 | 16 | 20 | 09 | 03 | 06 | 09 | 05 |
| 18 | 32 | 08 | 20 | 03 | 20 | 29 | 15 | 33 | 12 | 06 | 32 | 01 | 07 | 22 | 01 |

It seemed to have worked.

None of the values in the bottom row had ended up less than zero or more than thirty-three, which meant they corresponded to letters in the alphabet. Those letters should reveal Svetlana's dying message: Р Ю Ж Т В Т Ы Н Я К Е Ю А Ё Ф А.

Not words. Katya bit her lip as she double-checked her calculations. It seemed to be a code. Svetlana may have died for the secrets hidden in this book, so she probably used multiple layers of encryption.

Katya tried shifting the letters three slots over and reversing the alphabet, but Svetlana was more likely to use a complex Vigenère cipher requiring a keyword. She would choose something not written in the book, something only Katya would be able to guess. To pair with the code from the nihilist cipher, the key had to be sixteen letters or a shorter word repeating.

Katya tore a second paper out of her poetry diary and created a *tabula recta*. It had the thirty-three letters of the Cyrillic alphabet written thirty-three times, each row shifting one character to the left.

```
А Б В Г Д Е Ё Ж З И Й К Л М Н О П Р С Т У Ф Х Ц Ч Ш Щ Ъ Ы Ь Э Ю Я
Б В Г Д Е Ё Ж З И Й К Л М Н О П Р С Т У Ф Х Ц Ч Ш Щ Ъ Ы Ь Э Ю Я А
В Г Д Е Ё Ж З И Й К Л М Н О П Р С Т У Ф Х Ц Ч Ш Щ Ъ Ы Ь Э Ю Я А Б
Г Д Е Ё Ж З И Й К Л М Н О П Р С Т У Ф Х Ц Ч Ш Щ Ъ Ы Ь Э Ю Я А Б В
Д Е Ё Ж З И Й К Л М Н О П Р С Т У Ф Х Ц Ч Ш Щ Ъ Ы Ь Э Ю Я А Б В Г
Е Ё Ж З И Й К Л М Н О П Р С Т У Ф Х Ц Ч Ш Щ Ъ Ы Ь Э Ю Я А Б В Г Д
Ё Ж З И Й К Л М Н О П Р С Т У Ф Х Ц Ч Ш Щ Ъ Ы Ь Э Ю Я А Б В Г Д Е
Ж З И Й К Л М Н О П Р С Т У Ф Х Ц Ч Ш Щ Ъ Ы Ь Э Ю Я А Б В Г Д Е Ё
З И Й К Л М Н О П Р С Т У Ф Х Ц Ч Ш Щ Ъ Ы Ь Э Ю Я А Б В Г Д Е Ё Ж
И Й К Л М Н О П Р С Т У Ф Х Ц Ч Ш Щ Ъ Ы Ь Э Ю Я А Б В Г Д Е Ё Ж З
Й К Л М Н О П Р С Т У Ф Х Ц Ч Ш Щ Ъ Ы Ь Э Ю Я А Б В Г Д Е Ё Ж З И
К Л М Н О П Р С Т У Ф Х Ц Ч Ш Щ Ъ Ы Ь Э Ю Я А Б В Г Д Е Ё Ж З И Й
Л М Н О П Р С Т У Ф Х Ц Ч Ш Щ Ъ Ы Ь Э Ю Я А Б В Г Д Е Ё Ж З И Й К
М Н О П Р С Т У Ф Х Ц Ч Ш Щ Ъ Ы Ь Э Ю Я А Б В Г Д Е Ё Ж З И Й К Л
Н О П Р С Т У Ф Х Ц Ч Ш Щ Ъ Ы Ь Э Ю Я А Б В Г Д Е Ё Ж З И Й К Л М
О П Р С Т У Ф Х Ц Ч Ш Щ Ъ Ы Ь Э Ю Я А Б В Г Д Е Ё Ж З И Й К Л М Н
П Р С Т У Ф Х Ц Ч Ш Щ Ъ Ы Ь Э Ю Я А Б В Г Д Е Ё Ж З И Й К Л М Н О
Р С Т У Ф Х Ц Ч Ш Щ Ъ Ы Ь Э Ю Я А Б В Г Д Е Ё Ж З И Й К Л М Н О П
С Т У Ф Х Ц Ч Ш Щ Ъ Ы Ь Э Ю Я А Б В Г Д Е Ё Ж З И Й К Л М Н О П Р
Т У Ф Х Ц Ч Ш Щ Ъ Ы Ь Э Ю Я А Б В Г Д Е Ё Ж З И Й К Л М Н О П Р С
У Ф Х Ц Ч Ш Щ Ъ Ы Ь Э Ю Я А Б В Г Д Е Ё Ж З И Й К Л М Н О П Р С Т
Ф Х Ц Ч Ш Щ Ъ Ы Ь Э Ю Я А Б В Г Д Е Ё Ж З И Й К Л М Н О П Р С Т У
Х Ц Ч Ш Щ Ъ Ы Ь Э Ю Я А Б В Г Д Е Ё Ж З И Й К Л М Н О П Р С Т У Ф
Ц Ч Ш Щ Ъ Ы Ь Э Ю Я А Б В Г Д Е Ё Ж З И Й К Л М Н О П Р С Т У Ф Х
Ч Ш Щ Ъ Ы Ь Э Ю Я А Б В Г Д Е Ё Ж З И Й К Л М Н О П Р С Т У Ф Х Ц
Ш Щ Ъ Ы Ь Э Ю Я А Б В Г Д Е Ё Ж З И Й К Л М Н О П Р С Т У Ф Х Ц Ч
Щ Ъ Ы Ь Э Ю Я А Б В Г Д Е Ё Ж З И Й К Л М Н О П Р С Т У Ф Х Ц Ч Ш
Ъ Ы Ь Э Ю Я А Б В Г Д Е Ё Ж З И Й К Л М Н О П Р С Т У Ф Х Ц Ч Ш Щ
Ы Ь Э Ю Я А Б В Г Д Е Ё Ж З И Й К Л М Н О П Р С Т У Ф Х Ц Ч Ш Щ Ъ
Ь Э Ю Я А Б В Г Д Е Ё Ж З И Й К Л М Н О П Р С Т У Ф Х Ц Ч Ш Щ Ъ Ы
Э Ю Я А Б В Г Д Е Ё Ж З И Й К Л М Н О П Р С Т У Ф Х Ц Ч Ш Щ Ъ Ы Ь
Ю Я А Б В Г Д Е Ё Ж З И Й К Л М Н О П Р С Т У Ф Х Ц Ч Ш Щ Ъ Ы Ь Э
Я А Б В Г Д Е Ё Ж З И Й К Л М Н О П Р С Т У Ф Х Ц Ч Ш Щ Ъ Ы Ь Э Ю
```

Using the code from the nihilist cipher in the rows, she tried potential keywords in the columns – her name, her mother's name, all of their aliases. When nothing fit, she moved on to places they'd lived, street names where anarchist safe houses were located, code names of operations and rallies they'd been involved in.

Katya put away her notes when Matilda Ivanova returned with the teapot. Though she hadn't yet found the keyword, cracking the first layer of encryption was a breaththrough – one step closer to uncovering Svetlana's secrets.

# Chapter 26

## *Dima*

When Dima returned to his barrack, he found his bed already occupied by an old man in a tattered three-piece suit. Holding a mirror, the man waxed his moustache, carefully combing the hair into perfect curves above his lips. He had feathery eyebrows and a mischievous sparkle in his blue eyes.

'Ah, there you are, Dmitri.' He set the mirror down on his knee. 'I've been waiting.'

Though he had no idea who this man was, Dima offered the stranger a warm smile as he sat on the bed opposite him.

'Andrei Sergeevich Armanov.' The old man stuck out his hand. When Dima shook it, Andrei Sergeevich pulled Dima closer, whispering, 'We have a mutual friend. Father Iosef.'

'Oh?' Dima studied the old man's face with interest.

'There are a few of us working behind the scenes, doing whatever little things we can for the poor souls who have been sent here.'

'What kind of things?'

'Well.' Andrei Sergeevich leaned in closer, whispering conspiratorially. 'For example, I borrowed the keys to the punishment cells and gave them to the monk, so you could be seen at the infirmary.'

Doctor Tarasov's treatment staved off infection and likely

saved Dima's life. He'd thought it was one man's kindness, but several people had risked their lives to help him.

'Thank you,' Dima said humbly.

'None of that.' The old man waved his hand as though swatting away the gratitude. 'I'm not here to be applauded for basic human decency. I'm here about the artists' unit.'

'Yes, Commissar Boky sounded amenable.' Dima had been deeply unsettled by Boky's easy acceptance of his proposal, even more disturbed by his comment about poetry being a motive for murder. Had he been talking about Dedushka's epic poem? Dima would never forget his grandfather's words the day the Red Army came to their *dacha*. *They've come for my poem, but I won't let them have it.*

'Never mind Boky,' Andrei Sergeevich said. 'He'll take credit for it, of course. But you planted the seed and you and I are the ones who will cultivate it.'

'You and I?'

'I certainly hope so.' Andrei Sergeevich's curved moustache twitched as he smiled. 'Your poster lifted the spirits of everyone who saw it.'

Dima was taken aback. 'How did you know it was me?'

'Never mind that,' he said. 'Just imagine how humanising it will be for the prisoners to go to the theatre – to wash their faces and put on their best clothes, to stand in line to have their tickets torn, to escape into a story for a few hours. We could give them laughter. We could give them dignity.' Andrei Sergeevich rested his age-spotted hand atop Dima's knee. 'We could give them hope.'

*That's how hope grows, in the soil of little things.*

Dedushka's words filled Dima's thoughts. He remembered the shoe polish and how good it had felt to print that art. His grandfather taught Dima that being a skomorokh was a

responsibility, a holy calling. Stories taught courage and em-
pathy – they had the power to vanquish despair and restore
humanity to its ideals.

Dima had been wary when Commissar Boky so easily agreed,
but Andrei Sergeevich's words awakened something in Dima's
soul. It would be challenging to pioneer a theatre on top of the
hard labour already required of him, but well worth the effort
if they could restore some dignity to their fellow prisoners.

He lifted his eyes to Andrei Sergeevich's and smiled at the
old man. 'When do we start?'

# PART III

## *Midwinter*

# *Loss*

DEATH IS NOT
A MOMENT, NOT LACK OF
BREATH, NOT SILENCE WHERE
A HEART ONCE BEAT. IT IS AN
INVERSED WORLD, LIKE PHOTOGRAPH
NEGATIVES THAT TURN ALL LIGHT TO
DARKNESS. WHAT IS GRIEF? I OFTEN
WONDER IF IT'S FRIEND OR CAPTIVE.
DOES SORROW CLOAK MY SHOULDERS TO
PUNISH ME OR TO HOLD MY SHATTERED
HEART      IN PLACE? A      BROKEN
BONE            HEALS            BACK
EVEN          STRONGER,          BUT
IS          THAT TRUE          OF
A FRACTURED      HEART? WHEN
IS IT SAFE      TO CUT THE
CAST OFF      MY SOUL?
IF          I UNSHIELD MYSELF,          IF
I LOVE          AS BEFORE AND          I LOSE
AGAIN, I          MIGHT DIE.          AGAIN, I
MAKE MYSELF          WEAK. I          MIGHT BREAK,
VULNERABLE TO                    EVERY SORROW OF
GRIEF.      DAILY,          MY HEART      PANGS.
I FEEL      LONELY,
LOST AND LONGING
FOR          CONNECTION.      EVERYBODY          HAS
THE NEED TO BE KNOWN,          SEEN AND TREASURED
BY ANOTHER IN                    FRIENDSHIP. TO
LOVE IS TO                    BE BRAVE AND
BARE ALL,                    TO RISK
MY SOUL                    FULLY

# Chapter 27

## *Katya*

On the third day of November, the anniversary of Svetlana's death, Katya lay awake long before the morning bell broke the stillness of the guesthouse. The air felt too heavy when she closed her eyes. It clung to her skin like soil, making it hard to breathe. No matter how resolutely she fought to keep the image at bay, Katya kept picturing herself in a coffin beside her mother's bones.

When the bell fell silent, women rose from their beds. They lit the lanterns. They yawned and stretched their backs, groaning with the soreness of yesterday's work. Soon they would change their clothes. They would bundle up and trudge through the night's snowfall to queue up for rations, just like any other day.

Katya couldn't make herself move. The air still weighed too much, like gravity held her body with all its might.

While staring at the absolute blackness outside the guesthouse window, Katya imagined night as a living being, stretching his arms out wider each day to envelop the archipelago in darkness. She also thought of the ice inching out over the sea. Soon the harbour would freeze, trapping them on this island for the next several months.

Katya's chest ached when she imagined darkness and ice closing around her, as earth encloses grave. Though Katya wanted to be fearless, a cold sweat dampened her forehead and palms at the thought of ending up like Svetlana.

'Are you awake?' The bed creaked as Tsisana sat beside Katya.

Her gentle fingers combed the hair back from Katya's face. It was only when the strands clung to her skin that Katya realised she'd shed tears. Tsisana didn't look much better – bloodshot eyes, puffy face, the tip of her nose red from crying.

Though Tsisana's work in the infirmary was lighter than hard labour, Smolensky regularly summoned her in the night. Each morning, when she returned, the light in Tsisana's eyes had dimmed a little more.

She had other worries, too. Yesterday, the steamer crossed the White Sea for the last time this season, bringing a final batch of prisoners. If Tsisana's husband wasn't among them, she'd pass the long winter months in the torment of not knowing his fate. If he *was* here, she would have to face his reaction to the abuse she'd suffered on Solovki.

Tsisana reached for Katya's hand and intertwined their fingers. Their gazes met, and it felt like their souls did too. They were both lost in grief, but, for this moment at least, they were in it together.

'Why don't you sit up?' Tsisana said, her voice coaxing. 'I'll do your hair.'

It took great effort for Katya to fight the pull of gravity. Tsisana scooted onto the bed behind Katya, gently working out the knots in her hair before combing the length of it in long, soothing strokes.

'Morning, girls.' Matilda Ivanova, always the first one ready to greet the day, leaned on her cane. 'The theatre troupe has its first meeting tonight. Are you coming?'

The prison had been abuzz with news of the artist's unit ever since Dima hung posters in the courtyard a few days ago. Katya hadn't seen or spoken to him since that night beside the ration line. Natasha – if that was her real name – never returned after she'd stolen the book from Katya in the forest.

'I'd rather not draw attention to myself,' Tsisana said. She persisted in wearing that hideous kerchief to detract from her exquisite beauty, though, of course, it hadn't saved her.

'You don't have to be onstage. Since I'll be the director, you can be my assistant. Or help some other way behind the scenes.'

'They asked you to be the director?' Tsisana's comb paused mid-stroke, and the dull sadness in her eyes gave way to a gleam of excitement for her friend.

'Well, not asked exactly.' Matilda Ivanova hedged, waving her hand as though dismissing that detail as unimportant. 'No one loves theatre quite as much as I do, nor is anyone quite as adept at bossing people around. At auditions tonight, I'll inform them I've decided to direct the play.'

'And if they don't agree?' Tsisana asked as she divided Katya's hair and began plaiting it down her back.

'Then I'll simply *direct* them back to their seats. I can be quite convincing, you know.'

'Oh, I know.' Tsisana twisted Katya's plait into a bun and pinned it. 'I'm tempted to come to auditions simply to witness your coup d'état.'

'You'd be very welcome. You too, Katya. We'll have to recreate the scripts from memory – we could use someone with your talent for words.'

Katya opened her mouth to say she couldn't possibly share her writing with others. *Mother would be furious,* she thought. She bit the words back.

Svetlana had been dead for a year. Why was her opinion still so loud in Katya's head?

Katya had dedicated her life to fighting for other people's

freedom, yet all the while Svetlana held absolute control over her. Even from the grave, she directed Katya's steps.

*Maybe I should stop listening*, Katya thought, but she had to know what it all meant – the cipher, the lemon ink code, the map and the book about Stenka Razin.

If Katya understood what her mother died for, maybe she'd discover how to live on her own terms.

'We should go find our breakfast.' Tsisana squeezed Katya's shoulder before climbing off the bunk to put on her coat.

Katya gathered the book of fairy tales, her poetry diary and all her loose papers into her school bag. Maybe she should be letting go, but these were the last pieces she had of her mother. She wanted them with her on this anniversary of Svetlana's death.

As they left the guesthouse, Tsisana linked arms with Katya on one side and Matilda Ivanova on the other. They trudged through calf-deep snow, headed towards the monastery for breakfast.

In the courtyard, snow had been shovelled into big piles around the perimeter, leaving a much smaller space for prisoners to assemble. The roll-call found them crowded like sardines.

Tsisana stood on her tiptoes, but she couldn't see over people's heads. The newly-arrived company was first at roll-call. As the guard went through the list of names, he called out, 'Rafael Fernández-Villaverde.'

'He's here.' Tsisana said the words on one long exhale, as though she'd been holding that breath inside her all the time she'd been in Solovki.

'I told you everything would work out.' Matilda Ivanova pulled Tsisana into a hug. Tsisana wept on the old woman's shoulder, her relief spilling out of her.

Katya grabbed Tsisana's hand and squeezed it. She hadn't

asked for Tsisana's friendship – in fact, she'd actively resisted it – but Tsisana had given it freely nonetheless. She tried to shed her own misery and be happy for Tsisana, but all she could think of was how fleeting their moment of commiseration had been. Katya was alone in her grief once more, and self-pity clung to her.

That black mood persisted when she went to work, mopping the corridors of the administration building with an almost tantric intensity.

Night fell long before the evening bell rang out. When Katya put away the cleaning supplies, she found herself heading towards the theatre auditions, though she couldn't say what drew her there.

Boky had designated a cathedral vestry for use as the theatre. The cathedral itself had been badly damaged in the fire, but the vestry, a side chamber where priests donned their ceremonial robes, had been largely spared.

Katya had to navigate ash and debris to reach the back of the burned-out cathedral. The thick oak door to the vestry stood open, charred on one side. About twenty prisoners had gathered for the meeting. Stepping gingerly over soiled vestments and the planks of a broken table, Katya joined the group.

Andrei Sergeevich was giving a speech about the theatre's potential and goals. Katya recognised a few other prisoners. Matilda Ivanova stood at the front, tapping the top of her cane with one impatient finger. There was another woman from their barrack, an actress from Novgorod.

Then, of course, there was Dima.

The moment she entered Katya became keenly aware of him. It felt as though an invisible cord stretched between them, held in tension so Katya felt his exact location in the room.

He must have felt it too, for he looked over his shoulder,

right at Katya. His lips curved into that lopsided smile, and no amount of determination could suppress the fluttering sensation in Katya's belly. Dima's face had mostly healed. With the swelling gone down, his cheeks and jaw had regained the angles that made his face so interesting to look at. His nose had healed crookedly. Rather than detracting from his beauty, it reminded Katya of how bravely he'd spoken up for her when no one else would.

Dima moved to join her. The tether between them became charged. Katya's cheeks heated. Dima's shoulder brushed hers and prickles of electricity spread across Katya's skin.

'We've chosen *The Hypochondriac* as our first production,' Andrei Sergeevich announced.

'No, no, no.' Matilda Ivanova rushed to the front, her cane clacking against stone with every step. 'Not that empty-headed comedy. We should choose something with substance.'

'Sorry, who are you?' Andrei Sergeevich pasted on a polite smile.

'Matilda Ivanova Witte, formerly the most ardent theatre lover in Petrograd and currently the new director of this group.'

'I'm always glad to make the acquaintance of a fellow thespian, but I'm afraid we already have a director.' Andrei Sergeevich pressed his hand to his chest. 'Me.'

'You forfeited that position the moment you suggested *The Hypochondriac* for the first production.'

Andrei Sergeevich took a calming breath before saying, 'It's a comedy, and the purpose of this theatre is to give people joy.'

'You'll only succeed in putting them to sleep,' Matilda Ivanova said. 'That play is unspeakably dull.'

'Dull?'

'Yes, dull. It's shallow, too. I wonder if Pisemsky entertained even a modicum of thought while he wrote it.'

'Then tell me, which play would you recommend?' Andrei Sergeevich crossed his arms, his moustache ticking with every irritated twitch of his lips.

'*Children of the Sun*,' Matilda Ivanova declared. 'It has depth, thought, and meaningful themes.'

'I don't think a play about a *cholera epidemic* will do much to raise people's spirits.'

'Why not? It will make them feel seen and understood in their suffering.'

'This theatre is supposed to give them an escape,' Andrei Sergeevich said. When the old woman opened her mouth to argue, he held up a finger and said, 'Perhaps you and I should iron this out privately.' To the crowd he said, 'Excuse us,' before motioning for Matilda Ivanova to follow him out the door.

'Well.' Dima turned to Katya, one corner of his lips curved up in amusement. 'I can't say I envy him.'

'Me either,' Katya said.

Katya gave him a meaningful look, then nodded away from the group, motioning for him to join her.

'I'm guessing you've had no sightings of Natasha,' she said.

'No.' His brow knit in worry. 'She never came back to the guesthouse?'

Katya shook her head, then confided what she'd discovered about Natasha using a different alias with just about everyone she met.

'Why would she do that?' Dima asked.

Katya had no idea. Maybe it was a game or an exercise – or maybe her mind cracked during those two years she spent being experimented on in the lab. Whatever the reasons for Natasha's duplicity, Katya simply wanted to find her and get the book back.

'Could you get hold of passes again, so we can look for her?'

'No promises, but I'll try.'

'All right, everyone, let's come together.' Matilda Ivanova shouted as she strode back into the vestry, moving improbably fast for a woman with a cane.

Andrei Sergeevich followed, looking both beleaguered and bemused.

'We have reached a decision,' Matilda Ivanova announced. '*I* will be directing, but we have compromised and decided on *Uncle Vanya* as our first production, with Andrei Sergeevich in the titular role.'

Andrei Sergeevich bowed humbly, but the irreverent spark in his eyes made Katya suspect that old rebel might not be outplayed as easily as Matilda Ivanova thought.

'I propose we hold our first performance on midwinter night. That will give us time to clean this mess up, write out scripts and hold several rehearsals. Any objections?'

Matilda Ivanova raised an eyebrow, daring anyone to contradict her.

'Good.' She clapped her hands. 'Then let's get started.'

# Chapter 28

## *Dima*

The dream began as it always did – a paintbrush falling from Dima's fingers, green paint splattering on the floor, and two red stains pooling on the canvas where his brother and sister had been. Before the nightmare played out, Dima turned to find Yelezar beside him.

'Hello again, fellow dreamer.' Yelezar had a boyish smile but ancient eyes that radiated an otherworldly blue light. He still wore old-fashioned clothes and a story cloak embroidered with living threads.

Dima looked in wonder at his many times great-grandfather, visiting his dreams for the second time. As a skomorokh, Dima often had prophetic dreams that revealed memories of the past or glimpses of the future. He'd never interacted with anyone else in his dream world, and he wondered how this was even possible. Was Yelezar a memory passed down through Dima's blood, or had his dreams carried him beyond the constraints of time to when Yelezar still lived?

'This is a horrid dream,' Yelezar said. 'Why do you keep coming here?'

'When I fall asleep, this is usually where I end up. It's not like I choose to be here.'

'Of course you choose. *You're* the dreamer – look.' Yelezar waved his hand, and the scene around them changed.

Yelezar and Dima stood at the top of a crenelated watchtower, looking out over a frozen river. Fog surrounded the fortress. On either side of them, watchmen peered into the freezing mist for any signs of an enemy.

'Where are we?' Dima asked.

Before Yelezar could answer, a loud noise shattered the dream. Dima gasped as he sat up in his bed, banging his head on the bunk above him. The door to his barrack had been flung open while he slept. An icy gust swept through the room as five drunken soldiers stumbled in. They brought a sour smell with them, as though they'd been sweating vodka for days.

Dima's stomach dropped when he spotted Nogtev and Smolensky. He still felt the echo of every blow received during that beating his first day on the island. Fear coated the back of his throat.

'Line up, you wretches,' Comrade Nogtev shouted, slurring heavily. 'Time for inspection.'

Dima gulped. The men of his company reluctantly got out of their beds and inched towards the centre of the room. They formed a semicircle around the guards. Dima kept his head down, holding his hands behind his back to conceal their trembling.

'Count them off,' Nogtev ordered.

Pulling out his bat, Smolensky moved down the line of prisoners. He jammed the end of the bat into each man's chest, knocking them slightly off balance as he called out numbers.

*Push.* One. *Push.* Two. *Push.* Three. *Push.* Four. *Push.* Five. *Push.* Six.

At the seventh prisoner, Smolensky started again from one. A cold sweat broke over Dima's skin as every number brought Smolensky nearer to him.

'Four,' Smolensky shouted to the prisoner beside Dima.

Dima held his breath as Smolensky's boots stepped into his line of sight.

'Look what we have here.' Instead of shoving Dima, Smolensky used the end of the bat to forcibly raise Dima's chin. 'Hello again.'

Dima had no choice but to meet Smolensky's gaze. He shuddered at the delight in the man's eyes, at the smile the sliced across his lips.

'I gave him that crooked nose.' Smolensky leaned to the side to let his comrades admire his handiwork. 'What do you think?'

Two of the younger guards whooped and hollered. They clapped Smolensky on the back, as though Dima's disfigurement was something he should be congratulated for. Dima squeezed his eyes closed to hold back the angry tears threatening to spring forth. He had no choice but to stand there like a curiosity on display, no choice but to rein in every human reaction while they made mockery of his pain.

'I think he's still too pretty,' one of the other guards said. 'Maybe you'll get another round with him tonight.'

'That would be fun.' Smolensky leaned in, so close that his rancid breath made Dima cringe. 'You're a five.'

Dima let out a long exhale when Smolensky continued down the line, but he couldn't relax. When Smolensky finished counting, both the guards' excitement and the prisoners' fear became palpable.

'I'll do the honours.' Nogtev held open his meaty hand, and another guard placed a small cube on his palm.

Dima's heart sank as he realised their fate would be decided by dice.

'This is a random inspection,' Nogtev looked over the prisoners with bloodshot eyes. 'If your number is called, gather your belongings and follow us to the inspection site.'

Dima had heard of these 'inspections' being carried out in other barracks. None of the men who were taken away ever came back.

Dima's soul rebelled against the indignity of a fate decided by dice. He wished for a glorious death, for the opportunity to show courage or selflessness, for an end that gave meaning to everything that came before.

But he might not get that chance.

Nogtev tossed the die. It seemed as though time unspooled, the moment stretching out to prolong the prisoners' uncertainty and fear. The small cube skittered across the uneven floorboards and came to rest beside Smolensky's boot. Slowly, he picked it up. His eyes flicked to Dima's. That malevolent smile turned Dima's bowels to ice.

'Step forward if you received the number . . .' Smolensky looked at the die. 'Four!'

The man to Dima's right whimpered, but still it took a moment for Smolensky's words to make sense. Four, he'd said, not five. Not Dima, the man beside him.

Dima looked at the terrified man and felt a sharp stab of sympathy. How could this happen, men taken away for no reason, never to return? Dima longed to speak out, but he clamped his jaw shut. It filled him with shame, but speaking up now wouldn't change anything for these men – it would only ensure Dima joined them in the grave tonight.

Dima forced himself to look into the doomed man's eyes. The least he could do was be a witness to this injustice, even if he was a silent one.

'We don't have all night,' Nogtev barked.

The guards fanned out, aiming their rifles at any of the fours who hadn't moved. The man beside Dima was shocked into action when Smolensky approached.

'Too bad we won't get that second round tonight.' Smolensky patted Dima's back in mocking consolation. 'Maybe next time.'

The man beside Dima quickly packed his suitcase. As he brushed past Dima, he pressed something into his hand – an open envelope. The address on the outside had been written in a distinctly feminine script.

'Please,' the man said, and Dima understood. He wanted Dima to write to his loved ones, so they would know what became of him. With a nod, Dima promised he would.

Seven prisoners had been assigned the number four. The guards rounded them up like sheep and led them out into the merciless winter night. When they were gone, the stunned survivors returned to their bunks. Some lay down, some sat with their faces resting in their hands. Nobody made a sound. For the rest of the night, none of them slept.

These 'inspections' took place more frequently in the days and weeks that followed. It seemed the administration had decided to thin out the prison population for the sake of winter stores. Labour and threats of violence were hard enough to endure, but knowing you could be murdered at any time, based on the random fall of dice – it was too much for the mind to comprehend.

There were also disappearances. Guards pulled random prisoners from their beds and took them to Sekirka Hill, where a lighthouse church had been converted into a place for special punishment. Rumours claimed those sent to Sekirka suffered a fate worse than death.

As winter came in full, typhoid moved through the monastery with an axe in hand, felling prisoners left and right. Doctor Tarasov and the nursing staff had dark circles under their eyes as they worked tirelessly to save as many as they could.

By December, there was another outbreak – one of despair.

A haze of darkness surrounded Dima's vision, even when the sun crested the horizon, casting dim light for a few hours before slipping away once more. The long winter nights felt like a metaphor for what their lives had become – cold, dark and empty.

The artists' unit became Dima's lifeline. He chopped down trees in the frozen forest all day. Then, despite his hunger and exhaustion, he spent his last strength building stages and painting sets. Dima couldn't do much to make things better, but this small thing he did with all his heart.

# Chapter 29

## *Natasha*

Natasha followed the now-familiar path to Gleb Boky's bedroom door. Lately her life had fallen into a predictable rhythm. She spent her days at the cabin translating Yelezar Danilov's book into Russian.

Every night her feet carried her here.

Every morning, when she considered whose bed she had shared, she cursed herself as a fool.

The stream of power in this partnership seemed to be flowing one way, and it wasn't to Natasha. Boky had yet to keep his promise of sending Katya to the cabin, and Dima Danilov still lived.

Natasha paused outside of Boky's door. Closing her eyes, she breathed a few times until she'd mastered her frustration and rage. Only then, she knocked.

'Enter,' Boky said.

Natasha stepped through the door to find Boky pouring two glasses of wine. The table had been set, and Natasha's stomach grumbled as the scents greeted her: steaming sausages and potatoes, roasted root vegetables and freshly baked rolls. Boky provided better food than she'd had since before the Revolution. He also gave her extra clothes, writing supplies and access to the bathhouse whenever she wished.

Boky treated Natasha well, but she wouldn't wait much longer for him to keep his word.

She must not have done as good a job mastering her rage as she'd thought, for Boky took one look at her and smiled his wolfish smile.

'I think you'd better tell me what's on your mind.' He handed her the wine glass.

When she tried to lower her eyes, he tilted her chin up with his thumb. His nail elongated into a claw that nicked her skin.

Natasha raised her head to avoid being sliced as she stepped away from him. She drained her wine in one long gulp.

'Uh oh.' Boky took the empty glass and refilled it. 'What did I do wrong?'

'It's what you didn't do.'

He stepped towards her, and static prickled over her skin. He gave her the refilled wine glass and watched her drink that, too. Then he set the empty glass aside. Lust filled his eyes, and his suggestive smile warmed her blood. He pulled out her hair pins so her auburn waves fell loose. Then those devilish lips were on her collarbone, kissing their way up her throat to whisper in her ear.

'I told you.' He pressed her back against the door. She gasped when he pushed his thigh between her legs and spoke in a low tone, nearly a growl. 'You have to be patient.'

Natasha stiffened, trying not to respond to his body against hers, but the heady mix of rage and lust turned her blood molten. She fisted the front of his shirt with both hands, forcing him to face her fury. Her teeth clamped together as she matched his growling tone. 'You've been saying that for weeks.'

'It's still true.' He rested his forehead against hers. Their lips were nearly touching, his smirking, hers tightened in a hateful grimace.

She despised him, but it was a hungry kind of loathing, a craving Natasha couldn't resist. Natasha's anger made her feel alive. It was the only thing about her that still felt real.

Maybe that's why she pressed her lips to his with all the fierceness of her wrath. Natasha kissed him hard, her teeth clenched. Her fingernails dug into his chest as she pushed off from the door.

When they reached the bed, Natasha shoved him so he fell backwards onto it. He looked up at her, dark excitement glittering in his eyes. She made him wait a long moment before she began, very slowly, to undress. She unbuttoned her coat and let it fall from her shoulders. Then she opened her blouse with agonizing slowness, tormenting Boky by holding him in suspense.

By the time she was naked, a haze had settled over his eyes. She turned a leisurely circle, making him admire her body – a body she had no intention of letting him touch until the power between them balanced out.

'What happened there?' He nodded toward the puckered scars beneath her shoulder blades.

'You've read my file.'

'Reading a report isn't the same as hearing someone's story.'

She looked at him over her shoulder, eyes narrowed. Natasha might share this man's bed, but she knew where she stood with him. He was her enemy, likely the most dangerous one she'd ever had. Sharing her body with him was one thing, sharing her past was quite another.

'You first.' She motioned towards him with her pointy chin. 'What happened there?'

'What, these?' He held up both hands, waggling his scarred fingers. 'Souvenirs from my visit to the Peter and Paul Fortress. The tsar's minions had rather creative ways to welcome their guests.'

His voice and his eyes held equal amounts of poisoned spite, all of it focused on Natasha. In that moment, Natasha understood that Boky loathed her as much as she did him. She came from two royal lines of aristocrats and, at the time of her arrest, she'd been attempting to assassinate Vladimir Lenin.

Boky's stone-cold glare made her shiver as he rose from the bed. Natasha stood naked before him, but he made no move to touch her. Instead, he undressed as slowly and methodically as she had a few moments earlier. Unlike Natasha's sensual teasing, his every movement held a challenge. At no time did he avert his eyes from their intense staring match until he'd removed every bit of clothing.

'Take a good look.' Boky turned in a circle, displaying the criss-crossing scars on his back from an old flogging. 'See what I suffered to bring the Revolution about. There's nothing I wouldn't do to defend it from those who wish to put things back the way they were before.'

*People like Natasha.*

'Do we understand each other?' he asked.

Natasha nodded. Boky despised her with a soul-deep hatred, and the feeling was more than mutual. She had no affection for this man. Circumstances had thrown them together – unlikely allies with daggers where their hearts should be.

'Good.' He raised his chin in challenge. 'Then come here.'

'I might. If you do what I want.'

'What do you want, Natasha?'

When he said her name, danger prickled over Natasha's skin and a breeze blew through her, stirring the embers of desire. She hated that her body responded to him like that. What had started out as a campaign of manipulation had become Natasha's guilty pleasure.

'I want you to tell me why you're keeping Katya in the

monastery. And why Dmitri Danilov is still alive.'

A long beat of silence followed.

'You said we would share information as well as meet each other's needs,' Natasha reminded him. 'If you're keeping secrets from me, I assume you no longer need this.'

She gave him one last glimpse of her body before bending to pick up her clothes. Boky's hand caught her wrist, the movement impossibly fast.

'Don't do that,' he growled.

Still clutching her wrist, Boky stepped toward her. Their bodies almost touched. Natasha could feel the static energy between them, the building of a tempest that could destroy them both.

'Dmitri is too valuable to kill,' he said at last. 'I understand why you want him out of the way, but Yekaterina doesn't let many people get close to her. Of course, I had hoped *you* would be the one she let near.'

'I would already be near her, if you'd done what I asked.'

'Perhaps,' he said after a long beat of silence. 'Give me a few more days to consider my options.'

Boky must be planning to use Katya's friends as leverage.

Natasha couldn't help but admire the cunning that conceived of such a plan, and to dread her own part in it. Since she'd failed to worm her way into Katya's heart, did Boky see Natasha as expendable? If he didn't send Katya to the cabin, Natasha's life could be at risk.

At least she still had her wolves, and nothing in Boky's actions indicated he knew of her hold on them.

To survive this place, Natasha had to be careful – and twice as cunning as the treacherous man before her.

'Come here,' he ordered her again.

Natasha suspected he'd lose interest if she let him dominate her. Since she'd failed to fulfil the role he brought her here for, that interest might be the only thing keeping her alive. Natasha lifted her chin as she stepped toward him. She pressed her body to his, but her eyes defied him, displaying every bit of her resentment.

He smiled bitterly. Natasha wrapped her arms around his waist. She trailed her hands up his spine. Instead of using her fingertips to awaken his desire, she ploughed his skin with her fingernails.

'You're ruthless,' he said, sounding pleased.

Boky grabbed her face in both his hands and kissed her. His hands roved over her body, and his tongue pried open her clamped jaw. He held her like a thing to be devoured and she fed him on the abundance of her rage.

When at last they came together, it was impossible to tell if they were making love or waging war on one another.

# Chapter 30

## *Dima*

On midwinter night, Dima stood outside the Assumption Cathedral, waiting to walk into the theatre with Katya. He watched the prisoners arriving. Perhaps he imagined it, but he thought they carried themselves a little taller, bolstered by the simple dignity of standing in line to have their tickets torn for a night of entertainment.

Dima felt Katya's presence before he spotted her in line, walking arm-in-arm with a dark-haired young woman. Though her companion had one of the loveliest faces Dima had ever seen, he only had eyes for Katya.

Tonight Katya had plaited her hair into a coronet. Despite the oversized clothes, the hairstyle made her look like a queen crowned in gold. She was laughing at something her friend said, which brought a lively sparkle to her eyes.

Dima tried to capture that expression in his memory to sketch later on.

'Good evening.' Dima bowed as they approached.

He offered his arm, and his heart skipped a beat when Katya accepted it. They walked as a trio. Katya introduced her friend as Tsisana, a Georgian countess. It surprised him that she'd befriended an aristocrat. It encouraged him, too. Did that mean she no longer despised him because of the title he'd been born to?

They had their tickets torn and entered the cathedral. Dima and the other members of the artist's unit had worked hard to transform the burned out building into something magical. A row of lanterns led the way from the cathedral entrance to the vestry.

The theatre was crowded inside, but as cosy as they could make it. Having no chairs, they'd created seating by setting wooden planks atop of upside-down buckets. Dima had built the stage with his own two hands and done his best to make sets with the materials available to him.

Katya had recreated the script, which had mostly been dictated from Matilda Ivanova's memory of the play.

Dima was glad both he and Katya were stage crew rather than actors, allowing them the chance to sit in the audience tonight.

'There he is.' Tsisana said the words upon a gasp. Her dark eyes simmered with some mix of excitement and trepidation as a dark-haired man approached them through the crowd.

'That's her husband, the Mexican ambassador to Egypt,' Katya explained.

Hearing the word ambassador made Dima picture a glorified clerk, not the young, swashbuckling figure before them. Tsisana's husband did not walk – he strutted. He had tan skin, a rugged, close-cropped beard, and immaculately styled black hair. Sparing a smile for everyone he passed, the ambassador winked as though all the world were a joke and he was inviting them to be in on it.

Dima liked him instantly.

Tsisana bit her lip, trembling and fighting back tears as she stepped into his open arms. They held each other for a long moment. When they broke the embrace, Tsisana clung to his arm as though he might disappear from her sight if she let him go.

'This is my husband,' she said, preening with pride even as unshed tears made her eyes glassy. 'Señor Fernández-Villaverde.'

'Rafael,' he corrected. Katya offered her hand to shake, but he instead kissed it gallantly.

'Nice to meet you. This is my . . .' Katya cast an uncertain glance at Dima, as though unsure what to call him. *Friend? Date?* Finally she said, 'This is Dmitri Danilov.'

Rafael shook Dima's hand.

'We'll let you enjoy your evening,' Tsisana said before she and her husband walked off, their heads bent together in conversation. Katya and Dima found a place in the second row and sat down, waiting for the theatre to fill up. They'd placed a few rows of cushioned chairs at stage left for the heads of administration. Commissar Boky was already seated with Nogtev and Smolensky on either side of them. Several other senior guards were here as well.

Before long, the makeshift curtains opened and the play began.

Andrei Sergeevich took the stage with flair, his moustache waxed into two perfect curves.

Dima had watched the rehearsals enough to know that Andrei Sergeevich had memorised every line. Yet tonight, the script was merely a guideline to him.

He arrived on scene with a bouquet of autumn roses for Helena. Instead of throwing the flowers down and running away when he found her kissing Doctor Astrov, he punched the doctor and swept a squealing Helena into a passionate embrace.

Later he sent Matilda Ivanova into a fit of rage when, instead of firing his pistol at the professor, he shot Nanny. Falling to his knees, Andrei Sergeevich promised to keep the samovar warm and begged her to forgive him with her final breaths.

By the end, Andrei Sergeevich had only to step onto the

stage to send the whole audience into a fit of laughter. The ridicule died away when the actress playing Sonya burst into tears as she delivered the final lines.

'We shall live through the long procession of days before us, and through the long evenings. We shall patiently bear the trials fate imposes on us; we shall work for others without rest, both now and when we are old. And when our last hour comes, we shall meet it humbly, and there, beyond the grave, we shall say that we have suffered and wept, that our life was bitter, and God will have pity on us. Ah, then dear, dear Uncle, we shall see that bright and beautiful life. We shall rejoice and look back upon our sorrow here, and we shall rest.'

Sonya knelt and dropped her head into Vanya's hands. The actress rushed back into her lines before Andrei Sergeevich could interject himself into her monologue.

'We shall see all evil and all our pain sink away in the great compassion that shall enfold the world. Our life will be as peaceful and tender and sweet as a caress. I have faith. I have faith. We shall rest.'

As the actress's words fell silent, not a sound could be heard in the theatre. A solemn weight dropped into the soul of every person there. Tears prickled Dima's eyes as the curtain inched closed and the audience erupted in applause. The clapping morphed into a synchronised beat. As one, the audience rose from the makeshift benches to give a standing ovation.

'It's incredible, isn't it?' Dima spoke close to Katya's ear. 'Do you see how art brings people together? Right now there's no difference between guard and prisoner – or anarchist and aristocrat.'

He nudged Katya, and her lips curled up at the corners. Dima grinned, inordinately pleased with himself for making her smile.

With a happy sigh, he looked out over the audience. Art was the great leveller, the highest form of hope. Tonight it had restored a bit of dignity to a crowd of weary prisoners.

That feeling, like a fizz bubbling up in Dima's stomach, made him want to do even more. Perhaps that's why he did something so foolish – he reached for Katya's hand.

Instead of pulling away, she surprised him by intertwining their fingers and holding on tight.

Aside from Uncle Vanya, the night's performance was set to include two musical acts and a traditional Cossack dance. That meant the guards would be occupied for a while yet.

'Come with me,' Dima whispered in Katya's ear. 'I want to show you something.'

Katya didn't resist as Dima led her out of the cathedral. Cloaked by darkness, they crossed the courtyard to the hermit cells. Dima couldn't see her expression when he instructed her to drop into the hole of the punishment cell where he'd spent his first week on the island, but she only hesitated a moment before releasing his hand and lowering herself down into it.

Dima dropped in after her. He felt for her in the dark and took her hand.

'Where are we going?' she asked close to his ear. Her voice vibrated along his neck.

'You'll see.' He laced their fingers together and groped in the darkness until he found the door leading out into the hallway. Feeling along the wall, he guided Katya upstairs. When they were safely in the printing workshop with the door closed behind them, Dima lit a lamp.

Katya looked around with bewilderment.

'I thought we might create something together – your poetry, my art.'

'I can't,' she said. 'My words could be dangerous.'

'Dangerous how?'

She bit her lip. After a long beat, she said, 'My mother warned me my poems could have unintended consequences. She planned to train me in the arts of symbolism, but never got around to it. So I don't know how to write without weaving magic through the words, and I don't know what will happen if people read my poems.'

Dima thought back to one of his grandfather's lessons. As Christians, they believed words held the power of life and death. *God breathed that same creation power into Adam,* Dedushka had said. *That breath of life is in our lungs also, and mankind is still tasked with naming the world, shaping reality through every word we speak.*

Even people with no magical aptitude could speak things into existence and change situations by the power of their words. As a charovnika, Katya's words might be more potent than the average person's, but that seemed all the more reason to share her talent rather than hiding it away.

'Is it possible your mother had another motive for wanting your poetry to stay hidden?'

'What do you mean?'

'Not to be rude.' Dima touched his chest in a gesture of humility. 'But from the way you talk about her, she sounds a little controlling.'

'Yes, but I don't see why she would lie about that. Unless . . .' Katya bit her lip and thought. 'Actually, lying to me about something so important is exactly the kind of thing my mother would do.'

A storm of conflicting emotions swirled behind her eyes, and Dima wondered how complicated it must be for Katya to both love and hate the woman who raised her, especially now that Svetlana was dead.

'How about an experiment?' Dima motioned toward the shelf of stone slabs. 'I'll prepare for printing while you write a poem, and we'll see if the words have any effect on me. Then you can decide whether or not you want to publish it. No pressure.'

Katya looked sceptical, but she pulled her leather diary out of her schoolbag and curled up in the corner of the room with it on her lap.

She closed her eyes, her brow furrowed as she chanted the zagovor that would bring her mind into awareness of the Otherworld. Dima was struck by a profound sense of deja vu. Months ago, he'd dreamed this exact moment and sketched it in his journal – Katya bent over her poetry diary, her expression almost furious.

When he'd drawn her, he thought her face was contorted because of the intensity of her concentration. Now he wondered if Svetlana had something to do with that look.

It encouraged him that his dreams were coming true. That meant they were on the right track, following the path that destiny had laid out for them.

Dima turned his attention to the stones. He pulled one out on the trolley and ground the surface with grit to erase the previous image. When the stone was ready, he too closed his eyes. His skomorokh magic came alive inside him, and a picture formed in his mind.

Instead of drawing with the beeswax crayons, he used the lantern's heat to melt one atop of the stone. He spread the wax until the entire surface turned black. The top half of the stone became the night sky. Dima used a watered-down solvent to create the illusion of swirling galaxies. With the point of a razor blade, he removed spots of wax to create stars and constellations.

Dima outlined the elegant towers and onion domes of one of the monastery churches, using a thick crayon to darken it into a silhouette against the night sky. In the foreground, he used the razor to draw two people with their backs to the viewer. One carried a lantern, and Dima used solvent to portray the light it cast. The couple held hands, their faces turned up to the sky. Their breaths billowed upward, creating frozen sparks that mirrored and then joined the stars.

The right side of the foreground remained blank, leaving room for Katya's poem.

Dima glanced over his shoulder and found her watching him, her lips curved in amusement.

'You dance while you draw. Did you know that? It's like you can't hold still.'

'Art makes me happy.' Dima shrugged away his embarrassment, even as a flush rose to his cheeks. 'And I'm not sure you're one to talk, seeing as you scowl when you write. You get a bump above your nose, right here.'

He touched the place between his eyebrows, and Katya laughed.

'My friends always told me I'd never have to fight, but simply concentrate – then my expression would make my enemies flee in terror.'

Dima nodded toward her journal. 'Did your terrifying concentration give you a poem?'

'Yes.' Katya reflexively covered the words with her fingers. 'But I don't think I should publish it.'

'I'll be the judge of that.' He extended his hand with a dramatic flourish, but Katya pressed the diary to her torso, concealing the pages as she came to stand beside him. Her jaw dropped when she saw what he'd created.

'But how did you . . .' She turned to Dima with bewilderment. 'How did you know to draw this?'

'What do you mean?'

232

Katya took a deep breath, then handed her diary to Dima. A tingling sensation spread over his skin as he read Katya's poem.

> Though horror is your daily bread,
> and your cup is filled with sorrow.
> Though your loved ones are as autumn leaves,
> and death falls all around.
> Though your days are bleakest winter,
> though the sun withholds its warmth,
> though your land knows only twilight,
> darkness deepening day by day.
> There is hope for all who listen
> to the whispering of stars.

Tears prickled Dima's eyes at her words. They fit perfectly with his drawing. It made sense that the little sparks emanating from the couple's frozen breath could represent the whispering of stars, that crackling phenomenon in winter when breath turns to ice. *The breath of life*, he thought, remembering Dedushka's lesson. Her poem coupled with the image he'd drawn spoke to Dima of the power of words. People still had the ability to name the world. No matter how dark their circumstances, they could speak hope into existence, their words sparking light like stars in the night sky.

'Katinka?' The emotion rising within Dima made his voice sound choked.

'Yes, Dmitri?' Katya arched her brow.

He held up her poetry diary between them like an object of reverence. 'This is beautiful and important, and I think you should publish it.'

Katya swallowed hard as she took the diary from Dima. She picked up the razor and wrote out her poem in bold script.

Dima watched her, smiling unabashedly at her fearsome look of concentration. A lock of golden hair fell in her face, and she swiped it away leaving a mark of crayon.

She set down the razor. 'Happy?'

She faced Dima with a fire in her eyes and the little cleft visible in the stubborn set of her chin. When Katya raised an impatient eyebrow, Dima realised he hadn't answered her. He'd also been staring at her again.

'Yes,' he said. 'I'm happy.'

'Now what?' Katya motioned towards the lithograph machine.

'Watch and learn.' Dima smiled as he picked up a jar of talc and set to work printing their art.

# Chapter 31

## *Katya*

Katya's chest hurt. Just as circulation returning to a limb gives the sensation of pins and needles, this thawing of her heart brought exquisite pain. Tears prickled the backs of her eyes as she admired how perfectly her poem fit within Dima's artwork. She didn't know why she felt like crying, why she felt so much in general all of the sudden.

She'd been numb the past few years, hollowed out by grief and disillusionment until her life was reduced to a display case in the museum of loss. She was trapped inside it, looking out through the glass at people who still remembered the taste of food, people who laughed without the sound sticking in their throats and who dreamed in colour instead of shades of grey.

She would have stayed like that if not for Dima. He'd burst into her world like a flaming meteor, threatening to melt the walls of ice that kept Katya safe. Like a fool, she felt drawn to him, though she knew she would likely be burned.

Even now she couldn't stop watching him. He bobbed and swayed as he brushed talc over the stone's surface and painted on a shiny layer of gum arabic. Dima turned those mundane tasks into the steps of a dance, moving to the rhythm of music only he could hear.

'*Voila.*' He set down the paintbrush. 'Now we need to let it dry before the next step.'

Katya had been watching over his shoulder. When he turned to face her, they stood uncomfortably close. Katya should have put space between them, but she found herself arrested by his gaze. In the lamplight, Katya noticed the reddish hues in his brown eyes. Layers of deep mahogany and richest cognac shifted like kaleidoscope patterns as he glanced from her eyes to her lips and back again.

Dima smiled. The Russian language needed more words because 'smile' couldn't capture the complexities of what Dima did with his lips. For the past few weeks, Katya had been mentally cataloguing his various smiles, wishing she had the vocabulary to describe their nuances.

His current smile was little more than a curve, subtle and sensual. As he tilted his head, a note of amusement drew one corner of his lips up higher.

'You have crayon on your cheek.' He raised a hand to wipe it away, but paused before touching her. 'May I?'

Katya's mouth went dry. She nodded. Dima twined a loose strand of Katya's hair around his finger before gently tucking it behind her ear. Cradling her jaw with his fingertips, Dima brushed his thumb across her cheekbone. Her skin came alive beneath his touch.

'There.' His voice sent a pleasant shiver down Katya's spine.

He started to move away. Katya didn't know what came over her, but she reached for his hand, stopping him with the barest brush of her fingertips.

Dima's gaze flicked to hers, a question in his eyes. She answered him by bringing her free hand to his face. He exhaled shakily as he leaned into her touch.

That thawing feeling in her chest turned to pins and needles.

It ached with a pain she wanted more of. Dima's fingertips left her hand, sliding up her wrist and the inside of her arm, leaving a trail of sensation in their wake.

Dima lowered his head but then waited for her to make the next move.

'Kiss me, Dima,' she whispered, using his nickname for the first time.

His expressive lips curved into that same sensual smile as before. Instead of matching her urgency, Dima took his time. His lips lightly brushed hers, the first tentative paint strokes across an empty canvas. He caressed her hair as he deepened the kiss, slowly, sensually. Even this Dima turned into art.

Katya melted into his embrace, kissing him back with a desperate hunger. Her chest hurt so badly she couldn't take a breath, and then she went stiff in Dima's arms as logic flooded in.

At once she remembered all the reasons this shouldn't be happening. They were prisoners on this island, trying to uncover a deadly mystery while Boky watched their every move. Katya wasn't supposed to fall for Dima, because what would happen if he died? Katya might be strong, but she didn't think she could survive one more loss.

'This is a terrible idea,' she said breathlessly.

'Probably.' Dima smiled against her cheek. 'Though I can't say I'm not enjoying it.'

Katya's breath returned, swelling painfully inside her lungs. When he leaned in again, she pressed a hand to his chest.

'I can't do this.' Katya backed away, shocked to alertness by how cold it was outside of his embrace. 'I'm sorry. I just can't.'

Dima's brow furrowed with confusion. Katya turned away, not able to face the pain she saw in his eyes. She tried to remember her reasons for not wanting Dima's friendship, though they seemed less important than they had before. Did it really matter that he was a Cossack aristocrat? Dima couldn't control the family he was born into. No one could.

'Wait.' Katya nearly gasped out the word. Something had sparked in her mind at that phrase, *the family he was born into.*

'What is it?' Dima's brows drew together, his expression a mix of confusion and disappointment.

'The keyword to the cipher.' Katya crossed the room in three steps, pulling the book of fairy tales out of her schoolbag with shaking fingers.

Few people knew that Svetlana hadn't been born with the name Efremova. Svetlana's father married her off when she was only seventeen years old, claiming she was too spirited for her own good. Svetlana's husband died an untimely death not a year after they were married, which Katya suspected her mother may have had a hand in. Rather than returning to her father's estate, Svetlana went to Petrograd. She used the money she inherited from her husband to enrol in university and never looked back.

No one knew Svetlana's maiden name was Balakina – no one except Katya.

Dima hurriedly spread a sealing product over the stone's surface before joining Katya. Despite the awkwardness of their broken-off kiss, they huddled together on the ground in a corner of the printing room. Dima held up the lantern as Katya opened her book of fairy tales and unfolded the notes containing the *tabula recta* and her many attempts at cracking the cipher.

Katya flattened the paper on her knees. Below the *tabula recta* she'd written the code she'd uncovered by putting the page numbers Svetlana touched and 'Listen to the whisper of stars' into a nihilist cipher:

Р Ю Ж Т В Т Ы Н Я К Е Ю А Ё Ф А

Now she wrote her mother's maiden name below that.

С В Е Т Л А Н А Б А Л А К И Н А

Katya inputted the letters into the table, with her mother's name as a key on the left-hand side, and the code corresponding on the top row.

```
А Б В Г Д Е Ё Ж З И Й К Л М Н О П Р С Т У Ф Х Ц Ч Ш Щ Ъ Ы Ь Э Ю Я
Б В Г Д Е Ё Ж З И Й К Л М Н О П Р С Т У Ф Х Ц Ч Ш Щ Ъ Ы Ь Э Ю Я А
В Г Д Е Ё Ж З И Й К Л М Н О П Р С Т У Ф Х Ц Ч Ш Щ Ъ Ы Ь Э Ю Я А Б
Г Д Е Ё Ж З И Й К Л М Н О П Р С Т У Ф Х Ц Ч Ш Щ Ъ Ы Ь Э Ю Я А Б В
Д Е Ё Ж З И Й К Л М Н О П Р С Т У Ф Х Ц Ч Ш Щ Ъ Ы Ь Э Ю Я А Б В Г
Е Ё Ж З И Й К Л М Н О П Р С Т У Ф Х Ц Ч Ш Щ Ъ Ы Ь Э Ю Я А Б В Г Д
Ё Ж З И Й К Л М Н О П Р С Т У Ф Х Ц Ч Ш Щ Ъ Ы Ь Э Ю Я А Б В Г Д Е
Ж З И Й К Л М Н О П Р С Т У Ф Х Ц Ч Ш Щ Ъ Ы Ь Э Ю Я А Б В Г Д Е Ё
З И Й К Л М Н О П Р С Т У Ф Х Ц Ч Ш Щ Ъ Ы Ь Э Ю Я А Б В Г Д Е Ё Ж
И Й К Л М Н О П Р С Т У Ф Х Ц Ч Ш Щ Ъ Ы Ь Э Ю Я А Б В Г Д Е Ё Ж З
Й К Л М Н О П Р С Т У Ф Х Ц Ч Ш Щ Ъ Ы Ь Э Ю Я А Б В Г Д Е Ё Ж З И
К Л М Н О П Р С Т У Ф Х Ц Ч Ш Щ Ъ Ы Ь Э Ю Я А Б В Г Д Е Ё Ж З И Й
Л М Н О П Р С Т У Ф Х Ц Ч Ш Щ Ъ Ы Ь Э Ю Я А Б В Г Д Е Ё Ж З И Й К
М Н О П Р С Т У Ф Х Ц Ч Ш Щ Ъ Ы Ь Э Ю Я А Б В Г Д Е Ё Ж З И Й К Л
Н О П Р С Т У Ф Х Ц Ч Ш Щ Ъ Ы Ь Э Ю Я А Б В Г Д Е Ё Ж З И Й К Л М
О П Р С Т У Ф Х Ц Ч Ш Щ Ъ Ы Ь Э Ю Я А Б В Г Д Е Ё Ж З И Й К Л М Н
П Р С Т У Ф Х Ц Ч Ш Щ Ъ Ы Ь Э Ю Я А Б В Г Д Е Ё Ж З И Й К Л М Н О
Р С Т У Ф Х Ц Ч Ш Щ Ъ Ы Ь Э Ю Я А Б В Г Д Е Ё Ж З И Й К Л М Н О П
С Т У Ф Х Ц Ч Ш Щ Ъ Ы Ь Э Ю Я А Б В Г Д Е Ё Ж З И Й К Л М Н О П Р
Т У Ф Х Ц Ч Ш Щ Ъ Ы Ь Э Ю Я А Б В Г Д Е Ё Ж З И Й К Л М Н О П Р С
У Ф Х Ц Ч Ш Щ Ъ Ы Ь Э Ю Я А Б В Г Д Е Ё Ж З И Й К Л М Н О П Р С Т
Ф Х Ц Ч Ш Щ Ъ Ы Ь Э Ю Я А Б В Г Д Е Ё Ж З И Й К Л М Н О П Р С Т У
Х Ц Ч Ш Щ Ъ Ы Ь Э Ю Я А Б В Г Д Е Ё Ж З И Й К Л М Н О П Р С Т У Ф
Ц Ч Ш Щ Ъ Ы Ь Э Ю Я А Б В Г Д Е Ё Ж З И Й К Л М Н О П Р С Т У Ф Х
Ч Ш Щ Ъ Ы Ь Э Ю Я А Б В Г Д Е Ё Ж З И Й К Л М Н О П Р С Т У Ф Х Ц
Ш Щ Ъ Ы Ь Э Ю Я А Б В Г Д Е Ё Ж З И Й К Л М Н О П Р С Т У Ф Х Ц Ч
Щ Ъ Ы Ь Э Ю Я А Б В Г Д Е Ё Ж З И Й К Л М Н О П Р С Т У Ф Х Ц Ч Ш
Ъ Ы Ь Э Ю Я А Б В Г Д Е Ё Ж З И Й К Л М Н О П Р С Т У Ф Х Ц Ч Ш Щ
Ы Ь Э Ю Я А Б В Г Д Е Ё Ж З И Й К Л М Н О П Р С Т У Ф Х Ц Ч Ш Щ Ъ
Ь Э Ю Я А Б В Г Д Е Ё Ж З И Й К Л М Н О П Р С Т У Ф Х Ц Ч Ш Щ Ъ Ы
Э Ю Я А Б В Г Д Е Ё Ж З И Й К Л М Н О П Р С Т У Ф Х Ц Ч Ш Щ Ъ Ы Ь
Ю Я А Б В Г Д Е Ё Ж З И Й К Л М Н О П Р С Т У Ф Х Ц Ч Ш Щ Ъ Ы Ь Э
Я А Б В Г Д Е Ё Ж З И Й К Л М Н О П Р С Т У Ф Х Ц Ч Ш Щ Ъ Ы Ь Э Ю
```

Her breath hitched when she saw the result.

В А Л Е Н Т И Н А К Р Ю К О В А – *Valentina Kryukova.*

'I know that name,' Dima said, his voice hushed and reverent. 'She's a hermitess living on Solovetsky Island. Father Iosef said your mother asked about her when she came to the monastery last year.'

Katya took a moment to process that. The cipher led to a person, someone who lived here in Solovki. All the heaviness Katya had felt just moments ago turned to air. She'd finally solved the cipher, and now she knew exactly what she had to do next.

# Chapter 32

## *Natasha*

Natasha tried to concentrate on the manuscript set out before her, but her eyes kept drifting to look at the door. She'd received a message from Boky. *Stay at the cabin. The anarchist will be joining you shortly.* Tonight Dima would be killed. Then Boky would chase Katya into the forest, where she'd be forced to take refuge in the cabin.

Soon, very soon, Katya would be trapped where Natasha could watch her every move.

While she waited, Natasha tried to focus on Yelezar Danilov's book. The section she'd translated today marked Razin's transition from pirate to revolutionary. After a summer of raiding, the River Wolves had wintered in Yaitsk.

Tsar Alexei sent multiple battalions to try and reclaim the fortress. Each time, his *streltsy* defected, killing their commanders and joining the River Wolves as free men. Stenka Razin's numbers swelled.

A pounding on the door startled Natasha.

That would be Katya. Natasha smiled as she swaggered towards the door, but her smile faded when she opened it. Smolensky lurched through the doorway, shaking snow from his shoulders and boots.

'Marius,' Natasha greeted him, a question in her voice.

'The plan went awry,' Smolensky said. 'Yekaterina and Dmitri left the theatre early. Most of the guards attended the performance, so we think they left the monastery through an unguarded gate.'

With every word, Natasha's mood darkened. She'd waited weeks for Boky to get rid of the skomorokh and deliver Katya to this cabin. She had no intention of being thwarted now.

'Where did they go?'

'No one knows.' Smolensky lowered his head at her look of displeasure. 'We couldn't pick up her scent.'

Slipping off her shoes, Natasha took up her violin. She untied her hair so it flowed loose, then stepped into the protective chalk circle she'd drawn on the floor. She began to play – not the melody of Katya's sorrows, as she had before, but an improvisation.

Natasha closed her eyes. In her mind, she saw Katya and Dima as viewed from above, both of them bathed in starlight. They trekked through the night-dark forest, kicking up sprays of powder snow. Moon rays glinted off the frozen surface of the sea, somewhere to the right, and the pair approached an *izba* nestled in a birch grove. Welcoming orange light shone out of the windows.

Natasha's bow stilled upon the violin strings, and the vision faded. She blinked as the cabin came back into focus – the crackling fire, the desk littered with pages of translation and the Polish guard watching her with simmering hate.

Natasha plucked carefully selected herbs out of the bundles hanging from the ceiling. A dried thistle perfectly represented Katya's defiance and surliness. Twin pine needles symbolised Natasha's connection to the anarchist. Natasha twined the needles around the thistle's stem, using stalks of bindweed and rue to hold them in place.

Natasha sliced her palm. Holding the herb bundle in her bleeding hand, she chanted in Old Russian. When her blood soaked the herbs and began dripping on the floor Natasha tossed the bundle onto the fire. She continued chanting as she inhaled the smoke. Every intake of breath strengthened Natasha's connection to Katya. She could sense the anarchist's direction the way a compass points true north.

'Come with me,' Natasha ordered Smolensky as she pulled on her winter coat and stepped out into the night.

# Chapter 33

## *Katya*

Katya and Dima found a small, wooden *izba* nestled in a birch grove. It was a quintessential Russian cabin with latticework surrounding the south-facing windows.

Katya took a moment to catch her breath. Svetlana's cipher led her here and perhaps all the question marks Katya carried in her heart would have answers set beside them at last.

They climbed the stairs leading up to the cabin's door and knocked.

From inside came sounds of movement. Katya's stomach knotted as footsteps drew near. A latch clicked, the door opened, and Katya stood face-to-face with Valentina Pavlovna Kryukova.

She was taller than Katya. Valentina Pavlovna's grey-streaked brown hair framed her delicate face. With feet turned out in a ballet stance and a long dancer's neck, she was one of those women whose beauty had matured into regal elegance.

The dissonance between Katya's expectation of a hermitess and the reality standing before her left Katya momentarily dumbfounded.

'Is this the custom among young people these days?' Valentina Pavlovna's curious green eyes glanced from Katya to Dima and back again. 'You knock on a stranger's door, and when they open it you stare at them without saying anything?'

Dima nudged Katya with his elbow. All the traditional greetings and polite words of introduction fled from her mind. Emotion clogged Katya's throat as she choked out three words. 'I'm Svetlana's daughter.'

'Oh,' the woman said gravely, studying Katya's face. 'You'd better come inside.'

Valentina Pavlovna let them pass.

In many ways, the interior was that of a typical *izba*. An enormous, white-plastered stove with a sleeping platform above it took up much of the space. There was a red corner decorated with icons and embroidered towels, a table with bench seating, and walls lined with shelves containing various jars and utensils. A spinning wheel sat below the window and a line of dried herbs hung above it. There were also a few modern additions – a brass-horned gramophone in one corner and walls decorated with several posters and show bills from ballets all across Europe.

Valentina Pavlovna rubbed her arms against the cold as they shook the snow from their coats and removed their boots before stepping inside.

'Welcome to my home, Katya. I've heard so much about you, I feel like we're friends already.' Valentina Pavlovna held Katya's shoulders and kissed both her cheeks in greeting. She turned to Dima. 'And who do we have here?'

'Dmitri Danilov.' He offered his hand to shake. 'Call me Dima.'

Rather than shaking it, she took his hand in an iron grip and felt his bicep. 'You have a dancer's build. Has anyone ever told you that? And a Danilov – how interesting!'

'I'm afraid I have two left feet,' Dima said.

'People who believe they can't dance have simply never met

the right partner,' Valentina Pavlovna said decidedly. 'Perhaps I could give you and your girlfriend a lesson.'

'I'm not his girlfriend,' Katya said.

Valentina Pavlovna raised one perfectly plucked eyebrow in disbelief.

'Have a seat.' Valentina Pavlovna gestured to the table. 'I know exactly what you need: music, food, and—' She whispered something in Dima's ear.

He smiled conspiratorially. 'I won't say no to that.'

'Actually, we shouldn't stay long.' Katya stood her ground while Dima hung his coat up on a peg and scooted onto one of the benches. 'We just have a few questions. Then we ought to be heading back.'

Ignoring her objections, Valentina Pavlovna glided across the room, putting a disk on the gramophone's turntable and winding the motorised crank. After a few opening notes of orchestra music, a deep operatic voice poured through the brass horn.

'I hope you like Chaliapin.' Valentina Pavlovna put a hand over her heart. 'Dear Fyodor. We had a love affair, you know, back in Tbilisi, where we both got our start.'

As interesting as that sounded, Katya didn't want to make conversation. She needed to know why her mother sent her to this bizarrely elegant woman living alone in the wilderness. And then she needed to get far away from Dima before the temptation that came over her earlier became too strong to resist.

'Fyodor Chaliapin was your lover?' Dima leaned over the table, eyes alight. Clearly he was not in tune with Katya's goal of moving things along.

'Oh, yes.' Valentina Pavlovna sighed dreamily. 'Until fate had its say. He became a famous operatic bass, while I travelled the world as a prima ballerina. Paris, Rome, London, New York.'

'That sounds fascinating.' Dima tapped the table, as though his fingers itched for a pencil to sketch Valentina Pavlovna.

'It was. I attended elegant soirees, became an artist's muse, had scandalous liaisons with wealthy men – and women.' Valentina Pavlovna winked at Katya. Then she sighed again, swaying slightly to the music. 'But you never forget your first love.'

Valentina Pavlovna danced past Katya on her way to retrieve something from a shelf, asking, 'Why are you still standing there, *lapochka?*'

Katya tried to think of a polite way to ask Valentina Pavlovna to get to the point. 'I don't mean to be rude, but—'

'If you don't mean to be rude, then *don't be rude.*' Valentina Pavlovna ushered Katya to the table, aiming her at the bench where Dima sat.

Dima scooted to allow as much space between them as possible, but it wasn't enough of a gap for Katya to avoid that magnetic force making her aware of every tap of his finger or twitch of his knee.

After rummaging through a big ceramic jar, Valentina Pavlovna brought a handful of potatoes to the table. She offered Katya a knife. 'Would you be a dear and peel these?'

'I'm not much of a cook.'

'That makes two of us.' Valentina Pavlovna placed the knife in Katya's hand and patted her arm consolingly.

'Besides, we don't have time to stay for a meal.'

'No one's going to notice if we're gone until tomorrow morning,' Dima said.

'That settles it. You'll both stay the night.' In a graceful movement, Valentina Pavlovna reached for a high shelf and pulled out a bottle of clear liquid. Dima smiled when Valentina Pavlovna shook the bottle in playful demonstration – that must have been what she'd whispered to him about.

Valentina Pavlovna set three shot glasses on the table and sat down across from them, uncorking the bottle and pouring them all a shot. Dima took his without complaint, but Katya hesitated. She couldn't get drunk with Dima. It had taken all her self-control to break off their kiss. This was no time to let alcohol strip away her inhibitions.

'Thank you, but I really shouldn't.'

'To Svetlana.' Valentina Pavlovna raised her glass in toast. 'One of the most courageous women I've known.'

Dima raised his glass while Katya paused, fingers lightly resting on the shot glass she'd slid halfway across the table. Despite her reservations, she couldn't refuse to toast her dead mother.

'To Svetlana.' Katya raised the glass and took a sip. The homemade vodka, like liquid fire, singed her throat on the way down. A coughing fit overtook her, and her eyes watered.

Valentina Pavlovna refilled their glasses and raised the next toast before Katya could refuse.

'To new friendships and the twisted tapestry of fate.'

That was another toast she couldn't politely refuse. Forcing a smile, Katya raised her glass. She only took a small sip while Valentina Pavlovna and Dima drank their glasses empty.

Valentina Pavlovna arched her brow. 'If you do not drink deeply, our friendship will be shallow.'

With a sigh Katya downed the glass. She didn't cough this time, but her tongue felt numb and her stomach hot. With opera music drifting around her, Katya closed her eyes, head spinning. Valentina Pavlovna moved to refill Katya's glass a third time, but she pre-emptively put a hand over the cup.

'I shouldn't drink more. Not if I'm going to cut up these vegetables and keep all my fingers.'

'Nonsense,' Valentina Pavlovna said. 'Why do you have ten fingers if one or two aren't expendable?'

Katya's eyes widened, and Valentina Pavlovna laughed.

'Oh, girl. It speaks of the tragedy of our age that young people are so very serious.' She set down the bottle with a sigh. 'But fine. We'll wait until the meal to drink more.'

'Please don't make me wait longer to find out why my mother wanted me to see you.' Katya's voice cracked. 'I don't mean to be pushy, but I have to know. Did she leave a message, or . . .'

'She left *me*.' Valentina Pavlovna reached across the table and squeezed Katya's hand. 'Svetlana Efremova came to my *izba* in search of a story, one deeply rooted in this island's past. I reached into the richness of Solovki's history, untangling the knots of story until I found the thread your mother sought – the same thread she asked me to share with you.'

'Do you mean you can know every story that ever happened in a place, because of your magic?' Katya asked.

'That's not as difficult as you make it sound, especially in a thin place like Solovki. All I had to do was visit that moment in my sleep.' Valentina Pavlovna's green eyes sparkled. 'I thought you'd know more about skomorokh magic, considering your boyfriend is a Danilov.'

'He's not my boyfriend.'

Valentina Pavlovna smiled as she put the cork back in the bottle of vodka. 'I may be getting old, but I'm not blind.'

She cast a meaningful look at Dima, who lowered his eyes, and then at Katya, who suddenly felt as though her skin didn't fit her right. But her embarrassment didn't matter in the scheme of things, not if they were on the verge of learning Svetlana's secrets.

'Will you recite the story for us?' Katya asked.

'Later,' Valentina Pavlovna said. 'First we will eat – and drink – for we have a long night ahead of us.'

At dinner, Valentina Pavlovna regaled them with tales of her glamorous life – dancing every part a ballerina could dream of, travelling the world in style, having multitudes of adventures with friends and lovers. She was the kind of woman who said yes to every invitation and never held herself back from a new experience. Valentina Pavlovna Kryukova would try anything, risk everything, lose all her fortune in an ill-thought endeavour, win it back and promptly lose it again. She hadn't just survived – she'd *lived*.

Katya listened with growing discomfort. Valentina Pavlovna's stories glittered like glass, showing how dull Katya's reflection was in comparison. Katya had survived more than most people could endure, but was she really living?

'I'm surprised you ended up here.' Dima pushed aside his empty plate. 'You seem the least reclusive person I've ever met.'

'True.' Leaning back on her bench, Valentina Pavlovna tilted her head and sighed. 'But, at the end of the day, I'm still a skomorokha. The blood of the bear flows through my veins, and no matter how far I roamed or how fabulous a life I led, there could be no home but Russia. A few years ago Motherland called my name, and I had to come back. I had to come here, specifically, though I didn't know why at the time.'

'Do you know why now?' Dima asked.

'I believe I do.' Valentina Pavlovna's eyes met Katya's across the table. *Destiny*, they seemed to say. *A meeting brought about by the weaver of fate.*

The hair on Katya's arms stood on end, and a prickle moved up her spine.

'It's time,' Valentina Pavlovna said.

With the crackling fire filling the *izba* with warmth and light, Valentina Pavlovna cleared her throat and began to tell them the story.

# The Story of Nikita Minin

Cloaked in the darkness of a late spring night, a hooded monk crept between the buildings of the Solovetsky Monastery. In one hand he clutched a stolen key, in the other hand, a dagger.

Nikita Minin prowled up to the edge of a large courtyard and paused before stepping out into the open. He listened for danger but heard only the rush of blood in his ears. It pulsed to the too-fast rhythm of his heartbeat.

Cautiously stepping into the open, Nikita hastened to the elegant building where Father Superior lived. He slipped inside, counting his steps in the darkness as he made his way to Father Superior's study.

Nikita gently clicked the door shut and rested his back against it. Darkness filled the room, ink-black and impenetrable. He breathed the stale air and listened for movement in the house.

Just when he thought he'd avoided detection, a voice spoke from the darkness.

'Hello, Nikita Minin.'

Nikita gasped in a breath and held it.

'I know you're there.' The voice was thin and breathy, weathered as the ancient stones dotting these islands. And the man that voice came from was a relic in his own right – the Prophet of Solovetsky Island. Some claimed he was two-hundred years old, kept alive by the magic leaking out from the ground the monastery was built upon.

Nikita tightened his grip on the dagger.

'Did you think the Almighty would not see the evil plans in your heart?' the Prophet asked. 'Turn away from this. Return to your bed, Nikita Minin, and repent from this blasphemous endeavour.'

Pulling out the candle he'd tucked into his belt, Nikita lit it. The flame pushed back the darkness, revealing the Prophet standing an arm's breadth away from Nikita, his blind eyes clouded in white.

Nikita strode to Father Superior's desk. On the wall behind it, concealed by a tapestry, was an iron box built into the wall. Nikita pushed the tapestry aside and fitted the stolen key into the lock.

'It is not a true relic.' Stretching his arms out in front of him, the blind prophet groped towards the sound of Nikita turning the key in the lock. 'If you take that object from its place of safekeeping, you will unleash an evil on this world that's been contained for two hundred years.'

Inside the safe, Nikita found a book, ancient yet perfectly preserved. Its power sang to Nikita's blood.

'Don't,' the Prophet warned, panic in his voice.

But Nikita had already taken the book. He pressed it to his chest, right beside his heart.

'You snake.' The Prophet lunged forward. He almost got hold of the book, but Nikita shoved the old man into Father Superior's desk. The Prophet fisted Nikita's robe and held tight, groping for the relic.

That's when Nikita lifted the dagger. He only meant to threaten the old man, but suddenly the Prophet gasped. Something warm and wet flowed over Nikita's hand. He'd thrust the dagger between the Prophet's ribs. The old man groaned, his knees weakening.

Prying the old man's fingers off of his robe, Nikita pushed him to the ground.

'I curse you,' the Prophet said in a pained voice. 'May all your plans come to naught. I curse you to the depths of hell.'

His words sent a chill through Nikita, but no curse could harm him, not now that he possessed the *Volkhovnik*. Clutching the book tight, he left the Prophet to die alone. Nikita slipped back out into the night, making for the harbour and the fishing boat that would take him far away from here.

# Chapter 34

## *Natasha*

Natasha knelt in the snow, looking in through a window at the light and warmth of the skomorokha's *izba*. The cold had hardened Natasha's skin into porcelain, and snow dappled the loose locks of her hair. She clamped her jaw to keep her teeth from clattering as she watched and listened.

When Natasha first arrived, she'd noted the way Katya and Dima no longer appeared like individual units. They were a pair, like the twin pine needles Natasha had burned in her tracking ritual. For a moment, the ache of loneliness had nearly driven her to knock on the door and ask to be let inside.

She'd remained alone in the dark, listening through the glass as the skomorokha told the story of Nikita Minin. Five years after her tale, Nikita Minin had become Patriarch Nikon – the man whose treasure ship Stenka Razin plundered.

All the pieces fit together now.

The Cossack pirate had possessed the *Volkhovnik*, the most powerful book of magic ever written. Svetlana Efremova had been searching for the *Volkhovnik* for decades, since before Katya was born. Somehow Svetlana must have discovered the Cossack connection and come to Solovetsky searching for the truth about Stenka Razin. Did that mean the *Volkhovnik* was here too, hidden on the archipelago?

Whoever possessed that book would decide Russia's future.

*It's always been a woman who saved Russia.*

Natasha thought back to the schoolroom in her father's palace in Strelna. Aunt Sonya had only been there a few days when she lumbered into the classroom, her arms heavy-laden with thick volumes of Russian history. These she dumped onto the table in front of Natasha.

Relieved of the heavy tomes, Aunt Sonya straightened her vest and smoothed her skirt, looking like a squat bird preening its feathers.

'They're so big.' Despair settled over Natasha as she slid the topmost book off the stack. It was too heavy for her to hold up, so she let it thump onto the table in front of her.

'It's always been a woman who saved Russia.' Aunt Sonya placed her hand atop the stack of books, spreading her fingers and leaning forward to fix Natasha with a stern look. 'Someday that task may rest upon you, so you'd best be ready.'

Aunt Sonya began to pace the length of the classroom, giving Natasha her first of many lectures on the achievements of royal women who came before her.

The Rurikid dynasty wouldn't have lasted three generations if it hadn't been for Princess Olga of Kyiv, whose legendary vengeance destroyed the men who murdered her husband. She guarded the throne like a lioness until her son came of age. Because of her, the dynasty continued for nineteen more generations.

When Sofia Palaiologina, the last princess of Byzantium, came to Moscow, she found a city made of wood. Her husband was a weak ruler of a vassal princedom, paying tribute to the Golden Horde of Mongols. She brought Venetian architects to design a capital worthy of being called the third Rome and stopped her husband from paying tribute, insisting their neighbouring princes pay tribute to them instead. The Russian Empire grew from the seeds she planted, and it was through her bloodlines the rulers of Moscow began calling themselves Caesar, or Tsar.

Aunt Sonya continued her list. Sofia Alekseyevna ruled for twenty years when her brothers were too young or weak to wear a crown. Elizabeta Petrovna wrestled power from the hands of a foreign regent and brought the Enlightenment to Russia. Natasha's great-great-grandmother, Yekaterina Alekseyvna, continued Elizabeta's reforms and established Russia as a world power.

'You are born for greatness, Natasha.' Aunt Sonya knelt down to look Natasha in the eye. 'You come from a line of powerful women, and your father's lineage makes you the thirty-third generation descended from Rurik. Three is a portentous number, a number of divinity and completion.'

'I don't know what that means.'

'It means you need to prepare, so that if it falls to you to save Russia, which is likely, you will be ready.'

Over the years, Aunt Sonya groomed Natasha for greatness. Her mother's family planned for Natasha to marry a Romanov, strengthening that failing line and giving Russia the strong empress it needed.

The Revolution destroyed those plans. Then, for a while, they seemed unnecessary. After the February Revolution, the tsar abdicated. An interim government took power, in which Natasha's father had a significant role.

Her father pushed for a radical liberalisation of Russia. They established freedom of speech and of the press, abolished capital punishment and removed all legal repressions against minorities. A group of suffragettes came to the Winter Palace to demand the women's vote only to discover Natasha's father had given it already. It never occurred to him to deny women an equal voice in their government.

He had the old blood to appease the bourgeoisie and the democratic ideals to lead Russia into the twentieth century. He was the right man for the time.

'Perhaps I'm not needed after all,' Natasha had said one day that spring.

'It won't be a man to save Russia,' Aunt Sonya had replied with certainty. 'It never is.'

Aunt Sonya was proven right. Her father's reforms went too far for the upper class and not far enough for the revolutionaries. By July he'd been forced out of the government, and by October a second wave of revolution swept across Russia, changing the political landscape for ever.

Now Aunt Sonya was dead, Georgy lived in impoverished exile, and Natasha found herself a prisoner on an island in the far north.

But if Natasha found the original *Volkhovnik*, the throne of Russia would be hers for the taking.

She couldn't risk the others finding it first. Boky would use the book's power to create his communist utopia. He would strip away Russia's very soul and turn her into a country of mindless slaves.

Katya wouldn't do much better. She would use the book to dismantle the government and give the people freedom. That might sound good in theory, but it could never last. Katya would sow chaos and create even more death in a land already saturated by bloodshed.

Russia needed a tsarina, someone who had spent her entire life preparing for leadership. Natasha would use the book to carve out power for herself, but she wouldn't be an autocrat. Having been shaped by her liberal father as much as by Aunt

Sonya, Natasha envisioned a constitutional monarchy with her at the head, leading Russia into her next golden age.

All she had to do was find the book.

Svetlana had cut off the end of Yelezar Danilov's manuscript, the part that likely revealed where the *Volkhovnik* ended up after Stenka Razin's failed revolt. The clues to find it were likely given to Katya.

Natasha needed an alliance with Katya if she was to have any hope of finding the *Volkhovnik* before Boky did. That meant weakening Katya by isolating her

Dima Danilov had to die.

Then Natasha would be the only person Katya could turn to. After Dima's execution, Natasha would console Katya, befriend her, and – once they found the *Volkhovnik* – betray her in the end.

Natasha left her perch below the window, retracing her footsteps in the snow. Marius Smolensky waited in the shadows beyond the circle of birch trees. The skomorokha's wards were designed to keep unclean spirits at bay, so Smolensky hadn't been able to accompany Natasha to the house. His eyes had a lupine gleam as he watched her approach.

'Summon the pack,' Natasha ordered. 'We have work to do tonight.'

# Chapter 35
## *Dima*

The fire in the stove had dwindled by the time Valentina Pavlovna finished her story. Gusts of winter wind swept around the cottage and rustled the branches of the birch trees outside. Dima sat on the bench beside Katya. They'd each had two more shots of vodka. Now his blood felt pleasantly warm, his head light.

'So there you have it,' Valentina Pavlovna said, 'the story your mother wished for you to hear.'

'*The Book of the Wizard*,' Katya said reverently. 'I thought she'd given up on finding it.'

'I don't believe "giving up" were words in your mother's vocabulary,' Valentina Pavlovna said.

'True.'

Dima considered what this meant. His dedushka's research had led him to believe Stenka Razin came into possession of a powerful relic during one of his pirate raids. Could that be the *Volkhovnik*?

No wonder Dima had dreamed of Katya so many times. Yelezar Danilov's holy calling had been to record the deeds of his generation's hero, Stenka Razin. Perhaps that's why Dima had been drawn to Katya, a girl whose courage and determination were larger than life. If she found *The Book of the Wizard*, she could become one of the most significant figures in Russian history.

When he'd arrived on this island, Dima hoped to find a story worth telling.

He'd thought Yelezar's was the story he had been born to tell, but now he realised this was about something more than tracing the threads of events that happened long ago. The story Dima had been looking for was the one he and Katya were living right now.

'I've never heard the name Nikita Minin,' Katya said.

'No,' Valentina Pavlovna agreed. 'But you've likely heard of the man he became after stealing the *Volkhovnik* – Patriarch Nikon.'

'The *Volkhovnik* must be here on the archipelago.' Katya rose from the bench and started pacing, her expression settling into a fearsome look of concentration. 'Did she tell you anything else, like where she hid the last part of Yelezar Danilov's manuscript?'

'No, but she did give me a message to pass on to you.' Valentina Pavlovna smiled sadly. 'I'm supposed to say, "My little turtle."'

'Oh.' Katya's voice sounded pained. Her eyes glistened in the lamplight.

Dima resisted the urge to go to her, to wrap his arms around her to offer comfort. Katya being Katya, she took a steadying breath and pressed the grief deep inside herself.

Dima had seen who Katya was, had glimpsed her courageous soul. He didn't want to be forever outside her walls of self-protection. He wanted true fellowship, a meeting of souls – he wanted to be let in.

Instead of clouding his mind, the vodka seemed to have made everything clear. Katya's political affiliation didn't truly matter. She'd captivated him since that very first portrait.

Was it foolish to think that on this island of death and torment, they might find a bit of joy in one another? Was it too much to hope that Dima might experience love before his life was over?

'I'm turning in.' Valentina Pavlovna pressed a hand over her mouth to conceal a yawn. 'I believe the rest of the night belongs to you young people. I'm a deep sleeper, but feel free to put on the gramophone if you want more privacy. You'll find extra bedding in the trunk over there.'

As Valentina Pavlovna pointed to the trunk in the corner, she winked suggestively before climbing up to the sleeping platform above the stove. That piqued Dima's curiosity. The alcohol made his head swim when he stood up. Dima took a moment to steady himself before going to rifle through the trunk. Bed linens, blankets, a couple of pillows, and – *oh*.

'There's only one mattress.' Dima lifted it from the trunk and rolled it out on the floor. It was wide enough for one person. He rubbed the back of his neck, looking at the mattress and then at Katya. She stood with her arms crossed, shifting her weight from one foot to the other. Not wanting her to feel uncomfortable, Dima offered, 'I can sleep on the floor.'

'No,' she said, 'we'll share.'

Wondering how to interpret that, Dima studied Katya's face – the shadows accentuating her high cheekbones, the pointed chin, the full lips which she now worried with her teeth. She rubbed her arms, but she seemed more nervous than cold, especially as a rosy flush coloured her cheeks.

'I mean, we slept next to each other in the church, so there's no reason not to do so again,' she said. 'It doesn't have to mean anything.'

Dima watched her for a long moment. Then he said, 'What if I want it to mean something?'

Stepping towards Katya Dima let the heat of what he felt for her smoulder in his gaze. Her mouth dropped open in surprise, but she didn't back away. That encouraged Dima enough to keep going. 'I won't push you into something you're not ready for, but neither can I lie about what this is. All I want is to be near you.'

There it was. Dima had laid his heart wide open for Katya to either take or crush, but she stood frozen, her arms wrapped tight around herself. Dima sighed. Maybe the connection he'd imagined between them had been wishful thinking. Embarrassment coloured his cheeks. 'It's all right if you don't feel the same way.'

Katya closed her eyes. 'I'm afraid of what I feel for you.'

She took a shuddering breath. Even though she looked miserable, Dima couldn't suppress the relieved smile rising to his lips.

'I thought you were fearless.' He stepped forward and wrapped his arms around her back. Katya nuzzled his chest, still not opening her eyes.

'The people I care about die.' Her voice vibrated against his shirt.

'Everybody dies.'

'But I'm always the one left behind. I don't think I could survive that again.'

'What's the point of surviving if you're not going to live?' Dima tilted her chin up with his thumb. Hers was a life coated in the ashes of grief, grey with sorrow. How he wanted to paint colour into her soul again, if only she would let him. 'I think we both deserve whatever happiness we can find, for however many days we have left.'

Dima could see the fear in her eyes, but – Katya being Katya – she mustered enough courage to take Dima's face in her hands. Her touch was impossibly gentle, spreading sensation across his skin as her fingers slid along his jaw and then curled behind his neck. His arms were still wrapped around her back, but now he splayed his fingers over the fabric of her shirt. Dima pulled her closer. He felt her heart beating as rapidly as his own as she went up on her tiptoes and pressed her forehead to his.

Dima kissed her. And though their lips had been chapped by cold and thirst, the roughness made the sensation even more tender.

Dima trailed his fingers up Katya's spine and parted her lips with his tongue.

She let him in. Gratitude swelled inside his heart as her grip tightened on the back of his neck, as though desperate to have him closer. He obliged, pressing his body to hers until they were a tangle of limbs and lips. He kissed her as though he'd been drowning, and Katya was air.

They stumbled towards the mattress on the floor. Katya fisted his braces and shirt, pulling him along with her as she collapsed onto the mattress. Through their clothes he felt every curve of her body. He wanted to strip her bare. But he wouldn't. Not yet.

Dima didn't only want pleasure – he wanted connection.

Turning onto his side, he cradled Katya in his arms. Katya bit her lip as she met his gaze, their breaths mingling between them and their heartbeats echoing one another at their joined chests.

Dima kissed her forehead, her temple, the little cleft in her chin. He kissed along the line of her jaw and then down her throat, making her shiver.

'What are you thinking right now?' he whispered in her ear before kissing the tender spot behind it and burying his face in her golden hair. It smelled like smoke from the monastery, another reminder of all she had survived.

Katya's reply was drowned out by a strange sound filling the night, high and haunting.

A wolf's howl.

# Chapter 36

## *Katya*

Three more wolves joined the chorus. Though distant, their otherworldly howls wove a ghostly melody into the night. Katya inhaled shadows along with her breath. They teemed inside her, darkening her thoughts, chilling her blood.

She'd given in to her desire but hadn't been allowed even one full night with Dima. Perhaps she'd tempted fate. Maybe he'd be ripped away from her just like everyone she'd ever cared about.

*No.* Katya closed her hands into fists. She wouldn't let Boky touch him or the wolves come anywhere near. Rolling out of Dima's embrace, she pushed herself up to standing.

'Wake up,' she raised her voice to rouse Valentina Pavlovna, but her words were also for herself. *Wake up, Katya. Time for a fight.*

For once, she was a step ahead of Boky. She knew her mother had been searching for the *Volkhovnik.* If she could locate the end of Yelezar's manuscript, she might find its hiding place, and then . . .

So many possibilities came alive in Katya's mind. The Revolution was supposed to bring light and freedom to Russia, to push power downwards and give people hope. Maybe it wasn't too late. With *The Book of the Wizard*, Katya could empower the resistance and help the people take their country back from the regime of criminals who held it in an iron fist.

Valentina Pavlovna lit a kerosene lamp. Its flame melted the darkness and sent shadows fleeing to the corners of the room. She climbed down from the sleeping platform with the lamp held in one hand, her greying brown hair resting on her shoulder in a long plait.

A howl resounded through the forest, closer than before.

'We can't stay here,' Katya said.

'Wouldn't it be safer?' Dima asked. 'Brace some furniture against the door and wait them out?'

'No.' Valentina set down her lamp and lifted a hurricane lantern from a hook on the wall. She prepared the lantern for use, refilling the kerosene tank and trimming the wick. 'Volkolaki have a beast's instincts, but a man's intellect. My wards won't hold them back for ever, and once they have the place surrounded, there will be no way out.'

Katya thought through their options. They couldn't return to the monastery, nor could they stay here.

'We should go to the anarchists,' Katya decided aloud.

Dima froze. A shadowed look passed over his face.

'It's our best chance,' Katya said. 'I'll use a spell to cloak us – wolves can't carry talismans, after all. Once we reach the political prison, my allies will protect us.'

'I can't go there.' Dima's brown eyes darkened, gleaming in the lamplight like liquid ink. His brows drew together in a tortured grimace.

Katya put her shoulders back and raised her chin, posturing for a fight. But then she remembered. Dima's grandfather, mother, sister and brothers had all been executed by the Red Army, very likely by an anarchist.

'We could go to that abandoned cabin by the coast,' she offered.

With a relieved exhale, Dima nodded his agreement.

Valentina Pavlovna crossed the room and pulled two pairs of skis and ski poles from a storage trunk, offering them to Katya and Dima.

'Aren't you coming with us?' Katya asked.

'I'll distract them while you get away.'

'Come with us,' Katya said firmly. 'There's no reason for you to be a martyr.'

Valentina Pavlovna stepped toward Katya, kissing both her cheeks before giving her a stern look. 'I can handle myself.'

Again, a wolf howled, its baying voice raising the hair on Katya's arms. Valentina Pavlovna's eyes met Katya's one last time. 'Go. Now.'

Leaving her behind felt wrong, but they had no time to argue. Katya pulled on her coat. She wrapped her scarf around her neck and donned her gloves and hat.

'Thank you for everything,' Dima said.

Valentina Pavlovna smiled wistfully as she waved them towards the exit.

As soon as Dima opened the door, a blustery wind gusted through it. He clutched the hurricane lamp and forged into the wind's fury. Katya followed him outside. The cold struck her with force, stinging her eyes and numbing her face instantly. She shivered as she attached the skis to her boots and used the poles to propel herself away from the *izba*.

They paused just beyond the circle of birch trees for Katya to cast a spell. She focused her thoughts on anything a wolf might follow – the scents of their bodies, the tracks of their skis, the smell of kerosene and the light of their lantern. Then she cast her cloaking spell to conceal them from their enemies' senses.

'*Krypton pros panta omma to blapton emas.*' Katya's breath steamed, and the cold crept down her throat as she spoke.

Wind blistered her lips, but she pushed all discomfort to the back of her mind and focused. *'Siopilon pros pav ous akouon en kake gnome. Akhyron pros ten rhina zetounta emas.'*

Her words wrapped around them like a cloak, allowing them to move through the forest unseen, untracked, unfollowed.

Pressing on, they skied through forests and over winter-hardened marshes, struggling in places the wind had piled the snow in deep banks. Finally they reached a canal where their skis glided over the snow-covered ice with little effort. They used their poles as spikes to keep from slipping.

When the canal opened up into a frozen lake, they paused to catch their breath and find their bearings.

'Which way?' Katya asked, her teeth clattering.

Shielding his face from the wind, Dima tried to gauge their direction, but low clouds concealed the stars. Beyond the lantern's radius of light, the darkness was impenetrable. They didn't have a compass, and sunrise might be hours away.

A howl rose in the far distance, its mournful cry carried to them on a gust of wind. Katya's concealment spell had worked. But though they were safe from fang and claw, the cold had a bite just as deadly. She could feel it already, the chill spreading through her veins like poison. Fatigue weighed heavy on her quaking shoulders, and her heartbeat weakened with every pulse.

Dima thrust a pole into the ice and pushed himself towards Katya, carefully interlocking their skis. He held his poles and the lantern in one hand and rubbed her arm with the other to stimulate blood circulation.

'I'll try a finding spell.' Katya shouted to be heard over the wind, and Dima nodded his agreement.

Snow began to fall.

Katya took a steadying breath, trying to calm her shivering

enough to focus on a spell that would lead them to the cabin.

From the darkness of the trees beside them, something growled.

Katya's heart skipped a beat when two yellow eyes gleamed out of the shadows. An enormous grey wolf prowled towards them, teeth bared. Katya's mind reached for the threads of her cloaking spell, but she couldn't find them. The effects of the cold had distracted her, and she'd let her spell slip.

The volkolaki had been quick to track them. Two more sets of eyes gleamed out of the night-dark forest.

'Take off your skis,' Dima ordered. He bent over and started removing his. Katya followed his lead, unstrapping the skis from her boots. When she straightened, Dima pressed the lantern's handle into her gloved hand. His eyes were wide with adrenaline, almost feral. 'I'll distract the wolves while you get yourself up a tree.'

'That's a terrible plan!'

'I'll be right behind you. Unless you can think of something better?'

Katya couldn't think at all. She should use another spell, but the onset of hypothermia had made her thoughts sluggish.

'Go,' he shouted. 'Run!'

She moved as fast as she could, struggling through deep snow. Dima followed after her, walking backwards as he wielded a ski pole like a bat. The wolves prowled towards him. Katya had to hurry. Once she got into a tree, she'd try to think of a spell to help Dima. She raced towards the edge of the clearing and the trees beyond. Their snow-laden branches made sinister shadows in the lantern light.

The pines and spruces didn't have sturdy enough branches for her to perch on, so it would have to be a birch tree. But how would she get up one without a rope? Katya threw her arms around a white-barked birch and tried to climb, but without hand or footholds, she slid back down. Her breathing became panicked as she darted between the trees, swinging the lantern as she looked for one to climb.

A yelp resounded through the forest. Dima must have attacked one of the volkolaki with the pole. She glanced over her shoulder. Instead of spotting Dima, she saw a wolf prowl towards her. A growl rose from low in its throat.

Katya swung the lantern at the volkolak. With a smash of glass, the flaming oil sprayed over the wolf's face and neck. It yelped and bounded away, the smell of singed fur filling the night.

Katya pushed herself up. Three more sets of eyes glowed out of the trees.

Katya couldn't get herself up a tree, and it seemed the wolves were after her, not Dima. Maybe she could save him by drawing them away.

Katya ran. Her breath puffed like smokestacks and the cold air ached inside her chest, but she pushed herself faster. She threaded through the forest with the volkolaki on her heels. When a growling wolf leaped in front of her, Katya was forced to change direction.

She came to a frozen lake. Ice creaked beneath her boots as she sprinted through snow. Rather than continuing when the lake stretched out into a canal, she scrambled up the far bank, fingers trembling as she caught a bendy young tree and hauled herself up.

Darkness settled around her as she entered the canopy of the forest again. Katya's breaths turned to gasps as she pushed her body to its limit. She ran beneath pine needles and shrouded moonlight, through cramping muscles and exhaustion.

She ran until she stumbled upon a cabin. Its windows glowed

with welcoming orange light. Katya paused in the clearing before it, trying to catch her breath. Was this the cabin by the coast where they'd brought the book?

A growl sounded behind her.

Breath steamed through Katya's lips, and the night surrounded her like a cloak of danger. As death prowled out of the forest in the form of three enormous wolves, Katya didn't have a chance. They'd catch her, and they'd kill her.

Katya rallied whatever strength she had left, channelling it into one last, desperate sprint.

She sucked in a breath and shouted, 'Help!' to the person inside the cabin. Then she dashed forward like prey. The wolves gave chase. The door to the cabin opened, and a woman stepped onto the threshold.

*Natasha.*

Raising her hands to the sky, Natasha began to chant. The air shifted violently. A flash blinded Katya, and she was thrown forward. She scraped her palms and cheek as she slid across the ground. A wolf yelped and whimpered. Another growled. Katya lay in the snow – breath panting, heart pounding. What had happened? She couldn't lift her head.

Moments later, Natasha stood over her, grunting with effort as she flipped Katya onto her back. A line of unnaturally blue flames separated them from the wolves. Without a word Natasha grabbed the shoulders of Katya's coat and dragged her across into the cabin, kicking the door shut behind them.

# PART III

---

## *Alliances*

# *Reflection*

```
        WHEN YOU LOOK
      IN THE MIRROR, DO YOU
     MEET YOUR OWN EYES? IS IT
   NOT PAINFUL TO SEE THOSE LIPS
  THAT KEPT SILENT, OR THOSE EYES
 THAT TURNED THE OTHER WAY? DO YOU
 ACHE INSIDE, OR IS YOUR CONSCIENCE
 SCABBED TO THE POINT OF NUMBNESS?
 SINCE YOU SHIED FROM THE PAINFUL
 TRUTHS, CAN YOU SLEEP UPON THOSE
 LIES YOU TRADED THEM FOR? CAN YOU
 STILL RECOGNISE YOUR FACE? IS THIS
WHO YOU IMAGINED YOU WOULD BE WHEN
  YOU WERE A CHILD? OR HAS THE SHAME
   DIMINISHED YOU, MADE YOU INTO
   A SHADOW OF YOUR OLD SELF? DO
     YOU EVER THINK ABOUT TRYING
       TO MAKE A DIFFERENCE? ARE
        YOU COMFORTABLE SHIFTING
         BLAME? AREN'T YOU
          ASHAMED THAT YOUR
          REFLECTION IN THE
         GLASS REVEALS A SOUL
       SHRIVELED UP WITH FEAR?
```

```
        WHEN YOU LOOK
      IN THE MIRROR, DO YOU
     HOLD YOUR HEAD HIGH? DOES
    THAT FIRE IN YOUR EYES BLAZE
   AGAINST INJUSTICE? DO YOUR LIPS
  SPEAK TRUTH, EVEN WHEN IT HURTS?
  IS YOUR CHIN RAISED, YOUR JAW SET?
 WHEN SOMEONE NEEDS HELP, DOES YOUR
  HAND REACH OUT? WILL YOU STAND UP
  FOR WHAT IS RIGHT, EVEN WHEN IT'S
 DANGEROUS TO DO SO? DON'T YOU WEAR
THOSE BRUISES AS BADGES OF HONOUR?
 DO YOU SLEEP SOUNDLY, KNOWING THAT
YOU DID SOME GOOD IN THE WORLD? DO
  YOU HOLD FAST TO YOUR HUMANITY
   BY REFUSING TO PARTICIPATE IN
   CRUELTY TOWARD OTHERS? DOES
     YOUR HEART BEAT IN RHYTHM
       WITH A SONG OF FREEDOM?
        DO YOU KNOW YOU'RE
          BLESSED THAT YOUR
          REFLECTION IN THE
         GLASS REVEALS A SOUL
       GLORIOUS WITH COURAGE?
```

# Chapter 37
## *Natasha*

Windblown strands of auburn hair framed Natasha's face with fire-like wisps as she stood over her enemy, unable to hold in a smile of victory.

Katya lay panting on the floor, bleeding and barely conscious.

With her body already emaciated, the chase through the forest had taken a hard toll, but at least she was here. Natasha would nurse Katya back to health and then extract the information she needed to find the *Volkhovnik*.

Natasha built up the fire. Filling a pot with snow, she melted it over the flames. Then she knelt beside Katya and dipped a cloth in the warm water. She gently dabbed the cloth against Katya's cheek, which had been sliced open when Katya slid across the ice.

Blood oozed from the wound. The pain must have cut through Katya's dizziness, for her bleary eyes focused. Seeing Natasha, Katya flinched away.

'Do you want me to stop your bleeding or not?' Natasha's pointy chin jutted out as she waved the cloth before Katya's eyes.

'I'm . . . bleeding?' Katya touched her cheek and tried to examine her blood-stained fingertips, but her eyes lost focus. They rolled to the back of her head as she fell unconscious.

Natasha stared at her for a long moment, her enemy helpless before her. Natasha could slit Katya's throat right now. Or she could curse her. She could make this Katya's last day on earth.

She'd fantasised about this exact situation dozens of times. Unfortunately, she needed Katya alive.

She appeased her resentment by roughly scrubbing the grime from Katya's skin and pressing her wounds with more force than was needed to staunch the bleeding. Then she left Katya lying on the bare floor before the fire, not even bothering to put a cushion beneath her head.

The bruises and aches she'd wake up with were the least of what Katya deserved.

With Katya passed out, Natasha took the opportunity to inspect the contents of her school bag.

Natasha made the mistake of opening Katya's poetry diary and reading from the beginning. The words seeped off the page, flooding Natasha with a torrent of emotions. The poetry carried Natasha along unfamiliar currents, navigating Katya's longings, hopes and fears.

What must it be like to feel so much?

Natasha knew how to mimic emotions, but reading the intensity of Katya's feelings made her aware of her own counterfeit. Natasha had been a lonely child raised by an aunt with steel in her veins. Instead of love, she'd been given expectations. Natasha's emotions had been carved out of her with surgical precision, as she was groomed for greatness, taught to be ruthless.

It surprised Natasha to see so many mirrors in Katya's words, especially when she wrote of her aching loneliness and the fear of never living up to her mother's expectations. One line in particular shook Natasha, an earthquake inside her skin.

*How long can I wear the mask she wants to see without forgetting who I am?*

Natasha used to ask herself that very question. Now she'd worn Aunt Sonya's preferred mask for so long it had melded to her face. Katya's words spoke life to the lost and lonely girl Natasha had buried long ago. Natasha slammed the poetry book closed, uncomfortable with the sensation of bones rattling in her psyche, flesh and sinew returning to pieces of herself that were better off dead.

Awakening emotion would weaken Natasha when she most needed to be strong.

Biting her lip in determination, Natasha opened the book again. This time she flipped to the pages Katya had used to try and decode her mother's cipher.

Katya cracked the first code using a nihilist cipher and the second layer of encryption with the Vigenère. There was one more cipher that Katya hadn't decoded – perhaps its solution would lead to *The Book of the Wizard*.

'Wake up.' Natasha poked Katya's ribs with the toe of her boot.

Katya moaned. Pain and exhaustion were apparent in her voice, but Natasha was done waiting. She prodded Katya again, harder this time.

Katya's eyes blinked open. She startled when she saw Natasha. Then she attempted to sit up.

'I wouldn't do that if I were you,' Natasha warned.

Katya stubbornly ignored the advice, even though she had to hold her forehead when her vision swam. She scooted against the cabin wall and propped herself against it to keep from toppling over.

'What happened?' Katya asked.

'You were being chased by three volkolaki,' Natasha said. 'I saved your life.'

That wasn't technically true. The wolves' instructions were

to separate Katya from Dima and herd her to the cabin. Katya didn't have to know that, though. Natasha had conjured a line of blue flames to give the illusion of her magic holding the beasts at bay.

'What have you been doing here the whole time?' Katya asked, looking around the cabin.

'Keeping my end of the bargain.' Natasha motioned towards the desk. 'I've translated the book.'

'We don't have a bargain.'

'I'd rethink that if I were you.' Natasha's voice deepened. The shadows within her darkened her gaze. 'Do you have any idea what will happen to Russia if Boky finds the *Volkhovnik* before one of us does?'

Katya paled at Natasha's mention of the *Volkhovnik*.

'Yes, I know all about *The Book of the Wizard,*' Natasha said.

Katya studied the room, her gaze trailing from the herbs hung drying from the rafters to the scattered contents of her school bag and the poetry diary open to the page where she'd attempted to solve Svetlana's cipher.

Her eyes narrowed into two blades of suspicion as she turned back to Natasha 'Who are you?'

'That's still the wrong question. Who I am doesn't matter.'

'It matters to me.' Katya crossed her arms, creating another barrier between them. 'I won't work with someone who lies about their name.'

'Bobrinskaya was my mother's name, so it wasn't really a lie.'

'Who was your father?'

'Who was *yours*?' Some of Natasha's simmering rage boiled into her voice. She raised an eyebrow, daring Katya to answer.

Katya sighed. She looked unspeakably tired – tired of secrets, tired of lies, tired of conversations that felt like battle.

'Forget I asked.' Katya took off her coat, rolled it in a bundle and lied down on it. She pinched the bridge of her nose, closing her eyes against a pounding headache.

Natasha's resentment was only widening the gaps between them. She should be building bridges.

'Do you want to know what they made me do in the lab?' she asked.

Katya sighed again. She draped an arm over her face to block out the firelight and muttered, 'Why not?'

Natasha hesitated so long that Katya cracked an eye open. Natasha licked her lips and combed her hair back with her fingers. She was usually unflappable, but she had to muster courage to brave this topic.

'The wolves. They used me to make volkolaki. At first the ritual didn't work. I hoped they'd give up on the idea, but Boky discovered the missing ingredient was human sacrifice.'

Katya didn't react, but Natasha could tell by her stillness that she was listening.

'I killed a man for every volkolak I created. And five others in failed attempts.'

There was a long beat of silence, broken only by the crackle of flames in the hearth and the roar of the wind outside.

'You did what you had to,' Katya said at last. 'At least that's what I try to tell myself.'

When Natasha saw the haunted look cross Katya's face, she thought perhaps they had more in common than lonely childhoods and demanding mother figures.

'There's something I've been wondering about since we came to Solovki,' Natasha said. 'Why were you so emaciated?'

She seemed to have had a very different experience than Natasha, who was given every comfort for the cage they kept her in.

'They withheld food and sleep whenever I refused to

co-operate, which . . . I resisted whenever I could, for as long as I was able to hold out.'

'Barchenko must have *loved* you.' Despite herself, Natasha felt a grudging admiration for the anarchist. She delighted in the image of that meaty old fraud banging his head against the fortress that was Yekaterina Efremova. 'Did you know that *Doctor* Barchenko never even went to medical school?'

'What?' Katya propped herself up on her elbow.

'He's a science fiction novelist. I found three of his books when I searched Boky's desk.'

Katya's eyes widened. She stared at Natasha for a long moment, and then she did the last thing Natasha expected. Katya laughed. At first she giggled, covering her eyes with her hand. Soon she bent over with laughter, guffawing so hard her whole body shook.

Natasha didn't know why, but laughter bubbled up inside her too. She put a hand over her lips but couldn't contain it. It felt like a purging, the horrors of the lab turned from a heavy weight in her soul into an object of ridicule. Several moments passed before they emptied themselves of hilarity, their laughter spent. Katya held her belly and wiped her tears with her sleeve.

A companionable silence fell over them.

'Why do you want to be my ally?' Katya asked.

Natasha bit her lip and looked away, thinking. Her voice went low when she spoke at last, threading enough truth into her words as to be convincing.

'Earlier, you said I did what I had to for survival. I've told myself the same thing a thousand times, but I didn't resist like you did. I made myself useful, invaluable – and I've hated myself every moment since. That's why I want to be part of whatever you're planning. It's high time I became a problem for them, too.'

Katya stared at Natasha for a long moment as though searching for some sign of deception. She must not have found one, for she extended her hand.

'I don't trust you,' she said. 'But I think we could help each other. Allies?'

'Allies,' Natasha said as they shook on it.

# Chapter 38
## *Katya*

Katya's flight through the forest had pushed her body beyond the brink, and it took several days to recover. She slept through long winter nights, rousing herself for the food Natasha brought from the monastery before succumbing to exhaustion once again.

Though Natasha urged her to concentrate on the cipher, Katya immersed herself in reading the translation of Yelezar's book, which distracted her from worrying about what had happened to Dima that night in the forest. She'd led the wolves away from him, so why hadn't he come to the cabin like they'd planned?

That question offered too many possible answers, none of them good.

To keep from imagining them, she turned her thoughts to the distant past. The Russian government in Stenka Razin's time was as oppressive as the Bolsheviki, if not even more so. Rather than throwing up his hands and calling the situation hopeless, Stenka did what he could to make things better.

Stenka was one man, but he inspired a movement that nearly toppled the tsar. Tens of thousands of peasants took up their shovels, axes and staves, following Stenka Razin up the Volga River towards Moscow.

Who was to say that couldn't happen again? Russia would only be too far gone when her sons and daughters stopped contending for her future.

Closing her eyes, Katya let those ideas burn like hot iron within her – searing her conscience, insisting she remember who she was. Her mother had been imprisoned or exiled four times before the Revolution, yet she never gave up fighting for what she believed to be right.

It was time to start acting like Svetlana's daughter.

Katya got up and paced the tiny cabin like a caged lioness, her roar stuck in her throat and her claws useless against an enemy she could not reach.

Boky wouldn't have been idle for all those days she spent resting. He was out there on the island, searching for the *Volkhovnik*.

Katya had to find it first.

The last section of the book had been cut off, and those final pages must hold the secret of what happened to the *Volkhovnik* after Razin's rebellion.

Where would Svetlana have hidden them?

Katya had solved most of the clues Svetlana left for her. 'Listen to the whisper of stars' combined with the blood-marked pages had led Katya to Valentina Pavlovna.

Then there was the lemon ink clue.

*1436*
келья

ГЦЪШРФЭИИГТСНЙБНБОМА

The first three lines had been intended to guide Katya to the map of the labyrinths and Yelezar Danilov's hidden manuscript.

What was that final line for?

Katya continued pacing as she unfolded the paper with her *tabula recta*. Could one of the keywords she'd tried with the other code work as a solution to this one?

Natasha sat down at the table, her red hair spilling around her as she finalised translations. She gave a little sigh of annoyance when Katya stalked past her for the twentieth time.

'I think I liked it better when you slept all day,' she grumbled.

'You were right,' Katya said. 'I need to concentrate on the cipher. And we need to make a plan.'

Natasha sighed again and pushed the curtain of her hair back so Katya could see the irritation radiating from her eyes. 'I have one.'

Katya stopped pacing. 'What is it?'

'You'll find out soon enough.' Natasha waved dismissively, then went back to writing.

'That's not how this works.' Katya flexed her fingers, annoyed by Natasha's vagueness. 'You said you wanted to be part of what I'm planning, that we would bring down the Bolsheviki together. So why are you still keeping secrets?'

'Maybe I don't want to spoil the surprise.' Eyes unblinking Natasha tilted her head to an odd angle. 'Plans, schemes – so many mysteries hidden in here.' She tapped a gnawed fingernail to her temple.

Natasha stood and shrugged on her coat. A gust of freezing wind swept into the cabin as she stepped out into the snowy night and disappeared into the forest without another word.

Katya let out a frustrated groan.

Maybe she'd made a mistake teaming up with Natasha, if that was even her real name.

It had seemed like the right choice at the time. Katya had only needed rest when she came to the cabin, and reading Yelezar's story had been important – Svetlana wanted Katya to find it for a reason.

Katya didn't trust Natasha, however, and she had no intention of waiting around to be let in on Natasha's plans. She spread her paper open on the table and set to work trying to solve the final cipher.

# Chapter 39
## *Dima*

Dima and Yelezar stood at the bow of the River Wolves' flagship, looking out at an endless sea. Dima closed his eyes, savouring the freedom of flapping sails, screeching gulls, and the salt-spray coating his skin in brine.

'It's so warm here.' Dima opened his arms to bask in sunrays.

Yelezar was uncharacteristically quiet. Cracking an eye open, Dima studied him with a sideways look. His ancestor had matured from the excitable cub of a boy who first met Stenka Razin, but he was rarely so still and thoughtful.

'You've been dreaming for a long time.' Yelezar rubbed his chin, his eyes troubled. 'Not as long as I have, of course, but . . . don't you think you ought to wake up?'

At Yelezar's words, the sun dimmed. A chill seeped into Dima's hands and feet, becoming colder every moment. When Dima exhaled, his breath steamed.

'I want to stay.' Dima reached for the ship's railing. He held it tight, feeling the textured wood beneath his fingertips and willing it to be real. 'It's warm here.'

'We're not meant to live in the past.' Yelezar leaned on the railing, looking at Dima over his shoulder.

Why shouldn't he live in the past, seeing as he had no future?

Forming the question made him recall his existence outside

of this pleasant dream. He remembered climbing a tree and perching in the branches as wolves circled below – just as Yelezar had done when Dima first met him. Except it had been cold where Dima was. No, not cold – freezing. Stinging skin and numb fingers, violent shivers wracking his body as he struggled to hold onto the branch.

Then the shivering had subsided. His thoughts became as sluggish as his heartbeat. Trying to keep his eyes open had made Dima feel like Atlas bearing the weight of the world. Closing them was the last thing he remembered before he came here.

He was inclined to stay, dreaming alongside Yelezar.

Then he remembered Katya.

She'd run away with wolves at her heels, but had she escaped?

'How do I go back?' Dima asked.

'If I knew that, I wouldn't be here.' Yelezar smiled sadly. 'But it looks to me like you're already waking up.'

Dima held up his hand. His fingers were fading, becoming more and more transparent each moment as an otherworldly blue light spread over his skin. The cold sharpened until his limbs ached and his lungs burned with it.

Waking up with a gasp Dima found himself in a night-dark forest. His head pounded and his body felt sore from shivering. Lying in a bank of snow, he looked up at the twining birch tree he'd climbed to escape the wolves.

Had he fallen from the branches?

Examining himself for injuries, Dima gasped. His skin glowed with that same blue light as in his dream. The radiance quickly faded, dimming with every languid beat of his heart.

Dima sat up, brushing snow from his clothes. All around him, the forest was black and grey, the shapes of trees silhouetted in starlight. No sign of the wolves. Or of Katya. Pristine snow surrounded him – not a foot or paw print in sight.

It must have snowed a great deal while Dima slept for all the tracks to have been covered over.

Though Dima had felt pleasantly warm when he awoke, the cold soon nipped at his fingers and toes. Strange that he didn't freeze to death in his sleep. Dima decided it must be a peculiarity of his magic. One thing was certain: now that he'd woken, he'd need shelter. Then he had to find Katya.

Staggering to his feet, Dima wrapped his scarf over his nose and tucked his hands under his armpits to warm them. Which way had Katya run? He scanned the forest, but darkness cloaked potential landmarks.

Voices filtered through the trees along with a multitude of footsteps crunching over snow. Dima stumbled towards the sounds, struggling through the knee-deep drifts. Soon he spotted lanterns in the distance. Pushing aside snow-laden boughs, he stepped into the open.

A group of prisoners marched over a frozen canal, flanked by guards.

If Dima joined them, he'd eventually find his way back to civilization – except they were likely on their way out to the forest for the day's work. Dima wouldn't last ten hours in the freezing cold. Better to let them pass and find shelter on his own.

Dima stepped back, aiming for the cover of the trees. His foot slipped out from under him. With a yelp, he toppled forwards and slid down the embankment, landing hard on the ice of the canal.

'Get back in line,' one of the guards shouted.

Dima winced, holding his throbbing arm as he stood up. With no other choice but to fall in with the group, Dima put his head down and trudged along with them.

A time later, the wind picked up. The cold stung Dima's eyes, so he squinted while trying to get his bearings. They were out of the canal system, crossing a frozen lake. Ahead of them, the shadowed towers of the monastery filled the horizon.

He'd been wrong. The prisoners weren't starting their work day but rather heading back at the end of it. How was that possible? Dima couldn't have slept all night *and* day, could he?

Dima followed the group through the Nikolski Gate and lined up for soup rations, eager for something warm in his belly.

'Dima, is that you?' Father Iosef stood on the far side of the counter, distributing soup along with two other monks. He filled Dima's cup, then set down the ladle and joined Dima at the end of the line. 'Glory to God. We thought you'd been killed or transferred to the punishment cells of Sekirka.'

'I'm surprised anyone noticed I was missing.' Dima's fingers trembled as he lifted the cup to his cracked lips. He took a long sip, the soup warming him as he drank it down.

'Of course we noticed. You've been gone for three days.'

Dima choked on the soup. A coughing fit overtook him. His eyes watered and his mind reeled. Three days? Father Iosef must be mistaken.

'What day is it?' He asked between coughs.

'The twenty-fourth of December,' Father Iosef said.

Dima thought of the blue glow radiating from his skin when he awoke and of Yelezar's comment that Dima had been dreaming a long time.

Did his skomorokh magic keep him from freezing as his soul drifted into the Otherworld, like some kind of supernatural hibernation?

When Dima closed his eyes, a memory from midwinter night haunted him – Katya running for her life with wolves on her heels. Whatever had happened to her after that, Dima was too late to help.

'Have you heard anything about Yekaterina Efremova?' Dima clutched his soup cup in a fist, as though holding on tight to something might prevent grief from sweeping him away.

'Efremova?' The monk's face curdled.

'She's Svetlana's daughter,' Dima said, remembering too late how barbed Katya's surname would be for Father Iosef. 'But she's a good person and my friend. I'm worried about her.'

'I haven't heard anything.' Father Iosef put an arm around Dima's shoulder and guided him away. 'Why don't I take you to the infirmary so Doctor Tarasov can look you over? You're shivering and your face . . . it doesn't look good. Maybe one of the nurses will know something about your friend.'

So many prisoners had been felled by typhoid that sickbeds now lined the floor of the corridor outside the infirmary. Pale and moaning men lay shoulder to shoulder. The infirmary itself was just as bad. Every bed was full, and pallets had been laid out in the spaces between them.

When Dima and Father Iosef entered, they found Doctor Tarasov standing beside a patient, helping him drink. The doctor looked almost as bad as the sick man – pale-faced with dark circles gathering under his red-rimmed eyes.

He glanced up when he heard them and nodded in greeting.

'We may have a case of frostbite,' Father Iosef said.

'Right.' Doctor Tarasov gave a world-weary sigh. 'Have a seat in the office, Dima. I'll have my nurse look at it.'

Father Iosef took his leave, offering to go collect snow for the cold compresses Doctor Tarasov needed to treat the fevered men. Dima thanked them both and stepped into the small office attached to the infirmary that contained a cluttered desk and the bed Doctor Tarasov slept in.

A framed photograph sat atop of the desk. Doctor Tarasov had a wife and two young daughters.

Among the doctor's scattered papers, Dima found three copies of the art he and Katya created on midwinter night. Someone must have finished the job of printing them. Dima's fingers were stiff as he reached for a copy, amazed at what he and Katya had created together.

His recollection of that night had a hazy quality, like a dream – one that had too quickly turned into a nightmare.

'Where are you, Katya?' he asked the empty room.

'Hello again, Dmitri.' The nurse came in, carrying a bucket and a steaming kettle.

Dima recognised her as Katya's friend, the Georgian countess married to a Mexican ambassador.

Tsisana set down the bucket and kettle, then put her hands on her hips. 'I'd say I'm happy to see you again, but actually I was rather put out by your and Katya's disappearing act. It's cruel to make people wonder what happened. I was equal parts relieved and furious when her message came.'

'You heard from her?' Dima surged to his feet in his eagerness for news. 'Is she all right?'

'She's fine.' Tsisana assured him. 'Sit down, Dima. Let's see if I can send you back to her with all your fingers and toes intact.'

Tsisana set the kettle and bucket atop of the desk. Reaching for Dima's chin, she turned his face from one side to the other as she examined his nose.

'Not nearly as bad as it could be. Let's see your fingers.'

When Dima took off his gloves, Tsisana winced. Dima's hands were red except for the fingers, which had turned white in flaky patches.

'Right,' she said, as though bracing herself for an unpleasant task. 'I won't know how bad it is until we warm you up.'

She placed his hands in the bucket of lukewarm water, gradually warming them. Bringing in a second bucket, Tsisana gave his feet the same treatment. Once the cold had been driven from his extremities, she bandaged his fingers and toes one by one. Then she laid out a pallet on the floor by the desk, ordering him to rest.

Dima shouldn't have been tired after dreaming for three days, but the pleasant warmth spreading through him brought drowsiness along with it. His eyes grew heavy, and he soon drifted off into a dreamless sleep.

The next day, after Doctor Tarasov rolled out of bed to begin his rounds, Dima unwrapped his bandaged hands, finding raw, pink skin and several blisters forming on his fingertips. It would heal, though.

'How are you feeling?' Tsisana asked as she glided into the office.

'Much better.'

Seeing his bare hands, she tsked and immediately set herself to the task of wrapping his blistered fingers. Then she smiled at him, excitement dancing in her big brown eyes.

'I have a surprise for you. Put on your coat.' She clapped her hands like a drill commander and issued orders. 'Also your gloves, scarf and hat.'

When Dima was appropriately bundled, Tsisana hooked their elbows and near-dragged him out the door and through the infirmary. A layer of fresh snow blanketed the monastery. They followed a shovelled path to the gate leading to the lake harbour.

Tsisana's husband leaned against the dock's railing, chatting animatedly with two prison guards. Rafael wore an impeccably tailored double-breasted overcoat and a dazzling smile. With their forgotten rifles hanging ineffectually from their shoulder straps, the guards laughed at something Rafael had said.

'Ah, *mi amor!*' Rafael's face changed when he noticed Tsisana – shifting from the charming grin he projected to the guards to something softer. True affection shone out of his brown eyes, and the countess basked in the glow of his love for her as she stepped into his embrace.

He kissed the top of her head, and then offered Dima a friendly nod of greeting.

'We'll be going now,' Rafael told the guards, 'but here's a little token of my thanks.' Pulling two silver coins from his pocket, he used his thumb to flick them in the air, one towards each guard. Catching the coins, the men's eyes glazed over and took on a dreamy quality.

'Thank you, sir,' they both said in unison.

'It's my absolute pleasure,' said Rafael. 'Just remember, you never saw us leave.'

The guards nodded emphatically as Rafael laced Tsisana's arm through his and led her onward.

'Did you just cast a spell on them?' Dima eyed the dazed guards as he followed the couple along the snow-covered dock.

'It's his charm.' Tsisana explained. 'When he uses it, people do just about anything he wants.'

'But I never use it on you, darling.' Rafael kissed Tsisana's gloved hand.

'You never *have* to use it on me because I'm already thoroughly charmed,' she said, then turned to address Dima. 'The influence of his charm wears off when he's no longer in someone's presence, but the coins are charmed too. As long as the guards hold onto them, they'll do everything Rafael asked them to.'

'I'm surprised your charms worked,' Dima said. 'Katya told me most of the guards carry protective talismans.'

'You mean these?' Rafael pulled two beaded circlets out of his coat pocket and grinned.

'Did you steal those?' Tsisana smacked his arm. 'You promised me no more pickpocketing.'

'But I also promised we'd celebrate Christmas together. For that I had to charm the guards, no?'

Tsisana looked mildly appeased.

'We're celebrating Christmas?' Dima asked.

'I told you I had a good surprise.' Tsisana motioned towards the end of the dock.

When he walked out to the end of it, Dima saw two teams of huskies harnessed to sleds on the frozen lake. Andrei Sergeevich and Matilda Ivanova were bickering as they tried to situate two bags full of supplies into the sleds while leaving room for passengers.

'Not like that,' Matilda Ivanova scolded him. 'Turn it clockwise.'

'You're welcome to do this by yourself,' Andrei Sergeevich retorted with a huff, though he turned it the way Matilda Ivanova suggested.

'Is everything ready?' asked an impatient, feminine voice.

Dima turned to find Natasha striding towards him on the dock, her red hair tucked inside a fur hat. She stopped in her tracks when she saw Dima. All the blood drained from her face, making her freckles stand out in stark contrast.

'What is he doing here?' Her voice sounded strangled, and her eyes widened as though she'd seen a ghost.

'If you didn't want him to come, you should have specified that yesterday.' Tsisana hooked her arm through Dima's. 'Let's go.'

Natasha's lips thinned. Her eyes narrowed as she watched Dima and Tsisana stroll to the end of the dock. Her expression spoke of fear and hatred, but why? Dima didn't think he'd done anything to deserve such hostility.

When they climbed down from the dock, Dima greeted Andrei Sergeevich with a handshake and Matilda Ivanova with a kiss on her wrinkled cheek before taking a seat in one of the dog sleds. Tsisana took the place in front of him with a bag of supplies on her lap.

Rafael stepped onto the runners. Would a Mexican ambassador know how to drive a dog sled? Dima had only a moment to worry about this before Rafael shouted a command. The dogs took off and Tsisana was thrown back against Dima's knees. She laughed with delight as they glided over the frozen lake.

# Chapter 40

## *Katya*

Katya felt a tug in her spirit, a familiar yearning that could only be a poem begging to be written. She brushed her fingertips over the stack of blank papers Natasha left on the table when she went out yesterday.

Usually when Katya had a poem inside her, she worked in a frenzy, often forgetting to eat or sleep. Until it was completed, the poem consumed her.

This felt different – a gentle unfolding, like the opening of petals to the sun.

Before the printing room on midwinter night, Katya had only ever poured out her heart in her diary. Perhaps these blank pages could hold a different kind of poem – the epic poem Katya promised to write with Dima.

In careful handwriting, she titled it after Yelezar's book, *The Chief of Beggars*.

Then she thought of the storm the night Stenka Razin was born, summoning words into her mind. Rather than jotting them down as they came to her, she took the time to shape them into iambic tetrameter.

> One night upon the wildest steppe
> The winds were raging with a storm

As roofs were ripped from overhead
Upon a gust, a child was born

Leaning back to let the ink dry, Katya read the words aloud. Then she smiled, imagining Dima's expression when he read them.

Katya continued writing as the brief daylight began to fade.

She was startled by the sound of a barking dog. Katya clutched her chest as memories of the firing squad behind the women's barrack summoned ghosts. Fear spread up her spine, and she couldn't breathe for a moment.

She listened and heard more barks, then a high-pitched yip. That wasn't a single dog, but a team.

Katya hurried to the window, her breath fogging the glass. The south-western sky had faded to a murky grey, but Katya could just make out the shapes of the dog team, the sled and the people climbing off it. Instead of marching purposefully towards her like soldiers would, they bumbled about.

Natasha was the first to approach the cabin, a triumphant smile on her face.

'What is this?' Katya asked.

'I told you I had a plan.' Natasha bumped her shoulder as she pushed past her into the cottage. Katya froze at a familiar scent – wind, soil, pine, snow. Why did Natasha smell like Commissar Boky?

A suspicion unfurled inside her as she considered where Natasha had slept last night.

Katya set that thought aside as Dima approached, rosy-cheeked and bright-eyed in the cold. She let out a long exhale, releasing all the worries she'd held in her heart the past few days. He was all right.

There was an odd intimacy in their eyes meeting across the threshold.

Katya couldn't pinpoint the moment he'd stopped being a stranger. It happened gradually, but the warmth she felt while looking at him filled her up inside. Katya couldn't keep the sparkle from her eyes or her lips from curling upwards.

His answering smile, slow and sensual, turned the warmth inside her to heat.

Keeping to superstition, he avoided bad luck by stepping over the threshold before greeting Katya with a kiss on either cheek. Though they were chaste, the kind of kisses one gives to a cousin or aunt, the touch sent a shiver through Katya. She felt the vibration of his voice move through her cheek as he said, 'Happy Christmas.'

'Christmas?' As Katya counted the days she'd been here, she realised he was right. The Bolksheviki had changed the calendar after the Revolution and Christmas now officially fell in January, but most people still celebrated the traditional date.

'I have a few more things to bring in from the sled.' Dima met her eyes once more before turning back into the snowy twilight.

As Dima walked away, Katya recognised who else had come on the sled – Tsisana, Rafael, Matilda Ivanova and Andrei Sergeevich. Another surge of warmth spread through her at the sight of them. When she'd come to Solovki Katya had been determined to protect her heart from any unwise attachments. Yet, somehow, these people had become her friends.

Crossing the threshold, Tsisana pulled Katya into a fierce hug, saying how worried she'd been when Katya disappeared. Matilda Ivanova scolded Katya for not sending them word sooner, but she patted her cheek affectionately to show all was forgiven.

'Happy Christmas.' Andrei Sergeevich offered Katya a firm handshake, his waxed moustache lifting as he smiled at her. 'Nice to see you safe and well.'

Dima returned with two logs under each arm and Rafael brought two more. They arranged them around the table as makeshift seating. Rafael greeted Katya by gallantly kissing her hand before he and Dima went outside to unharness the dogs. Andrei Sergeevich sighed appreciatively at the warmth of the peat fire, setting down the sack he carried and stretching his hands towards it.

Matilda Ivanova reached for the papers on the table, but Katya beat her to them. She folded up the poem she'd been working on and placed it in her coat pocket while Tsisana pulled a linen sheet from one of the canvas sacks, and spread it out as a tablecloth.

'What are you doing?' Natasha watched in dismay as Matilda Ivanova set a candle in the middle of the table and a loaf of bread beside it.

The old woman gave Natasha a disparaging look. 'Preparing our Christmas party, obviously.'

'The party was just an excuse I gave the guards when I bribed them. I told you that.'

'What is this about?' Katya asked.

'Christmas is the best day of the year for divination.' Natasha dropped languidly onto a chair, her foot rocking with visible annoyance that increased with every plate Tsisana set on the table.

Katya sat on one of the logs.

Natasha leaned forward, her elbows pushing the tablecloth askew. Her eyes held a dare as she laid her plan out before them the way Tsisana and Matilda Ivanova were laying out plates of food.

'You're going to enter the Otherworld and cast a finding spell.'

'Enter the Otherworld?'

As Katya considered it, she thought she might already know what Natasha meant by that. She often felt like her soul was a doorway. Whenever she recited the zagovor to bring her mind into awareness of the spiritual world, that door cracked open. It seemed completely possible that one should be able to walk through it, though Katya had no idea how. That ability must have been one of the esoteric secrets carefully guarded by vedun warlocks in their secret societies. So why would Natasha offer her this knowledge?

'What are you hoping I'll find?' Katya asked.

'The *Volkhovnik*, of course.' The firelight cast her freckles in darker shades, like pinpricks of shadow.

Dima flung the door open. He and Rafael stomped the snow off their boots before coming inside. Dima pulled off his gloves and Katya noticed the bandages on his fingers for the first time. What had happened to him?

'This looks wonderful.' Rafael's eyes roved over the table and then landed on his wife. 'Thank you, my darling.'

'I'm afraid it's not as plentiful as a normal Christmas. No meat to be had, but we were able to bribe the guards for pierogi, bread and dried fruit.'

'Which we can eat *after* the ritual,' Natasha declared.

Matilda Ivanova wielded a wooden serving spoon, pointing it at Natasha. 'I didn't go to all this trouble for our food to get stale before we eat it.'

'Hear hear,' Andrei Sergeevich said, taking his place at the table.

When Katya's stomach gave a well-timed grumble, Natasha rolled her eyes but relented. They all scooted in around the tiny table, their knees bumping underneath it. Katya couldn't hold back a moan of pleasure when she bit into the pierogi and tasted the savoury potato and onion filling. The bread was still soft, the dried fruit sweet. Katya ate until her belly bulged and she thought she'd explode if she took one more bite. It was the first time since her arrest over a year ago that she'd eaten to satiation.

When they finished, Matilda Ivanova and Tsisana began clearing the table. Andrei Sergeevich and Rafael took turns singing carols in Russian and Spanish while Natasha scowled at them both. Katya stood to help with the clean-up, but Dima reached for her hand.

'Could you come for a walk with me? I'd like to show you something.'

Heat rose to Katya's cheeks.

'It's time for the ritual,' Natasha said.

'Just a few minutes more.' Dima pressed his bandaged hands together in a plea.

'Go on.' Matilda Ivanova waved them out the door. 'I won't be able to concentrate on any ritual until this mess is cleaned up.'

Putting on her boots and winter clothes, Katya followed Dima outside. The sky had cleared. Starlight made silhouettes of the evergreens and turned the snow a greyish blue. Their breath steamed as they walked a way in silence. Then Dima cleared his throat.

'I have something for you.' He pulled a rolled-up piece of paper from his coat pocket and offered it to Katya.

It was the art they'd created on midwinter's night – the monastery towers lit by starlight with Katya's poem written in the foreground.

'I thought you might like a copy as a keepsake. I, for one, never want to forget that night.'

Dima watched for her reaction, his bitten lip betraying his nervousness. Katya tried to speak, but tears crept up her throat.

Somehow he'd seen beyond the fortress she'd erected to keep people out, beyond the fire-breathing dragon that lived in her chest. He'd seen her poet's soul and given her the courage to open the door to that isolated tower. Because of him, she'd been bold enough to share her words for the very first time.

'It's beautiful,' she choked out. Then she pulled the folded paper out of her pocket and offered it to Dima. 'I have something for you too. Not a gift exactly, but I've started working on the poem about Stenka Razin. Our poem.'

At the words 'our poem', Dima huffed out a small, surprised breath. He turned the paper towards the moonlight to try and read it.

'This is great,' Dima said. 'I've been working on some lines as well. Maybe after the ritual we can combine them into one piece.'

Katya stepped closer, and Dima wrapped his arms around her. They both held tight, hearts beating against the other's ribs.

After a few minutes, Dima pulled halfway out of the embrace, still holding Katya but giving room for his half-lidded eyes to rove over her face. Their gazes met, and tension built between them. It ached inside Katya like a held breath. Looking up at Dima, she wondered if a kiss could feel like a deep exhale.

She slid her hands across his back, pulling him closer.

Their foreheads touched when Katya rose up on her toes. She closed her eyes and was about to press her lips to Dima's when someone cleared their throat.

Natasha had crept up on them, standing far too close.

'Come back inside,' she ordered. 'It's time to begin.'

# Chapter 41
## *Natasha*

Natasha prepared for the ritual, casting irritated glances at Katya and Dima all the while. The skomorokh should have died days ago. In bed last night, Boky assured Natasha no one could survive the winter forest for so long. Yet there he stood with that ridiculous smile on his face, making eyes at Katya from across the room while she chatted with Tsisana and Matilda Ivanova.

Their romance threatened this hard-won alliance.

Natasha had put in weeks of effort. She'd prepared this cabin and performed the ritual to bring Katya here. She had seduced Boky and gradually convinced him of her plan to isolate the anarchist. Then she'd swallowed down a lifetime of bitterness and spent these past days living with her oldest enemy – all for the chance of finding the *Volkhovnik*.

Natasha had no intention of allowing Dmitri Danilov to interfere. He was proving hard to kill, however. After the horrors of the lab, Natasha didn't have the stomach for taking matters into her own hands, but she'd thought of another way to drive a wedge between them.

Perhaps this night could serve a double purpose: divine the location of the *Volkhovnik* and expose Katya for the hypocrite she was.

A malicious smile curled Natasha's lips as she pushed the table against the far wall and bent down to retrace her faded protective circle.

'Can I help you with anything?' Rafael asked.

Natasha tipped her head to look up at him, from his polished leather Oxfords to the ironed pleats in his trousers and the brass buttons on his double-breasted suit. His black hair gleamed with pomade. His smile was just as bright.

'You can help by staying out of my way.' Natasha focused on redrawing the circle.

Every single person in this cabin was working on her nerves, but Rafael more than most. Maybe hearing him and Tsisana speaking French together, which was Natasha's mother tongue, reminded her of the bones rattling in the back of her mind ever since she read Katya's poetry. She'd buried the person she'd been before Aunt Sonya, but those sentimental parts of herself weren't as dead as she'd like.

Or maybe it was the party itself.

Natasha had spent two years locked in a cell. Sitting at a table with these loud and laughing people had made her stomach churn with nerves and the room feel like it was closing in around her. Her eye had twitched all through dinner. And oddly, she'd felt lonelier then than she ever had in the lab.

Natasha gritted her teeth as she placed the wood stumps in the circle. She set one at each point for north, south, and east. She had to put two seats at the west point, since Dima had thrown off their numbers. Matilda Ivanova and Andrei Sergeevich could sit together. Since neither of them was a practicing volshebnik, combining their spirits might balance out the power the other participants poured in the ritual.

Natasha directed each person to their seat, handing out four candles. She took her violin and stepped into the centre.

There she faced Katya. Did Natasha imagine the glint of suspicion in Katya's eyes? Something had changed between them, though Natasha didn't know what.

Not that it mattered. Natasha didn't care if Katya liked her, only that they found the book.

'Here's how this is going to work.' Natasha turned to address the group. 'I will play my violin for you. All you need to do is relax and follow the notes. They'll lead you into a trance where your soul can open to the Otherworld. Katya will draw from your magic, and those spiritual threads will serve as a tether as she and I cross to the other side.'

'I didn't understand what any of that meant,' Andrei Sergeevich said with a mischievous twinkle in his eye, 'but if it will prevent Boky from getting hold of the *Volkhovnik*, I'm keen to try it.'

Silence settled over the group as those words reminded them what was at stake. To convince them to come here, Natasha had no choice but to inform them about the purpose of the ritual.

'I don't understand,' Dima said. 'How will Katya draw from our magic?'

Natasha couldn't hold back a delighted smile. She'd hoped he would ask that question.

'It's a rare ability, one only found in Rurikid blood.' Natasha turned toward Katya. 'Isn't that right, Princess Lvova?'

Katya froze.

'Katya, a princess?' Tsisana laughed. Her merriment faded when Katya didn't join in.

As casually as one might comment on the weather, Natasha had cast one of Katya's deepest secrets out into the open. Now she watched her squirm.

'I thought you hated aristocrats.' Dima shook his head, as though his mind didn't want to accept Katya's hypocrisy.

'I do,' Katya said. 'Not any of you, but I hate the idea that some people deserve more in life simply because of the name they were born with. And I'm not a princess.'

Natasha smiled sweetly at her. 'If Prince Lvov is your father, then yes you are.'

'I've never even met him.'

Natasha snatched Katya's hand and ran a jagged fingernail along the veins of her wrist. 'But you have his magic in your blood.'

Katya yanked her arm free.

'Why so testy?' Natasha tilted her head, her voice honeyed. 'Did you not want them to know your true identity?'

'You're the one lying about your name.' Katya crossed her arms, tucking her hands behind her elbows. 'Who are *you*, Natasha?'

'That doesn't matter.' Natasha swatted the question from the air like an annoying fly.

'Fine. Instead of that, why don't you tell us whose bed you shared last night?'

So that's what had changed between them – Katya knew about Natasha and Boky.

Natasha swallowed ineffectually at the thickening sensation in her throat. She met Katya's eyes.

'I'm using him.'

'Maybe you're using us, too,' Katya said.

'That's what an alliance is.' Natasha gestured between them. 'I need you. You need me. We join our magic against our common enemy to ensure the communists never get hold of the *Volkhovnik*.'

The festive atmosphere that had filled the cabin shifted into something unbearably awkward. But the revelation had done its work. Dima leaned slightly away from Katya, watching her warily.

'Let's get this over with.' Natasha took up her violin. 'Everyone close your eyes and follow the music.'

No one responded at first. They all looked to Katya. After casting Natasha one last suspicious look, Katya squeezed her eyes closed. The others followed suit.

Even with her hypocrisy revealed, they still trusted Katya. Natasha could change that. She knew another secret, one far worse, but she'd wait until after the ritual to reveal it.

Walking seven times around the chalk barrier, Natasha chanted a protection spell in Old Russian. Then she invoked the spirits of north, south, east and west. For each cardinal spirit she lit a candle.

With those wards in place Natasha took up her violin. She played an improvisation, allowing the notes to flow freely and her mind to follow them into a trance. She could sense the other souls within the circle and willed her music to carry them along with her. Her trance brought her thoughts into awareness of the Otherworld. Her soul inched open.

'Draw our magic to you,' Natasha instructed Katya, shouting to be heard over the violin.

Natasha felt a gentle tug on the centre of her chest as part of the energy flowing into her from the Otherworld diverted to Katya. She set down her violin. Taking Katya's hands in hers, Natasha intertwined their fingers.

She began to chant an ancient Slavic invocation that had been passed down her maternal line for generations. She prayed it over Katya and herself, calling on their spirits to reach through the doorway of their souls and pull their consciousness to the other side.

Natasha's mind grew wings. She drifted. Journeyed. And when she opened her eyes at last, everything was entirely *other*.

Natasha still saw the cabin and the people seated within it, but she viewed them as though through a prism. Rainbow light surrounded them. Their circle of protection shone with silvery ribbons of light.

Already spirits gathered outside the circle, shadowy figures that hungered to enter the physical world. There were other spirits, too – the vengeful ghosts of the men and women Natasha sacrificed to create her wolves. She didn't dare to look behind her, though she sensed their rage at her back.

'Open your eyes,' Natasha instructed Katya.

Katya did so, and her glare morphed into wide-eyed wonder.

Here in the Otherworld, each person had a uniquely-hued aura – a cloud of energy superimposed on their physical forms.

Katya's looked like a winter sea, grey and blue, impenetrable in its depths. It rippled over the surface of her skin, revealing glints of steel.

Natasha's aura flickered and hissed with flames. Hers was a carmine soul – red as blood, hot as fire – but dark tendrils spread through it like black-as-midnight smoke. Those were the spirits of the volshebniki she'd sacrificed, bound to her for all eternity.

Shimmering threads connected Katya to those seated at the cardinal points.

Awe turned Katya's face radiant as she looked upon the spirits of her friends. Rafael had a gilded aura, the source of his golden charm. Tsisana's aura held all the varied shades of green found in a forest. More than colour, a *feeling* spread from her person, a nurturing sense of being loved, welcomed, accepted. She had a mother's spirit. Andrei Sergeevich's aura appeared like smoke, changeable and full of mischief. Matilda Ivanova burned like embers in a hearth, equal parts warm and fierce.

Katya stared at Dima the longest, which made Natasha's nerves feel like elastic stretched too far. Dima's spirit swirled with colour, like the sky in a van Gogh painting. He reminded Natasha of music, the way the colours shifted and swayed to an off-beat rhythm.

Natasha tilted her head, blocking Katya's line of vision to drag her attention away from Dima.

'I've attempted multiple divination rituals,' she said. 'Still the *Volkhovnik's* location eludes me. Something is concealing it – a talisman or protection spell, I'm not sure. But a spell cast here, in the realm of pure spirit, should be more powerful than any ward placed over the book.'

Katya considered this, inspecting Natasha's words as though they might contain a trap. Finally, she nodded her acceptance. Closing her eyes, she began to chant.

'*Narchi stapei moi ku yezhe sertse moye ishche.*'

The words were Old Russian. It translated to something like, *guide my steps to that which my heart seeks.*

Power gathered to Katya as she chanted. It flowed through the spiritual threads tethering Katya to her friends. It also materialised in the watery aura of her spirit.

An ethereal light shone within Katya, starting at her belly and spreading upward to her throat. That light trickled into her words, sparking as her breath carried them from her lips.

Each repetition of the chant made the words shine brighter. Katya's spirit began to levitate, rising away from her body. Natasha clutched Katya's hands in order to be carried with her. Though separated from their bodies in this state of astral projection, their spirits retained their shapes.

Drifting up through the insubstantial ceiling, they floated over the treeline. From above, Natasha observed several places where power gathered, shining in the Otherworld like aurora borealis. The spots of light appeared circular – were those the labyrinths?

The brightest light shone from the monastery itself.

Katya continued chanting, but they seemed to be moving aimlessly, floating first one direction and then the next.

Even in the Otherworld, something shrouded the *Volkhovnik's* location.

Natasha sighed her frustration.

Katya had made no progress on decoding the final clue. Now that this ritual had failed, Natasha couldn't see her next move.

'Let's go back,' she said.

Katya gripped Natasha's hands tighter. The immense flow of power gave Katya's skin a pearlescent glow. Her hair shone golden, and her eyes were like a goddess's, terrible to behold.

When she began another incantation, also in Old Russian, power infused her every word.

'*Lukavye glaza, lzhi ne izdavay. Dushish'sya v vozdukhe, yesli osmelish'sya. Pust' pravda zastavit tvoy yazyk.*' Wicked eyes, speak no lies. Choke on air if you should try. May truth compel your tongue.

Natasha's breath caught in her throat. She recognised that spell – Katya had tried to cast it in the forest the day Natasha first offered an alliance. At that time, she'd had to repeat the spell multiple times, building up power to make it potent, which had given Natasha time to get away.

Here in the Otherworld, a single recitation made the words wrap around Natasha's spirit. She tried to pull away, but she herself had spun this web. Now she was trapped in it.

'Who are you?' Katya's voice crackled around them, echoes of power causing metallic ripples to spread over the surface of her aura.

Natasha squirmed. She flexed her fingers to try and break Katya's hold on her, but words were already taking form. She'd held her name as a secret since the Revolution. Against her will, it rose from deep within her.

'I . . . am . . . Natasha.'

She clamped her jaw, holding her lips shut with all her might, but another word slipped through.

'. . . Georgiyevna . . .'

Above all, Natasha couldn't allow Katya to know her surname. On reflex, she reached for Katya with the might of her Rurikid magic, snatching the power forming a weapon against her. Katya's magic crashed into Natasha with the force of a tsunami.

The spell unravelled, and the colours of Katya's aura dimmed as her magic drained out.

Katya looked perplexed as Natasha chanted a reverse invocation, calling their awareness back into their bodies and slamming shut the doors of their souls.

They were back in the cabin, standing in the centre of the circle.

'What did you do?' Katya yanked her hands from Natasha's as though repulsed.

Natasha sighed. The failure and the fight had both exhausted her. A glance at the fading rune marks on the floor reminded her of that first divination ritual on the island. It had warned her secrets would be revealed if she forged an alliance with Katya.

Though Natasha had evaded Katya's spell, she'd still revealed herself as a Rurikida. Katya would discover the truth about her identity soon enough.

'Did it work?' Andrei Sergeevich asked.

'No.' Katya backed away from Natasha, her eyes narrowing into slits. 'Why are you so afraid of me finding out who you are?'

'Does your boyfriend know who *you* are? When he kisses you, does he know you're the daughter of the woman who murdered his family?'

Katya stumbled back a step, as though shoved by the impact of Natasha's words.

Dima looked as though they'd dealt him a blow as well. His face went very pale.

'That can't be true,' Katya said.

Natasha may have miscalculated. She thought Katya knew her mother had been there when Dima's family was executed.

The devastation on Katya's face said otherwise.

The candle fell from Dima's trembling fingers, extinguishing as it hit the floor. He staggered to his feet, grabbed his coat and left without another word.

Katya raised trembling fingers to her lips.

Tsisana rushed to put an arm around her.

'It can't be true.' Matilda Ivanova leaned on her cane as she stood up.

'I have to go after him.' Katya dabbed the corners of her eyes.

'Go.' Andrei Sergeevich made a shooing motion with his hands. 'We'll finish cleaning up here.'

Natasha winced when Katya cast her one last, hateful look before grabbing her coat. She shoved her books into her school bag, including Yelezar's manuscript and the journal of translation. Then she raced out the door.

Natasha needed Katya's help to crack that final cipher, especially now that the ritual had failed. She'd divulged that secret to put an end to Katya and Dima's relationship, but perhaps she'd gone too far. She had to convince her to come back inside. Natasha raced out the door, following Katya through the knee-deep snow.

Katya hurried after Dima, shouting, 'Wait.'

Dima turned to look back. He held up a hand, warning Katya to come no closer.

'I swear I didn't know.' Katya rested her hand over her heart.

'Please, don't,' Dima said. 'Just . . . I need some time to think.'
Dima strode off into the night.

'Come back inside,' Natasha suggested. 'It's freezing out here.'

'I might – if you answer my question.' Katya's gaze slid sideways. 'Who are you, Natasha?'

# Chapter 42
## *Katya*

'Who are you, Natasha?'

Katya whispered her question to the night, for she knew Natasha wouldn't answer. And the truth had already begun unfurling in Katya's mind, spreading poison through her thoughts. She'd looked at Natasha a hundred times, but had she ever truly seen her? Now, in the dim starlight, Katya studied her like a poem she wanted to memorise – not sweeping her eyes along the whole of the page, but pausing to note every line. The shape of Natasha's eye, the curve of her ear, the way her lips pressed together to hold in every secret.

The conviction deepened moment by moment, but Katya would have to wait to verify her suspicions.

'Come inside before you freeze,' Natasha ordered.

Katya took another step back.

Natasha obliterated their alliance the moment she tossed that accusation between them like a grenade. *Does he know you're the daughter of the woman who murdered his family?* Katya's heart stung with the emotional shrapnel of that revelation. She wished more than believed it wasn't true.

Dima had turned away from her, probably for ever, and whatever tentative trust Katya had in Natasha had blown away.

With her alliances broken, Katya only had one place to turn – the anarchists.

She tipped her head up to the sky, searching for the North Star. It showed her the direction of the Politicals' camp. She set off through the wilderness, never looking back at Natasha.

The trek to the north of the island took about three hours. Katya trudged through snowbanks, traversed iced-over lakes and threaded her way through forests and bogs.

Finally, she came upon a barbed-wire fence. Beyond it she saw a large brick building lit by the flames of a bonfire burning in the yard out front.

This had to be Savvatiyevsky, the political prison.

A gust of December wind carried laughter to Katya's ears. Politicals gathered around the fire, chatting and drinking from Thermoses. Several people skated on the frozen lake, some gliding gracefully, others barely able to stay on their feet.

The Politicals were celebrating Christmas. Katya couldn't help but think of the counter-revolutionaries huddled on their plank beds, praying their barrack wouldn't be visited by a guard with dice in his hand.

Her party had accepted the comforts of their captivity, even as their countrymen suffered unthinkable horror ten kilometres away. It shamed her, especially as she'd come here with the intention of joining them.

Katya laced her gloved fingers through the links of the fence. She rattled it with all her might, shouting until a man sitting at the edge of the bonfire noticed her. He flicked his cigarette away as he approached.

Katya recognised him as Maksim Kuznetsiv, a photographer, spy, and frequent paramour of Svetlana's.

'Katya?' Maksim's face was partially cast in shadow, but the light of the bonfire gleamed in the locks of blond hair protruding from the bottom of his fur hat. He grinned as he approached the fence, his round eyes sparkling. 'Is that really you?'

'Comrade Kuznetsiv.' Katya tried to sound dignified.

'Maksim,' he corrected with an indulgent smile.

'I've been misclassified,' Katya explained. 'You have to tell the guards I'm a Political. Tell them to let me in.'

Maksim winced as he curled his fingers through the fence. 'We revoked your mother's membership after Kronstadt, and yours along with it.'

That matched the dates in Katya's file, but it didn't make sense.

'Why?' Dread itched inside Katya's throat, making her voice husky.

'You didn't know.' The words came out upon an astonished sigh. Maksim's brow creased. 'We thought you and Svetlana were both in on it. Maybe it was just her.'

'In on what?'

'After Kronstadt, the government came for us anarchists. They knew our names, aliases, the addresses of our communes and safe houses. Svetlana betrayed us.'

Katya shook her head.

'I didn't want to believe it either, but I have photos. I followed Svetlana when she met her government contact, Gleb Boky. They were on *very* friendly terms.'

Katya thought back to her first conversation with Boky. *Your mother and I were great friends, you know.* Katya couldn't believe it. No one had been more committed to the anarchist cause than Svetlana Efremova.

'You're wrong.' Katya shook her head vehemently. 'You're wrong!'

Katya buried her face in her hands, trying not to cry. It couldn't be true, yet she knew it must be. In a moment, her world had become inversed, like the photographic negatives Maksim used to make in his dark room.

Katya squeezed her eyes shut to hold back the tears threatening to spill. *Anyone can be an informant,* Svetlana used to say. Katya never suspected her mother might be speaking about herself.

Svetlana had ruined any chance of Katya finding sanctuary with the Politicals. With no choice but to return to the monastery, Katya said a terse farewell to Maksim and headed south.

She tried to wrap her head around these revelations about her mother. Svetlana had murdered Dima's family and betrayed their closest allies. Katya shouldn't have been surprised – she'd experienced her mother's treachery first-hand.

She thought back to that dark February morning four years after the Revolution when Katya and Svetlana first made the short journey from Petrograd to Kronstadt. Katya had taken special care with her appearance that day.

When she came out of her room Svetlana had looked her up and down.

'You look pretty.' The words sounded like an accusation.

Katya thanked her, pretending not to notice the barbs in her compliment. It was easier that way. If Katya reacted, she might reveal the reason she'd woken up early to perfect her hair and makeup.

Stepan Petrichenko. He was a passionate idealist, a leading anarchist and an officer on the battleship Petropavlovsk. Though she'd never talked to him, Katya had heard him speak at anarchist gatherings in Petrograd and she wanted him to notice her.

Since the sea around Kronstadt had frozen over, Stepan awaited their boat at a small fort on one of the outlying islets. He stepped out on the dock to greet them. His smile flooded

Katya with warmth, despite the February cold. Svetlana gave Katya a sidelong glance, and a weight dropped in Katya's stomach.

*She knows.*

Stepan greeted Katya, then offered Svetlana his arm as they started their trek across the ice toward the fortress at Kronstadt.

Katya walked behind them, unable to join the conversation because of the roaring wind. Once in a while a gust would carry the sound of Svetlana's tinkling laughter, a laugh she only used on men.

Once they passed the giant warships frozen in the harbour, they entered the fortress and climbed a set of narrow stone steps that led to an upper level where the fleet's captains had gathered to hear Svetlana.

'You all have my deepest gratitude for inviting me here today.' Pressing a hand to her heart, Svetlana turned to bless the gathered leaders with the gleam of her countenance.

She laced subtle spellwork through her words as she listed the problems Lenin's policies had wrought: inflation, fuel shortages, famine, and then the most inflammatory issue of all, the mass arrests of protesting factory workers.

'Lenin is a wolf in sheep's clothing. He pretended to weep for the plight of the workman and peasant, but as soon as he tasted power, he made the Bolsheviki the new elite. He's worse than the tsar ever was. It's up to us now, my friends, my comrades and brothers, to defend the Revolution from those who have corrupted it. When the shepherds become wolves . . .'

'The sheep must lead themselves,' several of the officers answered in unison.

Katya remained in the background after Svetlana's speech while she and the sailors discussed their next steps. Eventually they agreed to write a list of demands to the government, a foundation upon which to negotiate. Some of the men doubted the Bolsheviki would be willing to talk, but Svetlana reassured them.

'There are ways they can be compelled to listen. You need only agree upon the wording of the resolutions – my daughter and I will do the rest.'

Svetlana smiled at them all, her teeth blindingly white behind her red lips. When she turned to Katya, her smile faltered. Was that resentment in Svetlana's eyes? Svetlana said *my daughter and I,* but in truth, Katya was the only one with magic strong enough to enact Svetlana's plan.

Once the wording of their demands had been agreed upon, Katya sat down beside the soviet's secretary. He offered her an inkpot, but she had brought her own. She pulled it out of her bag, swirling it so the reddish-brown liquid would be well-mixed. Katya had spent the past two weeks creating the concoction based on a recipe Svetlana gave her. It included bone ash, birch tar and a generous amount of Katya's own blood.

Then she sat down with a large sheet of thick brown paper. Everyone in the room watched her, including Stepan. Katya had never performed magic so publicly before, and she was determined to prove herself. More than that, she wanted to help the resistance. If she did her job well, this document could cause a ripple effect that would spread across Russia.

Katya closed her eyes and focused. She chanted under her breath, opening her soul to the Otherworld. She opened herself also to the other volshebniki in the room. She sensed three of them besides Svetlana. While she was strictly forbidden from using her mother's magic, even for a task as significant as this, she could use her Rurikid ability to draw power from the other three. Their combined magic would multiply the authority of her words.

For the next few hours, Katya wove spellwork into the document. She struggled to maintain concentration. The decreased rations had left her constantly ravenous. Her hands were cold and her head sluggish, but Katya fought through her body's weakness. She spoke incantations over every word, and her blood in the ink reacted to it, making the spell incredibly potent.

The sailors had agreed upon fifteen resolutions they would demand of the government, things like freedom of speech and of the press, equality of rations among all working people, and the release of political prisoners. They insisted new elections be held with secret ballots, which would end the Bolshevik monopoly on power.

People came and went from the meeting room in the hours it took Katya to work her spell.

When she finished, she sighed with relief and sank back into her chair, breaking her connection to the three other volshebniki. She slid the paper over to the secretary and looked around for her mother's approval, but Svetlana wasn't there. Neither was Stepan.

The secretary read over Katya's work, nodding all the while. Tomorrow they would present the document in an open meeting to the sixteen thousand sailors housed in the garrison. If they approved, it would be sent to the government.

Voices approached outside the door, and Katya perked up at the sound of her mother's tinkling laughter. Katya stood, smiling tiredly as she faced the door. Her smile faded when Svetlana entered on Stepan's arm.

Their faces were flushed, their lips swollen. Katya's gaze snagged on a red smear on Stepan's collar the exact shade of her mother's lipstick.

Katya cast her mother a deeply pained look, expecting to see shame or perhaps some sign that Katya was wrong to think her mother and Stepan had slipped away for a liaison. Instead her mother stared back at her with a vindictive smirk.

It required all of Katya's willpower to keep her composure as they took their leave from the Kronstadt leadership and left the island. She averted her eyes as Svetlana kissed Stepan goodbye.

'What was that?' Katya demanded as soon as they were alone.

'What?' Svetlana asked with feigned innocence. Her lips twitched with the effort of suppressing a smile.

Katya tried to hold her emotion in, so her mother wouldn't see how deeply she'd been hurt, but tears stung her eyes.

'Don't cry,' Svetlana said with disgust. 'I did you a favour. He's too old for you, and you don't need to be getting distracted by ideas of romance. We still have work to do.'

Katya turned away from her mother, looking out at the icy sea and the desperate city of Petrograd in the distance. Katya would do whatever she could to help Russia, but she would never fully trust Svetlana or look at her in the same way again.

# Chapter 43
## *Katya*

Katya arrived at the monastery just after the morning bell, exhausted and chilled to the bone. Rather than lingering in the courtyard for roll-call, she headed straight for the administration building and climbed to the third floor.

Her soul felt like an empty cistern. Natasha had used Rurikid magic to drain Katya's power.

*Who are you, Natasha?*

It was time to answer that question, once and for all.

Katya made her way to the file room. With her magic too drained to cast a spell, she used hairpins to pick the lock. Then she stood before the line of shelves, wondering where to start.

The Rurikid family line had dozens of offshoots. Katya had a creeping suspicion of who Natasha might be. Not wanting to accept it, she searched the files for anyone with a Rurikid name: Bariatinsky, Gagarin, Obolensky, Shumarovsky. Coming up empty, she finally had to accept her suspicion might be the truth.

Katya approached the shelf labelled 'L'. Natasha had introduced herself with *Georgiyevna* as her patronymic. Prince Georgy Lvov and his wife had no children – at least that's what Katya had always been told about her biological father.

Katya knelt down, running her thumb along the line of files.

She found one labelled: *Natalya Georgiyevna Lvova.*

For several minutes, Katya sat with the folder resting on her lap, barely breathing as the implications settled over her.

Natasha was Katya's half-sister.

She had a *sister.*

How could that be? Was Natasha's existence a well-kept secret, or had Svetlana known about it all along but kept it from Katya?

Though Natasha's file had as many blacked-out places as her own, Katya gathered a few important details. Natasha's mother was Countess Yulia Alekseyevna Bobrinskaya. Natasha's birth and her mother's death were listed on the same day in May, 1903 – a little over a year before Katya was born.

A grunt and then a loud scraping noise sounded outside the file room door.

Katya ducked behind one of the file shelves, but whoever was outside didn't come in. They had moved something in front of the door, something heavy. Attuning her ears, Katya heard footsteps departing down the corridor.

When they were gone, she rushed to the door and tried to open it. It wouldn't budge, no matter how she threw her weight at it. The sound must have been furniture being moved to block her in. Had Boky seen Katya return? In a panic, she went to the windows, but they were too narrow to squeeze through.

She had no way out.

*Think,* she urged herself. Taking Yelezar's book and Natasha's translation out of her school bag, she stashed them on a top shelf, obscured by file folders. Boky may have caught Katya, but she wouldn't give him information.

She paced the room until she heard the approach of heavy footsteps. There was a scraping sound as the furniture blocking the door was moved aside, then the door swung open.

Four guards rushed in. Two aimed rifles at Katya while two others gripped her arms and led her out of the file room, down the stairs and into Boky's office.

Commissar Boky stood by the window, looking out.

'Sit,' he commanded.

Katya remained standing.

He turned to look over his shoulder. She'd expected to be met with his fury, but the sly pleasure in his slate-grey eyes was a hundred times worse. His lips curved in the smile of a predator, and cold, primal fear spread through her.

Whatever game they were playing, she'd lost somehow.

'So you went to the anarchists,' Boky said. 'I did try to spare you the pain of that disillusionment.'

'How long was she your spy?' Katya's voice sounded raw, wounded.

'Long enough.' Boky took lazy steps towards Katya, then leaned against the back of an armchair, crossing his legs at the ankles. 'Your mother understood anarchist theories would never work in practice. People think they want freedom, but deep down most prefer to have someone tell them what to do. It's easier if another is responsible for your decisions, more pleasant if you have someone besides yourself to blame when things go wrong. Anarchists would create chaos and dissatisfaction, not utopia.'

'Is this the utopia you dreamed of?' Katya waved an arm towards the window and the prisoners gathered in the courtyard below. 'I can't say I'm impressed.'

Commissar Boky sighed and shook his head.

'This is my nightmare, but I haven't given up on dreaming. All of my efforts are towards delivering on the promise of the Revolution. If I'm to be successful, I'll need your help.'

Katya took a deep inhale, bracing herself for defiance. She

raised her chin and let hatred for Boky blaze from her eyes.

'A few weeks ago you and I agreed to answer a single question,' he said. 'I answered yours. Now I believe the time has come for you to answer mine. What have you learned about the *Volkhovnik*?'

'I don't know what that is.'

Commissar Boky stared for a long moment. Then he pushed off the chair and stepped closer, his steely gaze boring into Katya. 'What have you learned about it, Yekaterina?'

'I have no idea what you're talking about.'

'You don't want to lie to me.'

'Why, because you'll starve me? Beat me? Experiment on me?' Katya held her arms open in demonstration of what she'd already endured. 'Do your worst.'

'You don't really mean that.' Boky stepped toward the window and raised a hand. 'I'll give you one last chance to answer my question.'

'I can't tell you what I don't know.'

Boky closed his hand into a fist. Down in the courtyard, a gunshot rang out.

Katya started. Screams and wails rose to the window. Horror dawning in her heart, Katya stepped towards the sound. She looked out on the hundreds of assembled prisoners. At the front of the crowd, a man in a white medical coat had been shot dead on the cobblestones. Two other prisoners were lined up on their knees – Dima and a monk in a black cassock.

'Svetlana was very special to me. I've no desire to hurt her daughter,' Boky said, his face so close to her ear his voice's vibration rippled across her cheek. 'But I don't mind hurting *them*. The choice is yours – save them by telling the truth, or doom them by lying.'

Katya's vision swam. She gripped the windowsill to steady

herself as Boky lifted his hand again. Smolensky raised his pistol, pointing it at the monk.

'Wait,' Katya said, but her voice sounded far away.

Boky closed his hand into a fist. A ringing in Katya's ears drowned out the sound of the gunshot. Smoke rose from the pistol's barrel, and the monk fell forward. Blood dripped in rivulets from the back of his head down his cheek.

Sobs wracked Dima's shoulders. Katya was crying, too, though she couldn't remember having started. Her lips tasted salty and her heart beat like a frantic bird against the cage of her chest, as though trying to escape.

Boky touched the small of her back. She writhed as though maggots crawled across her skin. Katya bucked away from him, but he caught her upper arm and held her in front of the window.

Then he raised his hand.

Smolensky aimed the pistol at Dima.

Dima's sobbing stilled. A sober calm settled over him. He crossed himself and folded his hands in a gesture of prayer.

In the church on the island of labyrinths, he'd told Katya, *I want to live before I die.*

Now his life was in Katya's hands.

'Last chance,' Commissar Boky said by her ear. His fingers began to close into a fist.

'Wait,' Katya cried.

She'd tried to turn her heart to steel, tried to guard against friendship, against love or attachment in any form. But she had failed. Letting Dima bleed out on the cobblestones would destroy her.

'I'll tell you everything,' she said miserably.

'I never doubted you would.'

When Boky lowered his hand, Smolensky holstered his pistol

and kicked Dima onto the cobblestones. Katya's knees went weak with relief. She crumpled to the floor below the window, despising herself but unable to regret that Dima's tears were spilling on the ground instead of his blood.

'You act as if you're made of stone, but I know you're soft inside.'

Boky knelt beside her. Stray locks of Katya's hair stuck to her tear-stained face. She cringed when he brushed them away with his fingertips, tucking them behind her ear.

'Now you know it, too.'

# Chapter 44

## *Dima*

Dima knelt on the cobblestones, his face sticky with blood and grimy from the dried salt of tears. He couldn't move, couldn't tear his eyes from the two dead men beside him.

A hand settled on Dima's shoulder. Blearily, he turned to find Andrei Sergeevich standing over him. They were the only ones left in the courtyard. How long had Dima been kneeling beside the corpses?

'Come with me,' Andrei Sergeevich said gently.

Dima allowed himself to be pulled up to his feet. He turned to look at Father Iosef and Doctor Tarasov from this higher vantage point, but Andrei Sergeevich blocked his view.

'Don't torment yourself like that.' He threaded his arm through Dima's and led him away.

Shouldn't Dima be tormented? Father Iosef and Doctor Tarasov had been alive this morning. They'd been forced to kneel on the ground beside Dima. Why had they been killed and Dima allowed to live? It didn't make sense.

The worst part was how relieved Dima felt to have been spared. What kind of person feels that way after two good men have been murdered right beside him?

Andrei Sergeevich led Dima away from the courtyard, but still the scents of burnt gunpowder and blood coated his senses.

Dima's feet felt leaden. As they entered the infirmary, Dima's spirit sank even lower.

Every bed and pallet was occupied by a weak, moaning man – and Smolensky had shot their only doctor.

Andrei Sergeevich led Dima into the infirmary office and guided him to sit down. With a cloth and ewer, he cleaned the wound on Dima's cheek, received when Comrade Smolensky kicked him to the ground.

So much had changed since yesterday.

The joy and laughter of their Christmas party felt like a bright dream. After the ritual, it slipped through Dima's fingers, leaving only a nightmare.

Katya's mother killed his family. That truth painted dark smears at the corners of every memory the two of them had shared. He'd come to the island expecting to die. Instead he'd come alive as he'd followed the footsteps of his ancestor and discovered the story he was born to find – not the tale of Stenka Razin, but an unlikely love story, his and Katya's.

He was falling in love with her, but those feelings felt far more complicated than they had only a day before. His devotion felt like a betrayal of his family. With his heart pulled in two different directions, it felt like it would rip him apart.

'Rest for a while.' Andrei Sergeevich set the ewer aside and patted Dima's shoulder. 'I'll come back to check on you.'

Dima's gaze fell on the framed photograph sitting on Doctor Tarasov's desk, showing the doctor with his wife and two young daughters. Somewhere out there in the world, the doctor's family was going about their lives with no idea what they'd lost this morning.

A wave of sorrow crashed over him, bringing exhaustion along with it. Dima went to the pallet Tsisana had laid out on the office floor for him.

327

When Dima fell asleep, he found himself at the beginning of his usual nightmare. The paintbrush fell from his fingertips, and two red pools on the canvas marked where his siblings were missing from the painting.

'Yelezar?' he called.

'Hello again, fellow dreamer.' Yelezar materialised in the room, a wide smile on his face as his story cloak billowed around him. He tilted his head when his saw Dima's expression. 'Is everything all right?'

Dima shook his head.

'Well, I know how to change that.' Yelezar slid his arm around Dima's, hooking their elbows. 'What shall we dream together today?'

Dima knew the dream he needed, though the thought of it made his blood run cold. On Bolshoi Zayatsky, when he'd walked a labyrinth, he'd found himself in this nightmare. A gentle voice spoke to him then. *Just as a putrid wound must be scraped clean before being bandaged, so too must you face this remembered horror before you can truly heal.*

He'd refused to entertain the idea at the time, thinking if his wounds hadn't healed, they'd at least scabbed over. But watching Father Iosef and Doctor Tarasov die had brought back every horror, and learning that Katya's mother had been the anarchist who ordered his family's executions had broken something in his soul.

Dima needed to face his deepest nightmare, but he couldn't bear to enter it alone.

'I'd like to stay here, if you don't mind staying with me.'

'Are you certain?' Yelezar's otherworldly blue eyes studied Dima's face.

'Yes,' Dima said as bravely as he could manage.

'Very well, then.' Yelezar looked about them. 'What happens next?'

Dima turned away from the canvas, and the first part of the dream unfolded rapidly. They rushed down the hall, pausing when they noticed smoke pouring out of Dedushka's office. Dedushka told Dima to run. Yelezar ran with him down the stairs, where they nearly collided with Dima's older brother Petya.

Petya started to say something, but a pounding at the door interrupted him. Not a knock. It sounded like a battering ram. Petya's eyes widened with fear, and Dima's stomach turned to water. The door bent with each heavy blow, and then burst open with a spray of splintered wood.

'Run!' Petya shouted.

His brother dashed out of the foyer through the kitchen, while Dima stood petrified, his feet turned to stone.

*I'm here, too,* Yelezar reminded him. *This isn't real.*

A rifle came through the open door, and then the man carrying it, dressed in an olive-green uniform with red star patches on his arm. Five more soldiers swarmed into the foyer. The next thing Dima knew he was looking down the barrel of a gun.

'No!' Dima's mother raced down the stairs and knocked the rifle sideways, putting herself between Dima and the soldiers. When three soldiers aimed their guns at her, her voice rose to a panicked pitch. 'We'll co-operate. Please don't hurt us.'

One soldier lowered his weapon and yanked her towards the door. Then someone took hold of Dima. They dragged him outside, where a horse-drawn prison wagon had parked on the road in front of their house. Were they being arrested? Dima couldn't understand what they'd done wrong.

They were marched towards the road, but instead of being loaded into the prison wagon, the soldiers ordered them to stand in a line. There was Dima and his mother, their butler, gardener and two maids. Dima's younger sister Taya was led out of the house at gunpoint with little Sasha clinging to her skirts. Sasha looked around at the soldiers, his big eyes wet with tears.

Yelezar stood with them, his presence an anchor that kept Dima from being swept away.

'Where's Petya?' Taya's voice sounded so panicked it was almost a shriek.

Their mother shushed her and gathered the three of them into her arms like a hen gathers chicks. If Petya had escaped, she didn't want the soldiers knowing to look for him. Dima clung onto her and his siblings. Yelezar's comforting hand rested on his back.

'Be brave.' Dima's mother squeezed them one last time. 'If we do what they ask, we'll get through this.'

A voice called from the direction of the house, 'Look what I found, another Cossack rat.'

Blood dripped from Petya's nose, and his reddened face had started swelling. The soldier placed Petya in the line beside Dima.

The clacking of hooves resounded as a female rider approached on a tall, brown horse. She had a golden glow about her, and not just because of her blonde hair – there was a luminous quality to her skin, a radiant aura that made her impossible to look away from. She wore shiny boots, puffed military trousers, a pistol in a leather holster at her belt and a black patch sewn onto her uniform, marking her as an anarchist.

She swung her legs over the saddle and dropped to the ground, not deigning to look at Dima and his family as she approached the soldiers.

'You found him?' Her voice was mesmerising, smooth as velvet and surprisingly deep.

'Inside.' The commander hurried to speak before his comrades.

THE WHISPER OF STARS

'He was burning papers, but we stopped him for you.'

The anarchist's lips pressed into a tight line at that news. Her nostrils flared as she strode towards the house.

'Wait,' the commander called after her. 'What shall we do with these ones?'

He motioned towards Dima's household, lined up on the side of the road.

'Cossacks are to be exterminated.'

The anarchist hadn't so much as turned her head to look at Dima's family. She didn't care that they were human beings. If she'd really looked at them, she would have seen Maria Antonova, the best mother in the whole world. Or Petya, who had just received his acceptance letter to the Petrograd Mining Institute and planned to study engineering next year. Or Taya who hadn't even had her first crush. Or little Sasha, only nine years old, whose best friend was an old hunting dog named Arrow who he slept with every night.

The anarchist turned her back on them, headed for the house. Before she reached the door, a gunshot sounded from upstairs. Dima forgot how to breathe when he looked up at Dedushka's office window and saw blood splattered across the glass.

'Imbeciles!' The anarchist raced into the house.

*I'm sure that was the moment Dedushka died,* Dima told Yelezar.

*He probably tried to fight back,* Yelezar said. *I shared many dreams with him, and I knew him to be a brave man.*

'Form a line.' The commander paced in front of them until they'd done what he asked. 'Now stretch out your hands.'

He held a mangled iron cross. Moving down the line, he touched the cross to every person's skin – the butler's, the maids', the gardener's, Mother's, Petya's. None of them reacted to the metal. Dima held his breath when the commander stopped in front of him.

Dima braced himself for pain. He tried not to react when the cross touched his skin, but it struck him like a scorpion's sting. He stifled a pained yelp.

'This one,' the commander said, sounding pleased.

The two other soldiers grabbed Dima's arms. His mother screamed until one of the soldiers slammed his rifle butt into her torso. She doubled over, the breath knocked out of her. Sasha started crying, and Taya hugged him to her side and shushed him.

Dima didn't resist the guards leading him into the prison wagon.

*That's what I'm most ashamed of. I should have fought back, or at least said something.*

Yelezar followed Dima into the prison wagon, looking pensive.

As the commander tested the iron on Taya and Sasha, Dima peered out through the bars, his heart racing. Even though he'd heard what the anarchist said, some part of him expected that doing what they'd asked of him would make everything all right. They'd let his family go.

Instead the commander pulled the revolver from his belt. He shot their butler between the eyes. Then the maids. Then the gardener.

He stood before Dima's mother. She dropped to her knees and begged. Not for her own life but for her children to be spared. The commander took his time loading more bullets into the revolver's chamber.

That's when the transformation began. Dima's grandfather had told him about the kinship between skomorokhi and bears, how the ancient blood oath sometimes manifested in the ability to shapeshift. Neither Dima nor his grandfather had ever experienced that themselves, but, in that moment, the force of Dima's terror opened up something inside him.

Energy rushed through his limbs. Dima's clothes ripped at the seams. He screamed as his bones bent, shattered, remade themselves. Pain blinded him. As he writhed on the floor of the prison wagon, Dima heard the gunshot that killed his mother. His muscles bulged. Coarse fur sprouted from his skin.

Two more gunshots sounded. One for Petya. One for Taya.

The world came alive with scent – burnt gunpowder, his mother's blood, his sisters' tears, urine as Sasha peed his pants.

Now in bear form, Dima threw himself at the door of the prison wagon. It bent. Then it burst off its hinges. A final gunshot sounded – Dima was too late to save his little brother.

The soldiers trained their rifles on him.

'Stand down,' the commander ordered.

*They wanted volshebniki captured alive, so they could experiment on us,* Dima told Yelezar.

Instinct took over, and Dima fled towards the woods behind the *dacha*, his art satchel still strapped around his neck.

*Wait!* Yelezar leapt onto his back, clutching the satchel to hang on.

With a loping run, Dima made for the tree line. The landscape changed before he reached it. A haze moved in. Then, in the blink of an eye, Dima found himself back in his human form.

He and Yelezar stood in an achingly familiar wood-panelled office with tall windows, a cluttered desk and two leather armchairs facing a hearth with a crackling fire.

'You brought me to Kyiv, to Dedushka's office at the university,' Dima said, surprised that his words came out normally rather than passing from his mind to Yelezar's. Perhaps it was because they were in a dream Yelezar had spun rather than watching a memory play out.

'This was a happy place for your grandfather.' Yelezar plopped onto one of the armchairs. 'He dreamed of it often, so I thought you might be comfortable here too.'

'I love this place.' As surely as the fire warmed his skin, memories of Dedushka warmed Dima's heart, melting some of the dread and horror he'd just relived. He'd spent hours lying on his stomach before the hearth making practice sketches while his grandfather worked. As he'd grown older, he'd spent the first summer of his skomorokh apprenticeship on one of those leather chairs as Dedushka told him story after story about magic.

'What happened after you became a bear?' Yelezar asked, his words gentle but his eyes alight with the curiosity of a storyteller.

Dima sat on the second armchair, running his hand over the familiar feel of the leather.

He told of how he roamed the forest all summer, hibernated through winter, and, come spring, woke up in a cave near Kazan, human once more.

'After that I was plagued by guilt that I hadn't said anything or done anything.' Dima took off his hat and ran his fingers through his hair. 'I just let them put me in that prison wagon without saying a word.'

Yelezar reached across the gap between them, resting his hand on Dima's arm. He waited for Dima to meet his gaze before he said, 'What happened to your family wasn't your fault.'

'I know.' Dima lowered his eyes.

'No.' Yelezar squeezed his arm, insisting he not look away. 'Hear me. I watched those terrible events unfold, and I tell you the truth. You couldn't have saved your family. You need to forgive yourself for that.' Though his face was youthful, Yelezar's ancient eyes seemed to look into Dima's soul. 'It wasn't your fault.'

Those four words broke something inside Dima. His chest ached and his throat burned as tears filled his eyes. Dima covered his face as sobs wracked his body and the tears spilled out into his palms, salty as they touched his lips. Shame poured out with them, and the guilt he'd carried as a burden for so long.

Dima had blamed himself for what happened. Though he searched for beauty and goodness in the world, that heaviness of spirit was always within him. It weighed on his heart and plunged him into nightmares whenever he fell asleep.

His tears felt like a purging and Yelezar's words trickled through him like healing waters. It *wasn't* Dima's fault. Nothing he did that day caused his family to be killed. Likewise, there was nothing he could have done to save them.

That thought led him to another one – it wasn't Katya's fault, either. She wasn't her mother and loving her wasn't a betrayal of his family. Only his warped sense of guilt had told him that it was.

The voice in the labyrinth had been right. Reliving that memory didn't fix everything, nor did it diminish the horror of his family's tragedy. But it had given him perspective on his own role in what happened that day. Dima was a victim too, but he'd accused himself as harshly as if he'd been the perpetrator.

He could forgive himself. He could forgive Katya, also.

Perhaps, in time, he could heal.

# Chapter 45
## *Katya*

After divulging all to Commissar Boky, Katya collapsed. She was carried to a bed in the women's section of the infirmary. The trek to the political prison must have pushed her already ravaged body to the brink, and surrendering to Boky had broken something in her soul. Darkness seeped in through the cracks, filling her with a cold and hollow nothingness.

What had been the point of fighting? In the lab, no matter how much she resisted, Barchenko eventually got his way. Here on Solovki she'd struggled to outmanoeuvre Commissar Boky and ended up offering him her secrets on a silver platter. She'd thought she could find the *Volkhovnik*, thought she could use it to liberate Russia once and for all – instead she betrayed everything she believed in, all to save Dima's life.

Katya writhed on the mattress, tears leaking from her eyes like venom.

She had no awareness of how long she cried – minutes, hours, lifetimes? But then a warm and steady hand rested on her shoulder.

*Dima.*

Katya didn't bother to wipe her eyes. Let him see her wretched. Maybe then he'd stay far away from her and be safe. His face reflected Katya's anguish – eyes swollen and red-rimmed, cheek scraped from when he'd been kicked onto the cobblestones, lips pinched tight as though holding in poisoned thoughts.

Neither of them spoke for a long time.

The truth of Svetlana's evil actions had resurrected the ghosts of his past. Now he'd witnessed more horrors, all because of Katya. She wished she could apologise, but that would only add insult to injury.

'You don't have to be here. I'm sure I'm the last person you want to see.'

'Why would you say that?' Dima tipped her chin up and gently wiped her tears with his thumb.

'What my mother did to you . . .' Katya shook her head, unable to put her feelings into words.

'You're not your mother.'

Katya pinched her eyes shut. Another tear leaked out.

'What happened today?' he asked gently.

Katya lowered her head and bit the inside of her cheek. What happened? She'd become the thing she most despised – an informant – all to save Dima's life.

She felt like a cracking dam, like every barrier she'd set up to protect herself was crumbling. She could endure what hunger and rough conditions were doing to her body, but she wouldn't survive another blow to her heart.

Scooting back on the pallet, Katya wrapped her arms around herself. Time to put a stop to this while she still could.

'That night at Valentina Pavlovna's was a mistake.' Katya's heart was in her throat, and her voice came out strained.

Dima reached out, cradling her jaw with his fingertips. The touch brought back the memory of every kiss. Blinking away tears, she jerked away from his touch.

'I don't think we should see each other anymore.'

Dima's eyes narrowed in confusion, but something in Katya's

face made it clear she was building a wall between them.

'Why?' His voice went low and husky.

Katya took a ragged breath and mustered her last morsel of inner strength. She'd need it, because severing ties with Dima felt like ripping through nerves.

'I drank too much vodka that night. Sorry if I gave you the wrong idea.'

Shaking his head, Dima angled himself to look Katya in the eye. She lowered her gaze, staring at her hands in her lap.

'I don't believe you,' Dima said. 'You weren't drunk when you told me you have feelings for me.'

'I do have feelings for you, which is why I don't want to see you anymore.'

'Katya.' He said her name on a sigh.

She let herself look at him one last time. Her favourite part of his face was his least perfect feature. His nose had healed all wrong after his beating that first day on the island. Its crookedness reminded her he'd spoken up for her, a stranger, when no one else would. Because that's the kind of person he was.

Katya couldn't risk him getting hurt because of her.

'I'm an anarchist.' Katya tossed her head, raising her chin in pride. 'You're an aristocrat. We're better off as enemies.'

'Better off as enemies?' Dima chuckled darkly as he repeated her words. 'It didn't seem that way at Valentina Pavlovna's house or standing under the stars last night. What about finding the *Volkhovnik*? And the poem – I thought you wanted to help me write it.'

'I changed my mind.' Katya settled down on the pallet with her back to him, pulling the blanket up to her chin. With a note of finality, she said, 'Goodbye Dima.'

He waited as though expecting her to say something more. When she didn't, he rose with a sigh. Only when she heard his departing footsteps did she let the tears welling in her eyes leak out.

A bank of fog rolled across her mind, clouding everything. She could hardly put two thoughts together. Katya surrendered to numb forgetfulness. Her consciousness retreated to a place deep within herself, and she stared unseeing at a corner of the room.

# Chapter 46
## *Natasha*

Natasha strode into the infirmary. She held a scarf over the bottom half of her face, partly to shield her nose from the reek of sickness and sweat, partly to conceal any cracks in her façade. She couldn't afford to show weakness in front of Katya.

*She knows.* That morning, as she sat alone in the cabin meditating on what to do next, her fortune-telling ability reverberated with those two words. Natasha had inadvertently revealed her Rurikid magic, and Katya had followed that clue to the truth about Natasha's identity.

*Sister.* That bramble of a word twisted inside Natasha, full of thorns.

Natasha's ancestors, the Rurikids, ruled over Kievan Rus for twenty-one generations, nearly seven hundred years. Her mother's side, the Bobrinskys, descended from Catherine the Great. They'd carefully arranged their marriages to increase the chances of powerful sorcerers being born. Their vedun magic manifested most powerfully in the family's women, who didn't need secret societies or elaborate rituals to tap into their abilities.

*In times of crisis, it's always been a woman who saved Russia.*

Aunt Sonya must have told Natasha that a thousand times. At the end of the last century, with the Romanov line weakening and discontent simmering among the lower class, the Bobrinsky family purposely joined with the royal line of Lvov. Natasha's mother suffered ten miscarriages trying to bring a daughter into the world. When she finally carried a child to term, she died in the birthing room.

Natasha's existence represented generations of planning and a mother's ultimate sacrifice.

What did Katya's existence represent? Nothing but a theft.

Svetlana Efremova had taken advantage of Georgy Lvov in his grief. She'd seduced him. Then she had snuck into the palace library to search for the *Volkhovnik*. She didn't find *The Book of the Wizard*, but when she'd left the prince's bed with his seed in her womb, she'd stolen something else – Natasha's legacy.

This she passed onto Katya, her bastard daughter.

Despite their shared blood – no, *because* of their shared blood – Katya could only ever be Natasha's enemy.

But Natasha needed Katya to lead her to the *Volkhovnik*.

Navigating the narrow aisle of the sickroom, Natasha found Tsisana at Katya's bedside, speaking in a low, soothing voice. A weight settled in her belly when she saw the anarchist – body rigid, limbs unnaturally fixed, empty eyes staring blankly. Tsisana held Katya's hand, though Katya's fingers were stiff and outstretched.

'What's wrong with her?' Natasha asked.

Tsisana explained what had happened. After learning her mother had executed Dima's family, Katya had gone to the anarchists. They must have refused her, for she then returned to the monastery. Tsisana held back a sob as she described the executions of a doctor and a monk. Dima had been threatened also – that must have been enough to make Katya talk. After a few hours of interrogation, guards had brought her to the infirmary.

'She's catatonic. I've tried everything I know, but these

wounds aren't physical.' Tsisana brushed Katya's hair back with her fingers. 'I have no remedy for an injured spirit.'

In Natasha's first report to Boky, she'd described Katya as a fortress, one that wouldn't be able to withstand the battering ram for ever. Now here Katya was – besieged, breached, broken.

Natasha should be glad to see her enemy fall, but the void behind Katya's eyes made Natasha feel sick. Was this her fault?

Crossing to the Otherworld had consequences. Once a mind and spirit experienced the wholeness of being joined, that volshebnik would ache to return to that state. Perhaps Katya's despair had been so great that her consciousness slipped through the doorway of her soul to find relief in the world of spirits.

Natasha might be able to call her back, but she needed to know the extent of her spiritual wounds. What had Boky un-covered during Katya's interrogation?

Natasha would learn all she could before attempting a sum-moning because, if she failed, Katya could be lost for ever.

Leaving Katya to Tsisana's care, Natasha went in search of Boky. Smolensky told her Boky had gone to Sekirka, as he always did the day after executions if a volshebnik had been found among the doomed men.

Natasha strode into the guard station at the lake harbour, demanding they prepare her a dog sled. Three of the guards gaped at her, but the fourth was one of hers, a volkolak. Bowing to her, he ordered his bewildered comrades to do as she said.

Half an hour later, Natasha stood on the back of the sled, near flying over the frozen lake. Though she wore a fur hat, icy gusts tugged at the exposed strands of her hair until her chignon came unpinned and her auburn waves streamed behind her.

The dog team followed the frozen canals to the northwest of the island. Soon they came to an immense hill. It rose up out of the forest in a single peak, thickly forested with evergreens. A lighthouse stood at the very top.

Natasha ordered the dogs to halt. Boky's tracks continued, following a road up the hill. Natasha could approach the lighthouse more stealthily by way of a staircase leading up through the trees. She ordered her dog team to stay and climbed the steep wooden stairs.

At the top, she found a small monastery. The church had a single onion-domed tower with a lighthouse built into the cupola. A monastery residence was attached to the church, and Boky's dog team lounged in the snow outside it.

Concealed by the trees, Natasha watched the monastery for a long while. Two guards patrolled the grounds, neither of them volkolaki. She would need to be careful. Natasha heard the steady beat of a drum from inside the church and saw vague movement in the windows.

She waited until the guards passed on their rounds. Then she sprinted to the church, crouching down in the snow-dappled shrubs below a windowsill. She raised her head enough to look in through the glass.

The inside of the church had been transformed into a laboratory like the one at Lubyanka Square.

A partially nude man lay strapped to a table set in the centre of the altar. He struggled against his restraints and frantically tried to speak around the gag in his mouth. Another man, robed in black, sat with his back to Natasha as he beat a shamanic drum. A third black-robed figure moved about the altar, preparing some kind of ritual with brass vessels in the four corners and black candles placed between them.

Commissar Boky emerged from the baptismal pool completely naked, steam rising from his skin as he descended the steps to the altar and donned a black hooded robe.

343

Boky began a ritual, ringing a brass bell three times before stepping into the central square of the altar. He then rang the bell at each of the cardinal directions to welcome the spirits of north, south, east and west.

The sanctuary dimmed. A chill crawled up Natasha's back, and the wind carried a subtle malevolence. Boky chanted as he lit the black candles. Though Natasha strained, she couldn't hear his words over the beating of the drum.

Boky picked up a censer of incense. With it, he danced about the altar, working into a frenzy and chanting all the while. Shadows gathered around the altar. The smoke rising from the censer turned black.

When Boky pulled a dagger from the folds of his robe, the bound man's struggles became frantic. Boky plunged it into the man's chest without hesitation, piercing his heart. Dropping to his knees, Boky lifted a brass scrying bowl onto his lap, filling it with purified water from a pitcher.

Boky situated the bowl so his victim's blood dripped into the water. He stared into the rippling surface with trance-like concentration.

So this is what happened to the volshebnik prisoners, the ones led away from the firing squad behind the women's barrack. Boky brought them here. He used their blood in a black magic divination ritual.

Natasha's chest tightened. Her skin itched. The same man who had plunged the dagger into that man's heart had held her body close to his only two nights ago.

Though she'd known Boky's reputation, she'd never seen his villainy with her own eyes. Natasha could be ruthless, but Boky was downright evil. Natasha shuddered to think what he'd do with the *Volkhovnik*, should he get his hands on it.

Slinking down so her movement wouldn't be visible through

the window, Natasha crept away from the church. She'd have to risk calling Katya back without understanding what had caused her to break. Natasha needed that final cipher decoded. She'd do whatever she must to keep the *Volkhovnik* from falling into Boky's hands.

# Chapter 47
## *Katya*

Days passed with the sun making only brief appearances. Weak sunlight would trickle through the windows for a few hours and then vanish into seemingly endless winter nights. Katya slept and stared, unable to rouse herself. She heard people talking, but she couldn't assemble the fractured pieces of herself enough to listen or respond. Tsisana poured tea down her throat and spooned soup into her mouth. Katya's body survived while her mind hibernated, dark and barren as the cold January earth.

Then Natasha came to visit.

Katya was aware of her, but vaguely. Natasha slapped her cheek, but Katya didn't feel it. Natasha shouted, but the currents of Katya's despair carried the words away. Finally, Natasha took Katya's face in her hands and began to chant.

A jolt like lightning flashed through Katya's blood and thundered in her ears. The shock forced Katya's soul, mind and body back into alignment. She blinked and found she could look out from her eyes once more. The rawness of Katya's throat and the ache of her muscles proved she'd done her body no favours by sinking away, but she didn't care.

Natasha crossed her arms and smiled, inordinately pleased with herself. Katya wanted to be alone, but her jaw had locked shut and telling Natasha to go away seemed too much effort.

She stared at nothing and tried to drift away again.

'No.' Natasha grabbed Katya's chin. 'Every day Boky is searching for the *Volkhovnik*.'

*I don't care*, was Katya's first thought. But the second thought was sharper. *Half-sister*.

Katya worked her jaw loose and rasped out, 'I know who you are.'

'Good, you're finally catching up,' Natasha said nonchalantly. 'Here.'

Natasha dropped a folder on the bed. It landed on Katya's belly. Katya sat up when she saw that the label read *S.N. Efremova*. The label made the folder feel heavier, as though weighed down by all the love and betrayal that name symbolised to Katya.

Taking a deep, steadying breath, Katya opened the file. It contained three photographs.

Dizziness washed over Katya when she looked at the image of her living room the day Svetlana died. Though the photograph was black and white, she remembered the dark rust colour of the blood splattered across the living room wall. Back then she hadn't noticed bloody paw prints tracked across the floor. She squinted at the photo. An animal had walked through the blood. A dog, maybe? *Or a wolf.*

'Where did you get these?'

Natasha shrugged, her dark blue eyes glinting.

Katya bit her lip, letting the pain ground her nerves. How many times had she wondered what happened the day Svetlana died? Now the answers were at her fingertips.

She flipped to the next image. The photographer took the shot while standing in the living room facing Svetlana's office. The door hung crookedly from its hinges. Claws had scored the wood of the door frame, papers littered the office floor and an unusual amount of ash was spewed around the fireplace. Had Svetlana been burning papers before she died?

These pictures implied Svetlana was attacked in the living room, then perhaps managed to lock herself in the office. She'd had time to destroy evidence and leave messages in Katya's book of fairy tales before the door was busted in.

Katya hesitated to view the last picture. Closing her eyes, she breathed in and out a few times. She had knots in her shoulders and dread in her gut when she flipped to the final photograph – a picture of Svetlana's corpse.

Katya's hand quaked. Letting the photograph fall onto her lap, she pressed her fingers to her lips and tried to remember how to breathe.

Svetlana had wounds on her face and body, including a long slash of claw marks across her torso. But a bullet had killed her – and the gun that fired it rested in Svetlana's cold, dead fingers.

'I don't understand.'

'Yes, you do,' Natasha said, uncharacteristically gentle. 'She took her own life before she could be tortured for information.'

Katya pressed her lips together and closed her eyes. A tsunami of grief threatened to crash over her, but she turned her back on emotion and forced her mind to reason things out.

She thought back to the Kronstadt Rebellion, when everything went wrong.

Katya had stopped speaking to Svetlana after she slept with Stepan Petrichenko. She'd locked herself in her room for days, only coming out for food when she knew Svetlana would be asleep.

Her poems from those days were full of angst, the pages of her diary dappled with tears.

Then one day her bedroom door flew open.

Svetlana bounded through it, eyes lit with excitement.

'We did it.' Svetlana dropped onto Katya's bed, grabbing her hands and squeezing them. 'The Petrograd soviet has agreed to our demands, every last one. Your spell worked. They've sent the document to Moscow. Once Lenin and the other Bolshevik leaders read it, everything is going to change.'

Katya's heavy heart lifted at this news, but she kept her expression guarded.

'Let's go celebrate,' Svetlana suggested.

Pulling her hands from her mother's grip, Katya crossed her arms over her torso.

'Oh, come on.' Svetlana sighed, as though exasperated by Katya's surliness. 'What's the matter?'

'You really have to ask?'

'Fine, fine, I shouldn't have done that. Sorry if your feelings were hurt, but you know I'll make it up to you. Anyway, he wasn't good enough for my little turtle.' Svetlana cupped her cheek. 'He was too old.'

'He's closer to my age than yours.'

Svetlana dropped her hand from Katya's face and sighed again. 'You're angry, I get it. But look – the sun's shining and we did something historic. Let's go outside, at least. I can't spend another minute cooped up in this flat.'

'Fine.' Katya threw off her blankets. Swiping her clothes off the floor, she stomped off to the bathroom to get dressed and make herself look somewhat presentable. She slammed the bathroom door when she came back into the living room. Svetlana rolled her eyes, and Katya realised her mother would interpret her behaviour as a childlike tantrum. Svetlana couldn't fathom the depths to which her betrayal had wounded Katya.

Katya's anger drained away, leaving only acceptance. Svetlana would be Svetlana, no matter what. Her irresistible charm seemed coupled with an inability to recognise other people's feelings.

Though maybe she did know how Katya felt. When they left the flat arm-in-arm, Svetlana led Katya through the desolate streets of Petrograd, headed for the only bookmaker's shop still in business.

'I have a surprise for you.' Svetlana pushed open the shop door, and a ringing bell announced their arrival.

The shopkeeper greeted her warmly and handed her a package wrapped in brown paper. Whatever it was, Svetlana must have paid for it in advance. She held the package against her chest, making Katya's anticipation grow until they sat down on a bench at a waterfront park.

The sun shone down on their faces – a rare treat for early March. Svetlana's contagious excitement began to rub off on Katya, especially when she unwrapped the package. Inside the brown paper, Katya found the most beautiful journal she'd ever seen. It had a leather cover with thick, high-quality paper inside. Katya stared at it, shaking her head in amazement. She'd only ever had cheap composition books to write her poetry in.

'I love it.' Katya's voice sounded choked up. 'How did you afford this?'

With the cuts in bread rations, they were near starving. Everyone was.

'Don't worry about how much it cost.' Svetlana wrapped an arm around Katya's shoulders and squeezed her. 'I want to spoil you. You deserve to be celebrated – we both do.'

Katya let out a long exhale, releasing her bitter feelings. With Svetlana's arm still around her, Katya relaxed and rested her head on Svetlana's shoulder.

'Thank you, Mamochka.'

They sat in comfortable silence for several minutes, basking in the sunshine, until a distant explosion broke their reveries.

'What was that?' Katya asked.

Svetlana's face drained of colour. Katya followed her line of sight out over the frozen water in the direction of Kronstadt. A plume of black smoke rose ominously from the fortress. As they watched, another missile was launched from the northern shore. It arced through the sky, landing with a resounding boom.

Katya put her hand over her mouth.

'No,' Svetlana said. 'No, no, no, no.'

Svetlana rose from the bench and began pacing. Her shoulders crumpled when a third artillery blast struck the fortress.

'We have to go.' She grabbed Katya's hand and pulled her up to standing.

With her new poetry diary tucked under her arm, Katya tried to keep up with her mother's frantic pace. They went to Smolny, Katya's old school. It had been the base of radical activities the year of the Revolution. Now only small remnants of anarchist and socialist groups still met there.

When they gathered with the anarchists, they learned what had happened. The spell in the document Katya crafted had successfully compelled the members of the Petrograd soviet. But instead of sending the actual document to Moscow, Petrograd officials typed up a copy, one completely void of magic.

Lenin had been infuriated by the sailors' demands. His advisers suggested he send negotiators to Kronstadt. To everyone's shock, Lenin sent an army.

Katya would never forget the raw pain in her mother's eyes when she realised their plan had failed.

The Red Army laid siege to Kronstadt, first weakening the walls with artillery and then wasting the lives of their infantryman by making them run across the open ice and attempt to take the fortress. The sailors fiercely defended their stronghold,

351

killing tens of thousands of Red Army soldiers. Bodies littered the ice around Kotlin Island, but eventually the Red Army's greater numbers overwhelmed the island's defenders.

After eight days, the fortress fell.

Some of the Kronstadt sailors made it to Finland, Stepan Petrichenko included, but more than ten thousand died defending the fortress. Those who were captured faced the firing squad.

Everyone thought the resistance had died along with them.

Everyone but Svetlana.

Looking at the photographic evidence of her mother's commitment to the cause, Katya forced her mind to reason things out. If Svetlana had become a Bolshevik informant after Kronstadt, it wasn't because she'd turned her back on the anarchists. No. She'd gambled everything, betraying her friends and comrades for the chance to find a weapon powerful enough to stop the Bolsheviki for good – the *Volkhovnik*.

She must have informed on the anarchists in exchange for the papers they used to start afresh in Moscow and the money she would need to fulfil her quest of finding the book.

Svetlana had begun researching Stenka Razin after she discovered he'd possessed the *Volkhovnik*. In the weeks before her death, Svetlana took a research expedition to Solovetsky Island. She walked the labyrinth and found Yelezar Danilov's book.

When the Soviet fleet appeared on the horizon, Svetlana started the fire in the monastery's library to prevent the government from recreating her research. She cut off the end of Yelezar's book and hid the two parts, leaving a clue to the first part on the map Dima found. A cipher led to Valentina Pavlovna and the knowledge that the *Volkhovnik* may be hidden on this archipelago.

Somewhere she must have left a clue to the ending of Stenka's tale.

After destroying or concealing anything that might lead the Bolsheviki to the *Volkhovnik*, Svetlana returned to Moscow. She worked feverishly in the days that followed, but too soon the Cheka came for her.

Rather than telling Gleb Boky what she knew, Svetlana died to keep her secrets.

Because she trusted Katya to finish her work.

'I brought you soup and tea,' Natasha said. 'Also a bucket of warm water to bathe yourself.'

Katya worked her jaw loose and rasped out, 'Why?'

'Because we have work to do. You're going to get better. Then you and I are going to find the *Volkhovnik* before Boky does. Agreed?'

Katya stared at Natasha – fiery hair, stubborn chin, eyes the colour of dusk. What were her motives? What were her plans? Natasha felt less like a stranger and more like a deadly enigma.

'Agreed.' Katya said this to avoid confrontation, but she'd already decided she would never be Natasha's ally again.

When Natasha left, Katya took out her book of fairy tales. There was one clue she had yet to solve: the last line of the lemon-ink message.

*1436*
келья

ГЦЪШРФЭИИГТСНЙБНБОМА

The first three lines were meant to lead Katya to Solovki, where she would find the map hidden in a hermit cell. What was the purpose of the final line?

Katya remembered something Valentina Pavlovna had said. Svetlana gave her a message to pass on to Katya: *my little turtle.*

That had been Katya's nickname, but what if it was a keyword as well? моя маленькая черепаха. Twenty letters, just like the lemon-ink code.

Katya pulled out her *tabula recta* and copied over the code:

Г Ц Ъ Ш Р Ф Э И И Г Т С Н Й Б Н Б О М А Then she wrote 'my little turtle' below that.

М О Я М А Л Е Н Ь К А Я   Ч Е Р Е П А Х А

Katya inputted the code and keyword into the table.

```
А Б В Г Д Е Ё Ж З И Й К Л М Н О П Р С Т У Ф Х Ц Ч Ш Щ Ъ Ы Ь Э Ю Я
Б В Г Д Е Ё Ж З И Й К Л М Н О П Р С Т У Ф Х Ц Ч Ш Щ Ъ Ы Ь Э Ю Я А
В Г Д Е Ё Ж З И Й К Л М Н О П Р С Т У Ф Х Ц Ч Ш Щ Ъ Ы Ь Э Ю Я А Б
Г Д Е Ё Ж З И Й К Л М Н О П Р С Т У Ф Х Ц Ч Ш Щ Ъ Ы Ь Э Ю Я А Б В
Д Е Ё Ж З И Й К Л М Н О П Р С Т У Ф Х Ц Ч Ш Щ Ъ Ы Ь Э Ю Я А Б В Г
Е Ё Ж З И Й К Л М Н О П Р С Т У Ф Х Ц Ч Ш Щ Ъ Ы Ь Э Ю Я А Б В Г Д
Ё Ж З И Й К Л М Н О П Р С Т У Ф Х Ц Ч Ш Щ Ъ Ы Ь Э Ю Я А Б В Г Д Е
Ж З И Й К Л М Н О П Р С Т У Ф Х Ц Ч Ш Щ Ъ Ы Ь Э Ю Я А Б В Г Д Е Ё
З И Й К Л М Н О П Р С Т У Ф Х Ц Ч Ш Щ Ъ Ы Ь Э Ю Я А Б В Г Д Е Ё Ж
И Й К Л М Н О П Р С Т У Ф Х Ц Ч Ш Щ Ъ Ы Ь Э Ю Я А Б В Г Д Е Ё Ж З
Й К Л М Н О П Р С Т У Ф Х Ц Ч Ш Щ Ъ Ы Ь Э Ю Я А Б В Г Д Е Ё Ж З И
К Л М Н О П Р С Т У Ф Х Ц Ч Ш Щ Ъ Ы Ь Э Ю Я А Б В Г Д Е Ё Ж З И Й
Л М Н О П Р С Т У Ф Х Ц Ч Ш Щ Ъ Ы Ь Э Ю Я А Б В Г Д Е Ё Ж З И Й К
М Н О П Р С Т У Ф Х Ц Ч Ш Щ Ъ Ы Ь Э Ю Я А Б В Г Д Е Ё Ж З И Й К Л
Н О П Р С Т У Ф Х Ц Ч Ш Щ Ъ Ы Ь Э Ю Я А Б В Г Д Е Ё Ж З И Й К Л М
О П Р С Т У Ф Х Ц Ч Ш Щ Ъ Ы Ь Э Ю Я А Б В Г Д Е Ё Ж З И Й К Л М Н
П Р С Т У Ф Х Ц Ч Ш Щ Ъ Ы Ь Э Ю Я А Б В Г Д Е Ё Ж З И Й К Л М Н О
Р С Т У Ф Х Ц Ч Ш Щ Ъ Ы Ь Э Ю Я А Б В Г Д Е Ё Ж З И Й К Л М Н О П
С Т У Ф Х Ц Ч Ш Щ Ъ Ы Ь Э Ю Я А Б В Г Д Е Ё Ж З И Й К Л М Н О П Р
Т У Ф Х Ц Ч Ш Щ Ъ Ы Ь Э Ю Я А Б В Г Д Е Ё Ж З И Й К Л М Н О П Р С
У Ф Х Ц Ч Ш Щ Ъ Ы Ь Э Ю Я А Б В Г Д Е Ё Ж З И Й К Л М Н О П Р С Т
Ф Х Ц Ч Ш Щ Ъ Ы Ь Э Ю Я А Б В Г Д Е Ё Ж З И Й К Л М Н О П Р С Т У
Х Ц Ч Ш Щ Ъ Ы Ь Э Ю Я А Б В Г Д Е Ё Ж З И Й К Л М Н О П Р С Т У Ф
Ц Ч Ш Щ Ъ Ы Ь Э Ю Я А Б В Г Д Е Ё Ж З И Й К Л М Н О П Р С Т У Ф Х
Ч Ш Щ Ъ Ы Ь Э Ю Я А Б В Г Д Е Ё Ж З И Й К Л М Н О П Р С Т У Ф Х Ц
Ш Щ Ъ Ы Ь Э Ю Я А Б В Г Д Е Ё Ж З И Й К Л М Н О П Р С Т У Ф Х Ц Ч
Щ Ъ Ы Ь Э Ю Я А Б В Г Д Е Ё Ж З И Й К Л М Н О П Р С Т У Ф Х Ц Ч Ш
Ъ Ы Ь Э Ю Я А Б В Г Д Е Ё Ж З И Й К Л М Н О П Р С Т У Ф Х Ц Ч Ш Щ
Ы Ь Э Ю Я А Б В Г Д Е Ё Ж З И Й К Л М Н О П Р С Т У Ф Х Ц Ч Ш Щ Ъ
Ь Э Ю Я А Б В Г Д Е Ё Ж З И Й К Л М Н О П Р С Т У Ф Х Ц Ч Ш Щ Ъ Ы
Э Ю Я А Б В Г Д Е Ё Ж З И Й К Л М Н О П Р С Т У Ф Х Ц Ч Ш Щ Ъ Ы Ь
Ю Я А Б В Г Д Е Ё Ж З И Й К Л М Н О П Р С Т У Ф Х Ц Ч Ш Щ Ъ Ы Ь Э
Я А Б В Г Д Е Ё Ж З И Й К Л М Н О П Р С Т У Ф Х Ц Ч Ш Щ Ъ Ы Ь Э Ю
```

She wrote out the result. Пещера в центре острова – *A cave at the island's centre.* Katya stared at the words, a sense of wonder opening in her heart. From beyond the grave, Svetlana was still leading her, and now Katya knew where she had to go next.

# PART IV

---

*The Book Of The Wizard*

# *Claws*

```
                              I
                              AM
                  I          NOT          I
                 AM         ONLY         AM
                 NOT        BONES        NOT
                 ONLY                    ONLY
                 FLESH       LEFT        SINEW
        I                   BROKEN.                    I
       AM        BLUE      WHAT YOU      MADE         AM
       NOT      BRUISED.   SHATTER, I    WEAK.IN      NOT
       ONLY     VIOLENCE   FORGE INTO   ANY TRIAL,    ONLY
       BLOOD    CAN'T TAKE WHITE-HOT    MY SPIRIT     HEART
                MY STORY,   STEEL.      WILL STAY
       HARSH    FUTURE,                 TETHERED     GRIEF-
       SPILLED.  FIGHT.    NO SOUL      FIRM.        SHADOWED.
       LISTEN TO           IS MARKED                 MY LANTERN
       MY VICTORY.      FOREVER BY THE               WILL SHINE
       IT'S SINGING    CLAWS OF TRAGEDY.             WITH LOVE
       THROUGH MY    WE ARE FAR MORE THAN            DESPITE
        SCARS.      WHAT HAS BEEN DONE TO US.        PAIN.
              A BROKEN BODY HEALS IN TIME.
            IN GRIEF, FIND COURAGE. IN TRAUMA,
         DISCOVER YOUR FANGS. SORROW'S DARK CLOUD
        RESTS HEAVY ON A TORMENTED MIND, BUT EVEN
        SOUL-DEEP WOUNDS CAN BECOME PROOF OF YOUR
         GLORIOUS SURVIVAL.WHAT YOUR ENEMY MEANT
          FOR HARM, SHAPE IN WAYS THAT MAKE YOU
            STRONGER. THEY'LL NAME YOU BROKEN
              ONLY IF YOU LET THEM WIN.
```

# Chapter 48

## *Katya*

Katya awoke early one morning and trekked through knee-deep snow. In winter darkness, she stood shivering in the courtyard while the monastery awakened from its slumber. Katya had something to do today, something she dreaded.

She was going to talk to Dima.

Katya might have avoided him for ever if not for the encoded message. *A cave at the island's centre.*

While Katya had been in the infirmary, Dima had been busy. He'd added three journalists to the artists' unit and published the first edition of a weekly newspaper. Not only had Commissar Boky allowed the journalists to use the lithograph machine, he also gave permission for Dima and his journalists to be excused from labour one day per week. They received travel passes to visit various work sites on the island to collect news stories.

Katya needed one of those passes. That meant swallowing her pride and asking for help.

When the morning bell resounded through the monastery, she waited at the front of the ration line – the only place Dima couldn't avoid her. She rubbed her arms and shifted her legs so they wouldn't freeze stiff.

At last she spotted Dima.

Katya's chest panged at the sight of him, and her lips twisted into a pained wince. As always, his face captivated her. She could spend hours staring at the play of light and shadow across the lines of his cheekbones and studying the way the smallest movement of his lush eyebrows changed his whole expression. A black smear marked his chin, ink probably. It had been hard work, this newspaper, and all of it on top of the gruelling labour required of him each day.

Katya admired him more than anyone she'd ever met, and that admiration ached inside her chest now that she'd broken things off between them. She'd had to do it, though. Everyone Katya loved ended up dead, and she refused to let that happen again, especially now that Boky had fixed his sights on Dima.

Dima didn't say a word as Katya fell in beside him. He only lifted one eyebrow in surprise. This time, when his lips went crooked, it was in a frown.

'I'm probably the last person you want to see,' she said.

'I wouldn't say that, though I am surprised you're talking to me.'

He crossed his arms, inching forward along with the line. Dima's voice sounded raw, and his eyes looked wounded. She'd done that to him, injured him with her words that day in the infirmary.

'I need a favour.' Katya lowered her eyes, ashamed to be asking him for anything, especially now. 'I'd understand if you don't want to help me, but—'

'If you think I wouldn't help you, you don't know me at all.'

Katya bit her lip. She did know Dima. They weren't strangers anymore. Not friends, either. The boundaries between them were blurred in some places, barbed in others. But she'd known Dima would help if she asked.

'I solved the final cipher,' Katya said. 'I was hoping you could get me a pass to leave the monastery so I can follow where it leads.'

Dima nodded thoughtfully, taking it in. They were nearing the front of the line and only had a few more moments to speak.

'I'll get you a pass, but I have three conditions.' He held up a gloved hand and counted them off on his fingers. 'Firstly, I'm coming with you, of course. I want to know the end of my ancestor's story.'

Katya nodded reluctantly. She owed him that much, but being close to him felt like a torment after she'd broken things off.

'Number two is I want to check on Valentina Pavlovna before we go anywhere else. I've been sick with worry about what happened to her that night with the wolves.'

'I've been worried too,' Katya said, agreeing to this term.

'The third is non-negotiable.' Dima held up his third finger. 'The passes are for journalists. If I get one for you, you're on the paper. Every week, you have to let me publish something you write. No more hiding your talent away.'

His words made Katya nervous, but in a good way. She'd felt an undeniable thrill seeing her poem in print. Publishing her writing had always been a secret wish, one Svetlana had made her believe was impossible. Dima had seen that she *could* do it. Even after she'd broken his heart, he was still championing her to use her talents.

Katya's throat itched. She cleared it, lowering her eyes so Dima wouldn't see how much she'd been touched by his belief in her writing.

'It's a deal,' she said.

Though she didn't look at Dima, she saw in her peripheral vision how the crooked smile curved his lips and she tried to ignore the pang of longing in her chest.

'Good,' he said. 'Meet me after roll-call.'

Katya took her breakfast and joined her company, going to stand beside Tsisana.

'I owe you a debt of gratitude,' Katya said. 'You took such good care of me in the infirmary.'

'You don't owe me anything.' Tsisana bumped Katya's shoulder and smiled. 'Friends look out for one another. I'm just glad to see you up and about.'

Katya again felt that pins-and-needles sensation, like Tsisana's warmth was thawing the ice inside Katya's chest. Looking at her friend, she noticed a few changes. A smile, for one thing, and a lessening of the anguish she'd carried in her eyes. Tsisana no longer wore her hideous headscarf.

'How have you been?' Katya asked.

'Better, now that Rafael is here. I was afraid he'd be disgusted with me when he found out . . .' Tsisana lowered her eyes, a muscle ticking in her jaw as she swallowed the words she couldn't bring herself to say.

'It wasn't your fault,' Katya said fiercely.

'I know.' Tsisana let out a shaky breath. 'Rafael was furious, but not with me. To me he was gentle and kind, a perfect gentleman. He helped me come up with a plan for if Smolensky tries anything again.'

Katya started to ask what that plan entailed, but just then Matilda Ivanova clapped her hands and shouted to the women that it was time for roll-call.

After she'd received a check mark by her name, Katya met up with Dima, who had succeeded in obtaining two travel passes from the administration. They showed their passes at the guard station and were issued skis to carry them over the frozen canals.

They set off north.

The winds picked up by the time they reached Valentina Pavlovna's house, another winter storm rolling over the archipelago. Dima stopped abruptly as they crossed the yard. Katya followed his gaze to Valentina Pavlovna's door, and her heart sank.

It stood partially open.

Katya swallowed the lump forming in her throat as she and Dima removed their skis.

Climbing the steps to Valentina Pavlovna's door gave Katya a flashback of that awful November day at her flat in Moscow, how the stairs had creaked beneath her boots as she approached her mother's murder scene.

Katya couldn't dispel the remembered image of Svetlana's blood splattered across the wall. She held her breath as Dima entered the *izba* ahead of her and fumbled for a lamp. Soon light filled the room, along with the smell of kerosene.

There were no signs of violence.

There was also no sign of Valentina Pavlovna.

Snow had blown in through the open door, and frost coated the metal front of the stove. Three empty shot glasses rested on the table top, exactly where they'd left them.

She'd been gone ever since that night two weeks ago, but what had happened to her? She might have been captured, but Katya hadn't seen Valentina Pavlovna in the infirmary or women's barrack.

'Maybe she got away?' Dima looked sombre as he surveyed the empty house. 'There are cabins like this all over the archipelago. She could be hiding somewhere else.'

'I hope you're right,' Katya said, though her heavy heart believed otherwise. 'Shall we continue on?'

'We should wait out the blizzard.' Dima motioned to the open door and the wind howling through it. 'I still have blisters from the last time I got frostbite, and that's an experience I'd rather not repeat.'

Katya looked out at the snowstorm and sighed.

While Dima built up the fire, Katya swept the snow outside and shut the door. It was nearly as cold inside as out. Dima cast worried glances at Katya as they stood before the stove, waiting for the fire to do its work.

'You're shivering.' Dima unbuttoned his coat and opened his arms to her. Katya's mouth went dry, but she needed his warmth. She stepped into his embrace, threading her arms behind his back. He wrapped his arms around her shoulders and rested his cheek against the top of her head.

They fit together so well, in more ways than one. Though she couldn't rid herself of the image of Dima knelt on the cobblestones while Smolensky aimed a pistol at his head, neither could she forget what Dima said last time they came to Valentina Pavlovna's house. *I think we both deserve whatever happiness we can find, for however many days we have left.*

When Katya's shivering subsided, Dima said, 'Can I ask you a question?'

'Can I stop you from asking me a question?'

She felt him smile, but the rest of his body tensed and his voice came out strained.

'Is it only because I'm an aristocrat that you broke things off between us, or did I do something wrong?'

'You didn't do anything.' Katya held him close, tilting her head down against his chest so he couldn't see her face. 'Those two prisoners who were shot—'

'Doctor Tarasov and Father Iosef,' Dima said soberly.

'Yes.' Shame roiled in Katya's belly, and a bitter taste rose to the back of her throat. 'Boky killed them to make me talk. It all happened so fast. Smolensky was going to shoot you too, but I cracked. I told Commissar Boky about the island of labyrinths, about the map and the manuscript. I told him all about Valentina Pavlovna. I betrayed our secrets, my values, myself. But there's nothing I wouldn't have done to stop him from ordering that guard to pull the trigger.'

Dima inhaled long and slow. 'You saved my life.'

'Your life was only in danger because of my feelings for you.'

Stepping back from the embrace, Dima took Katya's face in his hands. His brow was furrowed, his dark eyes intense. 'I appreciate that you want to protect me, but you and I both know I'm never getting off this island. Even if we're doomed, I want to be with you for whatever time I have left. And I think you want that too.'

She did want that, despite the cold fear crawling up her spine.

'Be with me,' he said, the words whispered like a prayer. 'We're alone in an isolated cabin, and this might be the only chance we ever have.'

Katya met his eyes for a long moment, and then she nodded.

Dima kissed her forehead. He added a few logs to the fire then set a record on the gramophone and cranked up the motor. Jazz poured from the brass horn, gentle at first – a soft drum keeping rhythm, tentative chords on a piano, a saxophone belting out long opening notes, and a bass underpinning them all. When a soulful voice joined in, the words were in English. But it didn't matter. Jazz didn't need to be understood, only felt. And from the first moment she'd seen Dima in the lab, Katya knew he was a jazz song – all soul, emotion and unexpected twists.

If this was a night for being swept away, he'd chosen the perfect soundtrack.

Dima looked back at her over his shoulder. The knot in her belly turned to heat as his smile went crooked. Taking off his coat, hat and gloves, Dima combed his hair with his fingers before crossing the room and offering Katya his hand. 'Dance with me?'

'I thought you had two left feet.' She unbuttoned her coat and tossed it aside.

'Maybe I've found the right partner.'

Katya glanced ruefully at her frumpy clothes. She flattened the fabric of the too-big trousers over her thighs. Dima's eyes tracked her movements, and his lips curved into a knowing smile.

'You're beautiful.' Dima bowed formally, and offered his hand again, this time with a flourish. The intensity of his brown eyes made warmth rush to Katya's cheeks.

Katya opened her mouth, but only a shaky breath came out. As a charovnika, hers was a magic of words, but the heat of Dima's desire melted Katya's voice like wax.

She stepped towards him, never lowering her gaze from his. Dima took her hip, his fingers searing through the fabric of her clothes as he guided her forward, turning the narrow space between the entrance and the table into a dance floor. Katya's knees quavered, so she anchored herself to Dima's shoulder as they swayed to the music. He brought their joined hands in close, right beside his heart.

The song ended too soon. Dima stepped back in the brief silence between tracks, and Katya felt oddly shy as the opening notes of a slow song drifted through the room like intoxicating smoke.

He brought his lips to hers. It was a sweet kiss, one that demanded nothing of Katya, but heat pooled in her belly. As a saxophone wailed a mournful love song, Katya kissed him back, hard. If his lips were honey, hers were spice. He moaned. While his hand slipped into her hair, Katya skimmed her thumb beneath one of his braces, following the line from his shoulder to his waist. She broke the kiss, watching his reaction as she untucked his shirt and let her fingers rove across his back.

Dima bit his lip, eyes hazy with desire.

No one had ever looked at her like that. She'd been with a few boys before. Katya's poet's soul had sought connection, but it always ended in disappointment, the boy taking pleasure in her body and leaving her unsatisfied. She'd spend the following days feeling lonely, almost hollow, and anxiously counting down to her next period. Pregnancy wasn't something she had to worry about now. Hunger had stopped her cycles altogether. But was she ready to cross that line with Dima, to offer herself to him body and soul?

She wanted to. She'd never craved another person like this. Kissing him did nothing to quench her thirst for his lips on hers, and touching his skin only made her want him even more.

Dima untied the leather strap at the bottom of her hair and slowly undid the plait, combing her locks open with his fingers. He was so gentle when he touched her, so full of love every time he looked at her.

'Are you all right?' Dima's brow furrowed with concern, as if reading the inner debate written across her face. 'We can stop, if you want. Or slow down.'

'I don't want to stop.' She kissed him once, her heart pounding. 'And I want the opposite of slowing down.'

Dima tried to say something, but when Katya pressed her hips against him, only a strangled sound rose from his throat. On a long exhale, Dima closed his eyes and tilted his face skyward. He trembled as she kissed her way up his exposed throat. Katya's fingertips ventured up his back, and his arms wrapped tight around her waist. His breathing was shaky. When Katya's teeth nipped his jaw, Dima's whole body shuddered.

Dima lost his balance and tumbled into her. The force made Katya career backwards, giggling as she slammed into the table edge, clattering the shot glasses and bottle. He grabbed her hips to keep her from falling. But once she was steady, back half-tilted over the table, he didn't let go. A buzzing current poured through his fingertips, pulsating through her.

'Sorry,' he half-whispered, half-laughed.

'Maybe we should lie down before we break something.' Dima offered his hand. When Katya took it, he interlaced their fingers and led her to the mattress rolled out beside the stove. Then he paused, rubbing the back of his neck. 'I think that came out wrong. I didn't mean . . .'

Katya took off her sweater and dropped it on the floor. She still had a shirt on under it, but Dima's cheeks and the tips of his ears turned pink. Stepping closer, Katya fumbled with the buttons of his shirt.

'I didn't mean to assume,' he said. 'We don't have to do anything you don't want.'

His shirt now open, Katya put her hand on his chest, feeling the warmth of his skin and the race of his heartbeat. Dima was usually flirty and confident. Seeing him this flustered gave her an acute pleasure. She was nervous too, but she spoke with full bravado. 'There's nothing I don't want you to do to me tonight.'

Dima's eyebrows lifted with surprise, but it didn't take long for his lips to twist into a devilish smile. 'You're sure?'

Katya pushed the braces straps off her shoulders, and her too-large trousers fell in a heap around her ankles, leaving her legs bare. Dima's mouth dropped open like he'd forgotten how to breathe. She pulled her shirt over her head and slipped out of her undergarments.

Katya stood naked before him in the firelight, with jazz music spilling notes all around the room and a relentless winter wind howling at the door.

Dima's eyes traced the lines of Katya's body, his voice filled with wonder. 'You're a masterpiece.'

'And you're still wearing all your clothes.'

Dima chuckled as Katya slid the braces off his shoulders and forcibly removed his shirt. He took the hint and stripped before her. Dima was lean, his ribs marked by hunger. But labour had carved muscle into his chest and shoulders. Katya bit her lip. She loved the way his torso angled from his broad shoulders to his narrow waist, loved the pronounced V shape of his hips, which drew her gaze downward.

Gooseflesh covered Katya's skin, but her insides were molten. Her blood flowed like magma when Dima closed the space between them.

His dilated eyes were almost completely black as he guided her to the mattress. She lay on her back, and he hovered over her. Katya poured her heart into every kiss, but that only filled her with more yearning. Dima took his time. He made her body his canvas, sketching his love across her skin with his fingers, with his tongue and lips and teeth.

Dams burst within her – all the walls she'd built around herself crumbled. Her instinct was to resist, to fight, to seize back control. Without meaning to, she closed her hands into fists, and her body went rigid.

Dima looked down at her.

'Katya,' he said in that way of his that made her name sound like laughter. 'Everything all right?'

Blowing out a long breath, Katya forcibly unclenched her hands. She was so conditioned to pain that pleasure felt un-trustworthy, like a cruel joke. But this was Dima. Katya trusted him. She could let go of this one last barrier.

'I'm fine,' she said.

'Are you sure?' Dima brushed a stray lock of hair aside with his fingertips as he examined her face. When she nodded, he kissed her temple. He slid his arm beneath her neck and cradled her shoulders, rested his forehead against hers to anchor her with intimacy as his fingers trailed down her body.

Dima's thumb made sensation rush through her. As pressure built in her core, Katya's legs stretched out and her toes curled. With a deep exhale, she made her final surrender.

Flashes of hot and cold shot through her. Her back arched as she lost control, swept away by the spell Dima cast over her. His lips were by her ear, whispering words of love and comfort, but she was too consumed to make them out.

The pressure building between her legs flared, and it felt like being unmade. She couldn't breathe, couldn't think. Every cell of her body burned white hot. She moaned as the pressure shot upwards, and the scorching waves intensified.

All the while Dima was right beside her. Holding her. Loving her. Beaming at her pleasure when the climax passed and little aftershocks made her body spasm. Katya melted into the mattress, pulling Dima atop of her and stealing away his ridiculous smile with a burning-ember kiss.

She'd never felt so relaxed. Dima laid his face on her chest, his fingers making lazy circles over her belly as she closed her eyes. Though she let herself bask in the afterglow for a few minutes, they were far from done.

It was her turn to make him lose control. She wanted to overwhelm him with passion, to somehow turn every touch into poetry. Pushing him onto his back, she moved her body lithely over his. Her lips traced his collar bone, his throat, his jaw – her tender kisses like lines of a love letter.

She pulled him up to sitting and settled on his lap, wrapping her legs around his back. His arms caged her, crushing her against his chest. And his fingers dug into her back, as though no matter how close she was, he needed her nearer.

She gazed into his eyes as she guided him inside her. His eyes fluttered shut. His hands roamed her body as she rolled her hips, clinging to his neck as heat and pressure built between her legs again.

They moved to the rhythm of the music, a continuation of their earlier dance. A haze blurred Dima's eyes, his expression dreamy as pleasure overwhelmed him.

He gripped the backs of her thighs and tackled her onto her back. She dug her fingers into his shoulder and wrapped her legs around him. They clung to each other. Katya threw her head back, arching her spine as she relinquished all control. It felt like jumping off a cliff and landing in a sea of sensation, and this time Dima fell with her. In a moment his expression changed from an agonised grimace to a look of utter euphoria.

Dima threaded his fingers through Katya's hair and kissed her throat as his body convulsed. Then he collapsed onto her, out of breath. Katya took his face in her hands, kissing him as aftershocks made them both tremble.

Katya smiled as he rested his head on her chest. They lay in a tangle of limbs on the too-small mattress, a blanket draped over them.

'When they sent me here, I promised myself I'd experience as much as I could, *live* as much as I could, before they killed me. But I never dared to hope for this.' He kissed her temple and rested his head on the pillow beside hers.

Katya's heart swelled. She brought his hand to her lips and kissed his knuckles. The heat of passion had cooled, but an unfamiliar warmth remained inside her chest.

She watched Dima fall asleep, her thoughts keeping her

awake long after the gramophone went silent. Having something this good meant having something to lose. Was it a mistake to give her heart to Dima? Tonight had surpassed her wildest imaginings of what lovemaking could feel like, but she couldn't silence the voice saying this was all too good to be true, that grief waited around the corner, just like always.

Holding him tighter, she cast those thoughts from her mind. She would rather have spent this night with Dima than not, even if it crushed her later. Stubborn denial hadn't changed how she felt about him, so she might as well admit the truth.

She watched him a minute longer, the brush of his eyelashes, the way shadows gathered beneath his cheekbone. Gently kissing the bridge of his crooked nose, Katya rested her head on his chest. The fire had died down. A chill crept across her face, but Dima's nearness enveloped her in warmth. After more than a year of constant danger, his arms felt like a haven, the one place she would always be safe.

# Chapter 49

## *Natasha*

Natasha trailed Commander Nogtev through a narrow alley between buildings. When she was certain no one could overhear, she called his name. He turned, revealing the angry red blisters on his cheek and neck. He'd been badly burned while in his wolf form when Katya had smashed a lantern across the side of his head.

The camp director watched with bloodshot eyes as Natasha approached. He smelled of liquor, sweat and last night's vomit. Perhaps Natasha ought to prohibit his drinking, but she had more pressing problems this morning.

'Katya and Dima left after roll-call,' she said.

Natasha had translated the book, like Katya wanted. She'd fed her for three days in the cabin, and given her every resource she needed to decode the cipher. If not for Natasha, Katya would still be in the infirmary.

But the moment Katya found a clue? She'd gone straight to Dima.

Since Katya despised having Natasha as an ally, Natasha would show her half-sister the wrath she reserved for enemies.

'Smolensky reported that they left the monastery together,' she said, 'with passes *you* issued them.'

'Eh?' Nogtev swayed drunkenly, grabbing Natasha's shoulder to steady himself.

Natasha turned to look at his meaty hand, wincing with disgust as she removed it from her person.

Nogtev was singular among her volkolaki, and not necessarily in a good way.

He used to be a sailor in the Baltic Fleet, stationed on the battleship Aurora. In 1917, while moored in Petrograd for repairs, the sailors mutinied and fired the shot that began the October Revolution. That canon blast was the signal for revolutionary forces to storm the Winter Palace. It also caused Comrade Nogtev's hearing loss.

A few years later, when the Kronstadt sailors revolted against Lenin's government, Nogtev turned informant. That's what made him different from the other wolves. Hatred and rage drove most of them to violence, whereas Nogtev could shoot a man in the forehead and feel nothing. Nogtev had betrayed his fellow sailors to their deaths and thus committed a crime against his own soul, one so unthinkable that murder seemed mild in comparison.

Comrade Nogtev didn't rage against the prisoners like Smolensky and the others did. Because there was only one person he truly hated – himself.

Natasha understood why Nogtev drank to forgetfulness, but his foul breath and red, watery eyes filled her with revulsion.

'Why did you give Dmitri Danilov passes to leave the prison camp?' she asked, raising her voice enough for him to hear.

'Boky's orders.' Nogtev shrugged, as though it wasn't his fault he was either too drunk or too stupid to have informed her straight away.

Natasha bit the side of her cheek as she thought. Boky wanted Dima to be able to explore the island, probably hoping he and Katya would lead Boky to the *Volkhovnik*. His failure to mention this strategy to Natasha indicated that he too intended to cut her out.

With her alliances splintering, it was time for Natasha to make her move.

'Sober up,' Natasha ordered him. 'And spread this command among the pack. I want you all in wolf form, ready to come to my aid.'

Nogtev's eyes looked empty as he nodded in acceptance.

She watched Nogtev stagger away, hoping he wasn't too inebriated to carry out her orders. There was no time to seek out another volkolak. Katya and Dima must have decoded the second cipher. They were close to finding the *Volkhovnik*, and Natasha had no intention of letting them get there first.

Retracing her steps out of the alley, Natasha entered the administration through the small kitchen and made her way up the back stairway. She was surprised to see two guards stationed outside Boky's office, neither of them volkolaki.

Had something happened to put Boky on edge? Nerves fluttered in Natasha's stomach as she approached.

One of the guards opened the door for her to pass. Was this a trap? Natasha licked her lips and forced herself against all her instincts to step through the door.

Boky stood by his desk with Andrei Sergeevich, studying some sort of ledger.

'I don't see the problem.' Andrei Sergeevich shrugged.

'And *I* don't see how someone with a master's degree in mathematics could be such an incompetent bookkeeper,' Boky said with irritation. 'It's almost like you're doing it on purpose.'

'No, comrade.' Andrei Sergeevich's feathery eyebrows lifted, and he put a hand over his chest as though struck in the heart. 'It's not my fault the sums don't add up.'

'You'll make them add up, or tomorrow you'll find you've been transferred to hard labour.'

'As you like,' Andrei Sergeevich said as Boky thrust the ledger at him and waved him off. He limped to the adjacent room and closed the door.

A muscle ticked in Boky's jaw as he lifted his eyes to Natasha's. Though a chill moved through her, Natasha smiled. She swayed her hips as she crossed the room. Reaching for the lapels of his jacket, Natasha pulled Boky in for a kiss.

His lips were the gates of a fortress, barred shut. Taking Natasha by the shoulders, he placed her a few feet away from him, his cold grey eyes never leaving hers.

'What's wrong?' Natasha kept the smile plastered on her face, even when Boky's canines elongated. Clearly, something had soured between them, but showing her fear would only make things worse. Instead she raised her chin as she held Boky's gaze, as though she had nothing to hide.

'Yesterday you requisitioned a dog sled.' Boky clasped his hands behind his back. He paused for a long moment, his eyes boring into hers. 'Where did you go?'

Natasha quickly considered the lies she could tell, deciding on one that would turn the conversation in the direction she preferred.

'I had a hunch about where to look for the *Volkhovnik*. It turned out to be nothing, but I believe Katya may have solved the final cipher. She and Dima left the monastery together after roll-call.'

'I know where Katya is, just like I know where you went yesterday.' Boky turned away from her as though bored, shouting, 'Guards.'

Natasha was momentarily stunned as the office door flew open. She listened for any sign her wolves were coming but could only hear her heartbeat thrashing in her ears.

The guards roughly seized her arms.

'What are you doing?' She demanded, though she already knew. She'd known all along that she walked a knife's edge with Boky, that her life would be forfeit the moment he lost interest in her.

'It's a shame.' Boky's fingernails stretched into claws as he cupped her cheek and leaned in to kiss her forehead. 'We've had fun together, but I did warn you. That night in my office, do you remember what I said?'

Natasha shuddered as she recalled his words. *If I ever catch you spying on me again, it will be the last thing you ever do.*

She strained again to listen, but there was no sign of her wolves. Natasha never should have trusted Nogtev. What if he had passed out somewhere? Natasha could be dead before the volkolaki knew she needed them.

Black spots flashed in her vision as Boky's trap closed around her.

'Since you're so interested in what happens in Sekirka, I've decided to let you see it first-hand.' Boky smiled cruelly, showing his fangs. 'Take her away.'

Natasha let out a shuddering breath. The guards tightened their grips on her arms, but that's when she heard it – a low growl coming from the corridor outside.

Boky froze. He tilted his head, listening to the patter of claws on oaken floors.

Natasha breathed in a whiff of musk as her wolves burst into the office, quick as shadows. Natasha yanked her arms free from the shocked guards the moment before they were tackled to the ground.

'Stand down,' Boky ordered as the five remaining wolves surrounded him.

They growled, raising their hackles. Boky's face contorted

with rage. He pulled back his lips to show his fangs.

'I wouldn't challenge them if I were you.' Natasha strolled between two wolves, trailing her fingers along their coarse guard hairs. 'You're outnumbered.'

Boky looked at Natasha as though seeing her for the first time. Natasha revelled in his look of recognition. Did he know the exact shade of darkness pooling behind her eyes? Did he now recognise her as a formidable witch, every bit as dangerous as Boky – perhaps even more so?

He thought he'd foreseen every possible outcome, but Boky never anticipated this.

'What now?' he asked warily.

'That depends on you.'

Natasha flattened the lapels of his jacket. She tipped her face towards his, as she had dozens of times before. But this time she would not kiss him. Instead she bared her throat for a long moment, making it clear she no longer saw him as a threat.

The wolves growled. One of them gave an excited yip. They were eager to challenge the volkolak who had exerted dominance over them, but this was Natasha's contest to win. She let her glare slide around the circle, warning them to back off. Then she smiled at Boky.

'I could kill you,' she said, 'but you're the Bolshevik spymaster, the keeper of Lenin's dirty little secrets. It would be a shame to destroy such a valuable asset.'

'That would be a shame,' Boky agreed. He tilted his head away from her, hardly breathing as he waited to hear the other option she would offer.

'If you wish to live, I'll let you – on one condition.' Natasha circled behind him, trailing her fingertips along his jacket. She went up on her tiptoes to whisper in his ear. 'You'll have to join my pack.'

# Chapter 50

## *Dima*

Dima and Katya stood before a narrow cave opening leading into a hillside. Last night's storm left a fresh blanket of snow on the landscape. The crisp air was sharp and clean in his lungs, and Dima felt wonderfully alive.

He'd woken up with a smile on his face that morning, Katya still asleep in his arms. Gratitude swelled in Dima's heart. Despite the dangers both behind and ahead of him, he'd fallen in love on this island and somehow been lucky enough to have it returned.

Now Katya and Dima stood on the brink of uncovering Svetlana's final secret. They took off their skis and walked into the cave together.

Dima crouched to step through the low stone opening. As soon as he crossed the threshold, energy thrummed through the soles of his boots. Power crackled through the dense air, raising the hairs on the back of his neck.

'Do you feel that?' Dima held his hand open, and a tingling sensation spread through his fingertips and walked up his arm like a thousand spiders' feet.

Katya knelt down and pressed her hand against the winter-hardened earth. 'I feel a pulse, just like at Bolshoi Zayatsky.'

Ahead of them, the stone formed a perfect arch. The curving

tunnels leading deeper into the cavern appeared manmade. Was this a labyrinth? When Dima touched the stone wall, a jolt went through him.

'So many stories are connected to this place.' Dima closed his eyes. As his skomorokh magic awakened, thousands of mystical voices rose around him in a murmur.

This was a cave of mysteries, a gateway between realms.

Katya led the way into the labyrinth, running her fingers along the walls to find her way in the darkness. Dima followed, feeling like he waded upstream as currents of power dragged against him. The whispers grew louder.

'What is that?' Katya stopped short.

From deeper in the labyrinth came a strange rumbling sound. An odd, musky smell mingled with the scents of soil and wet rock.

'Is that a snore?' Katya asked.

Warning prickled up Dima's spine.

'I'll go first.' Dima turned Katya sideways and squeezed past her in the narrow tunnel. Faint blue light shone from somewhere up ahead. They crept along the tightening curves leading to the centre of the labyrinth.

There, in a round, stone-walled chamber, lied a snoring heap of fur and muscle bathed in an otherworldly blue light. It was the biggest bear Dima had ever seen, with golden, tattoo-like swirls shining out from its fur. The bear lay with its face outstretched, two round ears sticking up and a paw draped over its eyes. Its claws were curved daggers, each one longer than Dima's whole hand. Tremendous snores shook the cavern.

Katya grabbed Dima's elbow to pull him back, but he held his ground.

'We have to go,' Katya hissed.

Bears were most dangerous when awoken from hibernation, but this was no ordinary animal.

'Look.' Dima picked up a shirt off the ground – so soiled and threadbare it was hard to tell what colour it had been originally. The cut looked old-fashioned.

The cave went quiet – too quiet. Something moved. Holding his breath, Dima slowly looked up. The bear drowsily lifted its enormous head. Its nose twitched. Then calm, intelligent eyes opened – one brown, one blue.

'A skomorokh,' Dima whispered.

Katya clutched Dima's arm as the bear rolled onto its side and hauled itself up to standing. It loomed over them for a long moment before the blue light surrounding the creature flashed brighter, almost blinding as it pulsed out from the bear's heart. Its spine cracked and snapped. The bear threw its head back and let out a pained bellow that echoed through the cavern.

Standing behind Dima, Katya turned away from the blinding light as the bear shed its skin and emerged through the agony of transformation. Old and frail with a frizzy grey beard that reached to the floor, the naked man had tattoos of golden light swirling across his weathered skin. He stared in dismay, first at his wrinkled hands and then at the long grey beard covering the front of his body. Looking up, he blinked at Katya and Dima.

The man raised his hand and made the chironomic symbol of blessing, joining the tip of his ring finger to his thumb.

'Christ be with us,' he croaked.

'He is and will be.' Dima crossed himself and then began unbuttoning his coat, offering it to the old man.

The stranger took the coat and lifted his eyes to Dima's. 'What year is it, pray tell?'

'Nineteen-twenty-four.'

Eyes widening, the man stumbled back. Dima caught his elbow to steady him.

'Are you all right?'

The answer was clearly written in those anguished eyes – eyes that looked strangely familiar.

'I meant only to slumber through winter, and thereafter destroy the relic. But I wake to find centuries gone by and myself withered – verily, this body is become a relic in its own right.'

'Centuries?' Katya did a double take, then she shook her head to dismiss that idea. 'You must be mistaken, Dedushka.'

Dima's rational mind said no one could survive hundreds of years without food or water, yet Dima had slept for days when he should have frozen in the forest. On the otherworldly islands of Solovki, anything might be possible.

A sense of awe awoke inside Dima as he studied the old man's face.

'Yelezar?' Dima asked softly. 'Are you Yelezar Danilov?'

'Yes.' The old man looked up at him with milky eyes. He blinked. 'It's you.'

'You . . . know each other?' Katya glanced from one to the other, frowning as she tried to make sense of a situation that surpassed all reason.

'We've been sharing dreams the past few months.'

Katya's eyebrows bunched together. She bit her lip as she thought for a moment before asking Yelezar how long he'd been sleeping.

'Two-hundred-and-fifty-three years slept I.' Yelezar stared disconsolately at his hands, now wrinkled and dotted with age spots. 'What must Dorofeya have believed of me when I did not return? And our child . . .'

'You're shivering, Dedushka.' Dima took his coat from Yelezar's hand and draped it over the old man's shoulders.

Katya knelt on the pulsing ground, looking up at Yelezar. Dima could sense the questions waiting on her tongue, but she held herself back from interrogating the old man before he had a chance to get his bearings.

'I know a bit of what happened to your wife and son.' Dima pressed Yelezar's papery hands between his, gazing into his ancestor's cloudy eyes.

'A son?' the whispered words left Yelezar's lips on an exhale.

'Yes. Dorofeya named him Petrys, after her father. He followed in your footsteps as a minstrel. After Stenka Razin's revolt, Tsar Alexei labelled skomorokh magic a heresy. There was great persecution, so your family fled north.'

'How come you by this knowledge?'

'I'm a Danilov,' Dima said, 'descended from your line.'

Yelezar put a hand on Dima's shoulder, his eyes brimming with emotion and a small smile curling his lips. 'Perhaps that is why we found each other, and how I entered the dreams of your grandfather before you.'

'We read your book about Stenka Razin,' Katya said. 'Most of it, anyway. We came here looking for the ending.'

Yelezar glanced around the cave, the wrinkles of his forehead deepening in confusion. 'My book was here beside me when I fell asleep.'

Katya's mother must have found this cave during her research expedition and taken the manuscript with her.

'Could you tell us the ending, Dedushka?' Dima pressed his hands together in a respectful plea.

'How far into the story have you read?'

'We read about Stenka Razin's pirating years,' Katya said. 'And of his plans to bring an army to Moscow. It cut off before the campaign began.

'Ah.' Yelezar's cloudy eyes stared off into the distance, as though he could see through centuries.

Yelezar told how, in the spring of 1670, Stenka Razin's River Wolves left the Don once more – this time as an army. They began the long march up the Volga. A band of agitators went ahead of them, distributing propaganda leaflets in every city and town. The people of Kamyshin, Saratov and Samara threw open the city gates at the army's approach, greeting the rebels with bread and salt. Tens of thousands of peasants joined the march, armed with sickles, axes, pitchforks and staves.

Insurrection spread like wildfire as spring became summer and Stenka Razin moved steadily upriver on his way to Moscow.

'It all went wrong when we reached Simbirsk,' Yelezar said. 'The *voevoda* had a full garrison with two regiments of *streltsy* loyal to Moscow, and the tsar had sent Prince Bariatinsky to help guard the city with a detachment of heavy cavalry. It seemed impossible for the city to be taken by a peasant army.'

Yelezar looked up at them, pain radiating from his cloudy eyes.

'That's when Stenka decided to use the relic.'

Yelezar described how wielding the *Volkhovnik* changed his friend. Stenka stayed awake the night before the battle, poring over the ancient book. The next morning Prince Bariatinsky brought his cavalry into formation outside the city walls. Razin's peasant army prepared for battle.

Instead of giving a speech, Stenka Razin cast a spell over them.

Those ancient words pierced the souls of every man there, filling them with wrath. Their faces contorted into snarls. Fear vanished like smoke upon the wind, leaving only rage. Their primal vengeance found a beat, and the rebels thudded their weapons against the ground in unison, advancing on Simbirsk as one man.

When Yelezar looked over at his friend, he saw an evil presence within Stenka's eyes. By using the *Volkhovnik*, Stenka had yielded his body to the spirit of the book.

It possessed him.

The spell made their army unstoppable. The peasants fought with an unquenchable lust for blood. They obliterated the tsar's cavalry. Not long after, the gates of Simbirsk were thrown open, and the poor of the city came to welcome the rebels with bread and salt. Blinded by the spell of vengeance, the rebels saw only enemies. They cut them down with sickles and axes as they flooded in through the gates.

Hours later, Stenka and Yelezar entered Simbirsk themselves. Within the walls, corpses littered the streets. Fires raged on both sides of the Volga. Smoke filled the sky, and the river ran red.

'God have mercy.' Yelezar had said with tears in his eyes. 'What have we done?'

Looking out at the carnage, the spirit that now possessed Stenka Razin began to laugh.

Dima listened to Yelezar's account with growing dismay. He'd never heard of a book causing demonic possession. What was the *Volkhovnik*, really?

'After the massacre of Simbirsk, the tsar mustered all his forces to oppose us,' Yelezar said. 'With the help of the *Volkhovnik*, our army would have vanquished the tsar, but at what cost? I had to save my friend from the book's possession and protect the people from another wave of evil being unleashed. That's why I stole the book.'

'What happened then?' Katya sat cross-legged, eagerly leaning forward.

'What happened?' Yelezar offered Katya a brittle smile. 'I betrayed my dearest friend, deserted my pregnant wife and left behind thousands of desperate rebels on the eve of their slaughter – all to follow the voice of my conscience. The book had spilled violence and wrath into the hearts of our men and perverted the justice of our cause. There was only one way to save my friend, to save them all. The *Volkhovnik* had to be destroyed.'

'You destroyed it?' Katya asked breathlessly.

'No.' Yelezar's brow furrowed, and his glistening eyes became mirrors of pain. 'It can only be destroyed in the foundations of the Solovetsky Monastery, where it came from. But when I arrived on the island, the tsar's navy was laying siege to the fortress. They too were after the *Volkhovnik*. I hid it from them. Then I hid myself in this cave, waiting for the siege to end so I could finish my task. I passed the time by writing my account of Stenka's life. As weeks became months, I knew I would starve before the siege relented, so I shifted to my bear form to hibernate. Too deeply I slept.'

Yelezar again studied his wrinkled hands in dismay.

'What is the *Volkhovnik*?' Dima asked.

'To answer your question, I must tell you a story about why the Solovetsky Monastery was founded.' Yelezar closed his eyes, cleared his throat and began to speak.

***

In a time near forgotten, many centuries ago now, a monk named Herman went out in the wilderness in search of divine revelation. His spirit led him northward, until he came upon a chapel beside the Vyg River.

There he met a kindred spirit.

Savvatiy, also a monk, had ventured from his home in search of absolute solitude for contemplation and prayer. He was headed for the White Sea coast, planning to sail to an uninhabited archipelago rumoured to be the source of mysterious powers.

Herman agreed to accompany Savvatiy on his voyage. They sailed east until they reached the island we now call Bolshoi Solovetsky. There they erected a cross, built two hermit cells, and spent the next six years in contemplative silence.

Every day, Herman walked a stone labyrinth beside the coast, letting the movement draw him into a trance. Heaven opened up to him as he prayed within the labyrinth. Divine insight unfolded in his mind and he understood what it meant to be a son of God, how one could hold miracles in ones fingers or on the tip of the tongue.

Herman hungered to know more, to have every mystery of the world laid bare before his eyes. This thirst for knowledge led him to try something he instinctively knew must not be done – he walked the labyrinth backwards.

As he entered into his meditative trance, his spirit did not drift heavenward. Instead it descended to the depths of the underworld.

Wandering the shadowed realm, Herman encountered a wayward spirit, that of a man who had been a powerful wizard when he'd lived. The cross Herman wore protected him from the wizard's grasping fingers but not from his tempting words.

'Do you know the incantation to keep you warm, so that you need never collect firewood, peat or dung?' The wizard asked.

Herman resolved not to speak to him. As he walked away, the wizard recited an incantation. A pleasant warmth spread through Herman. It stayed with him when he returned to his body, and for the next three days he didn't need to light a fire.

The next time Herman walked the labyrinth backwards, the wizard awaited him. He gave Herman an incantation that sated his hunger and another that swept the floor of his cell, removing the distractions interfering with Herman's prayers.

'There's a way for you to gain all of my knowledge,' the wizard said. 'I can teach the secrets of life and death and give you words powerful enough to change a man's soul. You could cleanse the world of sin and heartache, make crops grow steady and wars cease.'

Something in Herman's spirit told him the wizard ought not to be trusted, but his words filled Herman's mind like a beautiful dream.

'How can I gain this knowledge?' Herman asked.

The wizard's reply so shocked and horrified Herman that he fled back through the labyrinth, vowing never to return. For many days he lingered in his cell, praying for temptation to be taken from him.

As time wore on, he wondered if he'd been too hasty in his refusal. The need for knowledge panged inside Herman like hunger, like thirst. He could no longer content himself with the small insights he received in prayer. The wizard had described heaven come to earth. Wouldn't such a blessing be worth any price?

So it happened that Herman knocked on the door of Savvatiy's cell for the first time in six years. Though visibly surprised by the interruption, Savvatiy offered Herman a friendly smile. Herman gestured urgently for Savvatiy to follow him to the labyrinth.

His guileless friend came with him as a sheep follows a shepherd. He took Herman's offered hand and allowed himself to be led backwards through the labyrinth. Trembling with fear as the dark side of the Otherworld came into focus and trembling even more when he saw the blade in Herman's hand, Savvatiy at last broke his vow of silence.

'Why?' he asked before Herman slit his throat.

Herman sacrificed his friend so the gateway created by Savvatiy's soul would remain open, and so all the bounty of heaven might flow through that gateway.

Only after he'd crossed back, when he heard the wizard's thoughts in his own head and the wizard's voice speaking through his lips, did Herman consider another implication.

The gateway led to heaven, yes – but it also led to hell.

***

Yelezar explained that Herman was possessed by the spirit of the wizard, an ancient practitioner of the darkest magic ever known to man. Herman sailed back to the mainland, hoping the spirit would be left behind, but it stayed with him his entire life.

On the mainland, Herman gave his confession to a monk named Zosima, who attempted an exorcism. The wizard's spirit could not be cast out.

Zosima returned to the archipelago with Herman and set holy wards around the gateway to prevent more unclean spirits from finding their way into our world. He founded the monastery that year, constructing the first building atop the labyrinth where Savvatiy's soul still remains an open gateway to the Otherworld.

The monks of Solovetsky Island became guardians against unclean spirits, as well as stewards of the great spiritual bounty spreading through the earth of the archipelago.

While Zosima pioneered the monastery, Herman spent the remainder of his life in an iron room, where he could not cast spells on his fellow monks.

'Many copies of the *Volkhovnik* have been written, and many have been burned,' Yelezar said. 'The original manuscript was penned by Herman during the long years of his imprisonment. In Herman's last days, the wizard's spirit left his body and infused himself into the book. Anyone who possesses the *Volkhovnik* will themselves be possessed by the spirit whose knowledge it contains. To wield the *Volkhovnik* is to be cursed – and eventually consumed.'

Yelezar abruptly stopped speaking, so the word 'consumed' echoed in the round chamber. Silence permeated the cavern, disturbed only by the thrum of an ancient heartbeat rising from the ground.

'I don't understand.' Katya dropped her head into her hands. 'Why would my mother go through so much trouble leading me to a spell book I can't even use?'

'Maybe she didn't know,' Dima said gently. 'Or perhaps she wanted you to find and destroy it. She knew Gleb Boky was after the book, and that he would use its power against the Russian people.'

'The book corrupts anyone who uses it,' Yelezar said. 'It must be destroyed in the monastery's foundations.'

'Then why didn't the monks destroy it centuries ago?' Katya asked.

'Solovki quickly became the richest monastic community in Russia,' Yelezar said. 'Pilgrims came from all over to have curses broken or sicknesses healed, and, in their gratitude, they gave the monastery gold. The power the monks wielded came from that open gateway. To destroy the book would close it, robbing them of their wealth and influence. The hegumen of Solovki instead decided to lock the book away where it could do no harm.'

'Until it was stolen by Nikita Minin,' Dima said, remembering the story Valentina Pavlovna told them. 'He used its power to become the church patriarch.'

'And stolen again by Stenka Razin during a pirate raid.' Yelezar's eyes regained a youthful sparkle at that memory.

'This feels like destiny.' Dima took Katya's hand. When she didn't pull away, he interlocked their fingers. 'All these threads coming together – the way the two of us met, the clues your mother left you leading to a book my ancestor wrote. I sense a divine hand in all these connections and coincidences. The book should be destroyed and the wizard's spirit returned to the Otherworld. We're the ones who can make that happen.'

'I know you're right.' Though Katya tried to sound brave, her voice cracked. 'But I was so sure the *Volkhovnik* was the key, the one thing that could save Russia from the Bolsheviki.'

'I see the battle waging in your mind.' Yelezar's long beard swayed as he leaned forward. He cupped Katya's cheeks, compassion shining out from his eyes. 'Come with me. I will show you where to find your path again, a place to search for answers and hope. If your heart is pure, you will learn where the *Volkhovnik* is hidden.'

Yelezar let Dima's coat drop to the ground. Blue light radiated from the centre of his chest, pulsing with the island's heartbeat. As it spread, turning his whole body radiant, Yelezar grimaced in pain. Dima rose to his feet and pulled Katya up to standing as Yelezar's skeleton reshaped itself.

Moments later, he towered over them, an enormous bear bathed in blue light. Yelezar lowered his head and shoulders, indicating they should climb on his back. Dima put on his coat before boosting Katya up. He climbed on behind her, hooking his arm around her waist. They held onto fistfuls of fur as Yelezar lumbered along the curving tunnels of the cave.

Outside, a rush of cold air swept over them. The sky had cleared, but a fresh layer of snow blanketed the forest, weighing down the boughs of pines and spruces. Already, the daylight faded. The western sky turned a burnt orange colour, and the first stars glittered overhead.

Lifting his muzzle to the wind Yelezar sniffed several times before loping off through the trees. Dima and Katya braced themselves against the cold as the bear sped up, carrying them south, then westward.

Yelezar slowed down when they reached the coast. Carefully listening to the ice, he crossed the frozen sea and Dima realised where they must be going. Sure enough, the little wooden chapel came into view, silhouetted in starlight against the darkening horizon.

Yelezar had brought them back to Bolshoi Zayatsky – the island of labyrinths.

# Chapter 51

## *Katya*

Yelezar set them down beside the small wooden chapel. Instead of shifting to his human form, the bear dipped his head, bidding Katya adieu. Then he lumbered off towards the labyrinths.

'I'm meant to follow him.' Dima brushed Katya's cheek with his gloved thumb.

Katya glanced at the chapel, remembering waking up with Dima beside the altar, how morning sun had bathed his face in golden light. Even now, she could taste the tender warmth of his lips when they'd shared that first kiss in the printing workshop. Katya wanted to steal him away from their problems, to go into the chapel and forget the world for a few hours – or maybe for a lifetime.

But reality couldn't be ignored. Katya knew which labyrinth she needed to walk. This time, she wouldn't be held back by fear.

'I'll see you after.' Dima tipped her chin up and kissed her softly, first on her lips and then on her forehead. Wind snatched away the warmth of his kiss the moment they separated and Dima jogged to catch up with Yelezar.

Katya exhaled, her breath clouding as she looked up at the stars. Her mother's final message warned her to listen, and now she had no options left except to do just that. Shivering in the briny sea wind, Katya headed in the direction of the labyrinths. Snow crunched underfoot, and a carpet of white blanketed the path.

She'd have to find her way by feeling, and that would be easier if she connected with the spiritual world. Katya recited her zagovor.

*'My soul, like the branches of the World Tree,*
*Weave the seen and unseen into one whole.*
*Be to me a gateway to the Otherworld,*
*That I may harness the powers of creation'*

As she chanted, the world around her blurred into obscurity. Her soul inched open.

She still heard the crunch of Dima's footsteps growing distant, still felt the wind lashing her cheeks, but when she opened her eyes again, everything changed. Wavering light rose up from the snow in spiralling lines, marking the labyrinths' locations.

Continuing along the wintry path, Katya found the labyrinth she'd walked before. The same one her mother had visited, and Stenka Razin before her. Their fates were all twisted up by whatever power was at work in this place. Maybe today Katya would understand why.

She paused at the entrance, shivering even as sweat gathered on her palms. As Katya stepped into the labyrinth, the wind ceased. Gravity turned sideways, guiding Katya into perfect warmth, a loving embrace. With northern lights shimmering around her, Katya felt seen, welcomed as a sister, as a daughter, as a part of something infinitely bigger than herself.

The power drawing her forward felt clean, pure – like something ancient and immense inviting Katya to yield.

Defiance was her first instinct, but she resisted the compulsion to raise her chin and put her shoulders back. If she fought this power, she couldn't follow where it led. Taking a calming breath, Katya stepped forward again. Every step sent vibrations through her. Though she walked on flat ground, it felt like an ascent. Each footfall raised her spirit higher, as though she climbed a spiralling staircase. Two realities met here, the physical and spiritual worlds interlocking.

When Katya reached the centre of the labyrinth, her eyes became a canvas upon which the island's magic painted her a vision. She saw herself on the edge of a cliff, a black abyss spread before her. Darkness overwhelmed her senses. The utter silence held unspoken threats, all the perils of midnight gathering in the shadows.

How could one woman stand against darkness so complete? What could be done when evil crept in like dusk, when the sun set on a whole nation? The Revolution was meant to be a beacon, but its light had gone out. Now the people were held for ransom by the beastly men who'd devoured their way to the top.

Katya had failed to stop them at Kronstadt. She'd thought the *Volkhovnik* might restore hope, but now she knew it was an evil object, one that couldn't be wielded.

'I don't know what to do.' Katya's voice crackled like the whisper of stars. Instead of freezing, her words sparked, giving off faint lights before the darkness swallowed them. A dam broke in Katya's chest and poetry spilled through her lips, the poem she'd written in the printing room that night with Dima. Katya didn't know if she was speaking to the divine presence in the labyrinth or the darkness she now faced. Maybe her words were meant for her own soul.

> *Though horror is your daily bread,*
> *and your cup is filled with sorrow.*
> *Though your loved ones are as autumn leaves,*
> *and death falls all around.*

*Though your days are bleakest winter,*
*though the sun withholds its warmth,*
*though you live in endless twilight,*
*darkness spreading day by day.*
*There is hope for all who listen*
*to the whispering of stars.*

Every word sparked as it left Katya's lips. The lights were tiny and flickering at first. As she continued, they joined together making stars and then constellations. They stretched out before her feet into a razor-thin bridge made of starlight.

Katya stepped onto the thread of starlit words with her arms stretched out like a tightrope walker.

Memories flashed through her mind. Matilda Ivanova boldly stepping forward to scold the armed guards who were demeaning the female prisoners. Tsisana chanting Hail Marys while healing Katya's throat. The women of her barrack promising to help bear the load of hard labour as she healed. They could have treated Katya as an enemy, but they cared for her instead. She remembered Andrei Sergeevich reading novels as a mild form of resistance, and Valentina Pavlovna raising a toast to life abundant even as wolves prowled outside her door.

Then there was Dima – so many memories of him drifted about her. How he'd spoken up for her when she was misclassified, how he'd helped pioneer the theatre and newspaper to lift the prisoners' spirits, how he'd given Katya the courage to share her words for the very first time. Heat washed over Katya's skin when she remembered making love to Dima in Valentina Pavlovna's house, how it had felt like coming home.

While Katya had been following her mother's footsteps in search of a weapon, Dima had written a poem – because he understood a truth Katya only now grasped. In the darkness, the only thing to do is light as many lamps as possible.

Following the trail of her words, Katya found the darkness wasn't as complete as she'd first thought. Lights twinkled here and there, the voices of other Russians, raised like lanterns in a black winter night.

Hope wasn't a volshebnika rising like the sun to save her nation with a powerful spell book in hand. No. Katya had seen things all wrong. The green and white lights of the aurora borealis swept out into the void, connecting voice to voice, light to light. Before Katya's eyes, the twinkling spots multiplied, becoming constellations of freedom, milky galaxies of creativity.

This was hope – a million voices whispering like stars, lighting the way with kindness and love, with wills that refused to bend and spirits that defied being crushed by grief. Russia's salvation lived and breathed in Dima, Tsisana, Matilda Ivanova, Andrei Sergeevich and Valentina Pavlovna. It shone out from every soul woven into the story of this land.

They didn't need Katya to save them, but she still had a part to play.

If Gleb Boky found the *Volkhovnik*, he'd extinguish those lights one by one. Katya's purpose and path were to find the relic before he did, and destroy it.

Calm settled over Katya, easing the tension in her shoulders and untangling the stress that had been knotted in her belly for over a year, ever since she saw the ambulance wagon outside her flat. Though the loss of her mother still ached and the disappointment of the Revolution's outcome stung bitterly, a sense of peace steadied her. Katya didn't have to carry the responsibility for saving Russia. She only had to do her part to shine.

When she closed her eyes, the world tilted and then spun. She tumbled backwards, freefalling through the centre of the spiral stairway before plunging into the physical world. Katya gasped, her eyes flying open.

She lay at the centre of the labyrinth, her upper body cradled on Dima's lap. Stars glittered overhead, and the moon cast silvery beams across the snow.

Katya sat up, stiff-limbed from the cold. She scooted to face Dima and found him pale and shivering in the moonlight. 'How long was I out?'

'It's been a few hours.'

'Hours?' It hadn't felt that long, but maybe the Otherworld distorted time. They seemed to be alone on the island. 'Where's Yelezar?'

'Gone.' Dima rubbed his arms to warm them. 'He vanished into the labyrinth and didn't come back. I think his time on earth is done.'

After centuries of hibernation Yelezar had reunited with his family and friends in the realm of spirits. Katya couldn't fault him for it, but how would they find the *Volkhovnik* without him?

Dima shivered so violently his teeth clattered. Katya stood and brushed snow off her coat. They went into the chapel. Dima found the ceremonial candles and rummaged through his satchel for a matchbox. He removed his gloves, but it took a few attempts before his cold-stiffened fingers could strike a match. As flickering orange light filled the room, Dima's face looked ashen, his lips blue.

Pulling off her gloves, Katya unbuttoned her coat. Dima's gaze rested on her face as she stepped towards him and opened his buttons one by one. Then she threaded her arms behind his back and pulled him tight against her. Dima wrapped his arms around her shoulders and rested his cheek against the top of her head. They stood that way until Dima's shivering subsided and colour returned to his face.

'We should make a plan,' Katya said. 'We haven't eaten all day, and without Yelezar it's not going to be easy to figure out where the *Volkhovnik* is hidden.'

'Didn't the labyrinth show you?'

Katya shook her head. 'No, but it showed me what I needed to see. If we survive this, maybe I'll spend more time on my poetry than trying to kill Bolsheviki.'

'I support that.' Dima tugged on her coat sleeve and stepped closer, desire clouding his eyes.

'Wait.' Katya pressed his chest to hold him back. 'What did you see in the labyrinth?'

A slow smile spread across Dima's face. 'I saw where the *Volkhovnik* is hidden.'

Katya's own smile grew, matching Dima's. If they found the *Volkhovnik*, they only had to smuggle it back into the monastery and destroy it in the open gate where it came from. They could end this. Tonight.

'Where?'

'Right here.' Dima motioned behind Katya. 'In an iron box buried beneath the altar.'

'How nice of you to say that out loud.' A honeyed voice trailed a gust of wind as the door blew open. 'It saves me the trouble of making you talk.'

Katya's body went rigid. Her breath halted as she slowly turned. Natasha stood in the doorway, pale with cold, her auburn waves blood-red in the candlelight. Wolves followed at her heels as she prowled into the church.

# Chapter 52

## *Katya*

Wolves circled Katya and Dima, hackles raised and teeth bared. Natasha stepped into the radius of candlelight, primal hatred shining out from her eyes.

'You've been careless, *sister.*' Natasha's voice dripped with disdain at that word. 'You forgot to cast your cloaking spell when you came to Bolshoi Zayatsky. My volkolaki tracked you easily.'

'Yours?' Though Katya tried to project calm, the panic closing in around her throat made her voice waver. 'I thought Boky—'

'The wolves are my creations.' Natasha stepped closer, closer, closer. Flickering light danced across her pale skin, casting her freckles as dark constellations, the antithesis of Katya's vision in the labyrinth. 'Making Boky their alpha served my purposes.'

Natasha stood eye-to-eye with Katya, and at once the fog surrounding her motives lifted, the shroud fell away and Katya saw her. Really, truly saw her. This sister of hers was not the harmony to her melody – she was a dissonant note. From the moment they'd locked eyes in the darkness of the guesthouse their first night on Solovki, there'd been tension between them, an uncomfortable strain that made Katya feel off-key.

Katya had only recently learned of their shared heritage, but Natasha had known all along. Connected by blood, divided by circumstance. Natasha was a true-born daughter, a princess disenfranchised by the Revolution Katya and her mother fought to bring about.

Natasha had claimed to want the same thing as Katya – the destruction of the Bolshevik regime – but perhaps their visions of what would happen afterwards stood in stark opposition.

Looking at her now, Katya felt the bone-deep vibrations of Natasha's hatred for her. Katya had been a fool to ever think they were allies.

'You're working for Commissar Boky, aren't you?'

'Wrong again.' At the danger in her tone, the volkolaki growled low in their throats. Dima held Katya tight in his arms as the wolves continued circling. Natasha raised her chin, proud and triumphant. 'Boky works for me now.'

Natasha snapped her fingers.

Several things happened at once. Four soldiers streamed in through the door, aiming their rifles. A wolf pounced. Dima yelped as it tackled him to the ground.

Katya gathered magic in her diaphragm, preparing to cast a spell.

Something metallic glinted in the corner of her eye as Natasha slid a hidden object from her coat. Katya only had time to gasp before an iron collar closed around her throat.

The iron sent a shockwave of pain through Katya's body as it ripped away her magic. She fell to her knees, eyes pinched in agony.

What had happened to Dima? Katya forced herself to turn, to look.

The volkolak pinned him face-down, but it hadn't mauled him. Not yet. Cheek pressed to the ground and blood trickling from his lip, Dima stared at Katya, his eyes wide and his forehead creased. They were trapped, surrounded by wolves and rifles. Katya couldn't reach her magic, but she forced herself to stand back up, to hold her head high despite her fear.

Commissar Boky prowled into the chapel, excitement gleaming in his slate-grey eyes as he stopped beside Natasha.

Katya stared at him, her heart pounding. She vowed that no matter what they did to her, or even to Dima, she would stand like a stone wall, unbreakable.

'Quite the reunion this is becoming,' Boky said. 'And I've invited one more guest. An old friend of yours.'

When Katya saw the man who entered next, her mortar began melting, her resolve crumbling. He had black eyebrows, white hair, drooping jowls – and deep scars running across half his face from the swipe of a bear's claws.

Doctor Aleksandr Vasilevich Barchenko was still alive.

'Yekaterina.' Her name sounded like a curse on Doctor Barchenko's lips, and horror opened inside Katya like a bottomless cistern. He'd never called her by her name before, only her number. The foul intimacy of hearing it dragged her mind back to the lab, to the revulsion of his breath against her cheek as his fingers closed around her throat.

Katya shuffled backward, but wolves blocked her retreat. The volkolak pinning Dima leapt off as two soldiers took Dima's arms, slapping iron cuffs onto his wrists before hauling him to his feet. With iron locking away his magic, Dima wouldn't be shifting to his bear form and rescuing them both. He met her eyes, and Katya's heart broke at the hopelessness she saw.

They were desperately trapped.

This couldn't be real. Closing her hands into fists, Katya drove her fingernails into her palms. Pain sliced through her skin and a whimper escaped her lips. Not dreaming. Not hallucinating. Not seeing ghosts. The man who'd experimented on Katya for ten months had come to Solovki, but how?

'The sea is frozen,' she said, bewilderment lacing through her terror.

'I've been here all winter,' Barchenko said.

*Of course.* Sekirka Hill had Barchenko's name all over it – the punishment cells, the prisoners disappearing, the whisperings that those taken to Sekirka suffered a fate worse than death.

Doctor Barchenko smiled as she worked things out, and the gruesome scars deepened and puckered. He'd lost an eye, but hatred shone out of the remaining one. 'Did you really think we were done experimenting on you?'

'But why transfer me?' Katya's voice walked the edge of tears. 'Why send me here?'

'We didn't just need you to find the *Volkhovnik*,' Boky explained in that calm way of his that hinted at danger below the surface. 'We need a powerful charovnika to wield it. You're a gifted spell-caster, but something had to be done about your defiance. So we brought you here, to break you.'

Dima grabbed Katya's hand and interlaced their fingers. Katya knew what would happen next. They'd torture Dima. Faced with the choice of helping her enemies or watching Dima suffer, Katya might not have the strength to choose the greater good.

Her vision in the labyrinth felt far away, like a pleasant dream corrupted by a nightmare. Katya's heartbeat pounded in her ears. Her eyes stung as she fought to hold back despair and put on a brave face.

'We need axes and shovels to dig under the altar,' Natasha announced. One of the soldiers darted outside to look for supplies. Her gaze sliced over Katya and Dima one last time before she turned to Barchenko. 'They're all yours.'

The small, cruel smile that bloomed on Doctor Barchenko's face sent ripples of panic through Katya. Barchenko led Katya and Dima out of the chapel. Smolensky and another guard prodded their backs with rifles to make them walk.

Dima held fast to Katya's hand, but she wished he wasn't here. She'd survived the horror of imprisonment in a lab once before, and she might have the strength to face it again if hers was the only life at stake.

Thinking of Dima in a laboratory demolished her hopes. It made her heart a ruin. She ached for the sketches he'd never put to canvas, the prison newspapers that wouldn't be published, the epic poem of Stenka Razin that would never be completed.

'I'm sorry.' Emotion clogged Katya's throat as they stepped out the chapel door into the freezing wind. 'I'm so, so sorry. I never should have let you near this.'

'No,' Dima said fiercely, squeezing her hand. 'No regrets, Katya. No matter what happens, I'm glad you gave me the chance to love you, even if it only lasted for one night.'

One night. That's all they'd ever have. Katya wanted a lifetime. She wanted the chance for the newness to wear away, for the heat between them to settle into comfortable warmth, the kind where every kiss felt like coming home. She wanted inside jokes and annoyance at each other's bad habits, the give-and-take rhythm of two lives merging into one. She wanted to see Dima's face with wrinkles, and for his fingers to run through her hair long after it had turned silver.

She wanted more time.

But Smolensky seized Katya's shoulders and ripped her from Dima's grasp. He shoved her down into a dog sled and handcuffed her to the rail. Iron bit into the skin of her wrist and throat, but she felt it everywhere – searing her mind, heart and soul.

Smolensky stepped onto the runners behind Katya, hooked a lantern onto the sled and shouted a command. Katya was

thrown backwards when the dogs burst into motion. Frigid
air lashed her face as the sled glided over the frozen sea. She
closed her eyes. Her ears filled with the hiss of sled runners,
and despair crept around the edges of her mind.

Though her situation seemed hopeless, Katya couldn't resign
herself to whatever fate Barchenko envisioned for her. When she
thought of Dima painting her skin with kisses, of Dima telling
her to turn around to the audience and see how art brought
people together, of Dima saying no regrets even as terror filled
his eyes – love filled her up so fully there was no place for doubt
or despair.

She had to save him. She had to save them both.

By the time the sled halted Katya had regained her defiance
and drawn from her well of determined spite. She would fight
them every step of the way.

Smolensky hauled Katya out of the sled, and her boots
crunched in deep snow. Beneath the fresh, crisp air carried by
the wind, a rotten smell lingered, the scent of decay. A steep,
forested hill rose before her with a wooden stairway leading
upward through the pines. Moonlight reflected off the snow,
lighting the forest in dim grey light.

Katya squinted at dark shapes in the snow at the bottom of
the stairs. She gasped. Corpses. At least a dozen bodies were
piled on either side of the staircase.

Smolensky grabbed her upper arm. A sensation of slimy
revulsion slithered through her as he spoke by her ear.

'They weren't worth the bullets it would have taken to kill
them, so they got a little push down the stairs. You'll join them
when we're done with you.' Smolensky shoved her towards the
steps and raised his rifle. 'Now up you go.'

Katya gripped the railing and began to climb.

The stairs led straight up the side of the hill. From the bottom she couldn't see where they ended. She took them one at a time, kindling her courage by summoning anarchist catchphrases.

*If the shepherds become wolves, the sheep must lead themselves.*

That sentiment took on a literal meaning here on Solovki, where Boky and his closest associates were volkolaki. The stairs groaned beneath her feet as she climbed.

*People have only as much liberty as they have the intelligence to want and the courage to take.*

Russia's best sons and daughters had been brave enough to die on their feet rather than living on their knees. Though they must have felt like ants facing down a giant or like stars trying to dispel the darkness of midnight, they raised their voices and their fists. Most of them became martyrs for freedom. Their blood watered this land.

In the depths of Katya's disillusionment, she'd thought their legacy had been stolen, that their battle cry had faded into silence as the fetters of communism closed around Russia. But she'd been wrong. Their voices still whispered, giving witness, lending strength. Katya wasn't a girl alone – she was a radical, one in a long line who dared to believe oppression was not the natural way of the world.

Many came before her, and others would follow in her steps.

As Katya climbed to Sekirka, she understood the Revolution hadn't died. As long as she had breath in her lungs, Katya could fight for a better future.

The Revolution still lived – in her.

With every stair she climbed, Katya rediscovered her resolve.

*Refuse.* Step.

*Resist.* Step.

*Rebel.* Step.

*Revolt.* Step.

When she at last reached the top of the stairway, a church

loomed over her, its white walls gleaming pearlescent in the moonlight. A single onion-domed tower rose from it with an unlit lighthouse built into the cupola. Smolensky grabbed Katya's arm, his fingers digging in hard enough to leave bruises. He dragged her towards the church where a lone figure awaited them with a raised lantern.

Petrova. Instead of a nurse's cap, the burly woman's frizzy blonde hair stuck out from the edges of a fur hat. Her cheeks were pink, her eyes victorious.

'I'll take her from here,' she told Smolensky.

Smolensky dug his fingers into Katya's arm one last time. 'Tomorrow I'll be transferred as a guard to Sekirka, so I'll get to see them break you. But tonight I'm in the mood for celebration. I think I'll pay another visit to that pretty friend of yours, Tsisana.'

Katya glared at him.

'She's very beautiful, don't you think? Though she might not be so pretty by the time I'm done with her. Perhaps I'll even let her husband watch.'

Katya threw herself at Smolensky, but Lyudmila Antonova caught her wrist in a vice-like grip before she could land a blow. Smolensky chuckled darkly as he strolled away.

*Please*, Katya prayed to a God she wasn't sure she believed in. *Please protect her from him.*

The nurse held the lantern aloft as she dragged Katya into the church. Angelic frescoes adorned the high, arched ceilings, but the space below them was anything but holy. Barchenko's lab equipment had been relocated here – chairs with leather straps, recording equipment and a table lined with gruesome metal tools.

The backdoor of the church led into a large monastery building with dark-panelled walls. Lyudmila brought Katya to an upper floor, where iron bars had replaced bedroom doors in the cell block. Katya caught glimpses as they passed, men and women with emaciated faces and traumatised eyes.

Katya stopped in her tracks.

Valentina Pavlovna lay on the floor of an empty room, one leg wrapped in bandages. She slept fitfully, her sweat-sheened face looking feverish.

Katya called out to her, but Valentina Pavlovna didn't seem to hear.

'Keep moving.' Lyudmila yanked Katya's wrist.

At the end of the hall, the nurse unlocked the last of the iron doors. She pushed Katya into the room with such force that Katya stumbled to her hands and knees. Katya glared up at Lyudmila Antonova, but the nurse only smiled.

'Welcome to hell,' Lyudmila Antonova said before slamming the iron door shut.

# Chapter 53
## *Natasha*

Natasha emerged from the Otherworld in a cold sweat. With trembling hands, she reached for her wine glass, nearly spilling as she brought it to her lips. Natasha drank deep, as though alcohol could wash away the terror of what just happened.

'I warned you,' Boky said without looking up from his book. He lounged on the bed, his outstretched legs crossed at the ankle.

He had indeed warned her. Natasha had decided to use the *Volkhovnik* nonetheless.

She'd been studying the book for a few days, holed up in Boky's bedroom. He slept on the floor now. After their mutual betrayals, Boky had ceded his will to Natasha in exchange for his life, but the intimacy between them disintegrated.

Natasha was too focused to care. The *Volkhovnik's* archaic language made translation exceedingly difficult. Natasha had pages of notes and annotations. She'd made a list of the book's contents, or at least the titles she was able to decipher.

Mistranslating a ritual's instructions could have devastating consequences, but when Natasha found a page on smiting one's enemy, she decided to take the risk.

She spent hours poring over the text. Whenever she came to a section she couldn't translate, a gentle voice whispered the solution. It reminded Natasha of when her foresight gave her warnings, except this voice didn't originate within her – it seemed to come from the book itself.

Natasha had performed the ritual, and all the while she felt a shadow alongside her. Afterwards, when she returned to her own body, she wasn't alone. That shadow had followed her, creeping beneath her skin.

*Your ambition sings to me,* the voice reverberated in Natasha's mind, dark and seductive. *Together we will build an empire greater than the Romanovs, greater than the Greeks or Romans – greater than any that came before.*

Natasha tossed the *Volkhovnik* into its iron case and slammed the lid shut.

That silenced it. She felt alone in her skin once more. Hopefully she'd acted quickly enough that the spirit hadn't gained a permanent hold over her.

A shiver moved up Natasha's spine as she stared at the iron box. Wine couldn't wash away the taste of corroded metal clinging to the back of her throat.

'You cannot possess power such as that without it possessing you.' Boky lowered the book he was reading. He surveyed her, arching his brow. 'Why do you suppose I went to such great lengths preparing Katya as a vessel for the book?'

Had that been Boky's plan, to make Katya use the *Volkhovnik*, so *she* would be the one possessed by the spirit within it?

Natasha couldn't think of Katya without picturing her chin up and her eyes blazing with defiance.

'Katya would rather die than be a slave.'

'Perhaps that was true a few months ago.' Rising from the bed, Boky crossed the room and poured himself a glass of wine. 'Now she has a weak spot.'

'Dima.'

Boky dipped his head in agreement.

So that's why he'd kept Dmitri Danilov alive. Brilliant, really.

Natasha had planned to wield the *Volkhovnik* on her own, carving out power for herself one ritual at a time. Now she understood that wouldn't be possible. Her throat still tasted like corroded metal, and she shivered at the recollection of sharing her body with a corrupt spirit. It had only lasted a few seconds, but Natasha never wanted to experience that again.

Natasha rubbed her lip as she considered her options. Using Katya in the way Boky suggested might be the best plan, but something in her rebelled at the idea of shackling her half-sister to such a fate.

Something else gave her pause – why was Boky telling her his plans now? Though bound to her in a vow of loyalty and obedience, nothing compelled him to offer up information she hadn't requested.

'Why are you helping me?'

'Do you know why I gave up an engineering career to be a full-time revolutionary? Why I endured twelve arrests, torture from the tsar's secret police and six years exiled in Siberia?'

Boky leaned against the back of a dining chair, sipping his wine. Natasha's gaze drifted to his scarred fingers. She shook her head.

'Before the Revolution, more than eighty percent of Russians were workers and peasants, men and women on the brink of starvation. Only one percent were aristocrats, yet they hoarded all the wealth. It wasn't right. And so I spent my life fighting for a society where people started on an equal footing, where the nation's bounty benefited all.'

With a sigh, Boky began to pace the room, taking a long sip of wine.

'The Revolution was supposed to bring justice – instead

we've created a new elite, those with party membership. This is not the Russia I fought for, the Russia I *suffered* for. With my party corrupted, I see the need for a third wave of revolution. I planned to use the *Volkhovnik* to bring that about.'

Interesting. Natasha had assumed Boky was a Bolshevik through and through. Was he truly planning to overthrow his own party?

'I'm not sure I believe you,' she said.

'Believe what you want. I could try to sabotage you, but what would that achieve? My fate is bound to yours. Besides, with you as tsarina and Katya wielding the power of the *Volkhovnik*, I could help you rebuild Russia into a nation we can all be proud of.'

Natasha rose from her seat, walking towards him and lifting her chin to look him in the eye. She sensed no deception. He ought to resent her for taking his free will, but he cared more about Russia's future than his own freedom.

'What else did you have planned?' Natasha reached out and ran a finger down his chest.

Boky smiled his wolfish smile, then he unfolded his strategy for her to see.

As Lenin's spymaster, Boky had full control over the party's intelligence. He'd realised four years ago that Svetlana Efremova was close to finding the location of the *Volkhovnik*. He kept her under constant surveillance – until she committed suicide rather than undergo interrogation about her expedition to Solovki.

He knew *The Book of the Wizard* must be on the archipelago, so, the next time he saw Lenin, he planted the idea of turning the Solovetsky Monastery into a prison.

Putting all of Lenin's enemies on this island served two purposes. It created an environment where Yekaterina Efremova could search for the book with Boky watching her every move. And it gave Boky a large group of test subjects already predisposed against Lenin.

He planned for Katya to use the *Volkhovnik* on the prisoners of Solovki.

'Think about it.' Boky cupped Natasha's cheek, his eyes radiating ambition. 'I've filled this prison with influential people – professors, writers, scientists, bankers. When we release them in the spring, you'll have an army of intellectuals singing your praises and preparing the ground for the final revolution.'

Natasha could picture it easily, the thousands of prisoners on the archipelago as loyal to Natasha as her volkolaki were.

All she had to do was sacrifice her sister. *Half-sister,* she reminded herself. She'd seen Katya as an enemy for most of her life – no reason to change that now.

Boky's plan was a good one. Let the book dominate Katya. They could use her love for Dima to control the spells she cast, and, through her, transform the prisoners of Solovki into loyal subjects.

Then, come spring, they would release the prisoners back into Russia, and Natasha would begin her rise to glory.

# Chapter 54
## *Katya*

The smell of roasting meat drifted up from the kitchen and through the iron bars of Katya's cell. Shivering in the corner, Katya's mouth watered. They probably left the kitchen door open as an extra punishment, so the prisoners had to smell the delicious meals the guards enjoyed.

The past two days, Lyudmila Antonova had given Katya cold water with a single boiled potato for lunch and raw potato peels for breakfast and dinner.

They did this to break her spirit. Making her wait seemed to be another of their strategies. Katya arrived in Sekirka braced for a fight, but instead she'd been locked away, forgotten. Was Barchenko too busy to torment her now that they'd uncovered the *Volkhovnik*, or was this another mind game?

Katya peered out through the bars, wishing for a glimpse of Dima. The cells were arranged in a squared U shape, connected by a railed walkway that looked out over the main living space down below.

Katya's cell was at the end of the hall, a corner room. She hadn't seen where they took Dima, nor could she look into Valentina Pavlovna's cell a few doors down. The injury on Valentina Pavlovna's leg had looked gruesome. She must have been mauled by a wolf while trying to distract the creatures so Katya and Dima could escape. Katya worried about her, especially because of the fever-sheen she'd seen on Valentina Pavlovna's face when they led Katya into the cell.

Katya paced her small room, as though constant movement would keep her darkest fears from catching up with her.

A board creaked in the hallway outside her room. Katya stopped pacing, listened. She heard footsteps, quiet almost-tiptoes that definitely didn't belong to Petrova. Silencing her breath, Katya strained to hear, and the pace of her heartbeat kicked up. She gasped when a black-cloaked figure crept up to her cell.

The figure pushed back the hood, revealing a beautiful heart-shaped face framed by long black hair.

'Sana?' Katya dashed forward and reached for Tsisana's hand through the bars. Grazing the iron stung her arm, but Katya didn't care. She held tight, studying Tsisana's face for signs of injury, finding none. 'Are you all right?'

'You're locked in a punishment cell, and you want to know if *I'm* all right?' Tsisana squeezed Katya's hand affectionately.

'Smolensky threatened you.'

'This time, I was ready for him.' Tsisana raised her chin, but there was bravado in her expression. Katya could tell she'd been scared.

'What happened?'

'I don't condone picking pockets, but I think I was justified in taking this when he came close enough.' Tsisana pulled a circlet of amber worry beads from her pocket and held it out for Katya to see. 'I slipped him one of Rafael's charmed coins, and that was that.'

'Are you sure you're all right?'

'I'm stronger than I look, Katyushka,' she said sternly. 'Besides, if he hadn't confronted me, we wouldn't have known you were here. Rafael made him tell us everything.'

Katya gripped Tsisana's hand tighter as gratitude swelled in her chest. Katya used to think protecting her heart from attachment would make her stronger, but this, right here, was true strength – having friends to fall back on when her knees gave out, friends to help her bear the load and come rescue her from a punishment cell in the middle of the night.

'You're getting me out of here?'

'Soon,' Tsisana said.

'They have Dima also. And my friend, Valentina Pavlovna.'

'I know. Andrei Sergeevich is spying on Commissar Boky and slipping us information. Boky has been holed up in his office all afternoon with Natasha and some doctor.'

'Barchenko.'

Tsisana nodded. 'They were discussing the different spells and rituals in the book, apparently searching for one in particular. They may have found it because Andrei Sergeevich said they're planning to bring the *Volkhovnik* here to Sekirka. We decided our best chance to rescue you will be after they move it. Then, hopefully, we can take the *Volkhovnik* as well.' Tsisana reached into her pocket and showed Katya five more amber circlets she'd snatched from Solovki guards. 'We have a plan.'

'How can I ever thank you?'

'Don't thank me. Just be strong, and be ready. Here.' Tsisana pulled a small, cloth-wrapped bundle from another pocket of her cloak and passed it through the bars. 'I'll see you soon.'

Pulling her black hood up, Tsisana crept back down the hallway, out of sight. Katya opened the bundle and found three big dumplings stuffed with egg and cabbage. After devouring the first two, Katya slowed down and savoured every bite of the final dumpling, enjoying the sensation of her belly filling up and her hunger losing its bite.

Katya licked the grease off her fingertips and then curled

up on the floor. A million thoughts raced through her mind, but she forced herself to dismiss them. *Be strong, and be ready.* Closing her eyes, Katya forced herself to rest so she'd be sharp and alert when the time came.

She must have slept a few hours before waking to the sound of Petrova's clomping footsteps. Katya blinked sleep from her eyes. As the nurse unlocked the cell door, Katya spotted the iron collar in her hand and fought against the urge to recoil. What a familiar dance – Katya shivering in a cell, Lyudmila Antonova locking away her magic and guiding her to Doctor Barchenko.

Images of the test subjects who'd died in the lab at Lubyanka rose unbidden to her mind, their tormented grimaces and red-veined eyes. Twenty-three volshebniki had died when Katya cast the spells Barchenko ordered her to. Dima would have been the twenty-fourth. Though Katya could picture the victim's faces, she focused on Dima's – the one she saved, the one who saved her in return.

Katya would be strong for him.

She stood as the nurse entered her cell and stretched out her neck compliantly. After shooting her a skeptical look, Petrova thrust the collar around Katya's neck. Grabbing Katya's arm, the nurse made to yank her, but Katya had already started walking, which threw Petrova off balance.

'What are you doing?'

'Going with you. Willingly.' Katya smiled sweetly.

'Whatever *this* is.' Petrova made a circular motion with her hand, gesturing toward Katya. 'And whatever you're trying to do, it's not going to work.'

'I'm not sure what you mean.'

Katya glided out of the cell and glanced over her shoulder, raising an eyebrow in a way that said, *Aren't you coming?* The nurse's brow furrowed in anger. She grabbed Katya's elbow and continued downstairs.

Katya struggled to suppress a smile. Getting a rise out of Petrova and Doctor Barchenko had been her only source of joy during those months in the lab. Who knew she could get one by feigning compliance?

With every worried glance the nurse shot her, Katya fought to keep her lips from curling upward. Her mirth died on the spot when they entered the church-turned-laboratory, lit by flickering candelabras.

Dima stood inside an iron cage, his limbs outstretched and fettered to the corners. Katya stopped in her tracks. Horror washed over her at the anguish radiating from his eyes. So much iron surrounded him, turning the magic in his blood into pain. With a groan, he let his head droop, and his eyes pinched shut.

*Be strong, and be ready,* Katya told herself as Lyudmila Antonova yanked her forward. Dragging her eyes away from Dima, Katya collected her wits. Smolensky stood beside the cage, pistol in hand. The nurse pushed Katya onto one of the exam chairs and roughly fastened her wrists and ankles with the leather straps. A second test subject already occupied the other chair – Valentina Pavlovna.

Blood had soaked through the silk nightgown the skomorokha still wore. Though they'd bandaged the wound on her leg, Valentina Pavlovna shivered on the chair and thrashed against her restraints. Sweat coated her ashen skin, and her eyes looked unfocused, delirious with fever.

As the nurse strapped her down, Katya glanced between Valentina Pavlovna and Dima, panic stirring in her gut. Where were Rafael and Tsisana? What if they didn't rescue them in time?

Katya couldn't catch her breath. Her heart pounded like a

battering ram inside her chest, and the sound of it filled her ears along with a high-pitched ring. Shifting in the chair, she tried to flex her trembling fingers as much as the restraints allowed, but they'd turned numb. A pins and needles sensation moved up her limbs, and her mind went blank.

As Doctor Barchenko strolled into the church with an ancient-looking iron box under his arm, every horror inflicted on her in the lab resurfaced from her memory. Katya wouldn't be rescued. She'd be used, her magic a weapon in Barchenko's hands, just like always. Why had she thought otherwise? Hope only ever lifted her up to drop her from a height.

Katya had tried to be strong, she'd tried to be brave, but as Doctor Barchenko opened the iron box and carefully lifted out the *Volkhovnik*, all her instincts reminded her of what she'd been in Lubyanka Square. A monster, something worse than the firing squad in the basement of the Cheka headquarters. She'd survived at the expense of others, but now the others in the room had pieces of her heart. To let either Valentina Pavlovna or Dima die would destroy Katya.

*No.* Katya drove her fingernails into her palms to shock herself out of survival mode, to silence her panic long enough for reason to have its say. Her friends were coming to help – she had to buy them time.

'Here we are again,' Barchenko said. 'Having you back in my lab feels like history repeating itself. Although, I believe that this night we'll *make* history.'

Candlelight bathed Barchenko's face, casting his puckered scars in shadow. As he reached into the iron box and reverently took hold of the ancient book inside it, dark magic crept through the church. A prickling sensation spread over Katya's skin, and a bitter taste lodged in the back of her throat. The power of the *Volkhovnik* sang to Katya's blood, a sinister melody of bloodlust and corrupted power. Mystical whispers fluttered through the sanctuary.

The *Volkhovnik* was a grimoire infused with the spirit of an ancient wizard. Those who wielded it had access to forbidden knowledge and god-like power. Now it had fallen into the hands of a fraud.

'I figured out why you'd get angry whenever I mentioned medical school.' Katya leaned forward as far as her restraints allowed. 'You're not *Doctor* Barchenko at all, are you? You're A.V. Barchenko, a science fiction novelist nobody's ever heard of.'

Ignoring her taunt, Barchenko set the book on his desk and prepared for the experiment. Katya's eyes darted to the doors, but there was no sign of Tsisana or Rafael.

Doctor Barchenko turned on the phonograph recorder.

'Twenty-first of February, 1924. Volkhovnik Trials test one, featuring subjects Numbers Two and Thirty-one.'

Hearing Valentina Pavlovna's full and gleaming life relegated to a mere number sparked something in Katya. Her defiance awakened. Though her heart still pounded, she forced her breath to slow, in and out. *Be strong, and be ready.*

'Here we come down to it,' Barchenko said to Katya. 'If this experiment works, we'll create utopia.'

'What experiment? What are you going to do?'

Those were the wrong questions to ask, judging by the smile spreading across Barchenko's face. His scars deepened with the movement as he said, 'You'll find out soon enough.'

Pulling a folded paper from his pocket, Barchenko smoothed it out on the desktop, studying the writing for a moment before looking at Katya with his one good eye.

'You know what will happen if you don't co-operate.' Barchenko waved a hand toward Dima, who slumped in his restraints.

Katya gave Barchenko a look of purest hatred and defiance.

'I see you intend to do this the hard way.' Barchenko turned to address Smolensky. 'Shoot his knee out. Or, better yet, his right hand. We'll see how her artist gets on without fingers.'

'No!' Panic surged through Katya when Smolensky took aim at Dima's hand. The leather straps bit into her skin as she struggled to break free.

'Shoot him,' Barchenko ordered.

'I'm sorry, Comrade.' Smolensky had a witchy gleam in his eyes. 'I can't do that.'

He turned the gun on Barchenko.

The door swung open. Five armed guards rushed in, surrounding the room. They aimed their weapons at Barchenko and Petrova. The nurse raised her hands in surrender.

'What do you think you're doing?' Barchenko sputtered angrily. 'Stand down, men.'

The guards did not stand down.

When the door opened again, Rafael swaggered into the church. Tsisana and Andrei Sergeevich followed behind him. With a sigh of relief, Katya leaned back on the chair and tilted her head up to look at the angels on the ceiling. Maybe there really was someone watching over her. Tsisana gasped at the sight of Valentina Pavlovna's condition and rushed to give her aid.

Andrei Sergeevich snatched the keys from Smolensky's belt, unlocked the cage, and began freeing Dima from his fetters.

'What is this?' Doctor Barchenko growled.

'This, my dear doctor, is the tables being turned.' Rafael circled him once, walking like a proud matador, before veering off towards Katya.

Barchenko tried to follow, but Smolensky shook his head in warning and moved his finger to the trigger.

'Delightful to see you again, Katya.' Rafael unclasped the straps around her wrists and ankles. Then he offered his hand with a flourish.

'I didn't think you were coming.' Katya let him help her up to standing. Though her mind was relieved, her body still held all the symptoms of panic. A sob lodged in her chest, ready to burst out.

'I assure you, my sense of timing is impeccable.' Rafael winked at her, and then kissed her hand chivalrously before releasing it.

He turned his attention to Barchenko, ordering his guards to seize the fraudulent doctor and strap him into Katya's vacated exam chair.

Tsisana re-bandaged Valentina Pavlovna's leg, then pressed her thumbs against her temples and chanted Hail Marys until the fever broke. Valentina Pavlovna's eyes cleared. As Andrei Sergeevich freed him from the last fetter, Dima clapped him on the shoulder in thanks before rushing to Katya.

He met her eyes as he approached. The torture still showed in them, but so did relief. Wrapping their arms around each other, they held on tight. Katya rested her cheek against Dima's chest, and the sound of his heartbeat reassured her everything was all right.

Dima pulled back slightly, just enough to study Katya's face. She felt grimy after days in a prison cell, but he stroked her cheek as though she couldn't be more beautiful to him.

'You won't get away.' Strapped in the exam chair, Doctor Barchenko stared at her with a thunderous expression. 'Soon enough I'll be rescued and you'll be captured. You're going to die on this island.'

His words sent a shiver up Katya's spine. But she couldn't think about the years she might not have – only what needed to be done tonight. Her eyes fixed on the *Volkhovnik* resting on Doctor Barchenko's desk.

As she sauntered towards it the pulse of dark magic tempted Katya to take up the book. She stretched out her hand. Power curled around her fingertips, enticing her to take it, use it, smite her enemies with a single spell. But a glance at the wrinkled paper Barchenko had placed on his desk gave her pause. It contained words in Greek, with Russian notations scribbled here and there. The title had been translated: *To Alter a Human Soul.* This is what Barchenko planned to do to Valentina Pavlovna, what Boky intended for all Russians. They would use the *Volkhovnik* for mind control, for re-engineering the human spirit, taking away greed and rebelliousness, erasing every predilection for dissent.

The utopia they envisioned would be brought about by the enslavement of every Russian – they'd take away laughter, poetry, that innate instinct to rise out of adversity and strive for a better world.

They wanted the opposite of everything Katya believed in, the freedom anarchists had fought for. However tempting the power at her fingertips might be, a magic that could turn a human into a slave was not one Katya would ever wield. In one quick movement, she returned the book to the iron box and shut the lid.

'None of you will get away with this,' Barchenko warned.

'They must keep a gag here somewhere, no?' Rafael made a show of looking for something to silence Barchenko.

With Tsisana and Andrei Sergeevich bracing up her shoulders, Valentina Pavlovna limped forward. Katya and Dima embraced her in a hug as the guards dragged Nurse Lyudmila onto the chair Valentina Pavlovna had occupied. She cursed them with a thousand painful deaths as they strapped her in.

'Are you all right?' Katya looked Valentina Pavlovna up and down. Tsisana had used her koldun magic to break the fever, but Valentina Pavlovna's skin still looked pasty, and blood was already seeping through the new bandage.

'I'll survive.' Valentina Pavlovna lifted her head and put her shoulders back into a perfect dancer's posture.

'We have two sleds at the bottom of the hill,' Tsisana said. 'If we can get her down the stairs, she can lie down.'

'You won't make it a mile before the wolves devour you,' Barchenko said darkly.

'Forget a gag, I have a better idea.' Rafael pulled a golden coin from his pocket, flicked it in the air and then caught it again. He pressed the coin into Barchenko's hand. 'Sit here in silence and think about what you've done, the lives you've taken, the patients you've dehumanised, the pain you've caused. Do not release this coin or speak again until you've reckoned with your choices and resolved to be a better man.'

Barchenko's mouth opened, but no words came out. His brow furrowed in deep thought as Rafael faced the others.

'What now?' Tsisana asked.

Katya took a steadying breath and reached for the iron box. 'Now we destroy the *Volkhovnik*.'

# Chapter 55
## *Katya*

Katya stood atop of Sekirka Hill, watching the six enchanted guards carry Valentina Pavlovna down the treacherous stairs. While the rest of their party began their descent, Katya lingered. Here above the tree line, uncountable stars filled the sky.

A memory of Svetlana came to her then, so vivid she could smell the musk and floral spice of Svetlana's favourite perfume. They'd been walking to their flat in Petrograd from Smolny. As they crossed a park Svetlana said it was a perfect night for stargazing. Hand in hand they'd timbered backwards into a bank of powder snow, laughing like children. They stayed there a long while, Svetlana pointing out stars and constellations, telling Katya all kinds of myths and legends surrounding each one.

*But what are they really?* Katya had asked.

*Memories*, Svetlana said.

Katya had turned her head, cheek pressed against the blanket of snow. She loved to watch Svetlana talk, especially in moments like this when her beautiful face was open and warm, filled with wonder.

*The starlight we see takes years to reach us. Sometimes hundreds of years, or even thousands. Some of the stars we're looking at right now may have died centuries ago, but their light still shines out into the universe, reaching us long after they're gone.*

If starlight was memory, Svetlana shone brightly in Katya's heart, even now. Her mother might have been deeply flawed, a thorny rose who'd given Katya beauty and pain in equal measure. But for all her faults, Svetlana had been wise enough to keep the *Volkhovnik* from falling into the government's hands. She'd left Katya clues, trusting that the daughter she'd raised would see this through to the end.

'I'm listening,' Katya whispered.

She clutched the *Volkhovnik's* case under her arm, the iron prickling her skin even with her coat and gloves as a buffer. They still had to smuggle it into the monastery and find the gateway to the Otherworld. Daunting, but Svetlana must have believed Katya could succeed – that faith lit her heart with optimism.

She could do this.

They would end it all tonight.

'Coming?' Dima waited a few steps down.

With one last look at the starry night sky Katya breathed frosty air and descended the steps of Sekirka Hill with Dima. At the bottom of the stairs they gathered with the others to make a plan.

The guards had set Valentina Pavlovna in one of the dog sleds. She needed to be taken to her *izba*. Tsisana and Rafael would go with her, so Tsisana could treat Valentina Pavlovna's wounds.

Katya, Dima and Andrei Sergeevich would take the second sled back to the monastery.

Dima lit the lanterns hanging from the sleds. It was time to say goodbye. With so much danger before them, Katya didn't know if she'd ever see her friends again. She knelt beside Valentina Pavlovna. Reaching beneath the fur blanket covering her, Katya found Valentina Pavlovna's hands and squeezed them tight.

'Thank you for everything,' Katya said. 'I don't know how I could ever repay you for all your help.'

'That's easy.' Despite the pallor of Valentina Pavlovna's skin, her eyes sparkled. 'If you want to repay me, allow me to tell your story. There's nothing a skomorokha likes more than to write of a brave heroine who defies all odds to triumph over evil.'

'I don't feel particularly brave, but my story is yours to tell.' It was oddly comforting to know that, if the worst happened, someone would remember her.

'*Prashai*, Katya,' Valentina Pavlovna said, releasing Katya's hands.

*Da svidanya* meant see you later, but *prashai* carried more weight. It meant goodbye for ever and pled forgiveness for any wrongs done, so there might be no bitterness to taint their memories of one another.

Katya took an unsteady breath. Emotion swelled up inside her, stinging her eyes. For years she'd kept people at arm's length to protect her heart. But this grief felt bittersweet. She might not survive the night. If she did, she'd likely end up right back in the punishment cells. Knowing her friends would remember her meant more than she'd ever expected it would.

'*Prashai*,' Katya said through the choking sensation in her throat.

After squeezing Valentina Pavlovna's hand one last time, she stood and brushed snow from her knees. Then she turned. Lantern light cast a golden glow across Tsisana's lovely face.

'Don't even think about saying goodbye to me,' Tsisana said fiercely. 'I'll see you after.'

They threw their arms around each other and hugged tight. Pulling out of the embrace, Katya kissed Tsisana's cheeks.

Rafael bowed to Katya as he took his leave. Husband and

wife stepped up on the sled runners. Before they drove away Rafael gave one final order to the six enchanted guards.

'Up the steps you go. Release every prisoner in Sekirka, and lock yourselves in their place. And you.' Rafael focused in on Smolensky, his eyes hardening into steel. 'Beast that you are. Since you have brutalised those entrusted to your care, you yourself shall be brutalised. After you have locked yourself in a cage, I order you to relive every act of violence you have perpetrated on this island. But instead of being the one in power, I order you to see those moments through the eyes of your victims – to tremble with their fear and feel the pain of every wound you inflicted on them.'

While the guards began climbing the steps, Rafael made a dramatic salute. The dog team darted forward at his shouted command.

Katya watched until their lantern disappeared between the trees. She turned to the second sled and was about to walk towards it.

Just then, Smolensky slipped on an icy step. He tumbled down three stairs, and Rafael's gold coin flew from his pocket. It landed in the snow.

Smolensky stared at the coin for a long beat, then he turned to them, face contorted with rage. His eyes shone with a lupine gleam.

'Stop him,' Katya shouted, but it was too late.

Smolensky leapt off the stairs and sprinted for the tree line. Soon he would transform into a wolf and race to carry their plans to Natasha's ears.

'We have to hurry.' Katya jogged to the sled. Dima climbed in behind her, wrapping an arm around her waist.

Andrei Sergeevich stepped onto the runners. When he shouted to the dogs, the sled lurched towards the monastery.

Katya turned to look at Dima. The darkened forest streaked by, and the swaying lantern made a play of light and shadow across Dima's face. Out here, he looked so different than the other night – not a lover intoxicated by desire, but sober. Katya ran her thumb along the tense line of his jaw, resting it on the spot where his muscle ticked.

'You don't have to come,' she said. 'You could go to Valentina Pavlovna's *izba*. You could finish our poem. Make copies of it on the lithograph machine and send it out when the sea melts and the steamer returns to the mainland.'

'Katya.' He raised an eyebrow and gave her a pointed look.

'I mean it. I can take the *Volkhovnik* into the monastery's foundations by myself. There's no reason for you to risk your life.'

'I'm not going to leave you – now or ever.'

The fierce determination in his eyes said arguing with him was hopeless. Katya rested her forehead against Dima's. They'd started this together, they'd finish it together, to whatever end.

Andrei Sergeevich ordered the dogs to halt a few hundred metres from the monastery gates. From there they approached the monastery on foot. Katya cast her cloaking spell over them. Yet still, as she strode towards the gates, she prepared for a confrontation if the guards possessed amulets.

Only there *were* no guards.

Perhaps the men assigned to guard duty tonight were now enchanted and locked in Sekirka cells.

'Do you know where we'll find the entrance to the foundations?' Andrei Sergeevich asked as they crept into the courtyard.

Katya looked up at the three massive cathedrals in the monastery's centre. Their bulbous towers, silhouetted in moonlight, seemed to reach for the stars. As always happened when she stood here, Katya felt power radiating from the ground. One of the Solovetsky Gates had been open for centuries. Magic leaked through it into the soil, into the stone foundations, up into the cobblestones and the church walls.

The monks who came here with Zosima would have centred their holy buildings on that source of power. Katya studied the three churches with that in mind. The Transformation Cathedral – a six-storey church with five burnt-out cupolas – was the oldest of the three.

Approaching the doors, Katya tried to turn the ornate handle.

'It's locked.' She readied herself for casting a spell to unlock it but Andrei Sergeevich guided her to step aside.

'Then it's lucky you brought an old radical like me along.' Andrei Sergeevich pulled a ring of lock picks from his pocket, twirling it around his finger.

He had it open in seconds, and the three of them slipped through the door. Dima held up the lantern, but it barely penetrated the darkness of the vast cathedral.

It took several minutes to cross the church. They stepped onto the altar and there found a door surrounded by gilded panels that led into the back rooms.

'Did you hear that?' Dima tensed, listening. 'I thought I heard footsteps.'

They paused for a long moment, then Andrei Sergeevich's eyes widened. 'I heard it, too.'

At the cathedral entrance, two torch beams cut through the darkness, scanning from side to side. Warning prickled up Katya's neck.

'Natasha,' she whispered.

It had to be her. Smolensky, having overheard their plans, had escaped to warn her. Natasha would rush to intercept the *Volkhovnik* before it could be destroyed.

'Keep going,' Andrei Sergeevich said. 'I'll buy you some time.'

Katya wanted to protest, but the weight of the iron box she carried reminded her of what was at stake. The *Volkhovnik* had to be destroyed at any cost.

Katya squeezed Andrei Sergeevich's hand. Then she and Dima hurried through the door, leaving him behind.

They jogged down a long corridor that led through multiple chambers, now empty of riches the church once contained. Finally they came to an arched door made of wood planks so worn and weathered they appeared ancient.

'This has to be it.' The lantern gilded Dima's skin as he held it up and reached for the handle.

The door opened to a stone stairway, leading down into the monastery's foundations. With the iron case clutched to her chest, Katya rushed down the stairs. She couldn't think about Andrei Sergeevich and what might happen to him.

At the bottom Dima snatched Katya's free hand and tugged her onward. The darkness lifted as they raced into the church foundations, giving way to a faint, otherworldly blue light. Here the magic was so potent it buzzed over Katya's skin and warmed her blood.

They raced down a narrow alley between curving stone walls. The foundations of Solovetsky were a maze – a labyrinth.

'Something's wrong.' Dima faltered, his face contorting in pain. 'The magic – it's doing something to me.'

Dima dropped the lantern. It rolled unevenly away from them and sputtered out, leaving them in the dusky blue light trickling towards them from the centre of the labyrinth.

Somewhere far away a wolf's howl pierced the night.

'We have to keep going.' Katya threw an arm around Dima's back and braced him. They staggered on together.

Unlike the stone labyrinths on Bolshoi Zayatsky, the foundations didn't have a single pathway leading to the centre. The path forked and splintered every few meters, some passages circling back the way they'd come.

They took a wrong turn and hit a dead end. There Dima crumpled to the floor. Sweat glistened on his forehead, and his jaw clamped tight with pain.

'Leave me,' Dima groaned. 'You have to destroy the *Volk-hovnik.*'

'No,' Katya said fiercely.

The boom of a gunshot resounded through the labyrinth.

Katya stepped toward the main aisle and peered out, listening.

A growl echoed through the passageway – the wolves were in the labyrinth.

'We have to hurry.' Katya turned back toward the dead end, squinting to see in the shadows.

Dima didn't answer.

Katya strode back in his direction, but tripped over something. She dropped to her knees and felt the ground around her. Her fingers closed around a bundle of discarded fabric. Was that Dima's coat? A little further, she found his shirt, then the satchel with his sketchbooks inside. Katya felt along the ground. Unease strangled her voice as she called out, 'Dima? DIMA?'

From up ahead came a snuffling sound, followed by a grunt. Trembling, Katya pushed herself up to standing and staggered forward a few more steps.

A hulking creature stepped out of the shadows, its enormous eyes gleaming in the faint blue light. Katya let out a shaky breath as she realised what she was seeing.

Dima had transformed into a bear.

# Chapter 56

## *Natasha*

Natasha strode through the cathedral with rage in her heart and a pistol in her hand. Boky and Smolensky followed a step behind her, to her left and to her right. They shined torches to light her path to the altar. The six other volkolaki were in their wolf forms, padding along behind them as they awaited Natasha's commands.

She never should have trusted Barchenko with such an important task.

Natasha had chosen not to go to Sekirka. She didn't want to witness Katya's enslavement, lest she lose her resolve. Natasha didn't know how Katya and Dima escaped the lab, but she would stop them from destroying the book, no matter the cost.

As they stepped onto the altar, the torchlights revealed a man blocking the doorway to the inner church. He squinted when they shined the torches on his face, revealing an old man with feathery eyebrows and a curved moustache.

'Andrei Sergeevich,' Boky said, a thread of panic in his tone. 'Step aside.'

'I could,' Andrei Sergeevich said. 'I've done it often enough since the Revolution. I stood aside while my comrades claimed the Red Terror was justice running its natural course. I stood aside when Comrade Lenin claimed there could be no freedom of the press in a time of such rapid change. Too late I realised I wasn't only standing aside, but standing on the wrong side. Now, at last, I'll stand my ground.'

'Don't think I won't shoot you, old man.' Natasha raised the pistol in a two-handed grip.

'No,' Boky said. 'This man saved my life once.'

Natasha squeezed the trigger. A gunshot thundered through the cathedral, and the force of the recoil made Natasha stumble back a step. She inhaled gunpowder, stinging her nostrils. Wiping her nose on her sleeve, Natasha stole a sideways glance at Boky.

He stared down at the body, pale with shock.

'Move him out of the way,' Natasha ordered Smolensky.

The Polish guard set down his torch, grabbed the old man's wrists and dragged him aside. Then he opened the door for Natasha.

She stepped through it. When Boky made no move to follow, she ordered him, 'Come.'

The three of them descended into the monastery's foundations with the wolves at their heels and found themselves in a maze. Natasha paused to get her bearings. She closed her eyes and breathed until she felt it, the pull of power coming from the centre of the labyrinth.

Walking with her eyes closed, she let her spirit lead the way through the spirals of the foundations. The power gathering around her felt intimately familiar – it sprang from the same source as the magic she drew from the Otherworld when she played her violin or performed rituals. By the time she reached the central spiral of the labyrinth, she felt as though she were wading through it. Never before had she experienced magic in so concentrated a form.

Natasha opened her eyes, amazed by the ethereal blue glow

surrounding her. Its origin seemed to be straight ahead. The labyrinth ended in an arched gateway leading to a large round chamber made of stone. Blue light flowed out from a round, well-like hole in the centre of the room.

Katya and Dima were nowhere in sight.

Natasha smiled. Despite the old man's interference, she had beaten them to the gateway to the Otherworld.

'They're lost in the labyrinth.' Natasha turned to address her wolves. 'Find them.'

# Chapter 57

## *Katya*

Katya held utterly still as the bear snuffled her. The abundant magic of the open gateway must have forced Dima's transformation, just as it had that day in the lab.

He seemed to recognise Katya still. When he'd finished sniffing her, he nuzzled against her hip, nearly knocking her over with his enormous head. Katya clutched the iron case in one hand and used the other to stroke the bear's neck, her fingertips trailing through coarse fur.

A howl reverberated through the labyrinth.

'The wolves are coming,' she said. 'We have to go.'

The bear blocked her way when she tried to leave. He nudged her towards his shoulder, as though wanting her to climb on his back. Katya hesitated until she heard the tapping of claws on stone as the wolves prowled closer. She scrambled up. No sooner had she grabbed a handful of fur then he lumbered forward.

Setting the *Volkhovnik* on her lap, Katya grabbed fistfuls of Dima's fur, holding on with all her might. Dima picked up speed as he loped into the central aisle of the labyrinth. A glance behind revealed gleaming eyes – the wolves had given chase.

They were almost there. Katya's heartbeat fell in rhythm with the magic pulsing from the labyrinth's centre, and the ethereal blue glow lit their path.

This was the final stretch – a long passage leading to a stone archway.

Natasha, Boky and Smolensky blocked the entrance. They raised their pistols, taking aim.

A wolf vaulted at Dima, mauling his hind leg. With a pained bellow, Dima edged sideways, slamming the wolf into the wall. He roared as he charged into the gateway.

Three gunshots rang out before Natasha, Boky and Smolensky leapt aside. A bullet hit Katya like a punch in the belly. It drove the air from her lungs. Still she clutched Dima's fur with all her might.

Dima barrelled into a vast pillared chamber directly below the church altar, the thinnest place in Solovki. Here realms mingled and magic seeped into the world through the gateway opened by Savvatiy's soul when Herman betrayed him in the Otherworld.

Slowing to a canter, Dima approached a large, round hole in the middle of the room. That must be the gateway. All Katya had to do was throw the *Volkhovnik* inside it.

A snarling wolf sprang at Dima. Its teeth flashed before sinking into Dima's shoulder. Dima bellowed and spun, flinging Katya from his back. She skidded across the floor, the iron case tumbling with her.

Katya couldn't breathe. The bullet made a fire-like sensation ripple through her torso. She pressed the wound, and blood poured through her fingers. *Keep moving,* she ordered herself. Opening the iron case, Katya took hold of the book. She clamped her jaw and staggered to her feet.

Two more wolves attacked Dima. He swiped at them but couldn't knock them off his back. Blood dripped from his shoulder, leaking out from a volkolak's fangs.

'Enough.' Natasha strode into the chamber with Boky on one side, Smolensky on the other.

The wolves yelped and whimpered as Natasha's command compelled them. They ceased attacking Dima and circled behind Natasha, ready to defend their mistress.

Dima wavered unsteadily before toppling onto his side. He writhed as he began a reverse transformation. All of Katya's instincts urged her to rush to Dima, but she had to finish what they'd started.

With one hand pressed to her wound and the other gripping the *Volkhovnik*, Katya edged towards the hole. The circular opening looked like an enormous well – too deep to see the bottom of. The stones lining it glowed with deep blue light, as though they were made of crystal, or perhaps ice.

'It doesn't have to be like this,' Natasha's voice echoed in the circular room. 'Give me the book and neither of you will get hurt.'

They were hurt already. Dima's blood painted the stone floor as his body shifted, snapping and tremoring as it remade his human form. Katya pressed her wounded belly, but too much blood spilled out through her fingers.

The wound was likely fatal.

*It doesn't have to be.* A deep, seductive voice spoke into Katya's mind. *I could save both you and Dima. All you have to do is open my book.*

Dima had regained his human form, but lost consciousness. He lay sprawled on his belly, bleeding from wounds on his back.

Natasha aimed her pistol at him. 'Give me the book or I'll shoot.'

Time slowed as Katya glanced down into the gateway. If she gave Natasha the book, Dima might survive – but Natasha would use this power to subjugate Russia. If Katya wielded the book's power herself, she would be corrupted by the wizard's spirit.

There was only one choice. She had to destroy the book, though they might kill Dima, though these might be Katya's last moments on this earth.

Closing her eyes, she held the book out over the abyss.

'No,' Natasha and Boky cried out in unison.

The voice of the wizard was coy. *Your wound is fatal, Yekaterina. Without my help, you'll die within the hour. Are you truly willing to sacrifice your life?*

Coming here tonight, she knew it might be forfeit. She wanted to live. She wanted Dima to live. This was all so terribly unfair.

But if Katya had to die, her final act would be one of bravery.

'Give me the book.' Boky stepped closer.

She met his eyes – the Cipher, a man who let disillusionment poison his ideals, an engineer striving to redesign the human soul. He'd already destroyed thousands of lives. If he succeeded in making Natasha tsarina, worse deeds surely lay in his future.

Those stone-grey eyes always seemed to see two steps ahead of Katya. Not this time, though. He understood strategy, but not sacrifice; calculation, but not love.

'Here.' Katya held the book out to him, her face carefully blank.

When Boky's fingers closed around the other end of it, Katya exhaled. He frowned when she couldn't suppress a little twitch of a smile.

'What are you doing?' He tried to pull the book away, but Katya held tight.

With her free hand, Katya fisted the front of Boky's coat.

'Wait,' Natasha shouted.

Boky's eyes widened, but Katya was already leaning back. The spirit of the wizard screamed his rage into her mind. A gunshot rang out as Katya tumbled into the abyss, dragging Boky and the *Volkhovnik* along with her.

They fell – not into air, but into magic.

Katya lost hold of the book as she plunged, her stomach rising into her throat. Boky's screams were barely audible through the roar in Katya ears. Screwing her eyes closed against the rush of wind, Katya's other senses came to life. The abyss smelled of damp earth. Its warmth felt like falling into sunshine.

*Save us*, the wizard spoke into Katya's mind. *Take me in your hands and cast a spell before it's too late.*

At the bottom of the well, a labyrinth glowed golden. That must be Savvatiy's soul, left open to the Otherworld. When the wizard's spirit returned to the other side, the gateway would close. Then, at last, Savvatiy could rest.

All around Katya, magic shimmered. Boky writhed as he fell. Golden tendrils drew the shadows out of him like poison from a wound. The pure magic was stripping away his volkolak powers.

Light gathered around Katya also. Inside Katya's veins her magic sang. The light purged her of shadows, of all her haunted grief. The horrors of the lab, the disillusionment after the Revolution – all of it lost its dark edges as light flooded through her.

Gravity hurled them towards the bottom of the cistern. Once she hit the ground, it'd be over. Her survival instincts kicked in. It took all her force of will to shut out the screaming voice of the wizard and accept the choice she'd made.

Katya gritted her teeth and braced for impact.

# Chapter 58

## *Natasha*

The gun slipped from Natasha's fingers and fell to the ground with a clank. She hadn't meant to pull the trigger. Her whole body had tensed when Katya dragged Boky into the chasm, and the gun went off. Now Dima's face was contorted in pain. He pressed his hand over the wound to his chest. Blood spilled out through his fingers.

He wasn't dead yet, but he would be.

Natasha stumbled a few steps back. Her hands trembled and the room spun dizzily around her. She'd shot Andrei Sergeevich and Katya. Now she'd shot Dima also.

And yet, she'd still failed.

Katya held fast to her anarchist ideals and destroyed Natasha's best chance at saving Russia. Turning aside, Natasha met Smolensky's eyes. At least she still had her volkolaki. The six others prowled the chamber in their wolf forms.

The ground rumbled. Shakily, Natasha walked to the edge of the chasm. She looked over just in time to see the *Volkhovnik* hit the bottom.

The labyrinth flashed with golden light. Then it erupted.

Mere seconds before Katya and Boky hit the bottom, a burst of golden magic erupted like a geyser. The force of the explosion carried Katya and Boky upward.

Natasha stepped back, shielding her face.

Having been carried to the ceiling by the burst of magic, Katya and Boky fell to the chamber floor. They landed with a crunch of bones. Natasha couldn't bring herself to look.

The golden light crested over them like a wave, drenching the chamber in pure magic. Something tightened in Natasha's chest as the spiritual tethers connecting her to her volkolaki went taut.

Shadows leaked out of Natasha's chest like spilled ink, vanishing as the golden light absorbed them. The wolves whined and barked as their magic was ripped away. Whimpers became screams as the volkolaki rapidly transformed into men – their spines cracking and snapping as the stripping of their magic remade them.

Natasha's knees trembled. Tears leaked down her face as more shadows streamed out of her. She collapsed as the magical currents absorbed the last of her black magic and carried it through the gateway.

One by one, stones appeared in the floor, making the shape of a spiralling labyrinth as the chasm sealed itself shut.

It was over.

With the last of the stones closing up the hole, magic died away.

The six volkolaki who had been transformed writhed on the ground, naked and in agony. But Smolensky, who had been in human form, stood over Natasha.

He raised his pistol.

She lifted her hand to aim her gun at him before realising she'd dropped it after she shot Dima. Natasha was unarmed. Now the resentment Smolensky had for her would spill over into wrath.

She'd lost everything.

She'd failed Aunt Sonya.

She'd failed Russia.

'Kill me,' Natasha said.

'I don't think so.' A cruel smile spread across Smolensky's lips. 'You made me a slave to dark magic and used me as your puppet. I think you should have to live a long, *long* while.'

Natasha knelt there, frozen in horror as Smolensky unhooked a pair of iron handcuffs from his belt.

'Put out your hands,' Smolensky ordered.

Natasha's mind scrambled for some way out of this. The nerves made her eye twitch. When she tried to back away, Smolensky's nostrils flared. He lunged forward and swung the pistol. Pain burst across Natasha's temple as the gun struck her face. Everything went momentarily silent. Her vision spun until the pain of iron closing around her wrists brought everything back into clarity.

'Help the commissar,' Smolensky ordered the guards who had been transformed.

Though they were naked and in pain, they rose to their feet. Four men lifted Boky by his limbs and carried him out of the chamber. The spymaster was injured, but still alive. Natasha dared a glance at Katya, but her half-sister hadn't been so lucky. She lay on the ground, broken and unmoving.

'Walk.' Smolensky prodded Natasha's back with the barrel of his pistol, forcing her out of the monastery's foundations to face whatever cruel fate awaited her.

# Chapter 59
## *Dima*

The moment the gunshot rang out, Dima knew he was a goner. The bullet pierced through the centre of his chest and must have hit his spine. His legs wouldn't move. He couldn't even feel them anymore. Couldn't feel much of anything except for the cold.

His thoughts dripped through his mind like wet paint, all of them running together, blurring their shapes and colours. The room spun around him and a ringing sound filled his ears. Turning his head, he blinked until his vision cleared. The chamber was empty now, except for him and one other person.

*Katya.*

Her name became an anchor in the rushing current of his confused thoughts. She lay not far away from him, unmoving.

Dima had to get to her. Between the dead weight of his legs and the slickness of his spilled blood, he struggled to move. Straining hard, he managed to grip the edges of a cobblestone and flip himself onto his stomach. The movement made him nauseous. Bile crawled up his throat, and a cold sweat broke over his skin.

He was losing too much blood.

Dima raised himself onto his elbows and crawled forward. Every movement felt like a battle being waged, a struggle between his determination to reach Katya and the death creeping over him like a hungry shadow. He'd escaped death four years ago when his family had been killed. Today, it might catch up with him at last.

He finally reached Katya. Dima collapsed at her side, breathing heavily. He reached for her, then paused as he registered her injuries. She'd been shot in the torso, and the fall had devastated her body. She had deep gashes and a broken leg. Was she dead? The cold creeping into Dima's limbs spread to his heart – until she took a wheezing breath.

'Katya.'

Her eyes cracked open, and she looked at him blearily.

Dima used the last of his strength to gather Katya into his arms. Her breath caressed his cheek as he held her in a warm embrace.

# Epilogue
## *Solovetsky Island*

*3 OCTOBER, 1925*

*Dokhodiagi* is the name for living ghosts, for goners.

You'd think starvation was contagious by the way the other prisoners cringe and avert their eyes when I come near. It hurts that they won't look at me. I can't pretend otherwise. When you've danced through life at centre stage, breathing in admiration, it's hard to accept a failing body, a forgotten name.

But Death has come calling, as he must for us all.

It takes all my meagre strength to stay upright, hobbling to the front of the ration line with a tin cup clutched in my bony fingers. Like I'm a leper, the prisoners move aside to let me pass. It's fortunate, I tell myself. I might faint if I had to stand waiting, so I try not to let their repulsion crawl under my skin. I lurch towards the front of the line where a guard sits at a table, not bothering to look up.

'Name?' His impatient thumb rests at the corner of the papers stacked before him, as though my name means no more than the check mark he'll put beside it.

My name used to grace playbills at the best theatres the world over. It was praised in parlour rooms and publications,

444

whispered alongside a thousand rumours, most of them true.

Now it's not even worth full rations.

'Name.' the guard's voice hardens into a threat.

I should just say it and move on. I barely have the strength to collect my dinner, so it's absurd to expend energy this way. But I wait until his irritated eyes flick upward, until he's forced to look at me. To see me.

'Kryukova,' I say in a voice so hoarse it's hardly recognisable as my own. 'Valentina Pavlovna Kryukova.'

He huffs out a breath then flips through papers. Turning this unpleasant encounter into a check mark, he shouts the words I know are coming. 'Quarter rations.'

'Valentina Pavlovna Kryukova,' I say again, though I don't know why. To remind him I'm a person? To remind myself? To declare my existence so some memory of me might linger when I have passed?

I shake my head at the futility of it and move along.

Limping inside, I approach an imprisoned monk ladling watery gruel from a cast-iron pot. My stomach writhes at the rotten stench, but I extend my tin cup anyway. My hand trembles with the effort, and the monk's wrinkles deepen like battlefield trenches. Behind him, a guard nurses a bottle of vodka, his rifle resting over his knees. With a resigned sigh, the monk lifts a ladle of soup over my cup but only tilts it partway.

Starvation rations.

'Thank you,' I mutter. It's the cruellest thing I can say.

The monk's grim face tightens, the creases above his nose marking his heart's torment. It's him or me, I know. If he tilts the ladle fully, they'll shoot him and starve me anyway. I understand, but why shouldn't he feel guilty for dishing out starvation rations, even if I'm too far gone to meet an arbitrary work quota? Or any work quota? Should I fade into silence, my humanity ignored?

They expect me to die quietly, but what kind of performer would I be if I didn't muster a finale?

The package arrived from the mainland in last week's shipment: a ream of paper and a vial of ink. I hobble back to my barrack, alive with memories of the friends who are threads in the tapestry of this island.

When hope returns to Russia, these stories must remain. That's why I've spent my last roubles on supplies instead of buying food to last me through winter. With flour and oil I could survive a few more months, but through paper and ink my friends and I might live for ever.

Before my strength fails, I will follow the final threads of my tale.

The night Rafael and Tsisana rescued me from Sekirka, we separated from Katya, Dima and Andrei Sergeevich. I heard later that Andrei Sergeevich died from a gunshot wound when he blocked the way into the foundations of the Transfiguration Cathedral, giving his life so Dima and Katya might destroy the *Volkhovnik*.

Meanwhile, Rafael returned me to my *izba* in the forest, and Tsisana treated my wounded leg. Three days later, we were arrested and charged with conspiracy. The Mexican government arranged for Rafael and Tsisana to be released the next spring, and it comforts me to imagine the long and happy lives they're living.

Commissar Boky left for Moscow on the spring's first steamer and has not returned to the island since.

Natasha went with him, in chains.

Even on this remote island we've heard whispers of her. After Lenin's death, she moved into the Kremlin. She is now known as Stalin's witch, performing black magic rituals against his enemies.

And what became of Yekaterina Efremova and Dmitri Danilov? Here the ending is harder to follow, for rumours abound and the thread of my story has frayed.

Some say they died in each other's arms that night, others that they were returned to the punishment cells of Sekirka. But from time to time a prisoner will report seeing a bear in the forest. Some even swear they've glimpsed a blonde woman in the witchy twilight, riding on its back.

Perhaps Katya and Dima are alive and free. I like to imagine them that way. Whatever their fate, I've set their story to paper so those who come after might have courage, so their lives can be like the whisper of stars. Consider this my love letter to the future, my radical hope that our spilled blood will awaken the compassion of Damp Mother Earth, and none of these sorrows shall have been in vain.

## The Whisper Of Stars

I
CAN
HEAR
EVERY
WHISPER
OF MEMORY
IN MY SOUL.
DISTORTED BY
TIME AND GRIEF,
BUT NEVER FADING
COMPLETELY. EVERY
LIFE RIPPLES ACROSS
OTHERS, GENTLY CHANGING
THOSE THEY TOUCH. THOUGH DEATH MAY STILL A HEARTBEAT, IT CANNOT SILENCE THE
ECHOES OF THE DEPARTED. THE PAST SHAPES OUR LIVES, AND WE ARE THE ONES
WHO WILL MOULD REALITY FOR THE GENERATIONS TO COME. RESPONSIBILITY
RESTS UPON OUR TONGUES. A HUNDRED THOUSAND YEARS AFTER ADAM,
WE STILL HAVE THE TASK OF NAMING THE WORLD. WITH EVERY
WORD SPOKEN, WE WIELD THE POWER THAT BREATHED
LIGHT INTO STARS AND SPILLED WATER INTO
SEAS. NATIONS ARE SHAPED BY HUMAN
VOICES. WORD BECOMES THOUGHT.
THOUGHT BECOMES ACTION. VOICES
AND DEEDS BRAID TOGETHER INTO A
A ROPE THAT GUIDES HUMANITY EITHER
TOWARD THE LIGHT OF TRUTH AND FREEDOM
OR DOWNWARD, INTO          DEHUMANISING LIES
AND INJUSTICES.              IN DARK TIMES, I
LISTEN. VOICES              OF MARTYRS ARE
HEARD BEYOND                THE GRAVE. WE
LEARN TO BE                 BRAVE AS WE
REMEMBER.                   WE'RE LED
BY THOSE                    WHO ARE
STILL                       ALIVE
IN                                  US

# Author's Note

My interest in Russian culture and history began at an early age. I was born in Japan, where both of my parents were working for the US military as Russian linguists and cryptographers during the Cold War. My father lived in Kharkiv, Ukraine, for most of my adult life, and I had the great privilege of spending a semester in Kyiv as a university student. There I fell in love with the rich history of storytelling that began in Kievan Rus and spread throughout the Slavic world.

The week before I completed a draft of the book, Russia invaded Ukraine. Like most of the world, I was deeply shocked and grieved – and also very worried about friends in both countries. I debated putting the project on hold. After some soul searching, I decided the themes of overcoming disillusionment and resisting evil are especially meaningful right now, and that stories like Katya's and Dima's need to be told.

The original seed of an idea I had for this book came from a dream I had about an anarchist poet imprisoned in the Gulag. As I began the long research process, I zeroed in on Solovetsky Island in the early 1920s as the location I wanted to explore. Being a prisoner there is the worst situation imaginable – it's winter for nearly nine months a year, and so remote there's little chance of escape. Beyond the physical elements of dark and cold, the prisoners had to contend with filthy conditions, typhoid outbreaks, starvation, impossible amounts of physical labour and the knowledge that at any moment they might be beaten or killed arbitrarily.

Despite all of that, the human spirit prevailed. The prisoners of Solovki started a camp theatre, writing out scripts from memory. They played music, danced, gave lectures, conducted scientific studies of the island, curated a museum and published a newspaper. They inspire and humble me because, while faced with the worst situation I can imagine, they refused to let their humanity be stripped from them.

While Dima is a character I created, I tried to capture some of the resilient hope and unbreakable spirits of the prisoners who began these initiatives.

The newspaper of the prison camp was originally conceived by Nikolai Litvin and first published on 8 October, 1923, on the monastery's old printer by Isaac S. Slepian, a lithographer by trade. Other prisoners involved in the publication's early years were: B. Shiriayev, T. Tverie, B. Glubokovsky, B. Eme-lianov and Ya. Galkh. These men had the challenging task of operating within the limits of the administration's censorship and often being viewed as traitors by their fellow prisoners while attempting to reflect the truth of what was occurring on the archipelago. Litvin said the primary aim of the press was refuting the depersonalisation of man and protecting the individual from being turned into dust. Aside from providing information about the various camp stations and assignments on the islands, the press published poetry, essays, scientific studies and satire.

The prison theatre was initially created by G.I. Nikitin and held its first performance on 23 September, 1923 with a showing of Miasnitsky's comedy *The Treasure*. I pushed the date back and chose *Uncle Vanya* as the opening theatre production for story reasons.

According to *Theatre in the Solovki Prison Camp* by Natalia Kuziakina, I. Armanov, a provincial actor imprisoned on Solovki, drew from the popular book *Creative Theatre* by P. Kerzhentsev when defining the tasks and conditions of the theatre:

- Condition One . . . the theatre must serve as a place of moral and physical relief for the convict, tired by a day of hard work.
- The second condition for a theatre is to serve as a source of energy. The theatre should avoid anything that depresses or belittles, and should boost spiritual strength and energy.
- Third, the theatre should serve to develop the mind. Joy, good cheer and knowledge are the three props of a people's theatre.

My descriptions of camp life and depictions of guards and administrators are largely drawn from prisoner memoirs and from *Gulag Archipelago* by Alexandr Solzhenitsyn (the beginning chapters of volume two document the timeframe this story takes place). The speech that camp director Comrade Nogtev gives at the beginning of the story ('There's no Soviet authority here, only Solovki authority') was recounted by multiple prisoners as the wording used to demoralise new arrivals. Eye witnesses describe Nogtev as a violent alcoholic who had partially lost his hearing while serving aboard *Aurora,* the warship famous for firing the shot that signalled the beginning of the October Revolution.

Marius Smolensky is described by prisoners as a Polish Communist with a violent temper and a soul-deep hatred for the Russian people. He invented a type of curved bat that became known among the prison population as Smolensky sticks.

Gleb Boky is also an historical figure. In some sources he's described as an idealist, a true believer in communism who refused the luxurious trappings other party members laid claim to after the Revolution. He lived in a small flat, drove a government-issued automobile and dressed in plain military garb.

There seemed to be another side to him, however. The backstory I included of his experiences in Tashkent is based in truth. Boky contracted tuberculosis and, at the point of death, turned to an Uzbek shaman for help. The shaman gave him dog meat (rather than wolf meat, as stated in my story) to eat and then performed a ritual that apparently saved Boky's life. This sparked a lifelong fascination with the occult.

Returning to Moscow, Boky took up a government post as head of the Extraordinary Commission, the top-secret section of the Cheka. There he oversaw the Bolshevik spy network.

In 1921, Boky met Alexandr Barchenko, a science fiction novelist who reinvented himself as a 'doctor' after the Revolution. Boky created a top-secret laboratory in the Cheka building at Lubyanka Square, where Barchenko conducted experiments on Sami sorcerers, Buryat shamans, and all types of psychics and clairvoyants. They hoped to further the Communist hold on Russia through mind control.

Boky also oversaw the early years of the Gulag, though it's unclear how much direct involvement he had. Some sources call him the mastermind of the Gulag, others claim he had little to do with it. The prison at Solovetsky Island, then called a 'special purpose camp', was overseen by Boky's Extraordinary Commission. It is unlikely that Boky would have spent significant time on the archipelago, and he certainly wouldn't have wintered there. I took creative liberties in having him remain on the island for the entire story.

In later life, Boky maintained the solemn exterior of a communist bureaucrat, but allegedly he spent his weekends holding wild orgies at a *dacha* outside Moscow. His participation in tantric sex rituals and his collection of mummified penises earned him quite a reputation. In fact, Mikhail Bulgakov, in his novel *The Master and Margarita*, allegedly based his character of Prof Woland (A.K.A. the Devil) on Boky.

Gleb Boky was arrested during the Stalin Purges and executed on 15 November, 1937.

Katya and Svetlana are characters I created. I owe a great debt to anarchist historian Paul Avrich, whose work helped me form Katya's character as well as understand the world of Stenka Razin. If you're interested in learning more about the Russian anarchist movement of the early 20th century, I recommend his books *The Russian Anarchists* and *Anarchist Portraits*, as well as the writings of Mikhail Bakunin. Another helpful resource in understanding the anarchist worldview and experience at the time of this story are Emma Goldman's memoirs, *My Disillusionment in Russia* and *My Further Disillusionment in Russia*.

A few other characters were inspired by real people.

Several memoirists mention being imprisoned alongside the Mexican ambassador to Egypt who was married to a Georgian countess. I couldn't find official records of them (and the memoirists don't agree on the ambassador's name), but he's portrayed as a swashbuckling character who brought an interesting dynamic to the prison's early years.

Countess Matilda Ivanova Witte likely wasn't imprisoned in the archipelago, but one memoirist mentions a prisoner named Witte sentenced to hard labour because their name was deemed counter-revolutionary. I included the countess to demonstrate the arbitrary measures used to imprison the government's enemies and to add nuance to Katya's perceptions of aristocrats.

Natasha is loosely inspired by 'Stalin's witch', a woman named Natalya Lvova who I came across in my research. In the 1930s she lived in the Kremlin and held black magic rituals to curse Stalin's enemies. The Lvovs were prominent aristocrats, so I thought it would be interesting to consider who Natasha (the diminutive form of Natalya) might have been before working for Stalin. Her personality and background are invented by me.

Prince Georgy Lvov never had children. His wife, Julia Alekseyevna, did die in 1903 as the story states, though not in childbirth.

As mentioned, the work of historian Paul Avrich was a great help in my research of Stenka Razin's life and times, particularly his book *Russian Rebels, 1600-1800*, which contains a detailed account of Razin's pirating years and revolt. Yelezar is a fictional character.

The work of Estonian folklorist Felix Oinas was a great help to me in developing the magic system. He has several books and essays that may be of interest to anyone wanting to know more about Slavic folklore. Two other helpful resources are *Russian Magic* by Cherry Gilchrist and *The Occult in Russian and Soviet Culture*, which is a compilation of scholarly essays.

A great deal of research went into this story. I've tried to make the historical aspects as accurate as possible, but I take full responsibility for any errors or gaps in my knowledge. I hope that you've enjoyed exploring the world of this story as much as I loved creating it.

# Acknowledgments

Thank you Kristina Pérez for being such a smart, ambitious and fierce advocate for my work. You've made my dreams come true! Thank you also to Isabel Lineberry, Jack Mozley and the rest of the team at PLE.

I'm grateful to my editor, Rhea Kurien, who opened my manuscript the day it went on submission and stayed up all night reading. You understood exactly what I was trying to do with this story, and your excellent advice helped me achieve it. You're a star!

Thank you to my publisher, Sam Eades, for going the extra mile for your debut authors, and to the entire team at Orion and especially at the Gollancz imprint for championing my book. Thank you to all those who worked on this book. A huge thank you to Micaela Alcaino. I'm so honoured to have your beautiful art gracing the cover of my book.

Thank you to Umar Turaki for fifteen years of friendship, for reading everything I write, and for never wavering in your faith that my work would find its audience. To Ulan Garba Matta for being such a good friend and a trusted source of feedback. To Jessica Jade, my long-time critique partner, for your sound advice. To Janice Davis, my official thirst consultant. To those who read and gave feedback on all or part of the book: Kip Wilson, Genoveva Dimova, Erin Rose Kim, Shana Targosz, Kalie Holford, Nicole Chartrand, Emily Charlotte, M.K. Lobb, and Lindsey Hewett.

Thank you to Alexa Donne for creating Author Mentor Match, which came into my life at just the right time. To

Rebecca Schaeffer for your mentorship. You found me at my lowest and built me back up, for which I'm forever grateful.

Thank you to Write Club. You foxes are the absolute best.

Thank you to Evgeny Shulgin for your thoughtful feedback on my depiction of Russian culture. You may not know that you were also the inspiration for my poem titled Reflection. I aspire to the kind of courage that speaks out when it's safer to remain silent, that protests at the cost of one's freedom, and that, with a heart full of grief, leaves home and country rather than participating in an unjust war. You have my deepest admiration and thanks.

I cannot list all of the individuals who have mentored and helped me through the years, as there are too many to name. I do want to particularly mention Sandi Tompkins, who, many years ago, gave me a teddy bear as a reminder to turn off my internal editor and approach writing like a child at play. She'll never get to read my published work, but that bear still sits on my desk. In that way, her encouragement is part of every creative endeavour I undertake.

Thank you to my mother, who taught me to be ambitious. To my father, who gave me a love of language. To the rest of my family and friends for their support and love. To my Belgian family, who have been a constant source of encouragement.

To Rena, Roxanne, Valerie, and Victoria, my brilliant and beautiful daughters – I'm proud to be your mother and I hope that my journey to publication has taught you to keep after your dreams, no matter how long it takes to achieve them. To Martijn, for making my dreams your priority and for understanding the best way to woo me is saying, 'I'll watch the kids—you go write.' I couldn't ask for a better partner.

Thank you also to God, whose love transformed my life. From him and through him and for him are all things.

# Credits

Cristin Williams and Gollancz would like to thank everyone at Orion who worked on the publication of *The Whisper of Stars*.

**Agent**
Kristina Perez

**Editorial**
Rhea Kurien
Zakirah Alam

**Copy-editor**
Tara Loder

**Proofreader**
Andy Ryan

**Editorial Management**
Jane Hughes
Charlie Panayiotou
Lucy Bilton

**Audio**
Paul Stark
Louise Richardson
Georgina Cutler

**Contracts**
Dan Herron
Ellie Bowker
Oliver Chacón

**Design**
Nick Shah
Rachel Lancaster
Deborah Francois
Helen Ewing

**Finance**
Nick Gibson
Jasdip Nandra
Sue Baker
Tom Costello

**Inventory**
Jo Jacobs
Dan Stevens

**Production**
Paul Hussey
Katie Horrocks

**Marketing**
Javerya Iqbal

**Publicity**
Jenna Petts

**Sales**
David Murphy
Victoria Laws
Esther Waters
Karin Burnik
Anne-Katrine Buch
Frances Doyle
Group Sales teams across Digital, Field, International and Non-Trade

**Operations**
Group Sales Operations team

**Rights**
Rebecca Folland
Tara Hiatt
Ben Fowler
Alice Cottrell
Ruth Blakemore
Marie Henckel